This is a Love Story

This is a Love Story

Jessica Thompson

W F HOWES LTD

This large print edition published in 2012 by
W F Howes Ltd
Unit 4, Rearsby Business Park, Gaddesby Lane,
Rearsby, Leicester LE7 4YH

1 3 5 7 9 10 8 6 4 2

First published in the United Kingdom in 2012
by Coronet

A CIP catalogue record for this book is available
from the British Library

ISBN 978 1 47120 607 8

Typeset by Palimpsest Book Production Limited,
Falkirk, Stirlingshire
Printed and bound in Great Britain
by MPG Books Ltd, Bodmin, Cornwall

For mum, dad and Louise

CHAPTER 1

HE LOOKS LIKE HE
COULD SAVE YOUR LIFE.

Sienna

There are two people sitting opposite me on the train this morning.
A guy and a girl.
They must be in their mid-twenties.
The guy has thick blond hair, green eyes and sexy freckles dotted all over his nose like stars in a clear night sky.
He's really handsome but not my type. I feel about him the way I feel about Monet. I appreciate what I see. It's nice. But not really to my taste.
I'm guessing his name is Tom, or something like that, and he works in PR. I am drawing this assumption because he's wearing what looks like a designer grey suit with a salmon-pink tie.
I like to play this little imagination game sometimes. I'm sure I'm probably wrong most of the time, but it passes a train journey.
She could be a Claire, with long brown hair that's kind of stringy and ragged, but still seems like it's all part of a carefully planned look. She

1

has made an effort to seem like she doesn't give a shit. I'm a girl, I see straight through it. She wants everyone to think she just rolled out of bed like this.

She's got perfectly painted grey nail varnish on, and a pair of tight black jeans with expensive-looking nude ballet pumps.

Claire looks a bit more creative than her public relations man; it's the jewellery that gives it away – big chunky bracelets and an eccentric beaded necklace. I reckon she works in the art world, perhaps. Possibly not holding a paintbrush, but maybe in a gallery, having to explain to people what the artist meant by the scrambled splats on the walls.

She's probably well educated, with a family who live in Kent but holiday in the Cayman Islands three times a year.

I bet Tom loves her. It looks like he does. He has the aura of a man who won't be easily distracted. It's lovely.

One of her legs is up on his lap. She's reading the paper and he kisses her on the cheek every now and then, looking like these are the moments that make his world go round. On the way to work with the love of his life.

I let out a deep sigh as I realise I am staring. Plus, I'm being overly romantic. I'm sure they have the same problems as everyone else – you know, rows about snoring, map-reading and household duties.

But still . . . It dawns on me that I don't have a love like that at home. I have love, but it's different . . .

I'm thinking that maybe mornings are easier when you are Tom the PR man and Claire the gallery girl, and not me. Sienna Walker.

You might be woken by gentle kisses, and that special feeling of skin on skin that you soon take for granted.

Warm breath against your face and knowing that you're safe.

But not me.

My mornings are more like being dunked into a vat of cold water.

I flinch as the train pulls away from the station and I recall the start of my day, which I'm sure would've been much easier if I had woken up next to the man of my dreams like Claire, or whatever her name is, did.

The alarm went off at 6.30 a.m., a shrill, piercing scream that made my ears want to burrow inside my head and nestle in the padded, warm folds of my brain. I just wanted to sleep. I wanted to sink back under the covers, which are soft on my skin and smell like fresh daisies, and hide from the world. I contemplated calling in sick, but I haven't been in the job for long enough to be doing things like that.

Mornings and I do not go well together, a bit like cheese and jam, or hummus and chocolate. It's a bad combo.

I dragged my heavy limbs out of bed and pushed my feet onto the smooth wooden flooring, my fringe sticking up into the air like a mobile phone mast.

The soft cocoon I had been lying in was replaced by a cool draft and an urgent need to pee. Like a zombie I plodded into the bathroom and tried to make sense of the half-light.

After a few minutes of 'getting ready', which included stabbing at my mouth with a worn-out toothbrush and attempting to run a comb through my tangled hair, I felt ready for a shower.

I was wrong.

The water came out cold.

It was a little like someone had stored a night's quota of icy rainfall in a rusty bucket and tipped it all over me.

My eyes opened wide for the first time since waking, my pupils shrinking to the size of pinpricks as I attempted to deal with the shock. I jumped around to dodge the relentless bullets while I waited for the water to heat up but they were unavoidable.

Then there was the challenge of negotiating the leafy streets of my west London suburb and getting the train to work. In spite of the shock of the shower, I was still bleary-eyed, and so the pavement seemed to spread out in front of me like a chessboard.

Walking around London in the rush hour is like a platform game. The scoring system goes a little like this:

5 points for not stepping into the giant puddle that always collects at the bottom of Edgley Road.

15 points for successfully overtaking the elderly couple who are blocking the way, without walking into a lamp post.

10 points for avoiding the charity touts who lunge towards me outside the station and give me incommunicable guilt for scuttling away.

15 points for buying the last carton of orange juice at the local shop.

20 points for picking up a *Metro* before they have all been greedily swiped by the grab it for yourself, then throw it away ten minutes later commuter population.

The next challenge was finding a seat on the train. Play it right and you are in for a relatively comfy ride. Play it wrong and you will spend twenty minutes with your face rammed against the toughened glass window and a walking stick wedged into your coccyx.

The train arrived one minute after I got onto the platform, so I weaved through the people, left, right, left, right, and I made it.

But as I sit across from a picture of love that is making me feel acutely depressed about my situation at home, I realise that today, I am not in the best of moods.

Oh no . . . As Tom pulls a strand of Claire's hair away from her right ear and kisses it gently I have to look away before I go insane. So I glance to my left in a bid to escape this doe-eyed display.

But in doing so, my eyes meet directly with those of a man sitting next to me, who just happens to be staring at that moment.

He must be in his fifties, a skinny type with beady eyes and a pair of glasses with lenses so thick they remind me of the bottom of milk bottles.

He smiles awkwardly as he realises he has been caught staring. Because I like to think I'm a relatively nice person, I smile back as if to say, 'you know what? It's ok. Let's just forget about this and move on'.

I turn away and gaze towards the ceiling; it is obviously a safer option today. But I feel a presence again, my peripheral vision is telling me this. So I turn my head back and the man is staring *again*, almost boring his eyes into my cheek. This is no accidental gaze. He jumps as if he has been caught pilfering grapes from the supermarket.

'Oh err, ever so sorry about that, it's just you're very beau . . . '

'Just stop will you. Please?', I ask, turning red.

'Yes, of course. Sorry', he says in his well-spoken accent, somewhat crestfallen.

Welcome to train life. It is a circus and a zoo all at the same time.

I wonder why invasive behaviour of this nature irritates me so much. Blatant letching goes hand in hand with over-enthusiastic public displays of affection, offensive-smelling takeaways and unrestricted trumping.

It's only my third week at the new job and this daily ritual is all a bit of a shock.

The squash of the rush hour can do such strange things to normal people. Individuals who are usually quite calm find themselves gritting their teeth, muttering under their breath and trying desperately hard not to decapitate someone with an umbrella.

A woman to my right makes a phone call, and a loud one at that.

Man sitting next to woman grimaces.

This woman is so wrapped up in her conversation that she fails to notice we are approaching a tunnel and then, oh dear.

What a shame. The whole carriage breathes a sigh of relief apart from Tom and Claire who are so wrapped up in their bubble of love, ducklings and popping candy that they had no idea about it all in the first place.

For a moment we seem to achieve some kind of peace. An idle-looking young man who appears to have been rudely awoken halfway through a six-month hibernation shuffles back into the corner of his seat. His scruffiness makes me feel better – he has the look I was sporting within my first hour of waking.

Tense legs start to relax, and daydreamers turn their heads back to the windows, hoping for some kind of escape from this cattle cart from hell.

I balance my tea between my knees, pick up my copy of *Metro* and try to think of the things I have planned for the day ahead, but I am quickly distracted by a picture story of a squirrel on custom-built waterskis.

God, I love this paper.

Being a journalist myself, much as I dream of one day uncovering an earth-shattering revelation of the same magnitude as the expenses scandal, I'd be just as happy writing about small, cuddly animals engaged in bizarre activities like this one.

I look around at other *Metro* readers. Is anyone else looking at the squirrel? I wonder.

A lady in the row behind the star-crossed lovers is reading, but no, she looks quite sad.

No one is smiling, let alone laughing, and that can't be right because this is one bloody funny animal.

I keep scanning and my eyes rest on a desperately handsome man in a green T-shirt, sitting across from me, a couple of spaces to the right. He is smirking; in fact, he is so tickled by something that he has to clear his throat.

Wow. How did I not notice him before?

Maybe he got on the train just a few minutes ago when I was lost in my angry, bitter thought processes.

He looks like he would be tall standing up. Under the T-shirt I can make out a perfectly proportioned torso supporting broad, handsome shoulders, and atop it all is a face I can't bear to look away from. My heart catches in my throat and I swallow hard.

He has pure olive skin, dotted across his chin

with sexy stubble that creeps up his chiselled jawline like vines on a beautiful house. His features are strong and bold.

He doesn't look like a coward. He looks like he could save your life.

These hard, artistic features contrast with a pair of dangerous brown eyes that almost glitter in the artificial strip lighting.

Don't. Fall. Into. Them.

His lips are perfect, and startlingly like those of my favourite pin-up, Jake Gyllenhaal.

He has whirls of thick brown hair almost caramel in tone, waxed in different directions.

He looks like trouble.

I can already imagine what it might be like to kiss him . . .

I peer over the top of the page and he must sense me because he looks too.

Our eyes meet, and for a few moments all that stands between us are forty-five thin sheets of sooty recycled paper, two metres of stifling carriage air and a fat man who is nodding off on my left shoulder.

This is one of those Hollywood moments you see in the cinema, except I am supposed to be blonde and a size zero.

He is quite possibly one of the most striking men I have ever seen in my life.

As a Londoner, you come to realise that while this city is bursting at the seams with people of all shapes and sizes, it's very rare that someone stops you in your tracks.

Most people on trains try to lose themselves in the depths of a book, hide away behind a paper or enter the realms of a musical world. They just pass each other by. To actually make a connection, and a friendly one at that, is nothing short of a miracle.

So here goes.

I am either going to make a massive fool of myself, or one day we will tell the guests at our wedding how we bonded over a rodent with a love of water sports. That will beat the usual stories of blind dates and meeting at the gym.

Deep breath . . .

Squirrel?

I mouth it at him, my lips slowly forming the shape of this very silly word. My eyebrows are arched in an inquisitive manner.

Time seems to blur like a slowed-down film clip; I can hear my heart beating in my ears. Shit, shit, shit . . .

Suddenly one thumb is up and the most gorgeous man in this city, in fact possibly the world, has turned his copy of *Metro* to face me and is pointing towards our fluffy matchmaker.

He bites his bottom lip to stop himself laughing out loud, a row of perfect white teeth just about visible. This is sexy.

I flash him a flirtatious grin and draw my eyes away from his, my heart racing in my chest.

Play. It. Cool.

I keep pretending to read my paper, turning away

from the picture story as otherwise I would soon be laughing so hard I'd be squirting tea through my nostrils, and that would kind of ruin the look I was going for.

Aware that I have pushed my own boundaries by initiating this whole thing, I keep reading and reading as if I don't care, and try to work out what to do next.

The train stops once but I am pretty sure I can still see the lush green hue of his top from the corner of my eye. I must try not to look at him.

God bless peripheral vision.

Soon five minutes have passed and I'm satisfied that it is safe to proceed with eye contact number two.

I look up, but to my horror my handsome stranger has been replaced by an elderly man in a pea-green jacket. The couple has gone too. I quickly whip my head around the carriage, back and forth, and then once more just in case. He has disappeared.

The pensioner sitting in his seat looks happy and surprised at my attention. Not you, pal . . .

Great, I think, looking down at my feet. There goes the man of my dreams. Quickly I realise the naivety of my little fantasy and I feel embarrassed. It was a silly idea anyway. I shudder at how I went from nought to sixty on the love scale within a few minutes – not like me at all.

Besides, he was probably a raving lunatic. Laughing at squirrels? Whatever next, I console myself.

I am a desperate romantic. I love the idea of random collisions of the heart. I crave quirky meetings rather than the conventional way women get chatted up at bars and dragged home for a night of drunken fumbling with a man they barely know. 'We got talking through mutual friends at dinner' is dire. If you're feeling particularly dull, you could whip out the 'We met at work' tale.

Yawn.

There is a little Juliet inside me, hoping I will lock eyes with my Romeo on the other side of a fish tank or through the gap in a library bookcase. Hell, even if it's behind the condiments section in a supermarket I don't really mind.

I'm only twenty but I lament the day that good old-fashioned romance died. I'm not sure when it was. Some say we lost it when we fought for feminism, which is probably a relatively small price to pay for what we've gained.

But did we really mean to take it this far?

So far, in fact, that if a man sends you flowers at work your female colleagues will cackle and pretend to vomit, yet when they get home they will still berate their husbands for never buying *them* flowers?

My stop interrupts me from what was becoming a deep, downward spiral of thought.

Being the fickle young thing that I am, I have pretty much forgotten about my handsome stranger by the time I get to the bottom of my large tea and chuck the crumpled cup into a heaving bin on the platform.

It was a fleeting moment, a bit of sugar on my cereal. I have bigger fish to fry, a career to focus upon. No time for distractions, I tell myself. Plus, there is too much mess at home. Too much to cope with. I really shouldn't be looking out for other men.

My heart starts to flutter as I negotiate the pavements of Balham. The streets are cluttered with people, mothers and prams, lads in baggy jeans, the last dribs and drabs of City workers dashing towards the train station to head into central London. There are newsagents, estate agents and pound shops, the usual suspects with the occasional petite coffee shop sandwiched between them.

I love it here.

Cigarette smoke wafts in the soft spring air, mingling with the steam emanating from fresh bacon rolls on the plates in front of a couple sharing breakfast at a table I pass.

I'm really pleased with my new job. It has taken two years of hard work and painful rejections to get this entry-level role at The Cube publishing house. Climbing the career ladder has been difficult for me, so I've had to be pretty creative to catch the eye of prospective employers. I wasn't able to go to university, so I've had to ensure I've taught myself about things like web journalism, video and trying to keep my finger on the pulse in terms of social media. OK, it isn't the *Guardian* or *The Times*, but it's a good start and so far I have thoroughly enjoyed every second.

The Cube is a media group which produces a range of unusual publications read by *very* niche audiences. Some of them cool, some not so cool. This means I am writing about a host of quirky subjects, ranging from what's going on in the world of fishing (less fun) to testing fast cars (a lot more fun). Some of our publications are small and virtually unknown, others are read by thousands.

This job is perfect for me as I love writing. I still can't quite believe my luck. I weave in and out of the bodies around me in a strange kind of dance – ducking, diving and dodging. Schoolchildren swarm around and pensioners scuttle into shop doorways, newspapers tucked under armpits.

Something in me thrives on the energy of London. Despite the infuriating nature of this lifestyle, I can't imagine anywhere else I would want to be.

Every day it's the same: I come home, feet aching, eyes bloodshot, hair limp from a combination of the weather and the pollution, but I am inspired. As I lie in bed I can't wait for the next morning so I can take it on all over again. Even if the first hour is pretty painful.

After five minutes of dancing through the crowds I am close to my office, a small, modern installation down a busy side road. It is nestled between two restaurants, one Indian, one Italian. Their beautiful, garlicky aromas manage to waft into our air-conditioning system and I spend most of my time in the advanced stages of hunger. There is a small car park behind the office with a bench in the middle, and a homeless guy often sits there.

He's there right now, and as I realise I'm going to have to walk past him again, butterflies fill my tummy.

I noticed him the very first day I arrived. It was hard not to as he called out to me from a small, hungry mouth, almost lost in the brown and black streaks on his weathered face.

'Can you spare some change, love?' he said, a look of hope in his eyes.

I turned away and walked past him. I never quite know how to handle these situations, and I've got too much on my plate right now.

He doesn't look crazy, or on drugs, or any of those stereotypes. He smiles at me sometimes; I smile back. I don't have the time to get involved. I know that's bad.

I'm scared of him, really, and the reality of his life. He has icy blue eyes, so icy they make me cold. I don't like looking at them, so I turn away.

The first time I met him, I asked one of the women in reception who he was.

'Who are you talking about, love?' came a high-pitched voice from a blonde, middle-aged character behind the desk.

'You know, the guy sitting in our car park,' I explained.

'Hmm, I don't think we're expecting anyone today,' she said, rifling through a tray of papers in front of her.

Receptionist number two piped up, 'Oh, Sandra, you know who it is. It's Dancing Pete.'

'Dancing who?'

'You know, the homeless fellow who insists on sleeping out the back.'

'Dancing? Why dancing? I've never seen him dance, for God's sake!'

By now the two ladies were in a frustratingly slow-moving conversation. It was like observing a pair of peacocks, clucking away pointlessly behind a glass screen, waiting to be put down and made into exotic handbags.

'Homeless fella? I didn't know we had one of those,' Sandra squeaked, as if she was talking about a new franking machine or state of the art photocopier.

'Yeeessss. He's been hovering around for a couple of years now. Are you blind?'

I walked away from them mid-chat; they barely even realised I had gone.

But the situation bothers me again this morning as I walk through the rear entrance to our car park. I don't drive, but the cut-through saves time and you have to come through the back if you want to take it.

He is sitting on the bench with his head in his hands. He looks up as I approach, his face as sad as ever.

'Excuse me,' he calls out as I walk past, grimacing because I don't want him to see me, but he always does.

I stop in my tracks and find myself standing next to the bench, but looking straight ahead so as not to make eye contact.

I should have just walked on, I tell myself.

'Yes,' I say feebly, regretting my actions.

'Have you got any spare change?' he asks, as always – like the answer will be any different this time.

I say nothing and walk forward quickly, swipe my entry card to open the glass doors and step into the lift. I hear him mutter, 'I just wanted to get myself a cup of tea,' as I go.

The lift to the third floor is small and often smells of PVA glue. I don't know why this is. No one else seems to know, either.

'Hello, gorgeous!' says Lydia, the second I enter the office. She gently squeezes my left cheek, which she has done pretty much every day since I first set a shaky little Bambi foot into the office. I am glad to be distracted from the fact that I keep walking away from someone who clearly needs help.

Lydia is the office co-ordinator. A very important-sounding title for someone who potters about and does all the annoying things no one else wants to do. I think she is capable of more, though.

She has a wild shock of thick chocolate curls set against a freckled face and the most piercing green eyes I have seen outside the pages of a children's storybook.

She is all cuddles and warmth and exactly what

you need when you start a new job. Although she is only three years older than me, she just took me under her wing.

'Hey, Lyds, good weekend?' I respond, making my way over to my desk with a big smile.

Like a fairy, Lydia floats around me, whipping things out of my way. Before I know it my jacket is hanging neatly on the hatstand and my list of editorial tasks for the week is fanned in front of me in perfect order. I quietly wonder how many arms she has.

'Bloody excellent, thanks, Si. You will never guess what happened on Friday night,' she begins, a wicked smile on her face.

I start to scan three scribbled Post-it notes on my desk. And no, I'm sure I will never be able to guess what happened on Friday night.

I haven't known Lydia for long, but she seems to have a social life which revolves around eight-inch heels, copious amounts of Jack Daniel's, bribing DJs with cold hard cash to play eighties cheese, and then busting into kebab shops on the way home and making everyone inside laugh. These are just some of the tales I've heard.

She leans in and whispers in my ear, despite the fact that I have made no effort to guess what happened on Friday night. It could be anything. She really is that random.

'I got barred from that salsa club in Leicester Square,' she says, before giggling and standing back up proudly, one hand on a curvaceous hip.

How, I wonder, do you get barred from a salsa club? Violent clockwise turns? Stiletto rage? I offer no response but look at her with a raised eyebrow. I can't wait to hear this one.

'Well, basically, we had too much to drink before we got there, which wasn't a good start, and I fell down the stairs that lead to the toilet. They thought I was really drunk, but I wasn't, you know. I'm sure it was my shoes . . .' she trails off with an element of shame to her voice.

I switch on my computer and it whirrs into life like an aircraft. I'm sure they aren't supposed to sound like that.

'Oh God, did you hurt yourself?' I reply with little interest. The story isn't as exciting as I first thought it might be and I've got so much to do today.

'Not really. The heel snapped off one of my shoes, though, which made walking home a bit difficult,' she adds, twiddling a long, luscious curl with her index finger and glancing over at our office goldfish, Dill, who is looking with longing through the glass at the outside world.

Rhoda, our advertising features writer, bought Dill six months ago and treats him like a child. There are toys. Yes, actual toys for fish, floating around in the tank. She buys them at the weekend and brings them in on a Monday. I'm surprised she hasn't put up an alphabet wall-chart yet.

I smile widely and look at Lydia. I continue the small talk to stay polite but I am struggling not to laugh at the mental image of her tumbling from the dizzy precipice that is high fashion.

'So what was the damage?' I ask, feigning interest but distracted by the tremendous workload that lies ahead.

'Well, they were Kurt Geiger, love. So, like, £120,' she replies with a giant sigh.

I feel her pain.

Caffeine. I need caffeine. I rise slowly and head towards the drinks machine; a small queue has formed and within it the usual inane chatter has commenced. One thread goes along the lines of how we're due a really hot summer this year as the last three have been terrible, another analyses how many holidays are acceptable in a year before you're considered just plain greedy, and the final one – the most dire – is about speed cameras and how unfair it is that Mark Watson received a ticket for driving at 100 miles per hour rather than the 96 he claimed to have actually been travelling at. At last my turn comes and I get a large tea with one sugar.

I return to my desk and get to work, but I'm soon interrupted by a frenzied kerfuffle, which has broken out like a virus in the area behind me.

It is a large, open-plan space and my desk is one of eight in the middle of the room, which are separated by little partitions. To the left of my desk are three small offices with their own doors and windows. The rest of the space is taken up with the usual suspects: more desks, noisy fax machines, recycling bins and a huge coffee machine. Our boss's office is on a floor above ours, and has its own little stairs leading up to it like a tree house.

I keep looking at my screen, trying hard to concentrate. I doubt it is anything that would interest me. Normally I have a great ability to tune everything out, but there is talking, and lots of it.

Concentrate. Concentrate.

Suddenly a sharp elbow belonging to Lydia is jabbed into my shoulder and I realise she's standing next to my desk, grinning at me. Strange, contorted expressions that are meant to be subtle, as if to say 'Look behind you,' without yelling it out loud, which is what she clearly wants to do.

Oh, for God's sake, I think, as I reluctantly spin my chair 180 degrees and see a figure in the middle of the din. He is surrounded, ambushed by fussing colleagues. All I can make out is a shade of green. Lush green.

My heart skips a beat, then two. Three may be pushing it.

A couple of people move out of the way, and as I slowly scan from the middle of the T-shirt upwards, my eyes meet a familiar face.

Holy shit. It's squirrel man.

And if it's possible, in this stark, dentist's-chair-like lighting that we are bathed in, he looks even more gorgeous than he did earlier this morning. He does look decidedly miserable, though.

But why is he here? Who the hell is he? Is he being interviewed? Maybe he's here to fix something . . .

No, he looks too soft for all that, and everyone seems to know who he is. 'Lydia, who the hell is that?' I whisper into her ear, my right leg trembling a little.

'It's Nick,' she whispers back, giving me a wink.

Of course. Bollocks.

Nick went away just before my first day, so he's the only person working at The Cube I haven't yet met. I do know, according to the kitchen rota, that it is his turn to get the milk and sugar on a Tuesday, and that he drinks peppermint tea with caraway seeds. I always thought he sounded like such a pretentious shit from the way people talked about him.

Apparently, since Nick's been away, Kevin in accounts has been screwing up invoices and wandering around listlessly, Tom in editorial has tried to take on the role of leader of the pack and failed miserably, and Rhoda has even taken up smoking again. The lads all think Nick was incredibly funny before his girlfriend left him for someone else. If I hear one more account of the time Nick dressed as a tree and spent two hours in reception unnoticed, I may actually cry.

His girlfriend and the guy who 'snatched her away' both worked here, I'm told. What a mess.

Now I am no longer faced with working alongside someone who is a hysterical jackass (which would have been bad enough) but instead – even worse – a heartbroken shell of a man who will probably leave a trail of teary snot wherever he goes.

And this heartbroken shell of a man is the guy I almost fell in love with on the train this morning. Gutted.

Nick

Usually, returning to work is pretty dull, especially after a break in Ibiza. It certainly wasn't this time.

I have managed to avoid budget, boozy lads' holidays in recent years. Scarred by trips to Spanish islands in my early twenties that were great fun at the time, I now feel like they're the last places I would want to be. I've spent enough time spewing in cheap hotels, falling into swimming pools and twisting limbs while attempting drunken stunts on holidays like that. No more Shagaloof for me, thanks. It just isn't my cup of tea any more.

I prefer city breaks now, if I'm going away with the boys. We still have a hunger for exactly the same things – pulling hot girls, drinking too much and dancing – but we have more money these days so we do it in a different setting. Our recent trips have involved smoking weed in Amsterdam, eating the best steak imaginable in Paris, clubbing in Brooklyn, stuff like that. We aren't kids any more.

So it's either overindulgent stuff in cool cities, or exciting adventures in tropical climes like Fiji. I love sharing my favourite life stories under the stars with random backpackers I'll never see again.

But many of my friends are hurtling towards thirty, and I'm getting there too. The prospect of a milestone birthday and a stag party do funny things to the male mind.

'Come on, mate, you'll love it – and it's my stag do. So you have to come, really, don't you?' said Ross, punching me hard on the arm like an American jock when the idea of Ibiza was first floated. He acquired the habit of punching me on the arm at university and he's carried on ever since. He does it for pretty much anything: birthdays, holidays, Tuesdays . . . It's slightly annoying and he's definitely too old to do it now, but it's his trademark so I guess it can stay. I always reckoned if we failed to find nice women, we could live together as bachelors and never have to grow up, punching each other all over the nation's golf courses and the bingo halls of west London. But that was looking pretty remote now.

Ross is my best mate, who I met at university. I thought he was a bit of a dick at first – he was the loud, rowdy one who always had to drink more than anyone else and he was more successful with women, too, which made me massively jealous. He's a big bloke – not fat, but burly, with broad shoulders and messy hair that makes him look as if he's just stepped off a rugby pitch. Girls love that, I've learned.

After just six months of living with him in halls I realised that it wasn't a competition, and that actually, he was a pretty cool guy. He even taught me how to talk to women without stuttering or spilling my drink all over them. He's not the best-looking bloke I know, but he has this incredible confidence, which seems to take him everywhere he wants to go.

Obviously I *had* to go to his stag do, even if it involved sitting in a pile of steaming horse manure for three days. This was Ross . . .

Like I said, Ibiza – not a place I would have envisioned myself visiting these days. The prospect of packed nightclubs and vomit-inducing light sequences made me sweat just thinking about it.

I protested, I did, but they had me by the short and curlies. The whole lot of them had worked out a response to every attempt I made at suggesting different locations. Eventually, the old 'last chance to have fun before marriage' guilt trip, combined with a bit of Googling and the promise of lots of hot girls, was enough to seal the deal.

It was only a few days, I told myself, and if it was too dire I could always get lost in the historical Ibiza Town everyone bangs on about.

Packing my suitcase wasn't too hard: shorts, shorts, pants, more shorts and some shower gel. I wedged five books into my hand luggage; if they went missing en route I feared I might lose my only escape if things got bad.

I was pleasantly surprised – something about the atmosphere got me in the mood to let my hair down as soon as we landed on the island. It was scorching hot and I needed to have some fun.

After a pint or five too many I managed to tell Ross I loved him on more than one occasion, fall down a small flight of stairs one night, and tread on several girls' sandaled feet in nightclubs – one of whom slapped me in the face. I felt nothing.

It was bloody brilliant.

Although I returned to London with the dreaded Ibiza flu everyone talks about. They should vaccinate for this shit. I'm afraid if I keep blowing my nose like this I may look down at the tissue and find the damn thing sitting there and looking at me from a bed of translucent snot.

It seems that seven days of pouring various different beers and spirits down your throat like there's a fire in your belly is not that good for you.

In addition, I smoked a disgusting number of cigarettes and joints, leaving me wheezing like a broken chew-toy.

I am a lightweight. It's official. I had to have a week off sick, for God's sake. Getting out of bed this morning was a joke – I'm surprised I managed not to drown in the puddle of drool next to my face let alone actually reach across to the alarm.

But lurgy aside, returning to an OK job that I've been in for far too long feels like a big comedown. That combined with the fact that I'm twenty-seven.

And single.

Nor has Amelia flooded my doormat with letters documenting her shame and regret at leaving me for one of our colleagues, and I was pretty sure she would. I had fantasies of not being able to get into the house due to the sheer volume of letters she might have sent me.

Toby Hunter, for God's sake!

Toby joined The Cube three years ago when I was a trainee designer and Amelia was a writer. He was the new company lawyer, a young guy for his position. He and his wife became friends of ours – they would come over for dinner and everything.

I should have suspected something when Amelia kept going down with this bug and Toby would always get it too. I learned later that he was off sick on the same days. Both workstations empty at the same times. The idea was so preposterous that I just pushed it out of my mind. It was a *surely not* situation.

This bug was so bad, she said, that she couldn't get out of bed. And there I was, working away happily in the office when he was over there getting into it with her. It was Toby who quit work first. He said he'd got a new job at a blue-chip company. I believed him. Next thing I know, Amelia's bags were packed and she was sailing off into the horizon with floppy-haired, watery-eyed Toby Hunter. I only hoped he would be sailing off somewhere nice soon, in an ambulance . . . The whole thing made me sick. (Actually, I am a tad jealous about his law career. I'm fast becoming a bitter 'artist' who wished he'd studied something else.)

Amelia didn't even serve out her notice period.

Boom. Gone. Just like that. And all the while Toby's wife was coming round on Friday nights and crying into a hanky while we got drunk on Grolsch, wondering what the hell had hit us. She even tried to kiss me one particularly booze-addled evening. I soon put a stop to that. The whole thing was enough of a mess as it was.

Needless to say, it was all pretty embarrassing at work. Everyone knew what had happened. It was a messy home situation, which should never have leaked into our professional lives. Getting together with people at work is a huge mistake.

I feel like life has juddered to a grinding halt. The brakes have been applied, pretty sodding hard, and there are angry tyre marks on the road. People don't seem to be taking my position very seriously, either. I'm sure if she'd left me for someone a bit cooler, like a footballer or a musician, they would be rushing round with porn magazines and takeaway.

My career has hit the buffers, my love life is in tatters and most of my friends are now marrying/having children/having some sort of meaningful life. Ibiza and its aftermath did a good job of numbing the pain for a couple of weeks, but when I woke up this morning I was greeted by that horrible feeling in the pit of my stomach.

Doom, I think it is.

This is not what I envisaged when I left university. Full of the hope of youth, I thought that by the time I reached thirty I would be the CEO of some multimillion-pound company, with a sexy wife, two children and a car that required that special petrol just because . . . well, because it's a flash car, isn't it?

OK, OK, I know that's not very realistic. But at least I could be running my own design studio or something. I could have at least got that sorted.

Now I have just two and a half years to achieve all this and basically it's not going to happen.

I was considering this very situation on the train this morning, the same anxiety gripping my chest, when something odd happened. Flicking through my copy of *Metro*, I stumbled across a picture story about a squirrel on waterskis. Utterly ridiculous.

For some unknown reason, this was a temporary cure for my weary heart and I felt the sudden urge to laugh my backside off. You know, the kind of laughter that makes you accidentally fart or snort like a greedy pig. The kind of laughter that only comes when you are so depressed that suddenly the most inane things are funny enough to bring you to tears.

You can't laugh like that, though, on a stuffy train full of tight-lipped Brits. It wouldn't be acceptable. So I spent a few minutes holding in my amusement with great difficulty. The more I held it in, the funnier it became. My eyes were filling with water and my stomach muscles were jumping up and down furiously. Trying to divert my attention from the rodent I looked up and saw a pair of the most beautiful denim-blue eyes ever, peeping over the top of the same newspaper.

29

Wow.

My stomach filled with butterflies and she mouthed a word at me.

Squirrel . . . she said.

She was bloody gorgeous, with a thick, straight fringe just touching her eyelashes and the most healthy-looking, beautiful skin I have ever seen. Her hair was a chestnut brown and I just wanted to touch it. Not in a horrible, overtly sexual, pervy way, or even in a gay hairdresser way. In an *I'm not sure if you're real, so I just want to touch you to check* kind of way.

Jesus. Be cool, Nick, I told myself.

Just. Be. Cool.

I did the opposite and stuck my right thumb up at her. Why? Why would I do that? She seemed pretty horrified by me after that and went back to reading. Don't blame her, really. Thumbs are so eighties.

I sat for a few moments, trying to work out at which point during my life I lost the ability to be good with women. Nope – no idea.

A few minutes passed and she kept reading, not even a glance my way. I could feel myself burning up.

You may wonder why I was taking a chance meeting on a train so seriously. I wouldn't normally attach so much hope to it either, but there was something about her. She was the girl from my dreams. Sweet, understated, devastatingly sexy.

I was already teetering on the edge of feeling

really down, so I figured I would quietly get up and go to the toilet. Maybe a quick self-bollocking in the mirror and a splash of cold water on my idiot face would sort me out, and thankfully it did. A cigarette on the way to the office and a small, strong coffee, and I was composed again.

I needed to keep busy, and if I'm honest, I had missed the office crowd quite a lot. I was hoping to be at my desk on time, ready to create a new round of graphics for our weird magazines, but reception soon put an end to that idea.

'Niiiick!' came the shrill tones of Maria behind the welcome desk, her hands clapping together and an armful of bangles jingling around like sleigh bells.

'Hey, gorgeous,' I said, leaning over the counter to give her a gentle peck on the cheek. She loves this.

'Look at you! Look, Sandra, doesn't he look good all tanned?!' she cried, sharply elbowing her colleague, who was buried in a copy of *Elle*.

The encounter went on for about six and a half minutes. I won't bore you with the whole conversation because, like me, you will be angry that you lost this chunk of your life with no way of getting it back.

When I finally peeled myself away from the 'lovely' ladies, I figured I would take the stairs to the third floor. It was time to face the world again.

By the second floor I was exhausted – my chest was thick with cold and the wheezing was getting worse, so I decided to get the lift for the final flight. I stabbed the control panel impatiently before realising I had pressed the wrong button, then started jabbing angrily at both buttons in turn.

Come on . . . I even started tapping my right foot impatiently on the floor, a trait I abhor in anyone else.

Thankfully the lift soon turned up, but when I stepped onto the office floor, it was all a bit overwhelming – like the floodgates had been opened.

Tom came over first, his gangly limbs moving as if in a fight with each other. I have never known a bloke so clumsy.

'Nick, you're back!' he exclaimed, nervously slapping my back, and nearly tripping over his own shoelace.

'All right,' I said meekly.

Then almost everyone else came over at once, offering me tea, biscuits and all sorts of 'feel better soon, please' comments.

'So, go on then, how many girls did you sleep with?' asked Tom above the hubbub, rubbing his hands together excitedly. But I couldn't concentrate, because I saw someone in the distance.

It was just the side of her face, but she had the sexiest smile. She was worryingly familiar. Could it be?

No . . . surely not, I thought, trying to look away.

But then she turned around in her chair and I realised that it was indeed the beautiful girl from the train this morning.

I wanted to laugh.

I don't even really know what was so funny. I hadn't felt happiness like this in a long time, the kind of delirious joy that makes you want to dance with strangers on the street and throw handfuls of sweets to children. A far cry from the wallowing mess I had been this morning.

My mind was full of questions. Who was she? Why was she here? Why wouldn't my bloody stomach stop feeling like it was full of jelly? Did I have a good enough shower this morning? God, I hoped I'd had a good enough shower this morning . . .

I looked her up and down, half concentrating on Tom. Our eyes met and it was like an electric shock running right through my body.

'So, go on then, tell me!' Tom insisted, a look of glee on his face, oblivious to the vision I had spotted in the near distance.

'Er, none, mate,' I said quietly, turning to my left in a bid to escape to my office. Tom walked away with obvious disappointment, as if I had forgotten to bring him back chocolate-based treats from the airport. I had forgotten those too, actually . . .

Suddenly Lydia was in my path, smelling like a bunch of freshly picked flowers.

'Hello, sweets,' she said, a look of pity on her face.

There it goes again. The look. People have been giving me that look ever since Amelia shacked up with Toby. I just wish I could turn back time and never get involved with anyone at work.

'Hi,' I replied, glancing towards the floor and feeling ever so aware of squirrel girl, who was now standing next to her, also looking shy and – if I was reading it right – slightly pissed off.

'There's someone I need you to meet,' Lydia announced, beaming and stepping aside with pride, as if unveiling a new museum exhibit. She gave the beautiful girl a hard shove and she stumbled towards me reluctantly.

'Hi, I'm Nick,' I said, extending my hand to shake hers, but afraid that I might fall in love if she touched me.

'Sienna,' she replied in a well-spoken voice that made the hairs on the back of my neck stand on end.

The skin of our palms met. Hers was soft. Neither of us mentioned the train thing.

'I work here, I'm a writer – just started a couple of weeks ago,' she said, looking deeply embarrassed.

That was when my short-lived dream was shattered.

She *works* here? This is not good news.

This means I will probably spend a lot of time wanting something I simply cannot have. Office romance is not an option after Amelia and Toby's stunt. Toby was a colleague. I've learned that for some people there are no boundaries. All the time I was working with him, he was lusting after my girl. Planning his attack. Dreaming of taking her away . . .

So I made a promise to myself. I would never get myself into a similar situation again. People at work already knew far too much about my life and now I wanted to keep work separate. Plus I've had too many friends leave the careers they've worked hard for because the person who tore their heart out and stamped on it was sitting at the desk opposite them, stalking around the photocopier and taking minutes at every damn meeting. In a way, I was lucky that they both left. The office is hard enough without affairs of the heart.

A cold chill descended on me. It was over before it had even begun. What had I been thinking? I don't even know Sienna. She could have a boyfriend, she could be married or something. Christ . . .

'Well, have a good day, Sienna,' I said as I stepped into my office, red-faced.

But hold on a minute, maybe I was being too hasty. If Romeo and Juliet could fight for forbidden love, then surely I could ask her on a date?

No, I told myself. Just no.

As I closed the door behind me, I wondered how I was going to cope with this situation.

This was me, Nick Redland. Nick who has never felt anything stronger than shallow, trouser-tightening lust for a woman I have just met.

Even my own girlfriends have failed to provoke this much enthusiasm in me. Even Amelia.

I must be having some kind of breakdown, I decided. The post-holiday blues were doing something odd to me.

This was straitjacket stuff. I was being a loon. What was I thinking?

She was clearly much younger, and gorgeous, and probably wouldn't be remotely interested in me anyway, I thought as I looked in a small mirror hanging on the wall.

Small lines were starting to gather round my eyes, and I noticed how I was beginning to look more and more like my father every day. I sighed a deep cavernous sigh which emptied my lungs entirely.

I sat at my desk for a while, wondering if I should talk to a close friend about the strange thoughts I'd been having lately. This break-up with Amelia was really getting to me.

Ten minutes or so passed. I collected myself. Pulled myself together. I was being rude locking myself away like this. I stepped out of my office and stood there for a moment with my hands in my pockets, looking out of the window to my left with a view of the flats above the shops across the road.

'Incoming!' shrieked Tom. I turned round and was hit square in the face with a Hacky Sack. Ha ha bloody ha.

'Right, that's it,' I yelled back, breaking into a run. I charged towards Tom, who despite being in his early twenties has the waif-like appearance of a ten-year-old, all skin and bones and silly hair.

He tried to run but it was useless. I backed him into a corner, leaned down, picked him up and proceeded to parade him round the office like a baby, his legs dangling uselessly from my arms.

'Oi! Oi! Put me down, you twat!' he shouted, his voice becoming shriller and more baby-like by the second. Everyone in the office was laughing. A lot.

'Put . . . me . . . down!' he insisted, fighting his own laughter.

'Say you're sorry! Come on, Thommo, say, "Sorry Mr Nick, I will never throw a beanbag in your face again," I taunted, looking down at him with a huge grin on my face.

He wasn't able to apologise as he was laughing too much, his cheeks a deep shade of crimson and tears of mirth forming in the corners of his eyes.

I eventually put him out of his misery and into a large recycling bin for old envelopes and junk mail. I left him there for about five minutes, his body folded like a paper aeroplane. He was giggling too much to be able to lift himself up and out.

You can do pretty much anything in our office and get away with it, which made it a pretty comfortable place to be, and was probably why I hadn't done much to try and leave.

My boss leaned back in his seat, poked his head round the door of his office and welcomed me back. I was pleased he was greeting my return so warmly, considering I had managed to screw up a whole load of illustrations just before I left.

Once Tom's humiliation had reached fever pitch I walked over to the bin, pulled him out and put him back on his feet again, ruffling his hair to assure him that I was only kidding. He looked sheepish.

Sienna was not paying us the slightest bit of attention. She was clearly above pratting about at work.

I laughed. Maybe being back wasn't that bad after all; and no one else knew that maybe, just maybe, I had fallen in love today.

CHAPTER 2

'I BELIEVE IN LOVE, YOU KNOW . . .'

Sienna

It's been five weeks and two days since I met Nick Redland, and things have not settled down as much as I'd hoped.

I quietly wished, after the disappointment of the train incident, that I would calm down. So I saw this guy on a train who seemed to be perfect, but then I discovered he was a heartbroken prankster who works at the same place as me. Never judge a book by its cover. That's what they say, isn't it?

He's more than a bit irritating, with all his fooling around in the office. Ping-pong balls thrown back and forth across the room, salt in cups of coffee and joke-shop severed limbs in the paper tray of the printer. It's almost as if his main purpose in life is to make Tom laugh. He seems so immature for his age, plus he's damaged goods.

Heartbroken men are like wild animals, running around with hysteria in their eyes, desperately trying to knock the dents out of their egos.

But he's gorgeous . . . And it's hardly as if I discovered that he has a wife, two dogs, a semi-detached house in the country and a baby called Alistair.

As much as I try to stop myself, I keep finding myself thinking about him. I'm about as calm as Cameron Diaz in *My Best Friend's Wedding* when she's on the brink of orgasm at simply being offered a cup of tea.

He is single. Yes, single. And looks-wise, my idea of perfection.

But sadly I can imagine why this Amelia woman would have left him. Maybe he was annoying at home, too, and it isn't just a front for the office. I think that would be enough to drive me away . . .

I'm trying to rein in these conflicting feelings. I feel guilty for being so shallow, because essentially he isn't stacking up the personality points. I just fancy him. A lot.

Every time I find myself walking down the street with a grin so wide it looks like a saucer has been rammed into my mouth, I tell myself off a little bit. And to be fair, his pranks are pretty funny sometimes.

He wouldn't be interested in me, anyway. I'm pretty sure he's a fair bit older than me, plus he ruffled my hair the other day and told me how much I look like his sister.

That is never a good sign. Ever. It's probably his little way of saying 'Please get away from me, I just don't like you like that.'

He gives the same beautiful grin to the ladies at

reception; he pays the same amount of attention to Tom; he even feeds Dill, for God's sake. Nick does not look at me any differently to anyone else in the world.

The problem with silly men is they are funny. And funny does eventually make them quite sexy. It's a fact. Men who make you laugh instantly become hotter. And while he is immature, he makes me laugh a lot.

My best friend Elouise thinks I'm going crazy, and has told me to calm down. That's exactly what I'm going to do; she is the cool splash of water I need at the moment.

I've known Elouise since Year 7, and she is my hero. She is the calm in the eye of the storm. When gale force winds are battering away at me, nothing ever seems that bad after we've discussed it over a bottle of wine.

She's a beautiful blonde legal secretary with a cute nose, who's so attractive it's almost a bad thing. Men suddenly want to become her Superman so they act up when they meet her, but really, she just wants to find someone who will be there for her and stop playing games.

She has a little boy, who's three now. No one told her that if you're sick while you're on the pill you can get pregnant. We were just in our late teens when it happened. When she told me about it, I remember wiping the mascara-stained tears from her cheek and thinking it would be the making of her. I was right.

People sometimes judge her the wrong way, but she's one of the strongest, most intelligent people I know and every day I feel lucky to be her friend. I need to talk to her about this Nick situation again, tell her that it's not going away. She will know what to do. She always does.

I was feeling even more on edge today because I had a meeting with my boss at 1 p.m., and I had no idea what it was about. Anthony had never called me in for a one-on-one meeting before, so it felt pretty exciting, although he did sound quite stressed when he phoned first thing this morning. It was the first time he'd called me before 9 a.m.

I had been trying very hard since I arrived, so I hoped it was something positive.

But then with all the silly daydreaming, my mind had been wandering, so he might be about to sack me. My probation period hadn't yet drawn to a close so I was still on shaky ground.

Knowing that this chat was coming up meant the clock was moving particularly slowly, and each second seemed longer than the one before it. I wanted to climb up on a chair, push the hands forward and watch while the office revved into fast forward mode. I tried to make time go more quickly by turning the clock on my desk around to face the woven partition, and I even hid the one on my computer screen. If I couldn't see it, I decided, I couldn't clock watch.

Finishing a feature about running shoes took up a decent chunk of my time and I made enough rounds of tea to equate to at least an hour of prime faffing around time.

An hour before the meeting my mind turned to Pete, the homeless guy. Maybe I could reduce my nerves by focusing on someone else. Doing something good. That's what my dad says, anyway: 'If you're worrying about yourself too much, help someone who has real worries. Turn your anxiety into something productive.' The words were bouncing around in my brain, so I decided to act on them.

'Lydia?' I called quietly across the office, leaning back in my chair. 'You know that homeless guy outside?'

'Yes, love?' I heard her respond from a muffled place far away.

'Can I, erm, can I take him some tea, do you think?' I instantly felt like a fool. What had got into me?

A wild shock of hair crept round from behind a desk partition, followed by an electric smile and crazy eyes.

'Hmm . . .' She looked around her, left to right, scanning for authority. Then she leaned towards me, and in a gentle whisper this time, a cloud of fruity perfume wafting up my nose, said, 'Go for it, but I never said a word.'

And just like that she vanished again, taking her cheeky smile with her.

I got up and headed for the drinks machine, peering out of the window into the car park below.

Sure enough, he was there – a thin, bent figure sitting on the bench, but this time surrounded by four cans of beer.

There was no queue this time. I got a tea with one sugar. It was a guess, of course. I imagined that if I was sleeping on the streets during a damp spring night I would probably like a sugar too. I had packed some biscuits in with my lunch so I put two of them in my pocket for him. Chocolate ones.

I hid the drink inside my jacket as I walked away and into the lift. I was nervous. What if he was abusive? What if he was rude to me? He probably wanted money. Not tea.

I stepped into the lift, hoping I was doing the right thing. I slipped unnoticed through reception, pressed the release button on the big glass doors at the back, and headed out into the cool air of the car park.

He was sitting with his back to me, his head bent forward so that from behind it looked like he didn't have one. I looked at my watch; it was 12.05.

I walked quietly over to the bench and sat down next to him. He didn't look at me, but his wrinkled face was now angled towards the lukewarm sun that was marking the start of our summer. He was wearing a dark navy bomber jacket, faded and full of holes, a grey jumper underneath, a pair of ragged black jeans and some brown boots with frayed laces. He stank of beer.

'So, you're talking to me now, are you?' he said sharply.

Immediately I realised this had probably been a bad idea. I decided to ignore the question. 'Hi, I'm Si—' I started meekly but I was interrupted. It made me jump.

'I believe in love, you know,' said Pete, his eyes drifting off to something on the horizon. 'I even had it once,' he continued, shuffling nervously on the bench, his grubby fingernails playing with a thread hanging from his jumper.

'What's your name?' he asked, oblivious to the fact that I had tried to tell him just a few seconds ago. He had a gruff voice with a thick London accent, like he had been posh once but turned cockney somewhere along the line.

'Erm, Sienna. Your name's Pete, right?' I asked him, noticing that he was still unable to make eye contact with me.

He nodded softly to confirm his name. 'She died, though. She isn't here any more . . .' he started again, a tinge of hopeless despair in his voice. This was something of an overshare for a first-time meeting, but I kept quiet, looking at the beer cans around his feet. He must be drunk. He kept pulling at the thread and a small section of his jumper started to unravel.

I didn't really know what to say. 'You had a girlfriend who died?' I asked eventually, realising how stupid I sounded, because that was exactly what he'd just said. I pushed the tea and biscuits

45

towards him across the wooden slats of the bench. He took them quickly and put them to the other side of him, away from me, as if I was going to change my mind and ask for them back.

I realised there was more to his tired eyes than cold nights on the street and a lack of nutrition. I didn't ask too many questions.

We sat side by side and didn't say a word for ten whole minutes. Police sirens broke the silence occasionally; a twig fell from a tree and landed at our feet. He flinched.

Eventually I felt ready to ask something.

'Is that why you're here, Pete?'

'You could say that. She was my wife, actually . . . She got on the train to work one day. I thought it would be a day just like all the others. That morning everything was normal between us – two big glasses of orange juice and a kiss goodbye. It wasn't the usual route for her, though; she was heading for some work conference and they were staying at a hotel that night. But there was a disaster, a complete disaster . . .' He paused for a moment and bit his bottom lip.

'She was on a train that crashed in Oakwood Park. It was an ill-fated carriage and my girl was inside and I wish I could have stopped her from going that morning. My whole life collapsed the day she died. Ruined. I did some silly things after that, and people weren't as supportive as I hoped. So it boiled down to this, me alone in the city. It was ages ago now. Two thousand and fucking two.'

He kicked one of the cans at his feet and it rolled down the slanted concrete before nestling against the back tyre of a Vauxhall Vectra. The car park was small and seemed relatively peaceful compared to the hubbub on the main road at the front of the building, which you could just about hear.

There was room for twenty cars, the spaces surrounded by a neatly trimmed hedge with the odd crisp packet and drinks can wedged between its branches. I don't know why the bench was here. It wasn't exactly a great hang-out spot. The only other thing in the space was a big blue rubbish bin with a black lid.

So that was it, one man's demise in a nutshell. An edited-down, hacked-up sentence or two documenting what must have been years of agony for the lost soul sitting by my side.

The story was pulling at my heartstrings and again I wondered if this had been a mistake. I had only wanted to bring him a drink and some biscuits, but now I wanted to help him. Save him. I'm a bit like that sometimes, but it's a mistake because I already have too much responsibility in my life.

He seemed horribly accepting of where he was, almost as if a way out seemed so impossible that he was just sitting out the rest of his life now, waiting for it to end.

Watching, waiting, scavenging. Rustling around in bins for the answers among the city's useless solutions. No chance of hoping, wishing or even dreaming. His life had been shattered; the end was already here.

The hollow hopelessness of his situation sent a cold chill through me. I imagined the wreckage of the train, the bent shards of metal and billowing smoke. I imagined the newspaper photographers climbing over fences and using their long lenses to get another shot of tragedy. I imagined the staff crowding on the gravel by the railway line in brightly coloured overalls with reflective strips, hands behind heads, squinting with expressions of disbelief.

I don't know why I did it, but I put my right hand on top of his left one. Sometimes you just do things because they're instinctive. His hand was rough to the touch. He flinched.

'Why are you doing that, Sally?' he said, turning towards me with a toothy grin.

'Sienna,' I corrected him. 'I don't know. I just think you might have forgotten what it feels like to not be alone. I don't want you to forget. I think everything will work out for you . . . I really do.' Tears started to prick my eyes, and my bottom lip began to wobble as the words spilled out of my mouth like emotional soup. God, I was pathetic.

'Oh, love,' he said. His voice sounded tired. 'I'm all right. I'm a soldier and I keep her with me anyway, she gets me through.' He pulled a tatty leather wallet from his jacket pocket and dug his nails into a small inside section. The stale smell of beer crept across the space between us and into my nostrils.

'Here she is: my beautiful Jenny,' he declared, as he produced a tattered photo of a slim-looking woman with long blonde hair. It was stored in a bit of grubby cling film in a rather vain attempt to preserve her image. She looked clean and wholesome and happy.

I imagined what he must have looked like when he was with her, a fresh shave, a buzz cut and a suit. Maybe they'd even had a car and a newspaper subscription. I pictured them sitting together on a Sunday, Pete with the sports supplement, Jenny with the culture guide.

I looked down at my watch; it was now 12.20. I did something completely impromptu.

'Can I take that picture away for a moment, Pete?'

'No. I don't want you to take this the wrong way, but what if it goes missing? This is all I have and it's in a right state. It keeps getting rained on . . . It might not last much longer,' he replied, a hint of genuine fear in his voice.

'Well, that's just it, I'm going to make it better for you. Please just trust me and wait five minutes,' I pleaded.

'But why do you want it? Tell me,' he said.

'Just trust me, could you?' I responded, my heart rate picking up.

Before he had the chance to argue any further I plucked the picture from his fingers and stood up. A look of desperation crossed his face, as if he were begging me not to take away the last beautiful thing he had. He looked as though he barely had the energy to speak.

I turned and ran through the back doors and into reception. 'Can I use the copying room, please?' I asked Sandra hurriedly. I didn't want to prolong what must have been for him a period of unbearable worry. She was filing her nails and paying little attention to anything else.

'Yes, of course, sweetheart. Whatever,' she responded, not even glancing in my direction and flicking the file into the air flippantly.

I had to work fast; I had just five minutes to do something really special and if I fucked it up, I would spend the rest of my life trying to come to terms with the guilt.

I gently placed the photograph on the scanner, ensuring there were no greasy stains on the glass. Within seconds the image was replicated on a screen in front of me. I made it slightly larger, sharpened the colours a little and trimmed the edges. I clicked print, my right hand shaking slightly. Yes. This was going to be fine. I would just laminate this so it wouldn't get ruined, give it back to him and go upstairs again. End of. Then he could have it forever.

The printer coughed into life and after I pressed a couple of buttons, it started to whirr. I didn't know how to use it, but it couldn't be that difficult.

The first copy came out, her face printed on photo paper, and it looked as good as the original, if not better. I picked it up and smiled. Cool. So far, so good.

But then another copy came out. And another. And another.

Oh God. Where was the stop button on this thing? Shit.

The copies were building up in the tray now and they were coming out faster and faster. It must have made a hundred in a matter of sixty seconds. How had this happened? Jenny's face was taunting me. Again and again and again.

I stood there for a few minutes as the paper kept spewing out, the sheets now slipping over the edge of the tray and sliding onto the floor like a mini avalanche.

I was getting flustered. And when I get flustered I can't think straight. I had been at least five minutes; I had already broken my promise.

I looked at all the buttons on the machine, but none of them made sense. Lights were flashing, one green, one red. There was a large pink button that looked like it might end this situation, so I pressed it but nothing happened. I leaned over the machine and my eyes scanned frantically for a wire that might lead to a plug, but it all seemed to be built into the floor. Fuck.

More copies were pouring out now. It seemed to get even faster. Clicking and whirring . . .

Suddenly I heard the sharp banging of heels

across the tiled floor and the door behind me swung open. 'What are you doing, Sienna?' asked Sandra, who was now standing in the doorway looking suspicious.

I said nothing and flapped my arms a little.

'People need to use this room! What's going on?' she continued, her face now sour, the make-up so thick it looked as if it might fall in a pancake from her face and land on the floor with a wet slapping sound.

I thought I was doing a good job of hiding the papers, but the copier was still churning out endless Jennys.

'Hold on a minute, what's this all over the floor? You do realise you're only allowed to make ten copies a day and if there are any more, you need to get permission from IT? There must be hundreds here!' She was shouting now as she kneeled down on the floor and started trying to scoop up the sheets. Her jewellery was clattering away and her noxious perfume was making me feel sick.

'Look, I pressed the wrong button, I don't know how,' I stuttered, my cheeks now crimson.

She held one of the sheets as she stood up, looking at the small image of a woman she didn't know on the top left-hand side of the page. 'Who the hell is this? The company does not have the money to be funding your projects, Sienna. You do realise I'll have to report this? It's my job.'

I was beginning to feel really angry now. 'I told

you already, I made a mistake. How do you stop this?'

She ushered me out of the way as the printer kept vomiting copies of Jenny and pressed a single button. One last sheet dripped out, number 451. There was silence. She looked at me with pursed lips and a raised eyebrow. I was sure she was evil.

I opened my mouth to speak but a loud banging could now be heard from the reception doors.

'Oi. Oi! Give my photo back!' came an angry shout. We both looked through the doorway nervously. It was Pete. We couldn't see him, but I knew.

'What the hell is going on?' she asked, flinching as the banging got louder.

'Oh God. I'm so sorry. Just give me a second, will you?' I turned to open the lid of the scanner so I could get the photo out, but before I had the chance, Dave, our sports writer, appeared as if from nowhere.

'Guys, there's something crazy going on!' he said excitedly, a great chunk of his boy-bandesque fringe falling over his face. He swiped it away.

My stomach flipped.

'That homeless guy is going mental out there, throwing beer cans. Fucking cans of beer he's lobbing, at the windows upstairs! One of the windows to Ant's office has cracked – he's livid, man! They're going to call security!' he shouted with glee, as if this was the most exciting thing ever to happen in the office. Ever.

'Everyone is upstairs watching! They might even have to call the police,' he continued, slapping his hands together.

I looked down at my watch, still not taking responsibility for this shocking turn of events. It was 12.40.

'Oi! I want my fucking photo!' Pete's voice came again from outside reception, even louder this time. Then another sharp bang, and you could hear the glass outside rattling. This time it sounded like he was throwing beer cans at the reception windows.

Sandra looked down at the photo on the sheet she was holding and glared at me.

'Have you stolen this photo from Dancing Pete, Sienna?' Her eyes narrowed.

Dancing Pete, what a fucking ridiculous name. I started to shake. 'God no, of course not. I was trying to do something to help him!' I protested. But even I knew this sounded pretty weak.

Only I could fix this mess, so I ran out of the room and into the main reception lobby, my heels tapping against the concrete floor. The photo remained wedged in the scanner.

There he was, pressed against the glass, almost foaming at the mouth. I was terrified. I pressed the release button and he lunged towards me as the glass doors opened.

'You bitch. Give me my photo,' he yelled, pointing a shaking hand at me.

I ushered him outside and around the corner,

away from the crowd of people who were probably looking out of the office window from our
floor.

'Calm down, Pete,' I whispered, trying to diffuse
his fury. His lips were twitching and his eyes were
watering. A small line of drool was shining on his
chin from where he had been shouting. 'Look, it's
OK. Something went wrong with the printer. I was
trying to do something for you, with your photo . . .
Just stay calm, all right? I'm going to get it for you
now. Just go and sit on the bench and take a few
deep breaths, please.' I was shaking like a leaf now.

His eyes narrowed as they bore into mine and
for a few seconds we stood face to face in silence.
'The printer? What are you doing with it? Go on,
go and get it. But if you don't come back I swear
to God I will smash my way in,' he threatened,
flinging his arm, already loaded with one more
can of beer, to his side.

I dashed back into the copying room and asked
Sandra and Dave to give me some space. 'Sandra,
cancel security please, it's OK. I've sorted it out.'

She tutted and walked away. Dave dashed back
into the lift, a look of pleasure on his face.

I took a deep breath to calm myself, picked up
a pair of scissors and cut around the photo carefully. Then I laminated it, trimmed the edges and
looked down at the new version. It had been worth
it. She was gorgeous, and she was forever now.
The plastic was extra tough and sealed securely
on all sides. This meant that her memory would

not be washed away by the rain, cracked by the frost or faded by the sun.

The joy of this achievement was greatly overshadowed by the fact that I would probably get into a lot of trouble for this.

I stepped over the piles of copies lying all over the floor, ran back outside and put the old photo in his hands. He looked confused.

'Look, Pete, I have to go back inside now, but this is for you, OK? Please don't hate me. I was just trying to help.'

I placed the toughened plastic between his fingers but he still looked really angry as he pulled it towards his face and stared at it, nostrils flaring. He didn't speak, so I gently put my hand on his shoulder and squeezed, suddenly aware of how bony he was. 'See you soon,' I whispered quietly before turning around to walk away. A squirrel was standing in my path.

As I reached the doorway, I turned around before going inside. The outline of his back was shaking a little; his head was in his hands. I stood, looking at him for a few moments, when unexpectedly he turned and smiled, tears running down his face. Happy tears.

I swiped my entry card to get back into reception and walked past Sandra, ignoring her as she shouted at me. I stepped straight into the lift, which was conveniently wide open.

I stood there for a few seconds, my heart racing, before pressing the button for the third floor.

As soon as the doors opened, Lydia was there

waiting for me. 'What the hell have you done?' she asked with a half smile, both hands pressed against her lips as if in prayer.

'Nothing, all right, just leave it,' I said, tears stinging my eyes.

Nick

Amelia came round this morning, a crying, sobbing wreck on my doorstep. At first I thought there was an abandoned kitten in my porch, or a dog with a broken tail.

'What do you want?' I said, the door open only a crack and the chain still attached as I stood in my boxer shorts. I have always worked by the rule that if a stranger attacked me, I would not want to be just in my pants.

Amelia was a stranger, really. She looked different. Oh yes, that was it – I didn't love her any more.

People do look different when you fall out of love with them. But then again, I wasn't sure if it had ever been love I'd felt for her, or for anyone in fact. Since meeting Sienna, I'd wondered if all my previous relationships had just been a farce. I had never had that stomach-tingling feeling with anyone before I met Sienna. I had only picked up snippets of what love might be like from Amelia's pastel-coloured novels piled up by the toilet, mass-produced pop songs on the radio and shitty romantic comedies, and consequently brought the symptoms upon myself like a phantom pregnancy.

'Please leave,' I said frankly and calmly. I had known she would be back here one day, but I'd never expected to feel so cool about the whole thing.

'But Nick, please, I can explain. I made a terrible mistake and I love you . . .' She trailed off, putting one of her soft yet bony hands in the door frame in an attempt to reach my chest.

I did adore those hands. I used to hold the left one up to my face when we watched TV and just feel it against my skin, tracing her nails over my lips. Now I wanted them as far away from me as possible.

She was poison in disguise. A Barbie stuffed full of explosives. 'I think you need to leave,' I repeated, stepping backwards so her hand fell away from me.

She started to crumple, tears falling like snow-flakes from her brown eyes as she dropped to her knees in front of me. Waves of auburn hair fell over her face as she thudded to the ground.

I felt pretty sorry for her. I scanned the street scene behind her small, shaking frame. This was rather embarrassing, really. God knows what the neighbours would make of it. What must they think I've done to her?

A milkman walked past and glared at me. Mind your own business, calcium kid.

Quietly and calmly I shut the door on her and walked back down the hall. I needed to leave for work within the hour, by which time she had better be gone.

I made tea to the soundtrack of helpless sobs outside my window, so I turned up the radio. Chris

Moyles was not my favourite human being on the planet, but right now his inane ramblings beat the sound of my ex-girlfriend crying herself into a frenzy in the street.

The shower failed to wash Amelia away. This was becoming painful and despite how bitterly furious I was with her, I felt like a right bastard. I dressed, went back downstairs and let her in.

'Oh, thank you, Nick. Please, just hear me out,' she sighed as she stumbled through the hallway like a drunk.

We sat at the kitchen table, and she traced her fingers over the tablecloth she had chosen all those months ago at Portobello Market. Her nose was pink and swollen; her eyes were bloodshot. She had spoiled it. She had ruined everything.

'Look, I don't want you to tell me why, or how, or when – or certainly not where—' I started, but was quickly interrupted.

'It was at his place. I would never have done that in our home, Nick,' she blurted out quickly, as if that made it all OK. It didn't, and I didn't believe her for a second anyway.

Hunched over, she leaned towards me desperately, her shoulders pulled down under the weight of her shame. And how heavy that must have been. I flinched at the thought of her in some dirty, sexy embrace with him, and slammed my right fist down on the table. The anger was rising thick and fast in my chest, clawing at my throat and suffocating me.

59

'Just stop, will you? I've met someone else. Just take your stuff – all of it – and go. Post your key back through the door when you're finished, yeah? Oh, and the Radiohead album is mine.' I got to my feet quickly and stormed out of the house, ignoring the shouts behind me and slamming the door so hard I was worried the glass would crack. I noticed that my hands were shaking. Adrenaline was pumping so hard round my body I didn't know what to do with myself.

Of course I hadn't really met someone else – well, no one that I could call my girlfriend. Yes, I had met Sienna, and granted, I had fallen pretty hard, but it would have been a little psychotic of me to make out that she felt the same, because I was pretty sure she didn't. But it seemed like the best thing to say at the time.

I hoped Amelia would be angry at me, just like I was with her. It was the best way to move on.

The sun was out this morning and the birds were singing; spring was tracing its gentle fingers through my world, changing everything around me. My anger about Amelia started to peel away as I walked, like a snake shedding its skin. I took deep breaths and felt the cool air fill my chest. I wanted to get rid of all this stuff, leave it behind me and start afresh. Alone. Maybe I could just start again. Me, a carefree, single guy. A kind of fresh start.

The train journey was quick, smooth and incident-free. I needed today to be simple. I had a meeting with Anthony at 1 p.m., which had been worrying me a little. He hadn't said what it was about when he called first thing this morning, but he'd sounded pretty pissed off. Maybe I was due a telling-off. To be fair, I had been moping around with a face like a wet weekend.

A few weeks ago I had drafted some new ideas in terms of graphical direction for our magazines, something to really give us an edge. I felt it was time to pull these out of the hat, and if we were due for crisis talks, I was hopeful about proving to him that I was serious about my career. I would tell him I'd let things slip, but I was on the turn, surfing the wave, and everything would be just fine.

I was off to a gaming fair in America the next day and I was determined to redeem myself then, even though it would involve me, Tom and the company credit card. It was a huge distraction but I had to resist the pranks and binge drinking, I told myself. Suddenly my head was filled with images of Tom and me passed out and spooning in some luxurious hotel room after a few too many beers. I shuddered.

I was feeling pretty sick with nerves in the build-up to the meeting, but then something strange happened that completely diverted my attention from the fact that I might be about to be fired.

Just after midday, some homeless guy started kicking off outside in a big way. No one in the office knew why. He was yelling something about a photo. He was probably drunk, and he ended up throwing beer cans at the windows on our floor, managing to crack one of Ant's, who was predictably furious about the whole thing. We were all told to stay upstairs while security was called.

Of course, everyone in the office was delighted. They were huddled in groups, chattering away by the windows and watching as this lunatic rampaged around the car park like an angry bear. I stayed in my office.

It was pretty short-lived entertainment, however, and by quarter to one the whole thing had died down. Everyone was saying they had seen Sienna outside, calming him down and sorting things out. I don't know why she had been dragged into it all. It's a waste of time, to be honest, you can never *really* help people like that. I think it's best to just stay out of it. I could tell already that she was one of those good, kind people, and if she carried on getting involved we'd end up with all the homeless and dejected people in Balham sleeping in our cars.

The hand on the big rectangular clock was just about to hit one, so I gathered my papers and made my way to Anthony's office. I was nervous, a feeling that had been becoming all too familiar recently.

As I walked towards his office I spotted Sienna, walking slowly towards me with a shy smile painted across her features. She looked flustered and her eyes were a little pink, like she might have been crying. But she was still beautiful.

Her movements slowed right down, just like in

the films. She was wearing dark blue skinny jeans and a retro cardigan with frills on the sleeves. Her long brown hair was sleek and shiny, tumbling over her shoulders. Yet again, she was holding a cup of tea. I wondered if there was one permanently fused to her hand.

Our paths drew closer and closer until we both stood awkwardly outside Anthony's mezzanine floor. 'Do you want to get past?' I said, comically extending a gentlemanly arm to let her through.

She looked puzzled. 'Er, no. I'm going to see Ant. Why are you . . .?' she responded, a look of total confusion in her eyes.

'Oh, but I'm due to see him at one,' I told her, wondering if I'd got the time wrong. Then a cold wave of realisation washed over me.

She looked at her watch and shook it next to her ear, biting her bottom lip.

We stood there for a few moments, obviously unsure of what we should do next. Then she broke the silence.

'I think I'm in real trouble, Nick, about what happened earlier in the car park. Shit. Bollocks,' she said, looking as if she was about to cry.

I was really confused now. She couldn't have caused the whole thing, could she? If she had, then yes, she was right. Ant would probably send her packing, to be honest. He doesn't suffer fools gladly.

I opened my mouth to speak but I was interrupted. 'Right, you two, come on in,' said Anthony, his booming voice reverberating down the small flight of stairs leading to his den.

He ushered us in with a pair of chubby hands in an animated, impatient fashion, a look of distinct irritation all over his face. Then we stood there for a moment like confused pigeons, legs twitching.

'Well, come on, then!' he sighed in exasperation. He seemed really angry now. If Sienna was in some kind of trouble about this homeless guy, then why was I being dragged into it? Why was I in this room? It had nothing to do with me. And anyway, the meeting had been called early this morning, before the car park debacle. Maybe she had got into other skirmishes with this guy when I was away and this was the start of a disciplinary that I would have to be involved in. I did technically have middle management status . . .

Shit. That would be a disaster. Having to professionally punish the girl you fancy. Thanks a lot. My mind started wading through the awful possibilities. What if I eventually had to fire her? That wouldn't exactly be a great precursor to 'So, how about a date?'

Two chairs were positioned opposite Ant's leather throne, which was so large that I often feared he would one day get lost in it. And Anthony was not a small man. Big in size, big in voice, big in presence. His ears were big, his mouth was big, and even his bones were big, I was sure. At 6 foot 6, he towered over most people he met, and regularly made people jump when he walked into a room (which I had to admit, I found very funny).

Although Ant and I got on well, he could still inspire a certain terror in me. He reminded me of Mr Blake, an incredibly scary teacher at my school. While we had run circles around the others, chewing gum in class and answering back, Blake used to frighten the hell out of us.

As well as being chubby, which was his most significant feature, Ant's head was adorned with a big pile of brown curls that never seemed to be under any kind of control. He had dark, beady eyes and a round snub nose. But despite his booming demeanour, he had a nervous element to his personality. He found lengthy eye contact difficult and he tended to fiddle with things around him a lot, often pulling at the curls on the back of his head when he was thinking.

I didn't trust him entirely, but like everyone else I found myself slithering around him like a snake, in case he used his power against me in a moment of rage.

That was another thing: Anthony was angry. We regularly heard banging from his office on the main production floor as he slammed his fist on the desk, and shouted at some poor minion on the phone. We would just cringe and keep typing.

He plonked himself down in front of us, small beads of sweat gathering on his forehead from the sheer effort of the treacherous four-metre walk from his door. I was surprised he hadn't asked for sponsorship. Over his shoulder you could see a huge fissure in the window overlooking the car park.

Feeling slightly concerned that Sienna might see them, I tucked my ideas behind the clipboard I was holding. I didn't want her to think I was a brown-nosing loser panicking about getting fired (which is, incidentally, exactly what I was).

'Right, you two,' Anthony said again, moving a brightly coloured A4 photo frame out of the way and leaning back to reveal an oversized and very satisfied-looking tummy. One of the buttons had come undone, showing a flash of pale skin covered in coarse dark hair. Gross.

'We have obviously had some drama this afternoon,' he went on, turning towards the cavernous crack in the glass behind him, then looking back at Sienna with a frown. Yes, this was definitely what the meeting was all about.

She sank down into her chair, looking very guilty. I started to feel the panic rising as I imagined having to fill out procedure sheets and hold a meeting with her in a month's time to find out if she had learned her lesson, or whatever the course of action in these cases might be.

Ant started to speak again. 'But aside from that, which seems to be sorted out now, we have another problem. Tom called in sick this morning and he won't be able to make the trip to America.' He rubbed his chin with one hand.

I leaned back in my chair and looked down the stairs to Tom's desk. Of course – his chair had been empty all morning. I'd just assumed he was at a meeting. I was a bit pissed off that it might mean the trip was cancelled.

But wait. If Sienna had been called in, this must mean . . . Oh, please, say it means what I think it must mean . . .

'Sienna, I know you're relatively new, but I think you've settled in well so I want you to work with Nick on this one,' he announced. Sienna blushed a little and smiled at me as she put her cup of tea on Ant's chunky wooden desk.

'Sienna, I want you to create a series of articles for a ten-page supplement for *Digimax* on the annual gaming fair in Florida. Nick will be the man behind the illustrations and photographs. How does that sound?'

Silence filled the room as both our original assumptions were blown out of the water and replaced with something utterly wonderful. I wanted to break this silence like a small child. I wanted to punch the air with delight, leap onto my chair and ruffle my boss's hair with joy. The man who I'd previously viewed as a fat obstacle to my happiness was now worthy of carving into a statue and worshipping. He had gone from nagging me, making girls cry, and keeping us in late, to setting me up on a work trip with one of the fittest girls I'd ever seen . . . I wanted to run over to Sienna, pick her up and jump onto the plane with her now. My head was suddenly swamped with images of us waking up in a hotel bed together in one of those 'whoops' movie moments, where everything is sexy and turns out to be OK, and not shit, like reality.

Sienna looked flattered. Overcome. Delighted, even. But still, neither of us managed to actually speak.

Maybe I could take her on a date on the trip. The possibilities flooded my mind and I immediately told myself off because it was against my new 'colleagues + relationships = bad' rule.

'You two aren't in the mood for talking today, are you?' Ant chuckled, pulling out a can of Diet Coke from his mini fridge. The cool snapping sound of the ring pull cut sharply through the awkward chasm of quiet.

'Sorry, that's great news. Thanks ever so much. And I want to talk to you afterwards about what happened earlier . . . I can explain it all,' said Sienna, looking really nervous now. I noticed her feet shuffle inwards and her hands flex on her lap. Her body language radiated fear.

'Look, just forget about it. I don't know what happened, but we don't have time to worry about it right now. Pop into my office before you leave for the day. I do want you to go on this trip – I think it would be great experience for you,' he said, warming up a little after his brusque opening.

She turned her face towards mine and bit her lip. Damn, she was sexy.

'Is that OK, Nick?' asked Ant, leaning over the desk and waking me from my daydream as he pushed his sloppy jowls in my direction.

'Yes, yes, of course. It'll be great to work with Sienna on this,' I replied, trying to sound as cool as possible when actually I wanted to kiss him on the cheek and give him a 'best friends forever' bracelet.

Ant turned to Sienna. 'So, we need to book you some flights. You'll be leaving tomorrow morning and it's a three-day thing. All right?'

There was barely time for the poor girl to think, even if it wasn't all right.

'Yes,' she replied quickly. 'Actually, Ant, I need to just ring home and check, you know . . . that everything will be OK,' she added quietly, obviously trying not to be rude to me as I was clearly the party with the least information.

Ant nodded understandingly. He knew something I didn't, and I wanted in. Why would she need to check that she could go? Please don't tell me she lives with overbearing parents who won't let her come out and play . . .

If she has to check with her parents that she can go on a work trip, then they must be a nightmare. Does she still live at home? She's twenty. I started imagining the poor sod who comes back to her place after a night out and then has to endure an awkward breakfast with a pair of overprotective, prudish accountants or something . . . God.

But really I had no idea what she was talking about. I was making huge assumptions. Perhaps it wasn't her parents she lived with, maybe it was another man. I wondered again if she was with anyone. I'd never heard her mention anything, but she seemed so private anyway, I doubted she'd tell me. I prayed the situation, whatever the hell it was, wouldn't stop her coming.

Sienna dashed out of the room and then it was just Ant, me and the buzzing sound coming from his drinks cooler. 'Actually, I have some ideas I wanted to present to you, while we have a minute.' I started to hand over the twenty-page document I had prepared, hoping I hadn't typed a load of inane rubbish.

He jabbed the pages with his chubby digits, and it felt like an unwanted intrusion. There was already oil on the first page from where he had food on his hands. For Christ's sake . . .

'Hmm, this looks great, Nick,' he said in the slightly patronising manner of a parent responding to their child's cack-handed paintings.

This looks great? You haven't even bloody read it, you tosser.

'Well, there's quite a lot there. I was thinking you might need a bit longer to go through . . .' I tried to demand more of his time, but Sienna was back already.

She had a wide smile on her face. This must be good. Ant's attention was gone.

'Yep, I'm in,' she said briskly.

'Are you sure that's all OK?' he asked sympathetically, his greedy eyes looking her up and down.

He fancies her! He bloody fancies her! I must get

to the bottom of this. I hate not being the centre of attention, and I hate not being in the know.

'OK, well, that's just great. You can leave a couple of hours early to prepare. Just call me if you have any questions – and remember, Sienna, I need to see you just before you go,' he continued as he stood up to usher us out. 'One more thing: don't forget your passport!' he added, raising his voice a little. Another button popped, revealing a huge belly button. I wondered for a moment – if anyone got lost in there, would we hear their cries of distress?

As Sienna and I left his office, I wondered how to handle this. It was like a dream come true, but looking too happy would definitely freak her out, and I was still a bit pissed off that Anthony had dismissed my work. He didn't even know Sienna that well and all of a sudden it was like everything revolved around her. He would normally have read my ideas with interest, he was always encouraging creativity, but now there was something different about the office. The dynamic had shifted.

But still – how should I react to the news of our trip? Being too blasé would just make her feel alienated. I also had to be careful with my choice of words. Already I had told her how she reminded me of my sister. My sister? God knows why I said that. I think it was some kind of defence mechanism to push her away because I was worried she didn't like me.

However, telling her she reminded me of my sister

was probably the ultimate sin. Worse than saying she was cross-eyed, bad at spelling or pigeon-toed (she is none of the above, and even if she were all three I think I would still fancy her).

I have a habit of filling quiet moments with stupid chatter rather than intelligent vocal contributions to society. 'So, what do you think?' I said, turning to face her at the entrance to the main office floor, my hands shaking a little. I thought I'd been nervous before the meeting, but I was really nervous now. If I did anything stupid, everyone would see.

'Oh my God, Nick, I'm so excited!' She started to jump up and down, using my arms as support. Sparks of electricity danced between us and I felt them. Each and every one. I suddenly felt overwhelmingly tense in her presence and needed to excuse myself. 'Look, I have to go, got so much to do before tomorrow! Got to clear out the remains of my ex-girlfriend tonight!' I said unblinkingly. There was a pause and I noticed her expression had melted from a smile into a look of horror.

'I mean, erm, not her actual bodily remains – her clothes and stuff . . . Ha ha, got you there!' I said. Foot-in-mouth syndrome had taken hold.

She smiled again, but still looked slightly disturbed.

I cleared my throat and exited stage left before I truly hung myself. How was I going to cope with this? I wondered as I ducked into my office. It was total chaos in there: pens, paper and measuring tools spread across my desk like artist vomit. I set my out-of-office. It went something like this:

> I am out of the office from Thursday 21 April until Monday 25 April.
> Please direct any urgent enquiries to editorial@cube.co.uk.
> I will answer all other correspondence upon my return.
> Thanks.

What it actually should have said was this:

> I am out of my mind from now (Thursday 21 April) for the foreseeable future.
> Please direct any urgent enquiries somewhere else. I don't really care where, but don't bloody well bother me.
> Oh, and Amelia – please fuck off and die.

On the way out I walked over to Sienna's desk. She was typing so fast I feared I might go blind just watching.

'Sienna?' I whispered, concerned that I might frighten her to death. She did jump a little. 'I'm going home now, but I can come and pick you up in the morning, if you like? I'm not sure what time it'll be, but I'm guessing it'll be pretty early.' I pushed a small piece of paper her way with my mobile number scrawled on it in black ink.

She looked panicked. I wasn't surprised, considering I'd almost made myself out to be a girlfriend-murdering nutter.

'That's really kind – thank you, Nick. I'll, er, have a think about it and call you. I'm really looking forward to the fair,' she added.

Out of the corner of my eye I could see Dave, our camp sports writer, dancing around behind Sienna, moving his hips like an oversexed R'n'B singer and pointing at her, his tongue hanging out of his mouth. Then his fringe flopped over his face. Oh God, this was embarrassing . . .

Sienna must have sensed something was going on behind her and she turned her head around. But by the time she did, Dave was sitting still with a false look of diligence on his face, probably typing the letters XyXyXy all the way across the screen. Cheeky bugger.

'Right, OK then, see you in the morning,' I called and turned on my heels.

When I got home I dreaded what I might find when I turned the key in the door. Maybe Amelia had created a floor mosaic out of raw meat spelling the word 'Fuckwit', or even worse, taken my Radiohead CD. The very worst-case scenario would be if she was still here . . .

I slowly made my way into the corridor. 'Amelia?' I called out, the fear obvious in my voice as it echoed down the hall. Looking down at my feet, I saw the key gleaming on the mat. Phew, I was safe.

I shuffled cautiously into the kitchen and saw a folded-up piece of paper. I began to read.

Nick,
What can I say?
I ruined the best relationship I have ever had in my life and I will probably never forgive myself for this.
I am deeply sorry for the pain I might have caused you.
If it helps in any way, the person who is hurting the most in all this is me.
People like you don't come around often, and I may never meet another.
If you ever find a way to forgive me, I will be waiting.
Love you,
Amelia
x

Well, you had to give it to the girl, that was truly heart-wrenching. I looked at a photo of us pinned to the fridge with a Honey Monster magnet. We looked so happy. Behind us were the rambling hills of the Lake District, and the bright sun had created a white flash in one corner of the photograph. A flaw in an otherwise perfect moment.

The true enormity of what had happened suddenly hit me like a ton of bricks. My house now felt huge, even though it wasn't that big. A two-bedroom terraced place that seemed like a sprawling mansion now I was alone.

I had put the deposit down on it with money left to me by my grandmother. Mum and Dad helped out a bit too. I was lucky to have this house at such a young age, but right now I felt so alone in it. I would probably have to get a lodger now to help with the mortgage. Great.

I had thought I was too angry about what Amelia and Toby had done to feel sadness like this. I'd been so incandescent with fury that I'd hated the thought of her; only now was I starting to feel her loss.

I suddenly remembered what this stage of a break-up felt like; it was all coming back to me now. It was like a really bad stomach bug after a dodgy takeaway. At the time you feared you might die with your head stuck down the toilet and a hole blown out of the seat of your trousers, then just a few weeks later you had completely forgotten how terrible it was. It was as if the experience had been so traumatic that your mind had dulled its memory enough for you to get all cocky again. Otherwise you would never be able to walk down a street with a curry house on it again. And that would make living in London quite difficult. With feelings, it was tricky. One minute you might be making a coffee or shopping for milk and cereal, and then bam – out of nowhere the inescapable would come and sting you. Those emotions you'd buried under a heap of male egotistical bullshit.

All the crappy phrases your friends had reeled off to salve the wounds: 'Plenty more fish in the sea, mate,' or 'We never really liked her anyway . . .'

But I wasn't sure whether I missed her, or whether I was scared of my uncertain future.

The loud ticking of the kitchen clock only affirmed the fact that I was alone. I'm not a big boozer, I don't really drink on my own, but I poured a small amount of whisky into a glass and trickled some Coke on top.

I pulled a Marlboro Light out of my jacket pocket and lit it with a match. The smoke instantly surrounded me in our small, clean kitchen, dirtying every nook and cranny with its nasty brown fingers.

I sat there for what seemed like hours, feeling the numbing effect of the alcohol settling into my legs. Taking deep drags on my cigarette I experienced the familiar buzz of nicotine and I convinced myself I deserved it. I had totally earned this moment of hideous self-indulgence, but I would definitely regret it when I woke up at 3 a.m. to get to the airport.

Nick. Twenty-seven. Single. The labels spun round and round in my head.

Nick. Twenty-seven. Single . . .

My self-pity lasted for about an hour, then I decided I had to sort myself out. All that was left of my broken relationship was this note, the photo on the fridge and the tablecloth. I calmly picked up all three and put them in the bin. The remains. That's what I'd meant.

Suddenly my phone rang, but I didn't recognise the number. I let it vibrate frantically before I decided it just might be important. 'Hello?' I answered, slightly concerned at who it might be.

'Hey, Nick.' I recognised that voice.

'Oh, hello, Sienna. You OK?' I responded, immediately sitting down, embarrassed as I looked at the display of self-loathing all around me.

'I'm fine, thanks. Just wanted to check the details for the morning. Is it still OK for you to pick me up?'

'Yes, of course. I'll be round at quarter to four, if that's all right?'

'Great . . . I was going to ask you. Could you not ring the doorbell or anything, please? If you could just give me a call, I'll run out, yeah?'

'Oh, sure, of course. Wouldn't want to wake anyone up!' I joked.

There was a strange pause on the other end of the line.

'Can you text me your address? I don't have a pen handy,' I added, trying to break the strange quiet that had overshadowed our conversation, while simultaneously scanning the room for one of the hundreds of brightly coloured pens that seemed to be everywhere when I didn't need one.

'Sure,' she replied.

'What happened earlier, by the way, Sienna? You know, that crazy man outside the office?' I realised I hadn't asked before, and I really wanted to know.

'Er, nothing, don't worry. I'll explain later. So,

what are you up to?' she asked, swiftly changing the subject.

Oh God, cold sweat. Cold sweat. 'Just reading a book in French about the Revolution, actually,' I responded quietly. I cringed at my lie, but I had to. The reality of me drinking spirits and smoking myself to death over my ex-girlfriend was pathetic. Still, I could have chosen something slightly cooler than the scenario my brain had just selected at random – like coming back from boxing training or something.

'Oh, wow. That sounds fascinating,' she said. I could hear her smile.

'What about you?'

'Just packing,' came her reply, neat and tidy.

Damn. Why didn't I just say that? Now she was going to ask me questions about the French Revolution on the plane that I might not be able to answer.

'Well, I'll see you in the morning then, Si. Not long now!'

'No, not long at all. See you later.'

The line went dead.

All of a sudden I was filled with hope again, so I dashed upstairs to pack. My packing plan was a little more elaborate than the one I'd adopted for Ibiza. Fewer shorts, sun cream and novelty hats; more suits, gadgets and hair gel.

I loved events like this. I had never covered the gaming fair in America before, but I had done lots of similar trips and it meant spending a few hours taking pictures, then enjoying slap-up meals and nights out on the company credit card.

Sienna

The sun was rising slowly over the city of London and Nick and I were watching it through a tiny window to my left. Rich whirls of colour were bathing the fields around the runway in a warm glow. My thoughts were a mix of overwhelming excitement and serious worry. I hoped things at home would be OK.

When I took the job I knew I might have to go away for work every now and then, so Elouise kindly agreed to pop round and keep an eye on things when I did. This was really short notice, though. I definitely owed her a few babysitting sessions, even if I had a habit of teaching Luke naughty words by accident.

Last summer I was looking after him and we were playing in the garden. I managed to tread on a wasp, which stung me between my toes, forcing me to utter a tirade of words that turned the air blue. He stood and looked at me with his feet pointing inwards and a look of fear clouding his big green eyes. It wasn't until a couple of weeks later that Elouise mentioned he was saying the words 'holy' and 'shit' in close succession at church playgroup and couldn't work out where he had picked them up from. I went red.

As the aircraft moved around the runway before

zooming into the sky, we both sat quietly, waiting for take-off.

I was becoming quite scared, if I was being honest. Air travel was something I had never really got my head around. Obviously there were scientific reasons why this stupidly heavy lump of metal bashed together by human beings could stay in the sky. Bashed together by human beings. Thousands of feet in the air, suspended above vast expanses of deep murky water and sharp-edged mountain ranges. People. Mortals, capable of making mistakes. People always make mistakes. Day in, day out. We are experts in the art of the accident.

My stomach flipped as I heard the engines whirr loudly beneath us. Sections of the wings started to move, ready for the flight and our ascent into the unknown. Fear spread all over my body, washing down my legs like alcohol. I kept swallowing hard, again and again.

We'd had such an early start that neither of us had really woken up. A dozy breakfast and a couple of overpriced coffees in the departure lounge had done little to bring us into a state of consciousness. But this was working a treat.

Like a meerkat tanked up on Red Bull, I was well and truly alert now. I was still blushing at the thought of my display of clumsiness earlier that morning.

Nick had swung into the driveway of our block of flats and called my phone just as he'd promised. I'd tried to be calm and cool but managed to trip over my luggage in my near comatose state of sleepiness, falling to the hard, wet ground in front of him.

I used to take ballet classes. I used to be graceful. This morning I resembled a giraffe with its legs tied together as my foot got caught in the handle of my bag, sending me soaring into the air. My heart jumped in my chest and the force of my humiliation hit me before I hit the concrete. I'm not sure which was more painful. Why did this have to happen now? Why?

These had not been a good few days for me, what with the Pete incident, which I had just about squirmed my way out of. Ten pounds. That was my punishment for the copying incident. They said it reflected the cost of the ink and paper. The window was covered by insurance. I think I got off pretty lightly.

Anthony is an angry man and an unreasonable one at times, but he seemed to understand that it was a genuine accident and not much more was said after that. I was still embarrassed, though, and my fall didn't help. I felt like a first-class idiot.

Nick instantly jumped out of the car, reached down and picked me up as his headlights momentarily put my shame on a stage. His strength was no surprise with his build. He picked me up with ease, as though I was a rag doll. I was really humiliated and I felt angry with myself for a few moments, before I realised I was taking myself too seriously.

We sat in his car quietly for a minute. Nick was

the first to crack. I was unsure about whether I should laugh or bawl my eyes out, so I did neither and sat in silence, looking down at my bleeding palms. This would not help my mission to impress him. I looked and felt like an eight-year-old.

Then he started to laugh, and I'm so glad he did. It started off as a quiet snigger, which burst from between his lips, sudden and sharp. He was trying so hard to hold it in but it eventually developed into a full-on belly chuckle. He turned towards me, wiping his eyes with one hand, an apologetic smile on his face. Then I went, and we were both laughing so much we couldn't speak.

'Let me see those,' he said eventually, gently pulling my hands towards his chest. He softly turned my palms over and made a hissing sound when he saw the gentle drops of blood rising to the surface of my skin. I wasn't looking at my bleeding hands. I was looking at him, holding my hands. It struck me for a moment that this immature man might actually be able to take control of a situation, might help me.

'I know what to do!' he said, reaching into the glove box for a tissue. He quietly worked away, dabbing the blood from my palms and pressing new tissue onto them to make the bleeding stop. He wrinkled his eyebrows in concentration. I felt like my heart had slowed right down. Something in the depths of my soul shifted and moved. I didn't know if it was the aftermath of embarrassment or the eye-wateringly early hour that had left me feeling a little emotional. But with each sweep of that tissue, it felt as though he was touching my heart.

I had felt the rush from a boy before. That twinge of teenage horniness you feel when you kiss some stranger in the darkest corner of the nightclub, or the lift you get when a good-looking man buys you a drink at a bar. This was different. I felt like he was creeping into my heart and there was nothing I could do to stop him. I had only met him a few weeks ago, I thought he was childish and bruised, but still these feelings persisted.

I was trying not to let it happen, I really was. Everything about the situation was inappropriate and difficult. I worked with him. He was older than me. It was an embarrassing crush I could never really admit to. There were so many reasons, other people, that were stopping me from being with him. And why would he even give me a second glance, anyway? I suspected with a face like his that he was a ladies' man, that he must have women scrambling around to be a part of his life. I wondered if he knew what he was doing to me. I don't think he did.

As the plane started to lurch forward, I dug my nails into my palms and flinched when I felt the sharp pain of my cuts.

'You OK, Si?' asked Nick, turning his face towards mine, a lovely expression of concern dancing across his features.

'Yeah, of course. Why – are you scared?' I jeered,

poking him in the arm to deflect attention from my own crumbling state of mind.

'No, no, of course not! Just checking you weren't going to freak out or anything,' he added, with a frantic hand gesture that made an air hostess giggle as she walked past. He was so animated, his face capable of such incredible expressions. I wouldn't even know how to find the words to describe some of them, but I knew what they meant when I saw them.

The familiar smell of foil-sealed food filled the space around us as the aircraft built up speed. My stomach jumped as it started to lift, bouncing along the runway slightly as it launched itself into the air.

Please don't let go, I thought to myself, making a little order to the plane as it gripped onto the sky, wondering how my home life would be affected by my absence, and how my permanent absence would be a disaster. I bit my lip hard, and flexed my fingers. My head was full of images of the pilot swigging neat whisky behind the instrument panel, and the co-pilot smoking crack. Tears were beginning to form in my eyes. For God's sake, it wasn't even 8 a.m. and I had nearly cried twice. I was a wreck.

'You're scared, aren't you?' Nick turned towards me, his eyes wide. He looked a little concerned and reached out an index finger to my face, swiping a single tear away with expert precision and balancing his thumb on my right cheek so he didn't poke me in the eye. My breath caught in my throat. He looked a little surprised at what he'd done.

'Gosh, Si, I'm sorry. I shouldn't . . .' he said, as my tear slid off his finger and onto his lap. 'I think it's the claustrophobic spaces thing. It makes me go a bit funny,' he went on, looking down at his feet.

'No, no, no. I'm definitely fline. I mean, fine.' I looked at him with my fake 'everything's OK' expression, my cheeks turning red again.

He glanced at me suspiciously before turning his eyes towards the window again. The plane lurched from side to side as it positioned itself in its charge for America. It swung down sharply, giving Nick and me a view of patchwork fields, so far away now they looked like my grandmother had knitted them. It was stunning.

Something in our relationship shifted during our trip to America. As soon as we touched down on the runway, work took over and Nick morphed into a different man. It was a fascinating transition to watch, but I felt like a distant party looking in from the outside. He seemed like a totally different person away from the hysteria of the office and his broken relationship, and again I was reminded how far I was from really knowing him. I felt light years away from that stolen moment we had shared – a single tear wiped from my face just a few hundred feet from the ground when I felt like we were already lost in the clouds.

He took hundreds of photographs, then tucked

himself away in remote corners to upload them to the work server back home. He was a true professional. Passionate and confident. He wasn't just the office prankster he made himself out to be. I had been worried that he would throw me in a dumpster or something, or that one of his jokes gone wrong would land us both behind bars. But he was far from being that boy here. He was a man. And seeing this side of him made him even more attractive.

The gaming convention was everything I'd hoped it would be and more. I threw myself into interviewing and met everyone from the archetypal geek to the closet gamer. Businessmen with wives, busy schedules and incredibly fast thumbs from secret console sessions in the twilight hours, mingled with out-and-out joystick freaks. America was as brash, outrageous and eccentric as I'd always imagined it would be. And I saw enough nutcases in fancy dress to last me a lifetime. I grew particularly fond of a young man called Buck, whose job it was to wander around dressed as Sonic the Hedgehog, giving out Twinkies to passers-by. He asked for my number. I asked to see his face. He refused. I found this odd, so I avoided him after that.

On our first night I made a couple of calls home, checking everything was OK, then Nick and I had dinner at an uptown sushi bar.

'Can I ask you something? And if it's none of my business then just tell me to sod off, but is there something going on back home? You seem troubled,' he said out of the blue, massacring a sushi roll with his chopsticks. 'I get the impression there's some kind of problem – or is your dad just overprotective?' he went on, giving up and stabbing the fish roll through the middle before sending it to the depths of his stomach.

I had a split second to respond to this question and I did a very bad thing. I lied. I was worried he would be freaked out. It was better not to tell him.

'Oh, it's nothing. Just got a couple of things on my mind at home.' My blood ran cold as I realised I had been dishonest. Something in his eyes told me he didn't believe a word. But something stopped me telling the truth.

'So, anyway, tell me about your family . . .' I threw in a quick subject change, taking a gentle swig of my vodka and lemonade.

He was wearing a crisp white shirt with thin red stripes, matched with a pair of dark jeans and a brown belt. He looked so good it hurt.

'Well . . . Where do I start? I have two parents who are, remarkably, still together, despite what seems like a loud and theatrical bust-up every day for the past twenty years. I have a sister who mocks everything about my existence, and a dog called Mildred who just sits and looks at me adoringly. I'm closest to the dog by far – she makes the most sense. How about you?'

I love dogs. I love that he loves dogs. Maybe one day we can have a house in the country full of dogs. Oh dear, it had swung round to me again. Shit.

'Er, well. I'm an only child. I was always envious of people with brothers and sisters but I guessed I missed out on the rivalry and arguments, which is no bad thing,' I finished, smoothing my French Connection skirt down with my hands. I still felt like a scumbag for lying.

'Sounds interesting,' he said, gesturing to the waiter for two more drinks. Unfortunately the gesture was a little too energetic and mainly involved his right hand, which was clutching a pair of chopsticks and half a California roll. Said roll became separated from the sticks and flew through the air and into a woman's handbag in the process. We watched with our mouths open as it sailed across the way and dropped into the silky lining of what looked like a brand-new Mulberry bag.

He looked at me. I looked at him. We decided not to tell her. He was shockingly clumsy, and it was great entertainment.

The rest of the night was a happy blur. I hadn't laughed like that in a long time, and it seemed possible he hadn't either. My face hurt. I felt free for the first time in ages, like anything was possible.

We spent the evening charging round a strip of bars, throwing back brightly coloured shots and slamming them back down onto marble surfaces. It was a blur of bright lights, giggling and the scent of his aftershave, which made me hungry for him.

He was silly. Funny. Hilarious, in fact. It all got more amusing the more we drank. I dared him to eat the large slice of lemon bobbing in his drink.

He did it, in one, including the peel. He dared me to wear his shoes to the toilet and keep a straight face. I did.

Because I was tired after a long day, he gave me a piggyback down a long, straight avenue lined with expensive-looking planters brimming with luscious flowers. Neither of us knew what the time was. It didn't matter. It felt like the moon was looking down on us and smiling.

I tried to return the favour but he was heavier than I expected and my legs buckled under his weight and my laughter. After thirty seconds and a metre of staggering, the two of us landed on the pavement in a heap of hysteria and scraped knees. One of his legs was caught in a planter. I couldn't breathe as I lay on the cool stone, giggling loudly.

It dawned on me that a real friendship was developing. I had never had such a connection with a man before. Whilst I was deeply attracted to him, this was something altogether different, a one-off. I was sure he didn't feel the same. It dawned on me, even at this early stage, that I might be capable of loving him. Falling hard, and instead of laughing, crying. It scared me. I had never felt this before and it filled me with a terror of the same magnitude as my joy. I had never been 'in love' before. I didn't know how it felt to be loved like that. Love scared me. Closeness scared me. This scared me.

I made a decision during our trip to America; I realised this was a matter of the heart that I should keep close to my chest. For my own protection.

This connection had the potential to be too special to ruin it with the hurt of misfired romantic intentions. Plus we worked together. It would be messy. And while half of me wanted to tear off his shirt with my teeth, I also wanted him to be in my life for the duration. I didn't want him to be the one I avoided because he'd hurt me. If I was just his friend, then I would still be blessed. If that meant swallowing my pride and being his shoulder when he got hurt, or being the one he ranted at when he was angry, I was prepared to do it and to do it with dignity.

Surely the physical attraction would melt away in time? Women would come and go, but real friends wouldn't. I had only just realised how incredibly lucky I was to have even met him, and the smartest thing I could do was to gather myself together and recognise that.

I made a decision. I had to put a lid on my feelings and I had to do it now. Yeah, right.

CHAPTER 3

'I LOVE YOUR DAUGHTER. TERRIBLY.'

Nick

It has been over a year since Sienna came into my world and turned it upside down. I adore her more every time I see her. I still haven't told her this, though, and I've left it too bloody late now. So many times the words got caught in my throat and never made their way out and now we're in that horrible place. The friend zone. The arm's-length, hugging, air-kissing, hair-ruffling friend zone.

She dates totally unsuitable men – cowards who can't handle her, guys who lie, blokes who give her the runaround. But because she tries to see the good in people, she ends up involved with men who will never change and ends up feeling disappointed every time. Sienna doesn't have a clue just how gorgeous she is, either – which is probably a good thing because if she did, she wouldn't be the girl I have grown so fond of. That's what I like about her. The fact that she doesn't know.

One bad thing is that she listens to terrible music,

like The Kooks and the Pussycat Dolls. I think I even found some Backstreet Boys on her iPod once . . . This music thing, this *affliction*, was my mission for today. I bought a CD that reminds me of her every time I listen to it, and I think she needs to hear it. Obviously I won't tell her that those lyrics and gentle guitar melodies make me feel the way she does when she's by my side. But I just hope she feels that warmth every time she plays it. I hope it makes her happy.

She hasn't been her usual chirpy self just lately. She looks a bit tired and worn down and this worries me. I think it's to do with the chump she's seeing at the moment.He is, to put it frankly, a moron. I have to act all pally with him when we go to the same parties and stuff, when actually I want to jab him in the eye with a cocktail stick. He has this horrible self-appreciating air about him and he doesn't treat her right.

His name is Daniel House and he's a primary school teacher cum rock band twat. I hate him. He's twenty-five, has crazy dark hair which he waxes at silly angles, and wears pretentious vintage T-shirts with slogans on that he doesn't even understand.

Daniel House is another reason why I just know that Sienna would never feel for me what I feel for her. We couldn't be more different. His jeans are so skinny I'm convinced he must have blood-flow problems, and his pants hang out the back. I want to give him such a big wedgie that his boxers rip in the middle and come right up over his head. His friends call him Housey, for Christ's sake . . . Any man who is regularly addressed by his surname is definitely either from public school or an idiot – or more likely, both.

I don't understand why she likes him. I really don't. He is quite good-looking, I guess, for a bloke and all. But it still doesn't make it OK. I don't know what she sees in him, but of course I can see why he went for Sienna. She's so beautiful that men just swarm around her, but they never know quite what to do with themselves when it comes to the crunch.

Dan's gigs are crap, too. I've been to a few of them, trying desperately hard not to laugh, but then I turn and look at Sienna gazing adoringly at the stage and realise that I have to just, well, man up.

'So you like Che, then?' I said once, pointing to an image of the iconic man on his top at a pub lunch one day.

'Who?' he asked, looking puzzled at the blazing political imagery splashed across his chest.

'Guevara, the bloke on your T-shirt?' I looked him up and down, hoping for Sienna's sake that there was more to him than expensive clothes and chiselled cheekbones. I wanted to push his face into a large bowl of rice.

'Oh, yeah, he's one of my favourite guitarists,' he responded blankly.

I nearly choked to death on a sausage.

He regularly lets her down, fails to give her the attention she deserves and spends more time with his so-called band mates than he does with her.

Of course, she adores him. But then they always love a bad boy, don't they? 'That's just the way he is, Nick,' she protests when I tell her that he is the biggest knob I have ever met.

'What – a twat?'

'No, not a twat, just a bit, you know . . . busy,' she responds. She's usually looking away from me by that point, because she and I both know she's making excuses. I've caught her crying in the cloak-room at parties on a couple of occasions while he stands holding her waist and pleading with her.

He's on borrowed time and he knows it. I'm sure he wishes I would butt out, maybe even die in some freak skiing accident, but I'm not going anywhere. Plus I don't ski.

It was a warm Saturday morning. I slipped on a pair of stripy shorts, some flip-flops and a T-shirt, and made my way to her place.

As the heat started to really take hold, girls were everywhere, wearing less and less. I loved it. The sun was doing that magical thing of giving women gorgeous little freckles on their faces and making them wear tiny dresses and skimpy tops. There was skin everywhere – long sexy legs swaggering down the high street, a defined back set off by a plunging dress. It was driving me nuts.

As frustrated as I was by the situation with Sienna, I was really enjoying being single, even though I was twenty-eight.

Nick, single, twenty-eight. It had a ring to it. I loved it.

I'd been on a few dates, and some of them had been great. Nights of laughter and flirtation with pretty girls, occasionally ending in no-strings passion. I'd forgotten how much fun it was to be single. I hadn't really felt anything deep for any of them, though – it was all just good fun at the moment.

It was just two stops on the tube to Sienna's place, although in the past year that we'd been mates I'd never actually set foot inside. This was something I found very odd, particularly when she seemed to be so tied to home. She dashed off there sometimes after hurried phone calls, never telling me why.

Dan had gone to Amsterdam for the weekend with his equally silly friends and she'd mentioned something at work yesterday about spending the day watching old films, so I thought it would be a good time to surprise her and drop round that CD.

I walked slowly up the drive to her building, hoping I was doing the right thing. The sun was beating down on me; my palms were getting a bit sweaty. I pressed the buzzer and waited.

'Hello?' came a male voice.

'Er, hi . . .' I started, instantly regretting what I was about to do. Who was this guy? Her father, maybe? God knows – it had always been such a mystery.

'It's Nick. I'm here to see Sienna.'

There was a short pause. 'Oh, hello, come on in.'

There was another buzz and the heavy entrance

door opened for me. I tucked the CD into the back of the waistband of my shorts and made my way up the stairs. The corridors were dark and smelled of bleach. It was all very clean, white and functional.

The man was standing in the doorway, waiting for me. 'Nick. So good to meet you,' he greeted me with a warm smile. It was almost as if he knew me well. The greeting made me panic – I was about to have to ask a very embarrassing question.

'I'm sorry, but who are you?' I said, running my hand through my hair nervously.

He looked slightly taken aback as he stood there in checked pyjama bottoms and a baggy jumper. 'I'm George. Sienna's father,' he replied, a note of disappointment in his voice.

He was nothing like I'd imagined. I was pleased to finally meet the guy who had brought up Sienna. If he had a daughter like her, he must be one hell of a good bloke. I was slightly shocked by what I saw, though. The man in front of me looked fragile, pale and older than his years. The skin on his face had a translucent, paper-like quality, as though he hadn't seen the sun for a while. I couldn't put my finger on why that could be.

The little hair he had on his head was silver; his lips were small and wrinkled. I spotted a deep scar on his forehead. Maybe he'd had too many jars last night, or possibly I'd misheard his age when Sienna told me he was only forty-six. I'd expected him to be a tall, dynamic, powerful presence.

97

'Sienna isn't actually here, Nick, but come in. I've heard so much about you . . .' He trailed off, obviously slightly self-conscious about how keen he was sounding. I felt suddenly aware that I knew precious little about him. Sienna had never volunteered anything.

'I just brought her a CD as a surprise, thought I'd drop it by on my way into town,' I responded, trying really hard to be casual.

Way into town, my arse. Sienna and I only live two tube stops away from each other. It's the kind of distance you can drive in ten minutes, or walk in forty if you're feeling particularly energetic.

George ushered me in, revealing the living space they shared. It was a typical London flat, all on one level, with a small corridor leading from the front door to a large living room and open kitchen. It was modest in size, and seemed to go on past the kitchen as another corridor led further back, revealing an open bathroom door and two other closed doors beside it. They must be the bedrooms.

I looked back at George, who was standing by a running machine wedged against the wall near the entrance to the kitchen.

I could see Sienna's touches all over the main living space. Owl-shaped cushions lay on the chairs, stitched together with thick, black cord. They were beautifully quirky; they looked like they'd been found in a gift shop in somewhere like the Brighton Lanes. Her jewellery was scattered on a small coffee table, and a faint trace of her perfume filled the air. It all looked messy and warm and had oodles of personality.

The sofa looked worn and loved, and there were large shelving units on almost every wall, packed full of books and films. The DVDs included everything from *Pulp Fiction* to *Sex and the City*. You could tell a lot about a person by looking at their books and movies, but this was a bit of a mess. A history book here, a celebrity biog there. The themes conflicted so much, you could easily tell what belonged to Sienna and what belonged to George.

About ten black notebooks were stacked on the main coffee table, surrounded by small piles of pencils and their associated shavings.

It was a beautifully cosy den.

What looked like a black, padded crash helmet was sitting in the middle of the floor. It looked soft, not the kind you would wear on a motorbike, but the kind donned by boxers and rugby players with fucked-up ears. Surely he doesn't box, I thought – not when he looks like this.

'She'll be back soon, Nick,' George said as he made his way to the kitchen, slowly. Holding onto any available surface, he shuffled to the kettle and flipped the switch.

It dawned on me that something was quite wrong here. His trousers sagged sadly over his bum, as though they'd once had a lot more George in them.

'I can't believe I haven't met you yet,' I said to him, then suddenly worried that he would think I was creeping.

'It's nice to finally meet you too, Nick. Sienna seems to be having a great time at work. I'm so glad she's working with people like you . . . It's been really hard for her over the years – but you know that . . . Tea? Milk? Sugar?' He turned around, still gripping onto the work surface like it was a safety rope.

Really hard for her over the years . . . What did he mean by that? *But you know that . . .* I didn't know, she hadn't told me. I started to remember all the occasions we'd been out and how she would just disappear sometimes, putting it down to a variety of reasons. I'd just accepted it as a quirk, just the way she was, but now it seemed like my questions were about to be answered.

'Oh, just milk and one sugar please,' I responded, sinking into the sofa. I was quite disappointed that she wasn't here, but I just knew there was something going on. She'd obviously been holding something back from me. Something I needed to know about, and without her here I stood more chance of finding out.

'So, what are you doing at the weekend? Anything nice?' I questioned as the water boiled so violently it shook the kettle hard on the wooden worktop. Oh, that was original, I thought. Might as well have started talking about the sodding weather.

'Not a lot, son.' He laughed slightly, stopping himself by leaning over the mugs and holding his breath for a few seconds.

This made me nervous so I perked up in my

seat, watching him closely. I noticed several large bottles of prescription medicine on the side.

He continued, 'Well, you know, I can't do so much these days. Just reading a lot, trying to learn as much as I can about the world from books. It's not as if I can get out there. I write a lot too, in those black notebooks over there. I write about what it must be like to live, properly, you know?'

Something was clearly very wrong with Sienna's dad. But why hadn't she told me? Maybe he had cancer, I thought. I felt a wave of sadness rush over me. I wanted to run out, find her and hold her really tight, but at the same time I began to feel angry that she'd never told me. She can't be that close to me, I thought, suddenly feeling like she was a stranger and I was imposing in a world I'd never been invited to explore. Maybe I had made a mistake by coming here.

The sound of a teaspoon jangling inside a mug snapped me out of my panic spiral.

'I'm sorry, George, but I don't know what you mean by *these days*,' I said quietly, unable to keep up the pretence that I knew something I didn't – but should.

He went quiet; the stirring stopped. Sadness crept over his features and he looked even more tired.

I stood up and started to walk over to him. 'Here, let me get those,' I said, reaching out to relieve him of the duty. He turned to face me, both cups of boiling hot tea in his thin hands, and then suddenly, the most awful thing happened.

As if in slow motion, the life seeped out of his eyes and his legs gave way beneath him, like buildings crumbling under the force of an earthquake.

I tried, I really did, but it was too late. Every muscle in my body lurched forward to catch him, but I missed. I missed. I failed.

The cups of tea flew into the air, milky brown water spraying all around us before the china smashed into little pieces on the floor. What must have been searing hot liquid ran down my face, but I felt no pain.

His face was expressionless as he crashed to the ground. I feared he might break in half. The boiling hot tea was all over his legs, and he lay motionless on the lino. Silence swept over the room. Shit. Fuck.

'Shit,' I muttered, my whole body starting to shake. Chunks of vomit started to fill my throat. My vision suddenly became sharpened, my sense of smell heightened; I was experiencing everything in ultra-sharp technicolour.

Fight or flight, Nick. Fight or flight.

I dropped down to his side, my knees sliding through the tea all around us. I arranged his body into the recovery position, shaking so much that I felt as if I would pass out. He must have had a heart attack. Oh my God, what if he was dead? What the fuck would I say to Sienna, to everyone? Sorry, Sienna, I'm a meddling idiot who just couldn't stay away. I spent five minutes with your father and killed him just by being near him. Fuck's sake.

I pushed my fingers into the soft skin of his neck; he was still warm, but I couldn't feel his pulse. I tried to work out if it was just my fear and the blood rushing around my head that was rendering me useless at finding it. Tears started to slide down my face. What on earth was I going to do?

Oh shit, I thought, what if George had a delicate condition that somehow I had disturbed? And if he died, then would I be the cause? I looked up to the ceiling, hoping that I could renew my faith in God. Last time I'd tried this was when I'd bunked off Sunday school all those years ago and spent the collection money on cola bottles. But praying was pointless. I had abandoned it for far too long.

I pushed myself down towards his face again, whispering into his ear. 'Please George, no, please. I love Sienna, she loves you, and she needs you. Don't go anywhere . . .' I begged his motionless body.

'I love your daughter. Terribly,' I said, my voice now a hoarse cry.

I pulled my phone out of my pocket and tried to dial 999, but my hands were shaking so much I screwed it up. Twice. I was wasting valuable time.

I'd always hoped that in moments like this I would be the comic-book hero, knowing exactly what to do, breathing life into the dying, sweeping the hurt and the danger away, applying bandages in the blink of an eye.

I was a tit. A crying, shaking, useless lump.

When I finally managed to dial the number I tried to explain what had happened to the operator, but the words didn't flow as I'd hoped. 'Please, just come now, I think he's dead. Please hurry,' I rasped, my throat dry as sandpaper.

'OK, caller, please stay calm. Where are you?'

'Erm, flat 10, Orchard Court, Great Westfield Road, London.' Yes, that was it. I was being vaguely useful now.

'What is the emergency?' came the cold, calm voice at the other end of the line.

'Look, I don't fucking know. I'm with a man, he's collapsed, I can't feel a pulse, I think he's dead. Just come NOW, please!' I shouted, a little hysterical by that point.

They told me later they had achieved a six-minute response time. Those next six minutes felt like an age. I sat next to George in the puddle of tea, holding his hands and weeping like a hysterical child. He didn't move an inch the whole time. I was already wondering how I was going to tell Sienna. What if they thought I'd done something to him to cause this? Panic pulsed through my veins as I imagined myself behind bars.

I was so glad when they turned up, flashes of fluorescent yellow and green and those sturdy, black laced-up boots. Bright red kitbags and the sound of Velcro ripping through the air reassured me that everything might just be OK.

One of the paramedics pulled me away from George and sat me down. I felt like a small boy. I watched in silence while they worked away at him, feeling as though I was having an out-of-body experience. 'He's alive, mate,' one of them said, turning towards me with a wide grin on his face. He obviously thought I was a dick.

Then the same paramedic kneeled down beside me, his bald head shining under the strip lamp. 'Are you running around after Sienna now, then?' he said, looking at me with a half smile. 'I hope you didn't say anything embarrassing – he'll have heard everything you said,' he added, the smile spreading out even wider now.

I said nothing.

'She's a nice girl, isn't she?' he concluded, rolling up a green mat and securing it with a black band.

God, this bloke knows Sienna – he's talking about her and George like he knows all about their lives, and I'm still in the dark. What happened back there? I wanted to ask but this bloke was getting on my wick. I shook my head, still unable to speak.

'Chill out, he's going to be just fine, mate,' said the paramedic, slapping me on the back. Ouch.

I remained silent, just trying to take it all in. I felt anger rising in me again. Why hadn't she told me what the hell this was about? Did her boyfriend know and keep this from me? Did everyone know but me? Why hadn't she trusted me with this?

The paramedics knew George by name; they had obviously done this before. Many times, maybe.

I had a flashback; a cold, horrible flashback. *I love Sienna, she loves you, and she needs you . . . I love your daughter. Terribly.* Yes, that was definitely what I'd said, wasn't it? I'd told him I loved her. Oh dear God. This was so embarrassing.

I imagined how silly I'd sounded when it was all happening. How my raspy voice had made these foolish love declarations while the tears of a frightened little boy gushed down my face.

I'd thought we were so close and yet I didn't know anything. Even now. Bollocks.

Sienna

Bread. Milk. Jam.

I'd only popped out to get a few bits from the shop and I came back to utter chaos. I knew it was bad the second I walked round the corner because there was an ambulance outside our block of flats, blue lights flashing. From this point, although I couldn't be sure they were here for my dad, I had a feeling in my gut which told me they probably were. They normally were.

A few people had gathered on the grass outside the block, pointing up at our flat. They always did this. Village idiots . . . I recognised most of them. It was always the same people.

Jack wasn't there, though. Jack is our neighbour, a man in his early sixties who has helped me out a few times when Dad has fallen and I've struggled to get him up again. When I say helped, helped grudgingly is the best way of putting it. I've had to knock on his door at crazy times of night with no warning. I don't think it's gone down very well, but he's the only person who's ever really any use in these situations.

To our left is a frail old lady. I can't ask her for help, so it's Jack by default. I don't think he liked that at first. No one wants to be Jack by default, but I think he understands how hard it is for me now. He even brings food round if I'm away for the weekend, tubs of bolognese and risotto. Despite his initial reaction I've never really been embarrassed, because the most important thing at the time is making sure my dad is safe.

My pulse started to race. This was not an unusual occurrence, but it never got any easier. I always feared that his next fall would be his last. There was only so much padding we could put up around the house.

But nothing could have prepared me for what I saw when I made it through the door. Because there, sitting on the floor, was Nick. His face was puffy-looking, and he had clearly been crying. There was murky brown liquid everywhere. He was staring straight ahead, and patches of his hair were wet. He looked traumatised.

My dad was being lifted onto the sofa by two burly paramedics. He looked exhausted.

I didn't know who to deal with first.

'I'm OK, love,' my father called quietly, waving

his arms towards Nick. 'Nick came round to see you. I passed out while I was making us tea. He did a great job though, Si,' he added weakly.

This was a disaster. I had managed to keep this from Nick for so long. I really didn't want him to know about it. Anger rose in my chest. OK, I had been going to tell him one day, I really had, but I'd wanted him to get to know me for who I really was before any of these complications came into play.

Suddenly I felt my anger transform into rage. Why was he here? Why had he been trying to catch me out? And on top of everything, the look of sadness on Dad's face clearly showed that he was disappointed in me for not telling one of my best friends about him.

It was a mess. I went and sat next to Dad, holding his hands in mine and trying to be calm, even though I wanted to shout at Nick. 'No cuts this time, eh?' I leaned forward, inspecting his head. 'What did I tell you about wearing your helmet, though?' I nagged. 'You obviously didn't have it on.'

Nick continued staring into the abyss. He looked pissed off.

'I'll be back in a moment.' I leaned down and kissed my dad's head gently. I knew he would be OK. It was a routine fall. We were quite used to all of this.

What I wasn't used to, though, was being caught out like this. It was my business. I was fiercely protective of my business. I touched Nick's arm and he gripped his hand into a fist. I could feel his muscles contract under his skin. He flushed a deep red; he looked furious. Well, I was too.

I pulled him towards me to lead him into my room so we could be alone. At first he resisted, but I pulled once more, a little harder this time, and this time he followed.

'What on earth is wrong with your dad? Why didn't you tell me about this, Sienna?' he whispered aggressively as soon as the door was shut, tears welling up in his eyes.

Goosebumps appeared all over my body, and I realised he was gripping my right arm tightly. I yanked it away. 'You're hurting me, Nick. Get your hands off me,' I growled, shoving my index finger into his chest.

I had never seen him cry before. In fact, I hadn't really seen any man cry before, apart from my dad just a couple of times and that was under what seemed like exceptional circumstances. Why was he crying? He wasn't the victim here. He had no right to cry. The fire inside me spread and I could hold it in no longer.

'What the *hell* did you think you were doing?' I said as my breath started to quicken in my chest. I could feel the panic rising. Anger I didn't know I was capable of spread like wildfire.

He looked at me like I was someone he'd never met before, his eyes as wide as satellite dishes. 'What do you mean? I just popped round to say hi.

What's wrong with your dad?' he repeated, his voice getting louder.

'So you get the impression that there's something going on here, because life's a little complicated for me sometimes, and then you just come round without telling me? What the fuck do you think you're playing at?' I hissed, suddenly aware of how defensive I was being.

He flinched and stepped backwards again, almost knocking over my bedside table. My accusatory finger was trembling.

'Sienna, you have no idea what I've just been through . . . I thought he had—'

But I interrupted him again. 'What *you've* been through? You've got to be kidding. *I* go through this, Nick, every day – not you. I'm the one who has to wash him, cook for him, clean. Don't tell me about what *you've* just been through, OK?' I was pacing across the small floor space now.

Nick crossed his arms defensively, but I continued, shaking even more now. 'Dad has narcolepsy, all right? And before you start asking lots of annoying questions, it's a neurological disorder, which makes him fall asleep pretty much all the time. He also has cataplexy, which means that his episodes are triggered by emotions – happy, sad, you name it, and he's gone. Passed out. It's exhausting. You have no fucking idea, so how dare *you* cry!' The words coming out of my mouth were ugly and distorted now. I could feel shame starting to kick in, but it was too late.

'Jesus, Si. I didn't even know, for fuck's sake! You told me, if you actually remember, that you would be indoors today, watching films. *Remember?* I thought you would be here. I wasn't trying to catch you out!'

Suddenly a look of hurt overtook his anger and I felt a stab of guilt. Of course. That *was* what I'd told him. I flushed, but I was too far into my argument now to become the bad guy. There was no room for a U-turn now.

'And what was the paramedic talking about when he said your dad could hear everything?' he added, his voice a lot calmer now. He looked panicked.

I took a deep breath and tried to stop my arms shaking by drawing in a fresh gulp of oxygen. 'He passes out, but not in the normal way. He can hear everything that's going on and he remembers it all, basically. He just can't move his body. It's kind of hard to explain,' I responded, hating that I had to go over the details all the time for everyone. All the stupid questions. All the misplaced curiosity. I just wanted him to be away from me, and I knew I would have to be spiteful to achieve this.

'You're just like everybody else, Nick. Nosy. Sod off, get out of my house.' Tears began to run down my face. The truth was, I was embarrassed now. I felt like a bitter, poisonous bitch.

He rushed towards me and wrapped his arms around me tightly. I stood still as a rock, afraid to fall into him, because I could feel the tidal wave of emotion I'd held back for a decade building to a peak. I was scared of what might happen if I let it crash to the shore.

'Come here, please, Si. Just come here,' he whispered quietly in my ear, the bristle of his stubble scratching gently against my cheek. I could feel his heartbeat against my chest. His gorgeousness still hadn't faded. I still felt so in awe of him that his proximity terrified me. It made my chest tight and my adrenaline pump so hard I feared I would pass out. I started to cry. I tried to stop it but I couldn't.

'You shouldn't have to go through this alone. Why did you shut me out?' he asked.

It felt like years of tension coming to the surface, tension I never really knew existed. Eventually I gave in, and he pulled me into his neck. Still angry, I thumped a fist against his chest. I felt him swallow, hard.

'It's been so hard, Nick. You literally have no idea. I hate the way people treat me when they know. I never wanted you to look at me with pity. I didn't want you to know. I wish you'd never come here!' I hacked out the words between deep, overwhelming sobs. There were mascara smudges all over his neck.

'Si,' he said, holding my face with both hands and pulling it close to his. I hated this, hated the nakedness of this moment. There was nothing I could do to hide from him, the way I had hidden from so many others.

'Sienna, please don't ever keep things like this from me. You are literally the best friend I've ever had. I want to help you,' he continued, one hand now running through my hair. I brushed it away and pulled my hair to the other side so he couldn't touch it. I tried to look away; eye contact would mean the end of my guard and I was still angry.

'Look at me,' he whispered.

I turned my eyes to his, which were red from all the upset. His pupils were small.

'Sienna. I have to tell you something. I, I . . .'

We were interrupted by one of the paramedics, who had decided to barge in without knocking. 'Well, we're all done here, guys. Just keep an eye on him for the rest of the day, OK? He'll probably sleep for a while now. We had to deal with some slight burns on his leg, but they should heal in no time.' He tilted his head and gave me that look of pity I knew so well.

'Thanks so much – you've been fantastic, as always,' I replied, wiping my eyes and stepping forward to start seeing them out.

'No, don't you worry about saying goodbye, love. Enjoy the rest of your weekend,' he muttered, belatedly realising that maybe he had interrupted something rather important.

Suddenly, the room was quiet. I turned to Nick. 'Leave, please,' I said, trying not to shout. Words were still coming out of my mouth that my brain didn't really agree with. I was just so humiliated. I wanted him to be far away.

'But Sienna, come on,' he said, his hands reaching towards me.

'Don't make me shout, Nick. Go,' I repeated, turning away from him and sitting on the edge of the bed.

I heard the door click shut. I felt hollow inside. I wondered if we would ever be that close again. I wanted to run after him and beg him to stay, but I kept my mouth shut and my body still. Maybe it was just one of those moments when people come together like magnets, drawn into each other's arms by heightened emotions, but it never happens again. It slowly dawned on me that I had been pretty damn nasty. That maybe we would never recover from this.

After five minutes of silence I walked out into the living room and stood in front of my father, trying to take in the enormity of what had just happened.

'He brought this for you, Si,' said Dad, waving a CD in the air and breaking my moment of reflection. It glinted sharply in my sore eyes, reflecting the glare from the ceiling light. 'I think he likes you. You do know that, don't you?' he continued, looking more serious this time.

'What gave you that impression?' I asked.

He paused before saying, 'I can't put my finger on it, darling. I just know love when I see it. Don't be nasty to him. I heard you shouting, Sienna – that's not good.'

I looked at him with one eyebrow raised, and felt sick with guilt.

That night I listened to the CD. Beautiful songs from a band I had never heard before. I listened

114

to the lyrics and attempted to work out what he was trying to say to me, because I was still just too angry with him. I wanted to call him, to say sorry. But I couldn't.

Nick

There was only one way to get through this. Beer. And copious amounts of it, too.

It was time for a board meeting, and the venue of choice this evening was the beer garden at The Grand Union in Brixton.

The lads realised it was serious. I texted Ross first, hoping he hadn't planned an evening of staring into his wife's eyes in the bath and feeding her spring rolls with his toes. Of course he hadn't. He may have got married, but he was still Ross. My mate: dependable and always up for a beer. He successfully rounded up the troops and we gathered for an important discussion about how I was going to handle this situation.

To my disappointment, however, it started with a detailed analysis of just how much of an idiot I was.

'So wait, wait. Hold on a minute,' Ross exclaimed after a swig of his drink, commanding the attention of the assembled party like an army officer. He was definitely the ringleader of the group. A well-built man with square shoulders and a square jaw. A bit like a human Ken doll.

'What you're telling me is that Sienna's dad passed out and you thought he was dead and told him that you love his daughter?' he went on, his strong, hairy arms crossed over his chest.

'Well, it's not quite as simple as—' I tried to defend myself weakly.

'As what, Nick? 'Cause that's how it sounds to me!' shrieked my supposed best friend through now uncontrollable laughter, slamming his fist onto the table and spraying my face with London's finest ale.

Wanker.

The rest of the lads bowed their heads and sniggered like schoolboys. I was becoming the evening's entertainment. I might as well set up a podcast featuring daily updates of my romantic misdemeanours, complete with voting tool so we can decide exactly which point was my lowest. Maybe geeky Jon could map them out on charts for me, just to rub it in a bit further.

'For fuck's sake, you lot! You're supposed to be helping!' I shouted, secretly smiling to myself and throwing a peanut at Phil. He batted it away with his right arm. Those were some good reflexes. You had to hand it to them; they always made me laugh, even if it was at my own expense.

'No, honestly boys, I need some help.' I changed my tone so they would realise I was being serious. I hoped that now we were in our late twenties and early thirties we could discuss stuff like this. I was mistaken.

'Do I tell her before her dad does? If he hasn't already? Or do I hope that somehow he forgot that part?' The questions came spilling from my mouth between drags on a Marlboro Light.

'So what's wrong with him again?' said Simon, a thirty-five-year-old accountant with a penchant for fishing and smoking weed.

'Narcolepsy or something. It means he falls asleep a lot and can't control it,' I answered irritably. I was getting a little bit bored of explaining this. God knows how Sienna must feel.

'And he can hear every word you say?' Simon probed further, like some sort of heartbreak scientist.

'Yes, everything, apparently. The paramedic said so, Sienna said so and I Googled it too.'

'Wow! This is a crazy situation. Shots, boys?' said Ross, already starting to make his way to the bar, his attention returning to the small matter of getting pissed. A group of girls in the far corner pointed at him and giggled cheekily. He still had this incredible knack with women, despite being well and truly spoken for.

I shuffled uncomfortably in my seat; the humid evening air combined with my sticky predicament was making me sweat. Fake palm trees stood between the tables, fairy lights threaded through their plastic leaves. I wanted to climb into one and hide, just like I did at work once, but not in a 'ha ha' kind of way this time.

'What's the big deal about this girl anyway, Nick? This has been going on for ages and there are plenty of women registering an interest in you.'

This unhelpful input came from Richard. Richard who has never met Sienna. Richard who recently grew a handlebar moustache 'just for a laugh'.

'What about that fit girl who works in that recruitment office near me? Oh God, what's her name, Dave?' he added.

'Sophie,' replied Dave with a knowing smile, gesturing with his hands to emulate a curvy female shape.

'Yeah, Sophie. She fancies the tiny, chequered pants off you, Nick, and she is smoking hot,' Rich continued. The lads nodded in unison.

I wasn't going to listen. If they had it their way, I'd be frolicking with strippers and writhing in pools of unsuitable women at album launch parties. They're nearly all in serious relationships or married now and they seem to live through me, hooking me up with the various women they secretly want to do themselves.

'Hey, Nick, look at that girl over there . . . She keeps looking at you,' declared Simon, pointing towards a leggy blonde smoking a cigarette. She quickly swished her head in the other direction, layers of shining hair flying through the air.

Jesus, it was like Sixth Form. Men never grow up. Fact. Yeah, she was gorgeous, had legs that went on forever and probably kissed like a fallen angel, but there was only one thing I wanted. Sienna.

'Here you go, pal, get this down your neck.' Ross was back with a tray of shots, the neon-green liquid on the verge of spilling over the lip of the glasses.

I was drinking hideous amounts of alcohol, very quickly. Half of me thought I should stop, the other half wanted to continue, so I went with the latter. I threw it down my neck, wiping the viscous liquid from my fingers onto my jeans.

'Look, guys. This isn't funny. It's getting to me. Should I get a new job? Cut her out? Leave the country?' I was being dramatic now, but it was necessary to get their attention.

Silence descended on the group. Ross leaned back, his lumberjack shirt pulling at the middle where the buttons were. He had been working out lately and was starting to resemble a wrestler. 'OK, how do you feel about her?' he said, a lot more serious this time.

This was awkward for a pack of drunken men. Feelings had come to the table – real, raw feelings. My feelings. It was terrifying, but I had consumed enough alcohol to be able to spill the beans. They knew I was a soppy git now anyway, so there was no point trying to claw back my floundering reputation.

'She's perfection. I've never felt like this. I can't imagine anything I want more than having her by my side every day. It actually scares me.'

'Well, you need to tell her, dude – but properly tell her. As in don't tell her comatose father, yeah?' said Simon, pushing his glasses up his nose.

'Ross. When you met Sarah . . . How did you know you loved her? How did you know she was . . . well, the one?' I turned my gaze towards my best friend, hoping I could find the answers behind the thick veil of his drunken stupor.

The alpha male shuffled awkwardly and paused for a moment. He knew that I knew he was a secret ball of goo. I'd never told the lads that I walked in on him sitting in his underpants, writing a poem for his wife with Ronan Keating on in the background just a few months ago. I've certainly learned that I should knock from now on . . . It had remained a secret between us, and it was my greatest weapon when his piss-taking reached annoying levels. A simple pen movement with my right hand was enough to shut him up.

'Well, er . . . I just knew, I guess,' he responded quietly, running his index finger around the top of his pint.

'What do you mean, just knew?' asked Simon. He was clearly fascinated by this too.

'I just felt like everything was right with her, and the thought of being without her made me feel totally lost,' he finished, opening out his hands on the wooden table. 'It's just a gut feeling, you can't really explain it.' His big bear-like features softened and he smiled from ear to ear.

'Well, that's how I feel about Sienna,' I said bluntly. 'But then again, the fact that she kept that secret from me for so long is a bad sign. She can't feel the same, there's just no way. Then I face the humiliation of my office and the loss of a great friendship . . .'

'Friendship, my arse,' Ross blurted out. 'Guys and

girls are never just friends, not like you two are anyway. There's always one person who wants to jump the other one,' he continued, like some kind of love guru in a pub garden, dishing out advice and cigarettes to his crowd of desperate disciples.

Even men who weren't drinking with us were perking up their ears and leaning in our direction. One scruffy-looking lad had given up pretending to be polite and perched himself on the end of the table. He can't have been much older than nineteen.

A bad feeling washed over me and it wasn't just alcohol-induced nausea. I felt that I needed to get real and get over this. I, Nick Redland, was turning into a pathetic individual and I didn't like it. My friends were laughing at me. Instead of making me want to run out of the pub, bribe a taxi driver and rush to Sienna's house to declare my undying love for her, I wanted to be as far away from her as possible.

The heavy beat of house music disturbed my thoughts and Ross rose to his feet, waving his beer in the air like an Olympic torch. 'This is a tune, lads! Remember this one from Ibiza?' he shouted, wiggling his hips to the track. It was tragic. So tragic I had to join in.

Next thing I knew we were all at it, as if my love life was so impossible to solve that the only thing to do was dance it out. Badly. We were men. This came more naturally to us than talking about how we felt.

The rest of the night was a haze; a haze which definitely involved more beer, shots, and added beer on top of that. For the first time in ages I forgot about Sienna and just danced my troubles away.

When it was my turn to get the next round, I stumbled up to the bar with a half pint in my hands, knocking into a girl by accident. She turned around to give me a telling-off.

'Shit. I'm sorry, I'm an idiot. Bollocks, did I throw my drink over your dress?'

She peered down at her ensemble. It involved strips of unusual materials that looked as if separately they had been languishing miserable and lonely in a charity shop somewhere, yet when stitched together formed the most beautifully flattering dress. From her left shoulder a frog brooch stared at me. This is definitely what people talk about when they refer to girls dressing for other girls rather than for men, who are as perplexed as I am by the result. The mad dress, combined with her long, tumbling, messed-up hazelnut hair, gave her that affected arty air so many London girls have. Still. She was quite attractive. Either that or I was quite drunk. I prayed I didn't face a £500 bill for the frock that was probably made by starving children in some developing country. I would really resent that.

She softened. 'No, you're safe. You could buy me a drink to say sorry?'

Cheeky minx. 'Yes, of course. What would you like?'

'A single spiced rum and Coke, please. What's your name?'

'Nick,' I replied, noticing a delicate horseshoe necklace falling over her collarbone. It was very sexy.

She smiled at me, and it made my heart race. Suddenly I felt nothing but lust; it took over my whole body and almost rendered me incapable of speech. It rushed through my veins like a train.

'I'm Kate, nice to meet you.' She held out a hand, which I shook weakly, instantly regretting it. Her perfume was unusual; rich, mysterious and spicy. It made me want to get closer to her. Her nails were painted black; she had that high-maintenance yet totally distressed cool about her.

It struck me how long it had been since I had actually opened my eyes to the world. How long it had been since I was just, well, a happy-go-lucky bloke. There were plenty of attractive, lovely women out there. Maybe I was just limiting myself with my tunnel vision.

Ross waved at me behind Kate's shoulder and stuck his thumbs in the air. I ignored him.

It was a noisy walk to the bus stop, clattering heels and laughter. We stumbled arm in arm through the streets and clambered onto a night bus, kissing like teenagers at every available opportunity. We shared a portion of chips, doused in salt and vinegar.

My head was spinning as the double-decker negotiated the streets of London, heading west to my bachelor pad. It never really crossed my mind that she was coming with me – but it never really crossed my mind that she wouldn't, either. She definitely wasn't getting off the bus, that was for sure.

Just before our stop, she held me back against the seat by my chest and pushed her lips on to my mouth, biting my bottom lip gently. I felt light-headed, kissing her back despite the audience we had.

The last thing I remember was Kate's clothes being flung all over my house. Just like in the films, shoes, lingerie and her figure-hugging dress were littered across the hallway and stairs like a trail of incriminating evidence. I recall running my hands over her naked body in my bed, being kissed passionately by a stranger. We were twisted in the sheets, tangled legs and arms. Her hair smelled good, every curve of her body was perfection. She was beautiful.

I woke up in the morning and rolled over. I felt empty inside.

CHAPTER 4

'DOES IT FEEL WRONG?'

Sienna

'So why do they call you Dancing Pete?' I'd finally plucked up the courage to ask him. It was cold. Really bloody cold. And I was back here again in the car park at work. Maybe I was a glutton for punishment, but the memory of his rage had long faded and what I saw was the person behind all that, and I thought he was worth getting to know.

I had seen him quite a few times now. I picked my moments carefully. We had never really talked much about his life since the photo incident, just light chatter while I gave him things to eat and books to read. Funnily enough, I'd told him about Nick. I had no idea why. I hadn't planned to. It had just come out one day, organically.

Pete rubbed his hands together, breathing into his palms. 'Well, I just used to try and replace the pain of losing Jenny with anything I could to take the edge off . . .' he started.

I looked at him warmly, hoping I could get him to tell me more without actually having to ask.

125

'Funnily enough, it started with chocolate and stuff – you know, naughty food. When I first became homeless I did have some cash so I would spend it on as much chocolate as I could get my mitts on.'

This surprised me. I thought about the Snickers bar in my handbag and suddenly saw it in a whole new light.

'I missed her so much, I had to fill the gap with something, Si. I used to just stuff my face in the park – bar after bar after bar until I felt so sick that it took the pain away and replaced it with another kind of hurt.' He looked a little embarrassed.

My toes were starting to go numb from the cold, despite the thick black boots I was wearing, which were lined with sheepskin. We were deep in the middle of a British winter and this bench in the car park was an unforgiving place. I had tried to take him for a hot drink in a café, but I think he found the prospect of Starbucks, with its yummy mummies and frothy, skinny, whippaccinos, a bit too much. I could hardly blame him; even I felt massively inferior in that place.

'But then that wasn't really enough any more, I needed something else to numb the pain. So I started drinking . . . A lot. It was a progression from the odd bottle here and there to a constant state of inebriation.'

It struck me how articulate he was; he could express himself beautifully. I think that's why I found him so intriguing. I noticed he needed a shave again.

'People walking past would sometimes give me a bottle, and I scrounged enough money to buy myself alcohol but not enough to ever get myself anywhere or buy myself anything decent. So the short-term solution was to dilute my thoughts . . .'

I studied his nose; it was red and swollen from the years of abuse. I had never really noticed it before. His eyes were bloodshot, but you could tell he was still young – in his early thirties, I guessed.

'Then bottles of cider weren't enough any more, so I started to turn to the hard stuff. You know, vodka and that. From there came the drugs. Cocaine was too expensive, obviously, but there was a lot of weed around, pills – you name it, I took it.' He breathed in deeply and looked at me as if I was too delicate to know what had happened next. Then he continued, 'I just spent all my time in this crazy world, where everything was always spinning and twisting and jerking, and when it started to stand still again I knew that I was sober again and the pain would come back.' He chuckled quietly in disbelief at the memory.

'So basically you were self-medicating?' I said as a squirrel came and darted around at my feet before stealing a morsel of bread and speeding off up a nearby tree.

'Yeah, pretty much. Friday and Saturday nights were the worst. I would hang around outside bars, listening to the music, and I would just dance. People would come and dance with me; sometimes they laughed, sometimes they cried. I became a bit of an attraction for drunk people when they left bars and nightclubs.'

I imagined his slight frame jerking around in time to some distant bassline. I imagined the drunken louts pointing and laughing. I imagined the heartbroken girls taking his hand and moving with him in the darkness as tears rolled down their cheeks. I could imagine it all. He must have been like a comedy act for them. Someone to mock when showing off to their friends.

'I must have looked like a right idiot. The things people used to say, Si . . . It hurt so much, but I just didn't care. There's this one song, this song Jenny and I used to love. We used to play it in the kitchen and run around like wild animals. Those were some of the happiest moments of my life.' He smiled and the chill left my body just looking at him.

'It was called "You Get What You Give".' He paused, as if the next bit was too painful. Then he started reciting the words to himself: '*You've got the music in you, don't let go . . .*'

'I know that song. I love it! It's by the New Radicals, isn't it?' I cried, clapping my hands together with glee.

'Yeah, it's great, isn't it? Well, this one night I was outside the bar on the corner there, and it came on and I was so gone I thought she was with me. I danced and danced, it felt like it went on forever. I was even holding her close to me.' His eyes started to well up and he positioned his arms as though he were holding a girl. His girl.

His pain was so close to the surface, it was as if a tiny pinprick would see it all gush out like water from inside a balloon. 'What happened next?' I asked, finding myself so wrapped up in our conversation it was as if nothing else existed. The deadlines, the office, Dad, Nick – it was all just so far away now.

'The song ended and I realised it wasn't real. Suddenly, the song that had just given me so much joy brought out this agony inside, so deep even my drunkenness couldn't take the edge off. So I just kept on dancing, to an empty silence. Like a nutter. Trying to hold onto that feeling, you know?'

There was a moment of quiet. I suddenly thought about the songs Dan used to write for me. Songs he would play me on his guitar, record in his room, and then send to me in the post on a range of multicoloured discs. He only lived a few minutes away, but there was something romantic about the post – well, that was what he used to say. I knew how it felt when one of those songs came on through my earphones on the train. I knew the aching in the pit of my stomach. How I could almost smell him and feel him.

And Dan really was a bit of an idiot. He was never my husband, or the father of my child, or even someone I'd lived with and lost. I didn't even love him. I was testing the water. He was just this silly boy who made me cry a lot. A silly boy who lied, and filled the gaps with 'I love you' when he didn't know what else to say.

I'd got so sick and tired of his shitty mood swings, the amount of time he spent in the bathroom, and his lies, that I chucked him. It felt great. Getting so close to Nick had made Dan seem like a Nissan Micra parked next to a Lamborghini. It became a farce. I couldn't continue with it, and although I didn't stand a chance with Nick, I hoped that maybe I could find a man just like him. If there *was* anyone in the world like Nick . . .

On the plus side, Dan did write good music . . . although Nick strongly disagreed with me on this. I started to think about Dan again, his crazy hair and outlandish dress sense. I cringed a little inside.

I looked at my watch. Time was running out, as it always did when I wanted to talk to Pete.

'So, anyway. How's Nick?' he asked, breaking our reflective silence with something comparatively trivial.

'Great, thanks. We had a falling-out a while ago, and it was hard for a bit. I don't think either of us knew how to act around each other at first, but it was OK in the end. He's fine now,' I said, looking down at my tights and pulling off a bobble.

'Have you told him yet? You know, how you feel?'

'No, no, no, of course not. I'm trying really hard to put it to one side, you know. I just feel like too much is at stake.'

Pete looked frustrated. 'I don't want to pry, Sienna, but I think I understand your feelings for

Nick. It's love, and it's the kind of love I had with Jenny. I find it hard that neither of you will open your mouths to admit it. I'm sorry, that's just the way I feel.' He looked a bit guilty and a bit angry too. It was a strange combination to witness.

'I think too much has happened. He seems to be dating girls all over the place,' I responded. I knew, but hadn't quite admitted to myself, that all these dates, all these women who had come in and out of his life, had made him seem even more out of reach. Even more intimidating than he had been before. He hadn't told me much about them, but I knew the vague details behind each name. Marie, a doctor from Finsbury Park; Lisa, a graphic designer from Surrey Quays; and of course Kate, a tortured artist from Soho.

'Look, I have to get back to the office now,' I said, pulling a warm pasty out of my bag. 'Here, this is for you.'

Pete smiled and took the package, tearing it open in front of me and taking deep, satisfied bites out of the flaky pastry. It was the least I could do. He brushed his oily fingers down his trousers, leaving streaks of fat down the denim like tyre marks. The tissue remained untouched on his left knee. Oh well . . .

I felt constantly guilty for not taking him under my wing. I regularly thought about taking him home and giving him somewhere to rest his head, but with Dad, and the size of our flat, it was a strain the pair of us wouldn't be able to take. I was doing what I could, though – finding him hostels to stay at, bringing him clothes, books, bits of food, and what I hoped would be a small ray of light at the end of the tunnel.

He'd told me he'd managed to cut out the drugs now, although I never really knew for sure. The drinking was down too, apparently. Well, at least that was what he told me. There were certainly no cans of beer collecting around his feet nowadays, and he was looking better, if that was possible in his situation. I really felt hope for him.

Raindrops started to fall from the sky. The stormy atmosphere was giving me a headache

'Thanks so much, Sienna,' he responded between giant mouthfuls of pasty. 'Oh God, it's starting to rain. It's going to be a really cold one tonight,' he added, shuddering at the thought of it and looking towards the moody sky. 'I wish I had somewhere to go . . .' he tailed off, chewing even faster as the rain started to fall heavily.

I wished I could have him to stay with us, but *it just wasn't possible*. And although I could talk to Pete very easily, I couldn't bring myself to tell him about my father. He had too much to deal with as it was; telling him about someone else's problems just didn't seem right. But at the same time, this meant I couldn't give him a good reason why I wasn't offering him a roof over his head. I worried he might think I was selfish, or that I didn't care.

'Sorry, love,' he said then. 'I shouldn't moan, should I? Nothing you can do.'

'I wish there was, Pete . . . I'll see you soon.' I started to walk away, thinking of how different our lives were. Yet somehow we met in the middle and found common ground. Even if it was a bench.

The heat blasted through the door on my way in, making my contact lenses grip to my eyeballs like shards of glass.

'Sienna, darling, what were you doing out there with that man in the cold?' came the high-pitched inquisition from Sandra. The phones were ringing frantically but she ignored them.

I hate the way she calls me pet names: 'darling', 'love', 'sweet pea' – you know the kind of thing. It gives the impression that she's a nice, caring person, yet when I got into trouble she expressed no desire to help me. In fact, she reported me. I didn't trust her, but I had to keep the peace, so I gritted my teeth and made the necessary small talk.

'You're going to make yourself poorly if you carry on like that,' she said, finishing her sentence with a pearlescent pink pout in my direction. God, she was annoying.

'It's OK. I have lots of layers on.' I smiled unconvincingly, pulling at my Topshop jumper, which was quite frankly a useless barrier against the cold. It was one of those skinny-knit numbers, the arms a pattern of arty holes. Like most of my clothes, I had fallen deeply in love with it on a Saturday shopping trip with no real thought for its practical merits. A little like my taste in men.

'All right, love, I'll take your word for it.' She smiled back, falsely. 'Nick left this for you, by the way . . .' She pushed a small piece of paper across the glass desk with a naughty look on her face.

I swiped the note from her fingers and made my way up the stairs, opening it quickly in the quiet of the corridor. The paper had been secured with a little scrap of tape to keep his words away from prying eyes. It stopped me in my tracks and I felt a dancing in my heart. I love his writing.

> *I had to go to a meeting, Penguin, so I thought I'd scribble this down for you on my way out . . .*
> *Fancy a retro gaming session tonight?*
> *I ordered a Sega Mega Drive from eBay and I'm desperate to revisit the good times.*
> *Text me . . .*
> *Love, your favourite Nick*
> *xxx*

I didn't have any other Nicks in my life, but even if I'd had a hundred, he and I both knew he would be the best.

'Penguin' was a new one, though . . .

This would probably mean hours of hysterical laughter; I knew what he was like, he made me laugh all the time. But this was a first. This note seemed so full on, it was different . . . I suddenly felt really excited. A wide smile crept over my face. I'd hit the jackpot – I knew what this meant.

I'd never been to his before and this note sounded so personal. Maybe finally something might happen . . .

What the hell was I going to wear? Had I shaved my legs? Did I even have time to shave my legs? Shit. Shit. Shit. I whipped out my phone and told him I would see him at eight.

Nick

I had been awaiting the arrival of this parcel like it contained a vital organ. This was so exciting. The Sega Mega Drive: the curse of my university years. I would spend night after night on it, off my tits while deadlines passed me by. And what a great time it had been.

Somehow I still came out of university without repetitive strain injury in my thumbs, a first in classics and the ability to eat for a week on a fiver. Luckily I overcame my obsession before I trained as a graphic artist for my postgrad.

I held onto the black console, feeling the familiar curves of the plastic. It was basic. Basic and chunky and I loved it. It had just two bright red buttons and a large slot at the top for the games. Consoles nowadays could make you tea and wipe your bum at the same time.

The best thing was that Sienna was coming round too and I couldn't wait. We had talked about these consoles all those months ago at the gaming fair, and when I was twenty-one and beating the hell out of pixellated enemies in Street Fighter, she'd been in her teens and bouncing along the platforms of Donkey Kong. It was perfect.

She was due round in just a few minutes so I started dishing up the Chinese I'd ordered. Her favourite was shredded beef, mine was sweet and sour chicken. I knew she would definitely eat some of mine too, so I'd ordered extra.

There was a quiet knock at the door, three gentle strikes. The cold night air filled the hallway as I let her in.

'Sienna!' I shouted, as if I was surprised to see her, scooping her into my arms and giving her a big hug. Her little frame was buried beneath a trendy winter coat, which she threw off as she rushed into the kitchen. Her presence was a little like a miniature whirlwind. I could never quite keep up with it.

'Yes! You've bought my favourite!' she cried, clutching a huge bottle of cider for us to share. We carried the contraband into the living room, pulling the curtains shut and pushing the world out. It was just me and my favourite girl now.

A tiny lamp in the corner of my living room was all we needed; the TV was flickering a harsh blue light as it waited for the fun to start.

'I take it your dad's OK tonight?' I questioned, tearing the paper packaging on a bag of prawn crackers, the contents spilling all over the carpet.

'Yeah, he's fine, Nick. I think he was glad to see me out of the house so he could have some peace.'

She straightened her back as she answered, the memory of our row obviously still fresh in her mind. She started to shovel forkfuls of takeaway into her mouth. The girl can eat. I love that about her.

I opened the cider and poured it out, the cold liquid immediately creating a thin coat of condensation on the exterior of the glasses. I didn't know what to do first – gulp the drink, hog the food, or tell Sienna how I felt. (Although I wondered if I would actually pluck up the courage to do the latter.) This was wonderful.

'Nick, I've been talking to Pete again lately, you know . . .'

'Who's Pete?'

'That homeless guy who sits on the car park bench at work.'

'What do you keep talking to him for, Si? You nearly got into serious trouble over that.'

'I know, I know, but I keep feeling bad that I haven't invited him to live with me and Dad for a bit. I've been thinking about it for a long time.'

I suddenly felt a bit awed by her. Sitting next to me was a girl in her early twenties who seemed to have more room in her heart to care than anyone else I had ever known. She had enough to contend with looking after her dad; she shouldn't be worrying about how to mend everyone else's lives. She was so in tune with the world, so grown-up for someone so young that it scared me a little. However, I couldn't help feeling that her idea was a little on the naive side . . .

'I understand where you're coming from, but wouldn't that be too hard on you and your dad?' I queried.

'Well, that's just it. It would be really hard. The flat is small, and life is difficult enough for him already. But I still feel bad about it.' She looked at me, searching for answers in my silly face like she so often did.

Sienna was so kind I was convinced she must spend the majority of her life feeling guilty. If it weren't for her dad and the limitations of space, she would probably have a house full of homeless people, stray dogs, kittens, pigeons, and lonely elderly people she had helped onto buses. It was ridiculous.

I didn't know much about this homeless bloke, but I knew he was lucky to have her in his life. Despite her beauty there was not a drop of arrogance in her soul. And I knew why: Sienna was so gorgeous people just didn't tell her. How couldn't she know? That was what they probably thought. It was too obvious.

'Now, I have two games: Donkey Kong or Street Fighter. You choose,' I said, changing the subject, feeling the need to brush away the harsh realities of life and replace them with violent eighties video games.

She giggled and picked Donkey Kong. I knew she would. I pushed the game awkwardly into the console, feeling the familiar crunch as it sank into the bizarre mechanics inside. I took a couple of large swigs of my cider, kicking my trainers off into the corner of the room and nearly knocking down a tall lamp in the process. God, I was an idiot. She seemed to like it, though – it made her laugh that deep giggle that sometimes proved difficult to stop.

I held on to the controller like it was a newborn child, wondering how on earth to play the game. It had been a long time and my memory was failing me. Sienna looked worryingly ready, chewing her bottom lip and squinting at the grainy screen. There was no way she could win. It would crush my pride so badly it might never be fully restored. It would be almost as bad as the incident with her dad, and that had been bloody embarrassing. I had avoided her for at least a week after that. No – gaming was my territory . . .

'Right then, Si,' I declared, toasting her with my glass. She returned the gesture before settling down into the corner of the sofa.

The next few hours were a blur of cider and laughter. She tried to distract me in every way she could, even pulling my jumper over my face at one point. I still kicked her arse. The order of the universe had been restored and I was a happy man. There was so much shrieking and hysteria I was surprised the neighbours hadn't started banging on the wall.

The clock was moving swiftly towards 1 a.m. when we piled on as many layers as possible and headed out to the garden. I was clutching two rum and Cokes and a big, fat cigar.

We sat down next to each other on a towel I laid on the decking, and she rested her head on my shoulder. It was the perfect fit. The brutal cold made her body shake like a puppy so I put my left arm around her and squeezed her tight. I took a deep drag on the cigar, puffing the smoke out in perfect little rings. Maybe if I tried hard enough I could tell her I loved her like this . . .

No. That was silly. And impossible. Sienna needed me in her life. I suddenly felt myself backing away from the prospect of just telling her, finally. Suddenly all my self-persuasion retreated so quickly that I could barely hear the words that had been rattling around in my brain. I never wanted to be the one to break her heart, to disappoint her, to be late for dinner or to hog the bed. I never wanted to be the person to make her cry, or turn out to be a huge let-down. She meant too much to me for any of that. While I believed I could love her better than anyone in the world, I didn't really trust myself to be . . . well, good enough.

'Pass it here, warthog,' she said, pulling the cigar from my fingers.

I watched her as the smoke drifted from her lips. She seemed so pure to me that the contrast between her face and the smoke billowing from her mouth was verging on artistic. I could take a photo of this moment and put it in a gallery and everyone would just look at it in wonder. Who was this girl? What was she all about? Where had she come from?

'What's up, Nick? Are you all right?' She turned towards me. Our faces were millimetres apart and her breath was sweet. This would have been the perfect moment to kiss her. But I just couldn't.

'Yeah, I'm fine, dude, just chilling out.'

Dude? What a load of shit. 'Dude' was what I called her when I was scared and needed her to be my friend. 'Dude' was not the woman I had yearned for every single day since I'd first seen her face peeping over the top of a newspaper.

'Any nice girls in your life at the moment?' she asked me, turning her delicate profile towards the moon, which hung in the sky as if suspended by invisible string.

'Yeah, I guess so . . .' I responded, my mind scanning through the dates I had been on recently.

I wasn't really telling the truth – they weren't that nice. One of them had tried to drag me behind a bin for sex after just one date. Another one clearly had a few boyfriends and saw me as a bit of a plaything, which suited me OK but didn't really set me on fire. And then there was Kate . . . Beautiful, tortured Kate. I never knew that I had taken a broken doll home with me that night in Brixton; all I'd wanted from the evening was a one-night stand, but she needed fixing and she looked to me to do it. Kate was really the closest I could have got to someone serious over the past few months, but something was holding me back. I was tired of holding her face and telling her she was gorgeous, exhausted by the teary phone calls

141

from her at three in the morning. I should have seen our wild night as an omen; there was something in the desperation of our passion that indicated our shared vulnerability. I was hurting from my row with Sienna and needed the distraction, and Kate needed someone to make her feel beautiful again. I did, and it was like a drug to her.

'Who is it, Nick?' I felt her body tense up; I guessed she must be cold. We didn't talk about this stuff too often.

'Well, Kate's lovely. But I don't know if I can cope with the drama any more. She makes me feel a bit suffocated, really, but I can't just leave her to fend for herself. I'm too deep into the situation . . .' I paused, realising that I sounded like a bit of an arsehole.

'Does it feel wrong?' she questioned, quietly this time, as she pulled her coat over her knees.

I could smell her hair; a beautiful, appley scent. 'No, I don't think so. I think I like the idea of her, but the reality is too much to handle. She isn't my girlfriend, obviously . . . but she's almost made herself that by default. I feel like the choice isn't mine.'

I was surprised the words were spilling out like this. Talking to Sienna, my thought processes were coming out in some kind of neat and tidy order, when in my head they had been swimming around like alphabet soup.

'I think you should try harder, Nick. I think she might need you. Sometimes, people need you and it's so scary you push it away when actually you want it to be closer.' She looked at me and I suddenly felt the weight of a new responsibility. One I had tried to deny, but when Sienna put it so simply I felt I had missed something hugely obvious.

'Well, I'd better go now, my lovely,' she said, suddenly looking down at her watch.

The cold instantly bit into my clothes as her warm frame moved away from me. It was very late now and I could tell work would be a struggle in the morning. My head was spinning.

'Can you call a cab?' She looked up at me in the moonlight.

'Of course. You can stay in the spare room if you want?'

'No thanks, Nick, I should get back, really.' She wandered into the living room and I followed her inside. I heard her climb onto my sofa again as I opened the fridge for some chilled water. 'I'll call a taxi firm in just a second, Sienna,' I shouted down the hallway, but there was no reply.

I started shuffling through the papers on the kitchen worktop, looking for a taxi number, frustrated at my own lack of organisation. After a few minutes I finally found a business card. I picked up the phone and walked into the living room, but I was surprised to see her lying on my sofa, fast asleep. That was quick, I thought. She must be exhausted.

I didn't really know what to do, so I stood there looking at her for a few moments.

Her beautiful face was lit by the blue screensaver on the TV and she looked so peaceful.

I wondered about her dad and if he would be OK if she wasn't there in the morning, but I knew his social worker always popped in when Sienna left for work so I guessed he'd be all right. It was a difficult situation to gauge.

I couldn't bring myself to disturb her, so I went upstairs and pulled the duvet from my bed, carrying it down carefully so as not to trip on the edge and fall down the stairs, landing in a tangled heap at the bottom. That was exactly the kind of thing I would do. I gently laid it over her, noticing her ribs rising and falling as she slept, and crept quietly up to my room.

I lay under a thin sheet. It was cold, but it was OK. It was just fine because I knew that Sienna was here, safe and warm under my duvet, even if I wasn't under it with her. As I tried to drift off I thought about my life, and how far I'd come since the break-up with Amelia. How much of that was down to Sienna? I wondered. Just having her around felt like such a blessing I had to pinch myself. I slowly slipped into the land of dreams, my legs twitching occasionally and bringing me back to consciousness until I was lost in the satisfying murk of sleep.

I reckon it was about 3 a.m. when Sienna's silhouette appeared in the shadows of my room. I could only just make it out. The click of the door as it opened had brought me out of my dreams and through one eye I squinted at her hovering around like a ghost. Was she sleepwalking? I stayed quiet and played dead, wondering what on earth was going on. She stood still for a few minutes; my heart was beating so hard in my chest I could hear it on the pillow.

Should I say something? Walk over to her? I'd heard sleepwalkers lash out if you wake them . . . Then there was some more movement and she sat on the edge of the bed, letting out a loud sigh. It was an unhappy sigh – I knew her that well. There was another pause. Then silence. The black of the night. She gently spread the duvet over the bed so as not to wake me, and slid underneath its heavy weight. Her long hair swished against the pillow, a strand brushing my neck.

Sienna

It was nearly one in the morning and the cider had well and truly taken effect. I had that beautiful woozy feeling, the fine line between tipsy and drunk. All my cares seemed so far away. It was just Nick and I at his place, and nothing else seemed to matter. Nothing at all.

We had played Donkey Kong for hours, and it was an effective distraction from the tension that was building up between us. But now the console was off, I was well and truly switched on. My attraction to him was so overwhelming now it scared me.

'Fancy sharing a cigar outside?' he asked as we

stood in the hallway, pulling on a dark brown padded jacket with a green stripe detail on the arms as if I had already said yes. It was one of those trendy jackets you see on London men who prefer to use oversized cans rather than inner-ear headphones, read the *Independent* and keep their brightly coloured trainers dangerously clean. He had that look about him. It drove me crazy.

He found a jacket for me too, a big black Helly Hansen number that was several sizes too big and made me look as if I was ready for a ski trip. The smell of his aftershave washed over me as I zipped it up. I could barely contain my urge to just hold his face and kiss him, right there in the hallway.

Nick made two rum and Cokes in the kitchen on our way out, and selected a big fat cigar from a selection of five in his cupboard near the back door. He also grabbed a towel and laid it down on the decking outside. The air was so cold I had to zip the coat further up my neck, but the alcohol provided an additional layer of protection.

We sat down and Nick lit the cigar, the strong smell spreading all around us. The moon was so bright it was as if someone had left one of those economy light bulbs on, making everything look like the set of a vampire movie.

I started to tremble a little, shuffling my bum along the towel so I could have a little of his heat. Being this close to him was so torturous I could have cried, but at the same time I was happy. It was bittersweet.

Nick put his arm around me and squeezed as he started puffing out the smoke in little circles. They got wider and softer as they drifted off into the freezing night air. He looked like he was deep in thought. Distracted. Far away. I asked him to share the cigar, pulling it away from his fingers before he had the chance to reply. I knew this was cheeky, but I was nervous. Deep down, I knew that if we didn't get it together tonight, while the moon was full and the stars were glittering, we probably never would.

There was more silence, so I asked him if he was all right, turning towards him so our noses were almost touching. I felt the heat of his breath against my lips and stared into his eyes. I could kiss him. I really could. Right. Now. Well, go on then, I thought. Do it . . .

But it was too late, and he broke the quiet by saying: 'Yeah, I'm fine, dude, just chilling out.'

Dude? The moment was gone and he called me dude. Damn.

I asked him if there was anyone in his life at the moment, hoping we could get on to the subject that way, my breath creating puffs of whiteness against the crisp air.

'Yeah, I guess so . . .' he replied, squinting slightly to stop the smoke going in his eyes.

Oh dear. I bet there was someone I didn't know about. Maybe he was right on the verge of being in a relationship.

'Who is it, Nick?' I asked, desperate to be put

out of my misery. I hoped it hadn't shown. He started talking about Kate. I had vaguely heard her name once or twice. I think he met her on some night out in Brixton back when things were funny with us after that argument, but he'd described her as a 'tortured soul' when her name had come up in previous conversations. Tortured soul. This didn't sound like something he should have to contend with.

I asked him quietly if it felt wrong to be with her, and pulled his coat over my knees. Now we were talking about another woman, the cold seemed to seep into my bones.

'No, I don't think so. I think I like the idea of her, but the reality is too much to handle. She isn't my girlfriend, obviously . . . but she's almost made herself that by default. I feel like the choice isn't mine.'

I was surprised to hear him talking so honestly to me about this. For some reason we'd always kind of skirted around the details of our relationships. I'd always assumed it was because Nick was private about these things. And for my part it was because I wanted him to know that I was available if he ever felt the same. That's bad, isn't it?

Suddenly I was worried he'd picked up on my feelings for him. I started backpedalling to protect myself and said things to push him closer to Kate, in the desperate, secret hope that he would just say: 'There is someone else – it's you.' I felt instant guilt. This Kate girl, whoever she was, could have been perfectly lovely. Why was I wishing ill of their relationship? It was hideous and not like me at all.

I found myself spouting yet more bullshit as I then said, 'I think you should try harder, Nick. I think she might need you. Sometimes, people need you and it's so scary you push it away when actually you want it to be closer.'

Ironic wasn't it? I'd hoped this would be our moment, yet here we were, talking about someone else . . .

Nick

The appley scent of her hair instantly crept up my nostrils again. It was so damn sexy. I held my breath as she lay on the mattress next to me. One . . . Two . . . Three . . . Four . . . My lungs felt as if they were about to burst. I have always been terrible at holding my breath since I was forced to go on a school swimming trip and was pushed under the water by itchy Luke (don't ask about the nickname). Now every time an attack of the hiccups arrives I see his angry little face in front of mine just before he slammed my head into the drink and nearly killed me. Associated trauma, I think they call it.

I exhaled slowly and quietly as she turned her body towards mine, and once more I could feel the heat of her just like I had in the garden. My heart was now thumping so fast in my chest it was making me feel sick. I could smell the cigar we'd smoked on my pillow and felt decidedly ill. The cider and Chinese takeaway were sitting uncomfortably in my stomach. Oh God. Why did her mere presence make me feel like I was going to fall apart? And what the hell was she doing?

I worked hard at a fake roll so I could turn away from her, pulling the duvet under my torso in a selfish manner so she really would think I was asleep. Her body moved away from me once again. I was not entirely sure how playing dead would help me in this situation but it felt like the right thing to do at the time.

Yes, running away from it all was definitely better than facing it head-on. I had chosen this option so many times before and it had worked just fine for me. Unfortunately, however, my senses were so heightened by adrenalin that I was about a million miles away from any kind of sleep-like state. My eyes were out on stalks and the hairs on my arms and legs were standing on end. From the sound of Sienna's breathing, which was also pretty speedy, I guessed she was now lying on her back. She sounded stressed too.

Think about something else, Nick. Come on, anything . . . Penny sweets, elastic bands, fax machines . . . Sienna, beautiful Sienna . . . Broken toasters, instruction manuals, ferrets . . . But Sienna's here . . . Cam belts, WD40, baked goods . . . Your Sienna . . .

Damn it. It obviously wasn't working, so I let my mind wander to the place it wanted to go. I wondered what it might feel like to be brave. You know, to not be me. I knew I could never take advantage of her, but if I had some balls rather than the raisins they had been replaced with this evening, maybe I could turn around and pull her close to me with my right arm. Yes, that would be lovely. I could wrap my arm around her tiny waist and pull her across the sheets until her nose was touching mine.

And maybe, in my dream-like scenario, she wouldn't shriek, 'Urgh, Nick! What the fuck are you doing?' and whack me around the head with her sock, but just stay quiet and let her lips rest on mine.

Because this had been brewing for so long, neither of us would take the plunge with the kiss straight away; we would just lie there first, seeing how it felt. Maybe a few minutes would pass, and I'd be able to feel her breath on my face. I would take in every second like it was the real meaning of life, these moments that make the world go round. Then, maybe, if I was really lucky, she would kiss my bottom lip and tell me she loved me too and always had . . .

The scenario was so dream-like it was making me ache from the depths of my soul. It actually hurt. This was definitely love. Without a doubt. This was what those poets were talking about in the old-school literature that used to make me cringe when I was spotty, fourteen and fantasising about Miss Rogers in my English literature classes.

151

This was it. It was pulse-racing, heart-wrenching, dizzying love. The kind that touches every one of your nerve endings and renders you almost insane. The kind I could not give into easily because it already hurt like hell before lift-off.

The reality of this situation was that the love of my life was lying on her back, in my bed, at 3.30 a.m., and I was pretending to be asleep. What a hero I was. Come on out, Spider-Man. Where the hell are you now? Huh?

The darkness enveloped every corner of the room. My eyes scanned the space in front of me but it was as if a black ribbon had been tied around them. There was nothing but inky depth.

Then, suddenly, it happened. I felt a soft hand move under the sheets and snake round my waist. Not a dream, Nick, not a dream. This was definitely happening. My stomach muscles immediately tensed up so they felt like a row of seaside rocks. Well, that made it pretty obvious I was awake, didn't it?

I tried to relax my torso but it just wouldn't calm down, then I figured the permanently taut feel would do me no harm so I should just roll with it. I wondered what she was doing. She *must* have been sleepwalking . . . Then, using my stomach to grip on to, she pulled her body behind me and pushed her legs under mine. Wow.

We were Mr and Mrs Spoon, cuddling in the cutlery drawer. This was it. More than a year after meeting, she had finally broken the ice. Did she know what she was doing? But I didn't want to ruin it, so I stayed dead still. Holding her hand or trying to kiss her might have been too much at this stage.

Her lips touched the back of my neck ever so slightly and it set my heart on fire.

Calm. Peace. Quiet. A loud sigh rushed from her lungs as she finally dropped off, her legs twitching just like mine do.

I didn't sleep a wink. It felt like all my birthdays had come at once.

I imagined who I would tell first. Ross? Yes, it had to be him. He deserved a medal after putting up with all my pining and whinging. I could call him casually and tell him how Sienna and I had finally sorted things out, like I'd always known it was going to happen. He would probably take the piss, but he'd be happy for me.

I could call my mum and she might finally believe that I'm not gay (she'd been starting to express concern since Amelia and I had split up and I'd brought no one resembling a serious female partner to our uptight family parties).

The reception girls would love it too. They've been teasing me for ages.

Wow. Sienna, my girlfriend. Christmas drinks, executive gatherings, bar mitzvahs, whatever. Me and Sienna against the world. Joint bank accounts. Egyptian cotton. A Tesco Clubcard . . . My beautiful, wonderful girl.

Those three and a half hours in bed while Sienna's arm was curled around my body were possibly some of the happiest I have ever experienced. There was that time I got to ride a camel in Africa, and my first big promotion – oh, and not forgetting my three-and-a-half-hour marathon (now that was a cracker) . . . But none of them beat this.

She couldn't be asleep, you don't just cuddle people in your sleep. This was for real.

The sun was rising slowly behind my curtains and I stayed dead still, excited about what she might say when she woke up. It could go something like this: 'Morning, Nick, I hope you don't mind me doing this . . . I've just wanted to tell you for so long . . .' or even: 'Don't speak, Nick, just kiss me . . .' Yes, I quite liked the sound of the second. Let's go for the second. I knew this would work out. I just always had a feeling in my gut that we would sort this out. All along.

Then, at around 6.55 a.m. she turned around in her sleep. Bugger.

Now that her arm was away from my body, the little strip of skin that it had covered felt cold and, well, naked. I mean it was naked, but properly now. I had lost her. That's fine, I thought. She would wake up soon and we could talk, and I could tell her how long I had loved her, and all the silly things I'd said and done and why. Like the time I said she reminded me of my sister. I would definitely be explaining that first.

At 7.10 the alarm went on her phone, piercing the gloriousness of the early morning calm and the start of our new life.

'Shit, shit, shit,' she exclaimed, sitting bolt upright in bed, the duvet wrapped around her chest as if she was naked. She wasn't. Her fringe was poking up in the air in a variety of strange angles and she had a line on her face from the seam of the pillowcase. She dived to the side of the bed and scrabbled around for her phone, silencing it with what sounded like an angry fist. I jumped.

'Damn, Nick, sorry. I don't know why I got into your bed. My head hurts. Shit, bollocks!' she exclaimed again. A tirade of swear words and regret. Her cheeks were red.

I rolled over to face her, not sure I was really hearing this and suddenly very aware that I was only wearing my boxer shorts and the glory of the morning meant there was an erection that resembled a chequered tent in the southern part of camp pants. This was a nightmare.

This situation was becoming a never-ending, heartbreaking saga, and I wasn't sure if I could take it for much longer. It was push and pull, give and take, yin and yang, but all messed up. I felt like I'd been pulled from the top of a very high horse in Happyland and fallen into a pile of dog turd, face down. In fact, some of it had gone in my mouth. I was sure of it.

'Nick, please forgive me for getting into your bed. I work with you, for God's sake. I think I had a bit too much to drink, it makes me sleepwalk sometimes,' she said, pulling at my arm guiltily.

155

I yanked it back, a little irritated by now but trying really hard not to show it. 'Er, Si, I didn't even know you were here,' I bullshitted, even though I felt sure she must be able to hear the broken shards of my heart tinkling onto the floor. 'Anyway, it was really cold last night so it's cool,' I added, suddenly withdrawing my body to the other side of the bed and pulling on a pair of trousers, trying to hide my boner.

I was still without a top. Damn. Where was my top? I scrabbled around on the floor and found one, bashing my head on the way up on the sharp edge of an open cupboard door. I should have listened to my mum about leaving doors open. It was the kind of pain that made you wonder if your skull hadn't caved in to let your brain out for a quick stroll.

'Bollocks!' I shouted. That really bloody hurt. I gritted my teeth so hard I feared they might just crack and drop out of my mouth like pennies from a broken piggy bank.

'Nick! Come here!' Sienna cried as I stormed into the bathroom and shut the door. I sat on the toilet seat and pulled my head into my lap, gripping on to it hard to stop the throbbing pain. Breathe. Come on, just breathe. I was completely consumed by humiliating rage. Tears of pain and frustration started to fill my eyes. I felt like such a fool. It was a mixture of raw anger and deep disappointment and I didn't know which hurt more – that, or my head. God, she'd only put her arm around my waist and I was already doing the weekly shop with her. What an IDIOT! For a guy approaching his thirties I could be hideously naive at times. This was it. This was my wake-up call. It was time to get real.

There was a gentle knock at the door, like a little angel wanted in. It was hard to stay this incandescently furious with Sienna for long, but my embarrassment was prolonging my bitter feelings towards her. They stung like a fresh cut, and they weren't going away.

'Nick. Please come out. I'm worried about you . . .' There was a long pause while I considered whether or not this situation could get any worse.

'Nick?' she repeated softly.

I looked at myself in the mirror and saw an idiot with bloodshot eyes. My hair was flat on the top of my head while a couple of bits stood on end at the back like a radio receiver. I tried to gather the chunks of hacked-up male pride that were scattered all around me and walked to the door. I slowly opened it, peering through a tiny crack between the frame and the knotted pine door.

Sienna pushed her arm through and pulled me towards her. It was a stealth attack and I had no chance to block it. 'Come here,' she said, squeezing my body tight. I tried to push her arms away but it wasn't working.

She ran her fingers gently over my head, a sharp sting making my eyes water when she touched the sore spot. Chills ran up and down my body. I felt really exposed.

'Oh, Pookie, I can feel a bump,' she said, pulling me even closer.

I sniggered into her neck despite my concentrated sulking. It was a pet name we'd heard on a train once that had made me want to scream with laughter at the time. Now it was mildly tickling away the agony suffered by my battered ego.

'I'm OK, Si. You really are overreacting,' I responded, still pretending not to have been aware of the arm thing. If I couldn't handle a small bump to the head, then even more of my manliness would ebb away.

'Are you sure?' She straightened her body and faced me; I could see the fear in her eyes. She knew that I knew. I knew that she knew.

Her skin was all fresh from the morning, despite our drinking and smoking binge the night before. I was pretty sure I looked and smelled like a used teabag. Strands of dark hair tumbled across her face – the effect was as though she was looking at me through the sharp, thick leaves of a tropical plant. She was painfully beautiful.

For a few moments, we stood and stared at each other. It was then that things changed. That moment between Sienna and me was the start of a shift in our relationship. I had to stop loving her.

CHAPTER 5

'ISN'T IT TIME YOU,
WELL . . . GAVE UP?'

Sienna

'So I just fell asleep with my arm around him,' I said to a table of transfixed young women, half of whom had their mouths wide open. It was like a crazy golf course, only with very good-looking girls and minus the plastic plants and stuffed monkeys.

Elouise dropped her spoon into her bowl of potato and leek soup in shock, flinching when some droplets leaped onto her face. She wiped them away quickly with her sleeve, her eyes still stuck to me.

'He didn't come on to you at all?' she muttered in disbelief, as if this was a preposterous concept. A shred of leek still clung to her bottom lip.

'No,' I said quietly, pushing a chunk of potato around the bowl with my spoon and biting the inside of my mouth. It was a very bad habit of mine and something I only did when I was really stressed.

I kept fiddling with my food. The disappointment

was audible – a tut here, a sigh there. Womankind was in mourning. Well, at least the women in this room were.

'He didn't even really cuddle me back. I know he was awake too because his heart was beating really fast in his chest and he was doing that fake sleep-breathing thing men do.' I sighed. 'What was I thinking?'

My eyes scanned the collection of ladies assembled in front of me. I was hoping for answers to wrap this mess up once and for all.

Lydia dozily reached over to the bottle of wine and poured me a glass the size of a small bath. I gratefully accepted.

'Oh, Sienna,' she muttered, shaking her head in shame slash sympathy as the last few drops leaked from the neck of the bottle.

'Muuuuuuuuuuum!' came a shrill cry from upstairs, piercing the atmosphere at a perfect time. The looks of sadness were starting to panic me.

'Yes, darling?' El leaned back in her chair, her blonde locks sweeping over her shoulders as she angled her head.

We waited in silence.

'I want you to paint my nails,' came the innocent voice of my best friend's little boy from what sounded like the staircase.

She blushed. 'Sorry, ladies – I'll be back in just a moment,' she announced, rising quickly to her feet and running up the stairs in a pair of glamorous heels.

The rest of the table continued its silent protest of concern. Lydia was looking at me with a cock-eyed expression of pity, her auburn curls falling over her shoulders and resting on an army-green tank top set off by a delicate silver necklace. I'd sworn I would never tell her how I felt about Nick, but she'd caught me crying in the toilet once and I can't lie to save my life. I had snot on my top lip and everything. She had been surprisingly good, actually, not uttering such scandalous gossip to a soul. I doubted even Dill knew. I had since introduced Lydia to my friends, and she was now invited to anything we planned as a group.

Tess was running her index finger up and down one of the knives, her perfect little nose pointed towards the shiny glass tabletop. She was a stunning Korean girl I'd met at a taxi rank in Clapham two or three years ago. We'd shared a drunken journey back to west London and had been firm friends ever since. She had recently graduated from university and was on the job hunt, the stress collecting in little lines under her eyes. I knew she would be just fine.

Then my gaze moved over to Penny, who almost had a tear in her eye. Her wavy blonde hair was swept into a trendy and effortless-looking updo and her eye make-up made me instantly envious. She was a glamorous creature, working in a Kensington dental surgery to the stars, regularly giving us fantastic gossip about diva-like behaviour over the spit bowl. Now how *did* she do that thing

161

with the eyeliner flicks? I wondered about this for a good few seconds before smiling back at her. Her level of emotional involvement in my screwed-up love life was making me feel bad. She looked bloody miserable.

Before I knew it, Elouise was coming back down the stairs, her torn jeans tight against her slender frame. A pair of sparkling blue eyes hid an under-current of embarrassment and we all automatically knew not to mention the nail varnish thing. She covered it up with a lovely smile, the one that melted the hearts of men all over the south-east. Just one smile from Elouise is all it takes and men are putty in her hands. I've seen it everywhere we go together – checkout assistants and barmen, all reduced to over-compliant creeps, desperate to get her number and secure that coveted first date.

'Sorry about that, girls,' she exclaimed, breathlessly sinking into her seat. 'So what happened next?' She turned towards me, the rest of the girls' heads leaning into the centre of the table as I recommenced my tragic love story.

I took a deep breath and continued: 'Well, because he didn't cuddle me back, I figured I'd made a huge mistake, so I woke up in the morning and apologised for getting into his bed.' I cringed, my face turning crimson. 'I did the whole "I'd been drinking, I was sleepwalking" spiel – you know . . .' I poked at my wine glass before raising it to my mouth and taking a colossal gulp to numb the pain.

'And did you mention, you know, *the cuddle*?', said Tess, leaning back in her seat and wincing at the humiliation of it all.

Even Lydia was baring her row of perfectly straight white teeth in sympathy, like she was watching some kind of circus stunt gone wrong.

'No. I figured if I pretended it hadn't happened, he would just put it down to me doing it in my sleep, or being drunk, or both,' I retorted defensively. 'At least I know where I stand now.'

There was more silence.

'I've really fucked this up, haven't I?' I asked.

Penny leaned forward and squeezed my hand. 'Don't be silly. What about the time I cheated on my ex with his brother without realising they were related? Now that's fucking up,' she sniggered, clearly quite proud of her naughty accomplishment.

'They were identical twins, for God's sake!' shrieked Tess, elbowing her hard in the arm. The whole table erupted into laughter. 'And that has nothing to do with this situation. Sienna's a good girl!' she continued, pretending to scold Penny. I love my friends.

'But it gets worse . . .' I started once more.

The timer on the oven beeped loudly in the background as if trying to put an end to this tale before it could possibly get any worse. We all ignored it.

'He started getting dressed as soon as we woke up. He was digging around on the floor for a top, and on the way up he bashed his head on an open cupboard door. Really, really hard. Then . . . he locked himself in the bathroom,' I finished, raising my hands to my mouth in a bid to hide behind them.

They all gaped at me again.

'You really are a pair of idiots, aren't you?' said Penny, starting to laugh now.

Eventually her giggles became so strong that they were infectious. It was obvious she was trying to stop, her black-painted nails clawing at her face. I loved watching her laugh like that, even if it was at my expense.

Lydia caught it next, flapping her arms around apologetically. Then it was Tess who cackled loudly and melted into a heap. Elouise was the last to go, but she went all right, and with a snort followed by a look of shock that she was capable of making such a noise.

'Girls!' I shrieked. 'Come on! This is terrible, right?' I pleaded for some seriousness, but it was in vain.

My eyes were full of tears, partly because I had put myself out there with a man who clearly didn't feel the same, and partly because the whole thing was so farcical it *was* becoming hilarious. Still, it did hurt a bit that the girls were laughing.

The thing is, Nick's such a nice bloke that he'll go on pretending that he was asleep, which I know he wasn't. And I'm such a coward that I'll pretend to believe this lie, and we'll all live happily ever after.

When the laughter had died down and I had received an apologetic smile from each of my girlfriends, we got back to the serious stuff. It was Penny who had the bravery to utter this short but brutally honest sentence:

'Isn't it time you, well . . . gave up?'

There it was. She had thrown it into the centre of the table amid the elegant wine glasses and scrunched-up napkins. She had skipped the 'maybe he's intimidated by you', 'maybe he likes you so much he's scared' rubbish, and gone straight for the home run. El widened her eyes, looking at her as if to shriek 'You can't say that!' and slapping her across the leg.

They waited for my reaction, which could have been one of several:

1) To take great offence, storm out of the dinner party and ignore my friends for the next six months.
2) To take great offence but stay at the dinner party and start calling Nick again in a desperate bid to defy this cutting advice.
3) Start crying.

What I actually did was draw a deep breath, smile, and simply say, 'Yes.'

Because yes, it was time to give up. This *had* been a long-term, painful debacle. One big 'gaffe', as the papers would call it. A fuck-up. A two-Jags, blow-job-in-the-White-House, mislaid-expenses-receipt, whoops-I-just-set-my-own-house-on-fire, sodding disaster.

Nick was a man. A good one, but still a man. And men were highly sexual creatures. All of my male friends reinforced the notion that thinking about sex or sex-related topics was up there in the top five things they did each day, somewhere below breathing but just above eating. It really was that big a deal. I knew this was a massive generalisation, but if a man liked a woman, he did not pretend to be asleep when she put her arm round him in bed.

No, he didn't. He pounced on her like she was the last bagel in New York. Or at the very least he panicked, gave her a little kiss and pounced the next time, once he'd got over his own insecurities. So, Sienna Walker, it was time to get real.

'Yes?' said Elouise, leaning towards me and narrowing her lovely eyes. 'So you're just going to give up on the man you love?'

Ah, the man you love stuff . . . The go-get-em, fight for your fella, stake your claim cliché.

'Yes, actually, I am.'

Because my level of preoccupation with Nick was now verging on either 'mug' or 'stalker' (depending on how you looked at it), and that didn't make me feel particularly confident or attractive. Therefore, this was a great time to give up.

Lydia looked crestfallen. 'He's just been a lot happier ever since he met you, Si. I don't know how to explain it.'

Penny butted in: 'But maybe that's just friendship, Lyds. I really think he would have said or done something by now . . . There's no denying they have a special friendship, but I just don't think he sees it the way Sienna does.'

Ouch. Be strong. This was a bit like having each one of my toenails pulled off by a hydraulic torture machine, but I kind of respected her for it. I needed some tough love.

'Hmm, I don't know,' said Lydia, clearly starting to feel a bit riled by Penny's brutal lack of hope for the situation.

'What do you think, El?' I turned to my very best friend in the whole world. Her opinion would seal the deal.

'I think, my beautiful friend, that you should move on. I'm not saying he doesn't like you, I just think this situation is bad for you. He's clearly a bit confused,' she concluded nervously.

Yup, that was it. The post-mortem was over. The verdict? Get over it.

A few more glasses of wine and a night of playful banter passed in what felt like seconds. We talked about Elouise's son's little penchant for having his nails painted pink, which was presenting problems with the other boys at school. We talked about the pressures of the job hunt, the rat race, the career world. We talked about the pros and cons of settling down young. We even talked about pensions and mortgages, for God's sake (even though pensions and mortgages seemed a very long way off yet). The early twenties female mind is a confusing and panicked place, I can tell you that, but I think we all walked away feeling like a few things had been picked apart, analysed and put back in a better order than they had been before.

I certainly did, anyway. I had a plan to move on. I thought about my idea on the way home, turning it around and looking at it from different angles so I was totally clear.

I stepped out of Elouise's house into the crisp, cold, early hours of Saturday morning and pulled on a pair of gloves, the grey ones with the little heart buttons my dad had ordered for my Christmas present. A fox looked at me for just a few seconds and then darted into the undergrowth.

Nick Redland is just another guy. Nick Redland is just another guy. Nick Redland is just another guy.

This was the new mantra. I imagined writing the sentence like lines on a blackboard, icing it on a cake, even stencilling it on a wall in a dirty London alleyway somewhere and accidentally becoming a hero of the urban art world.

I could train myself out of all this. Like a smoker, I could cut down. Like a drinker, I could kick the bottle. Like someone in love, I could learn to redesign the route to my heart so someone else stood a chance in hell of navigating it. I *could* do this.

And that wasn't the only thing, either, I thought as I pulled my jacket tightly over my body, fighting off the abrasive cold that was biting into my skin. I was going to start eating really well. Salads for lunch, fruit juice and low-fat yoghurts. I was going to start going to the gym. Yes, that sounded like a great idea – four times a week would be good.

I was going to start reading Dad more intelligent books rather than silly ones so we could learn at the same time too. Work – yes, I was going to work harder. By the end of next year I was going to get a promotion. And I was going to stop biting my nails, smoking cigars at the weekend, drinking too much alcohol, drinking too much caffeine, lying in till noon, and leaving it three months before getting my hair cut.

I was going to start a new and better life and it might even involve regular manicures. In six months there would be a new and improved Sienna Walker with slimmer legs, shinier, sleeker hair and a better pay packet.

Good night.

On Saturday, Dad woke me up at 1 p.m. with a chocolate croissant and a double espresso.

Bless him for thinking of me, but this was not how it was supposed to start. I was meant to wake up this morning to find a pair of wings had sprouted from my back during my peaceful slumber. Then those wings were supposed to carry me all the way to the gym, where I would work out solidly for two hours without creating a single drop of sweat.

Oh well. I would have this and then start again afterwards.

'Good morning, Si,' he said, tentatively edging round the door with the tray. This worried me a little – not only was he narcoleptic, but his trousers were way too long for him, with great swathes of material gathering at his feet. I'd been meaning to take them to the tailor near work for weeks now, and I quietly kicked myself for not sorting it out sooner, feeling guilty for how preoccupied my mind had been recently. Dad and hot drinks were not an ideal mixture, as Nick had found out. Nick. Nick, who I am no longer in love with.

'How was last night?' he asked, perching on the edge of the bed, his small frame swallowed up by a red lumberjack shirt. His face looked quite fresh this morning; he looked really awake. This was good to see. He had been on some new medication lately and I had high hopes that it might change his life. Still, there was always a new medication, some new trial, but nothing had been earth-shattering just yet. We had a hospital appointment coming up soon.

'It was great, thanks, Dad. We had a lovely time,' I said between yawns, tucking my legs under my bottom and starting to consume the banned goods. The first wave of guilt crashed over me. 'We talked about loads of things and had wine and a really nice dinner. It was just great,' I repeated, a flake of pastry flying from my mouth to the floor.

My father smiled and I wondered if he ever missed

his old friends. They came round every now and then, but it was pretty hard for them to see him fall asleep every time they cracked a joke. In fact, they had been coming round less often recently. I hoped it wasn't a case of out of sight, out of mind.

'So, when are you inviting Nick here again? It's lovely when he comes for tea,' my father asked with a real look of hope in his eyes.

This was difficult. A little like explaining divorce to a child. 'Well, Dad, he might not be coming round so often now,' I started, tearing at the pastry until some crumbs of chocolate rolled onto my legs. I picked them off delicately to ensure I didn't end up covered in specks of brown goo. I felt he was alert enough to be able to handle such a serious conversation.

'Why, Sienna? You haven't fallen out with him again, have you?' he asked, looking panicked already. I could see the first wave of cataplexy prod at his body. He steadied himself by leaning forward and placing his hands on the dresser. A bottle of perfume rocked back and forth before standing still again. Maybe I was wrong about him being awake this morning . . .

'No, no, not at all,' I assured him hurriedly, then wondered what to say next. He had no idea how I felt about Nick.

Nick had been coming a couple of times a month to join us for dinner, which was usually followed by a long, profound conversation about something my dad had watched on a documentary or found when scouring Google for new and mind-boggling information. The visits were special for both me and my father, but for very different reasons. I felt that while Nick should still come round, his visits should be a little less frequent. I really needed to start watering down my relationship with him.

'He's just really busy with a few things at the moment, so it might be tough to do it so often. But we will still do it, Dad, honest,' I tried to reassure him but he was now collapsed on my bed, head first onto the green striped duvet.

I sat up and looked at him, holding my coffee and feeling the warmth of it in my hands. It struck me suddenly and poignantly how much I loved my father and how strange and unique our little world was. As I grew older I was learning to embrace our difference and feel really happy with just being us. But you could never really escape how bizarre it all was. Here I was, talking to my dad who was passed out at the foot of my bed, yet was capable of hearing and remembering every word I said.

As for my father's reaction to my news about Nick, it was sweet but it was hard for me too. I wanted to take a step back from Nick, and Dad had to be OK with that. I did so much for my Dad, I hoped he could help me now.

I put the baby-blue mug down on my bedside table, turned his body over so he could breathe more comfortably, and carried on talking, patting his right hand softly all the time. I knew he would be taking it all in, despite his state of exhaustion.

'To be truthful, Dad, there's something I need to talk to you about,' I continued, pulling my legs up to my chin.

Obviously there was no reaction from my father, so I carried on with my story.

'You know when you met Mum, you said that you fell in love with her straight away?' I asked, realising that under the circumstances any questions were pointless. 'Well, basically, I'm going to be brave and just tell you that I fell in love with Nick the moment I saw him. And, well, I don't think he feels the same.' My disclosure was making me feel a bit sick. It was nerve-wracking, pouring my heart out to him like this, even if he was otherwise engaged.

I looked down at him; his mouth was hanging open now. You could just about make out the outline of his eyes, hovering under his closed lids. What was I doing telling my dad about this? I wondered, pausing for a few seconds before starting to tell some more of my story. I guessed this was what mums were for, really, but mine wasn't around so I had to make do with a father in a coma.

'And it isn't his fault, Dad, of course, so don't get angry. Because he'll always be my friend, and he has always wanted the very best for me . . .' I looked up at the window. It was starting to rain. A lump built up in my throat. I suddenly felt very alone and this confession was making me more emotional than I'd expected.

'Basically, while he'll always be a friend to me, I need to get my head around the fact that he'll never be anything more. So I think a bit of distance is necessary. I hope you understand.'

The silence now seemed deafening.

'And he really does like you, Dad. He'll be back. He told me that he wanted to talk to you about crop circles next because he found some old photos from a farm in Minnesota or something.'

Dad continued to lie on his back, probably screaming out some advice or words of comfort in his head, but it was no good. He wasn't able to vocalise them.

I tilted my head and looked at him. This might be a long sleep, I considered, aware that he would usually have come round by now if it was a quick one. His hair was really starting to thin, and I felt a flash of fear about how quickly my life had gone so far and all the things I wanted to see, do and achieve in the rest of it.

The rain started to chuck down so hard I could hear it on the windowpane. A big fat tear rolled from my right eye and ran over my lip but I felt numb. I licked it away with my tongue, tasting its familiar saltiness. What a mess. What a terrible mess. I started to think of my mother, and what she might say about all this if she was around. But I couldn't even imagine. I had no idea who she was now, or how she might react to things like this.

My mother, Kim, a legal secretary, had shocked the whole family by leaving Dad when he was diagnosed with narcolepsy, and I was left wondering, at a young age, how she had managed to abandon us like that. I have only realised fairly recently that I've developed not only a burning resentment about this, but also a complex about whether or not I was just difficult to love. Now I'm older, I see babies turn into little girls, and then into young teenagers, through neighbours and children of older friends, and wonder how on earth she managed to walk away when she knew me for the time she did. Was I a difficult kid? Was I selfish? It can't just have been Dad's illness – other families get through stuff like that. By default, I assumed it must be something to do with me . . .

I suppose I could hardly blame her for being deeply frustrated by Dad's illness. I know I have been at times . . . An admission that always plagues me with guilt.

See, he wasn't like this when they met. He was a tall, slim man with a head of dark brown hair, sparkling blue eyes and a warm smile. I've seen photos of how he used to look; he had this cheeky vibe about him. You can barely see the resemblance now, apart from that smile. But then it all got a bit weird: Dad falling asleep on shopping centre floors, dozing in supermarket toilets and generally feeling too tired to do anything at all. It was a world away from the vibrant young man Kim had met at a music festival, rocking an angled straw hat and a pair of green wellies.

Everyone put it down to laziness at first. Even

when I was just five years old I started to notice it. All the other dads were active and ambitious, while mine was sinking into a hole. In the early stages of his illness we were all in denial, aware of the fact he was losing his grip, but putting it down to a phase of simple tiredness that wasn't going away. But if you looked back carefully, there had been plenty of warning signs. He told me that he once passed out on the floor playing kiss chase at school when he was seven, he regularly fell asleep during university lectures, and had a habit of sleeping through his alarm time and time again.

Still, everyone treated it as a quirk: young men often struggled to peel themselves out of bed in the mornings and the passing out could have been a host of things. Maybe he needed a holiday, we often thought. Was it a change of diet he needed, or even a new bed? Even depression was explored as a possibility. You hear about people staying in bed for days sometimes, hoping to wake up and find that the black dog that was sitting in the corner of the room has left.

But after countless visits to nutritionists, herbalists and even spiritualists, everyone was stumped. All apart from my mother, who thought he was making excuses to dodge the responsibilities of life. An illness that makes you sleep for no apparent reason? Surely not.

The consumption of hundreds of different vitamins and supplements was not working, and within just four years he was no longer able to function in the modern world. It was a quick downward spiral and I grew up with it. My first proper memories of my father were overshadowed by his unexplained illness.

The rows were tremendous. I used to tremble in my bed listening to the smashing of plates and sobs as Mum told Dad he was the 'laziest, most miserable creature she'd ever had the misfortune to know'. I will never forget those words. I was only nine, but I knew it was serious.

I remembered my mother's blotchy eyes hidden behind a pair of dark sunglasses as she drove me to school, a red, shiny nose poking out from the layers of chestnut hair. Her shoulders were always tense and hunched in front of the wheel. That's the clearest memory I have of her in terms of looks. It's not a happy one. Most of my memories before that are a bit of a blur, as if I got so angry at her I wiped a lot of them away. She also had a habit of biting her bottom lip with furious worry until it bled. 'It's just a cold sore, darling,' she would say – another lie to gloss over the truth.

By the time I was ten, Dad couldn't laugh or cry without collapsing onto the floor, sofa or pavement in a deep sleep. It finally dawned on everyone that something was seriously wrong. Doctors squinted through their thin-rimmed spectacles, neurologists made pointless, empty notes, and his case was passed around the best specialists in the country. No one could find the answers.

He spent more than his fair share of time in

brain-scanning machines or hooked up to a network of wires, but the frantic study of wobbly lines and charts proved to be nothing but an impossible puzzle. Narcolepsy was known, but not well, and a large number of medical professionals had never heard of it. The resentment between Mum and Dad got worse. In the end there were no more kisses, hugs or family days out. Their wedding picture was turned to face the wall. They kept telling me everything would be fine, but I knew the family unit was eroding and it would soon plop into the ocean like a small, deserted cottage on the edge of a crumbling cliff.

It probably wasn't terribly surprising that Dad developed an unnatural interest in documentaries on Sky; taping everything, watching it all again and again. His fascination with the outside world started there and then spread into his writing in hundreds of notebooks, where he explored what things might feel like as his memories got weaker. He had been writing in them ever since he'd got really ill. There were boxes of books in his room now, each stickered on the front and arranged in date order. I bought them for him so he could write about the bad dreams and visions that go with his cataplexy, about his frustrations and fears.

It was a wet Sunday afternoon when Dad made his discovery. He told me all about it when I was a little older.

An American documentary called *Sleep Wake* was being aired; he had drawn a circle round the listing with a thick red biro and double ticked it for good measure. He'd even set an alarm clock so he would be reminded, and put a video in the recorder to capture it.

The opening sequence showed a rich, green field in the sunshine, reminiscent of the opening credits of *Little House on the Prairie*. A cute fluffy lamb came bounding out into the natural playground and bam. That was it. The creature suddenly keeled over, lifeless, as if it had died. Dad said it was tear-inducingly funny but heart-wrenchingly sad all at the same time. The lamb soon jumped up again, but within minutes it was back on the ground, four little hooves twitching away.

Dad sat in front of the TV alone; I was at a friend's house, and Mum was gossiping with a neighbour over a bottle of wine. As the programme continued, his hands trembled at the sickening familiarity of what he was seeing. The viewer was introduced to Martha from Illinois who was unable to stay awake for more than five hours a day, passing out wherever she was. But she was obese, deeply unhealthy and obnoxious. He didn't want to belong to her world. He wasn't *like that* . . .

Two more case studies later and dad had his answer – narcolepsy. After this, he didn't hang about. The very next morning he slowly dressed himself and requested that Mum take him to the doctor's surgery. He wore a shirt this time; he wanted to be taken seriously. I remember this episode clearly.

Dad plodded slowly from the front door into the front seat of the family people carrier, holding on to the door frame at one point to stop himself from falling. Word had spread that something wasn't right, that he was ill in a most unusual way. He had collapsed in our front garden a few times. People talk. Neighbours stood still in their gardens, staring at him. Jack didn't, but he did give us strange looks sometimes. He wasn't one of the gossips, but you could tell that in his own way, he was curious about what he'd heard uttered over fences and landscaped borders on his way to get milk and bread.

Mum drove the short distance to the surgery, noticing a videotape in Dad's hands, his knuckles white as he held it tightly. I was sitting in the back.

'What the hell is that, George?' she asked with her usual contempt.

'I think I know what's going on,' he replied. 'I think I have narcolepsy.'

'Narco-what?' she said, flicking her fringe indignantly across her face. She threw her right hand into the air angrily, perfectly manicured nails glinting like sharp blades. The comment was followed by a deep sigh and then more silence.

The wait to see a GP seemed to go on forever. Mum flicked angrily through the glossy pages of *Hello!* magazine, barely reading the articles. I tried to talk to Dad but he wasn't very receptive. I remember noticing for the first time the deep crinkles across his forehead. He was ageing. As he tapped the black video case with his index finger, an elderly woman looked at him sternly from across the walkway with visible irritation.

'Mr Walker?' the petite receptionist called out from behind her glass pane. This was it. Dad got to his feet but he'd started to look really tired again. Mum and I knew what this might lead to. He tried to steady himself and take a few deep gulps of stale waiting-room air in an attempt to come back from the brink, but it was too late. The strength was pulled from his legs like a tablecloth whipped from beneath a banquet. Dad's body went crashing to the floor, his head narrowly missing the edge of a wooden table, hitting the carpet with a dull, hard thud. Mum sank to her knees to hold his head up, and for a second they looked how I'd always hoped they would. Together.

The waiting room was thrown into chaos. All ten occupants leaped to their feet and gathered round Dad, Mum and me; an atmosphere of panic had hijacked the space. 'Please, please, can you all just go away?' I pleaded. I hated this and how humiliating it was. It scared me as well. I was all too used to ushering nosy crowds away from Dad's limp form on the floor of some dusty public space.

'He doesn't look OK,' said an interfering woman – the same one who had glanced at him with such contempt just a short while earlier. She pulled her red glasses down her nose so she could take a better look.

'He must be having a fit!' another shrieked, so

loudly that even a hard-of-hearing lady in the corner of the room flinched.

Someone appeared with a glass of cold water and a chocolate biscuit, hovering uselessly in the background.

'Right, that's enough!' screamed Mum, her voice cutting through the hysteria in the small magnolia waiting room like a knife. The garbled, gossipy chatter came to a halt.

Suddenly Mum started to cry. 'This, everyone, is my husband!' she cried. I tugged her arm to stop her, aware that a major emotional breakdown was about to ensue. Even the reception staff were craning their heads like owls, jostling in the small window to get a good look, their ID badges rattling on the glass counter. It was like a train crash and no amount of arm-tugging on my part could stop it.

'This man was the most amazing person I had ever met,' Mum began, her voice wavering in the madness of it all. 'He made me feel like the most beautiful woman in the world. He was happy, ambitious, energetic . . .' I knew Mum was aware of the assembled audience, but a certain deadness in her eyes indicated a complete loss of control. As she spoke she flung her arms to the ceiling, a wristful of tiny silver bracelets clattering against each other. I went red.

'This man, my husband, is very unwell. None of us know what it is, and I can't cope, I can't . . . I can't do this any more. He isn't the man I married. Please, someone, help me!' And that was it, the show was over and she was curled up in a ball on the floor next to Dad's seemingly lifeless body. It was like the scene of a crime. Something had been lost, gone wrong, come unravelled, and this small family was failing to put the pieces together. Mum and Dad were like children. I had to clean up the mess.

Stern glasses woman put a tentative arm on Mum's back, rubbing it gently. No one really knew what to say. A few of the less voyeuristic members of the public crept back to their polyester covered chairs to immerse themselves in their newspapers; maybe the sports results or the latest stocks and shares might pull them away from the naked vulnerability of this emotional outburst. Others came close to the action, looks of genuine sadness and concern on their faces.

Tea was made, space was given and eventually Dad came to. His eyes brimmed with tears. He had heard everything. He sat down again and tried to hold Mum's hand tight, but she pulled away. I saw it. I will never forget it.

After a few minutes, when Dad was ready, he shuffled slowly to the consulting room, one hand gripping the bar screwed into the wall, the other still clutching the videotape.

We knew his doctor well by now. Rebecca Knowles was a young GP, she couldn't have graduated much more than five years previously. She had a delicate, heart-shaped face and mousy-brown hair, pulled back by a thick black headband. She looked mouse-like, but she was far from that. She had often expressed her frustration at Dad's worsening condition, cupping her face in her hands over her desk. This was such an unusual case and she had failed to crack it. She had admitted that it was becoming an obsession, amid the routine cracked ribs and throat infections.

'I know what's wrong,' Dad said, thrusting the video at her. I sat on a chair next to him. Mum was nowhere to be seen.

Dr Knowles sat upright in her chair with a look of bewilderment on her face, presumably wondering firstly what on earth Dad's diagnosis could be, and secondly where on earth she was going to find an old VCR player.

She said nothing but merely put her index finger in the air, as if trying to sense where the requisite clapped-out old machine could be. She moved left and right, clearly thinking as she went along. Suddenly, she darted towards a cupboard and pulled out an elderly-looking TV with built-in VCR, its lead and plug catching on a pile of paperwork, which came tumbling to the ground. Within a minute or so she had plugged it in and slammed the tape into the mouth of the box, which gratefully accepted the challenge, chewing away at the white cogs inside with hungry satisfaction.

The room fell silent as we witnessed for the first time what this big breakthrough could be. It emerged later that Mum was sitting in a toilet cubicle down the hallway, frantically drawing on a cigarette.

I remember looking at Dr Knowles; she was crying. 'Of course,' she kept saying, again and again. Dad was right.

We never saw Mum again after that.

Nick

There is a new girl in the office.

I noticed this straight away because our office is quite small and mainly full of miserable-looking people, and she is gorgeous.

Her name is Chloe. I'm technically allowed to like 'new girls' now, because I finally ended things with Kate. It was hard, but I couldn't be her support any more. It wasn't good for either of us. I felt sad for a few days, but relief was the overwhelming feeling. She wasn't very impressed, of course . . . But I know in time she'll realise it's for the best.

I guess it's too soon for me to be thinking about anyone else, but I'm a man. We can't really help but pay attention when a stunning female struts into the office. I'm single and now I've finally realised that things with Sienna will never be more than friendship, I am free.

It all started a bit like this. At about 10 a.m. today, I had fed Dill, done the tea round and swapped a few of the letters on Tom's keyboard when there was a voice from my doorway.

'Hi – Nick Redland, is it?'

The voice prompted me to look up from my monitor and see that it was coming from a pale face with sparkling brown eyes surrounded by a glossy blonde mane. The blonde mane was dotted with random, very tiny plaits and looked quite messy. Bed hair, I think the fashion magazines like to call it . . . but whatever. And the voice came from a pair of full, heart-shaped lips.

The face was unusual, actually. Not instantly stunning, but a grower. By this I mean that it took a couple of hours for me to fancy her, rather than the instant attraction that normally materialises when I see a woman I like. To be honest, I thought she was a bit funny-looking at first. Kind of feline. She had one of those pure but very naughty looks about her, which I eventually decided I liked.

'Yep, I'm Nick,' I replied with a smile, rising to my feet and shaking her hand. It felt smooth and slender.

'Ah, great,' she said, stepping into the room properly. I pulled my trilby from my head, suddenly feeling slightly embarrassed by it.

She was wearing a delicate navy dress with grey tights and a pair of black boots. Her hair was much longer than I'd initially thought – from the front, the wisps and curls just touched her shoulders, but when she turned around it fell further down her back. Smudged black make-up surrounded her eyes, making them stand out even more.

186

'I'm Chloe. I'm just here for a week as an editorial assistant – it's a work experience role.'

I was surprised. The thought of the company providing the resources and time for a work experience placement seemed pretty unlikely considering that I almost had to dress up as a French maid and beg Ant every time I needed a new ink cartridge for the printer. In fact, we'd had a policy introduced that stated we weren't taking work experience people any more. Letters were screwed up and thrown in the bin. Emails deleted. It was all very brutal. Ant said it was because we didn't have the time to train them now redundancies had been made, and that our focus should be entirely on our own workloads. What happened to that?

'Oh, OK, great,' I said, still confused. I looked through the doorway and up to Ant's office. He pushed himself back in his chair and gave me a smarmy smile. Gross . . .

'So you're an artist here, right?' she asked nervously. What else would a scruffy-looking guy in his mid to late twenties in urgent need of a shave be?

'Yes, spot on. What exactly will you be doing during your week here, Chloe?' I enquired, leaning back against my desk and noticing a dirty mark on my immaculate Onitsuka Tigers. Damn. I'd had these for eight months and managed to keep them scuff-free.

'Well, I'm here to help everyone, really. I'm hoping to get some really good experience here to help me get a job, but it's tough to break into the market now. I'll probably be making lots of tea, too.' She smiled.

At least she was realistic. 'So what do you do normally?' I asked.

'I'm signed up to an agency at the moment and they're looking for something permanent in the publishing world. I've just finished a master's degree at UCL. It's been pretty tough, really,' she admitted, playing with some old-looking gold bangles on her left wrist.

'Well, I wish you the best of luck, Chloe, and it's lovely to meet you,' I said, trying to push some positivity her way. I could remember the start of my career, and how soul-destroying it had been at times. Scrunched-up letters from various different failed applications, and the bitter taste of rejection with my breakfast. Humiliating interviews with pompous, overconfident young whippersnappers, hired because they were the director's relative.

'Have you met the gang yet?' I asked.

'Yeah, I've met most of them – just need to meet Sienna, I think it is . . . She works in editorial, I believe? She isn't in yet, I think she's at an interview or something.'

'Ah yes, Sienna,' I said knowingly. I was desperately trying not to give away the fact that I was trying to get over her, having loved her unconditionally for nearly two years.

I leaned in to speak to Chloe; she smelled of warm spices and I considered for a moment how much I loved women and their exotic scents and wacky jewellery, and how you can almost remember someone like they're right next to you when you smell a familiar fragrance on the train . . .

'Sienna will take good care of you. That's her desk over there.' I turned Chloe round and pointed towards the empty workstation. It was covered with photographs of smiling young girls in their early twenties in various glamorous nightclubs and bars, Sienna usually wedged in the middle, wearing some fantastic ensemble she had just thrown on.

I felt a brief wave of sadness again. It was like I had lost something when I made my decision to walk away. In many respects, I was grieving for the loss of hope. Hope that one day we could be together. I had spent most of the weekend vegetating in my house and watching old films with a packet of Marlboro Lights and a crate of beer for company.

'Oh, great – well I can't wait to meet her. Speak soon,' Chloe said before sashaying out of my office like a cat. She definitely wiggled her bottom a bit. Definitely on purpose, too. Hmm . . .

Finally, something new and exciting in the office. Even if it was only for a week. It was perfect timing, and the fact that she was leaving soon was also great news. That meant I might actually be able to ask her out on a date, have some fun, whatever. She was on work experience so it wouldn't contravene my 'no dating colleagues' rule, because in a week, she wouldn't be one any more. Ha.

A small orange bar flashed on the bottom right-hand side of my screen. It was an instant message from Anthony.

'WHAT DO YOU RECKON?'

Capital letters. The mark of a madman.

I played dumb. Again. 'About what?' I replied.

'THE WORKIE, DIPSHIT.'

How rude. 'Yes, she seems nice. I didn't think we were doing work experience any more. Has the policy changed?'

I saw him lean back in his chair and scratch the back of his head. 'WE WEREN'T. SHE CAME IN THE OTHER WEEK, TOLD RECEPTION SHE HAD A MEETING WITH ME SO I CAME DOWNSTAIRS AND SPOKE TO HER. SHE MANAGED TO PERSUADE ME. YOU CAN'T BEAT DETERMINATION LIKE THAT, PLUS SHE'S HOT, NICK. OPEN YOUR EYES AND ENJOY THE SCENERY.'

Jesus, this was so unprofessional. I deleted the conversation trail and opened a new window. I hated office sleaze and sexist banter and wanted no part of it.

I tried to get back to drawing, but it was a difficult and highly unproductive couple of hours. My mind was cluttered. Where *was* Sienna? It was reaching midday and she still hadn't arrived at her desk. In fact, I hadn't heard from her all weekend and we'd had that awkward situation on Thursday night. I hoped her dad was OK and that nothing had happened.

We spoke at work every day, of course, but I made a firm resolution now. I had to keep some distance. Things were going to change. I was back in the game – I needed to start dating again, find something new to distract me, eat better, exercise more. Change. Maybe I could finally learn how to play the guitar, or join that local football team I'd been thinking about for so long . . .

I looked up and spotted Chloe staring at me through the glass. She quickly turned away when she saw me. That was when it struck me that she was actually quite sexy, and thoughts of Sienna trickled from my mind. But I was keen not to look like the office perv. I drew my blinds and shut the door. Hopefully everyone would just think that I was creating something so amazing it required total silence and solitude to do it. The reality of the situation was that I was drawing circles all over the screen, filling them with random colours, then deleting them, over and over again.

I couldn't help but think about Sienna and where she could be. Eventually I lowered my head to the surface of the desk and tried to collect myself. Why wasn't she here? What if something had happened? What if she'd been on a night out and got abducted and somehow no one had noticed yet? What if she'd fallen wildly in love over the weekend with some American guy and jetted off to Los Angeles without telling anyone? Now come on, Nick . . .

There was a quiet knock at the door. It wasn't

Sienna because she had a specific knock and I could tell it from a mile off.

'Come in,' I said sadly, suddenly realising how miserable I must sound. I quickly pulled at my T-shirt to straighten myself out and put on a brave face.

The blonde bed hair was filling my doorway once more. 'Sorry, Nick, it's me again. Ant has given me a brief for you already, hope that's OK . . .' she trailed off quietly.

'Yes, of course, I should probably do some work, shouldn't I?' I chuckled, quickly deleting the window of scrawl I had been creating in my state of paranoia. I think she may have seen it, though. 'Take a pew.' I patted my hand on the empty seat next to me.

'Oh, OK,' she said, blushing slightly as she started to pull an A4 sheet from a brown envelope.

I put my left elbow on the desk and twisted my body towards hers. She had lovely dimples when she smiled. My eye suddenly caught a sexy-looking bra strap poking out from the top of her dress. It was black lace with what looked like a flash of blue silk. Wow.

'So, I was on the phone to the company – it's an outdoor sports group and they're creating extreme assault courses in treetops all over the country.'

She ran a pale pink fingernail down the page. I wondered how it would feel to have it running down my back. God, Nick, stop it.

'Tom's going to try it out and write about it for *WeekEnd* magazine, so we need some page design and illustrations to go with the photos,' she continued. 'Ant wants you to decide the format. We need it by Wednesday 5 p.m. at the latest. Um, I think that's about it, really . . .'

She turned to look at me and a tingle ran down my back. I squeaked like a teenage boy when I tried to speak. Shit. How embarrassing. She looked down at her lap and smiled.

I finally managed to get the words out. 'OK, great, thanks for that. I'll let you know if there are any problems so you can relay them.' She was fit. Definitely.

'Fab. Speak to you later.' She sashayed out of the office again and gently shut the door behind her.

My mind went into overdrive. Sex with Chloe in my office. Door locked, blinds closed. Pushing everything from my desk and onto the floor movie style, including my £3,000 Mac, and lifting her onto it. Yum.

Oh dear God. I was just as bad as the rest of them. Another orange bar flashed at the bottom of my screen. It was Tom. He had clearly not been able to fix his keyboard after my improvement works this morning.

Y+U F*NCY HER, RIGHT? BEC*USE IF Y+U D+N'T YOU *RE DEFINITELY G*Y.

'Sod off,' I wrote.

Sienna

Tick.

Tock.

Tick.

T.

O.

C.

K.

I couldn't wait for the clock to strike five today. I had only been in the office a few hours because of a morning interview in town, but the day had still gone very slowly. I was buzzing for the start of my new and improved life, which would involve me being a super sexy gym bunny.

Yup. I was totally ready. Eyewateringly expensive gym membership? Check.

Energy bars? Check. Fluffy miniature towel? Check. Great-fitting gym kit (yes, it is possible)? Check.

On Sunday I'd been to a quiet corner of Covent Garden and discovered a beautifully mysterious dancewear shop. I was able to find some kit that was relatively stylish, didn't cling to my body like shrink-wrap, and didn't give me camel-toe. It was almost a miracle.

But it didn't happen without a struggle. The woman in the shop was scary; in fact, scrap that, she was terrifying. An ex-professional ballet dancer – you could tell the second you looked at her, with her wiry, yet graceful frame and pursed lips.

'Hello, darling,' she purred, her jazz shoes sweeping across the wooden floorboards as she swayed from side to side.

Uh oh. 'Oh, hiya. Yeah, I was hoping—'

'STOP,' she interrupted me loudly, a tobacco-scented finger pushed hard against my mouth.

What the hell? I caught a glimpse of myself in the mirror. I looked terrified. How could I get out of here? I looked left and right, left and right, but she had me trapped between a tall mirror and an exceptionally scratchy tutu. I was half expecting to see the foot of a cameraman poking out from one of the changing-room curtains before he jumped out and shouted, 'Candid camera!'

'Are you married?' she asked, a sharp black eyebrow pointing towards the ceiling. Her lips, which had started to resemble a cat's bottom, were pursed together to create an effect you only usually see in female Disney villains.

'Er, no, but I don't know what this has got to do with—'

Again I was suddenly cut short. 'Why?' the sharp voice demanded.

'Excuse me? Why what?' I responded, starting to get a little defensive now. I only came out for bloody gym kit, not a cross-examination on my romantic failings.

'Why on earth aren't you married? You're beautiful,' she said angrily, shifting her weight onto her left leg as she looked me up and down.

I blushed. I was angry, flattered and embarrassed

all at the same time. And she, I was sure, was totally nuts.

'Look at you,' she said, seeming on the verge of fury. She spun the full-length mirror round, confronting me with my own terrified reflection. It was a bit like Trinny and Susannah, but even more rude and humiliating. At least she hadn't started manhandling my tits yet. Dear God, there was no one else in the shop. She might kill me and sell me to the pub round the corner as cheap meat. But there I was, a frightened thing caught in the headlights of this strange woman's tirade.

Here were the vital stats. Sienna Walker, 5 foot 7 inches tall, nine and a half stone, long dark hair, black and pink hi-top trainers and a nice, thick-knit cardigan over boy-fit jeans. A fairly regular, run-of-the-mill girl in her early twenties in off-duty London trends. So what?

'You want to know why you aren't married?' she said, leaning close to my face now. The odour of stale Chanel No. 5 bombarded my nostrils. Yuk.

'Because I'm young, busy and not that both-ered?' I responded with venom. I had clearly found one of these old-school women who felt that life was supposed to begin and end with washing your husband's dirty Y-fronts with a bar of whale fat and a broken mangle. I don't think so, missy.

'No, of course not,' she shrieked now, flapping her right hand through the dusty air and narrowly missing my nose with a sharp, red fingernail. This was verging on assault, surely?

She walked behind me and I noticed her grey wispy hair was piled into a bun that looked as if it was about to fall off her head. A powder puff, if you will. I should have just stormed out of the shop but I was curious; maybe even a glutton for punishment. What *was* she getting at?

'It's all because of this,' she uttered in disgust, pulling at the loose material of my jeans and yanking one of the arms of my cardigan, leaving it hanging limply from my wrist.

Then she walked to my left-hand side. 'And this,' she continued, lifting a strand of my unkempt hair into the air and dropping it as if it was a rat's tail.

Well, she had a point. I was looking pretty low-maintenance today, but still . . .

'It is clothing like this which is an insult to the gift that is being female,' she said with real conviction. 'What's your name?'

'Sienna,' I replied, still feeling pretty riled by the intrusion.

'You, Sienna, are a strikingly beautiful young woman. You have been blessed with a present.' She ran her index finger under my chin and tilted my face upwards until I could feel the heat of the ceiling light bulbs on my eyelids. I hoped she didn't talk to all her customers like this.

'Well, that's very kind of you. I think I should go now . . . I just wanted some gym clothes . . .' I trailed off, starting to turn towards the door and some level of normality.

'No. You mustn't.'

197

Oh dear. I was definitely about to be made into a burger. No one would know where I was. My face would be on milk cartons all over the country.

'Why?' I asked, feeling more than a little confrontational now. I decided I must not be afraid of this woman, even if she did resemble an ancient cut of shoe leather.

'I want to give this to you,' she said, pulling a thick drape of velvet away from a corner of the wall and revealing what was probably one of the most beautiful dresses I have ever seen in my life. No joke.

The low light cast dark shadows on swathes of jewel-green fabric. I couldn't figure out what kind of material it was at the time. All I knew was that it was the kind of texture I'd only dreamed about when I was a little girl, yearning to be transformed into a princess, just like in the films.

It had a sleek halter-neck, which plunged down the middle in a steep V and then met a delicate corset waist section. This then flowed into a rippling skirt, which I imagined would trail behind the wearer like a wedding dress. But it clearly wasn't a wedding dress. It was a dress of utter temptation. It was sexy, actually. The proportions were perfect, the colour was perfect, the cut was perfect.

And this was a very sneaky sales technique . . . I wasn't having any of this, I decided, turning towards the door again. I couldn't wait to tell the girls about my crazy encounter with this woman.

'What do you think?' She smiled, beckoning me back.

'Well, it's absolutely stunning, but I'm actually only here to get some gym kit, so if I could just have a browse over there that would be great.' I was trying very hard to be polite.

She shook her head with frustration and rushed the garment towards me suddenly. Swinging it through the air, she laid it to rest in my arms, which I had involuntarily stretched out to ensure it got to me safely.

Her eyes were so illuminated, so alive, it looked as if they might burst into flames.

Layers of green silk rippled in my hands. It took my breath away. It was old but on-trend. Vintage but cutting-edge. Rachel Zoe would have probably chased me down the street and gouged my eyes out with a toothpick for this one. It was bloody gorgeous, and probably hideously expensive to boot.

'Yes, like I said, it's lovely. I really have to crack on now, though,' I said, looking down at it. But love had already taken hold. I had fallen for it hook, line and sinker.

'It's yours. I want you to have it,' she said, her coldness suddenly melting into a warm, broad smile. 'It used to be mine, Sienna. I fell in love the night I wore it and married him soon afterwards. I've been waiting for the right girl to take it on, and you, I just have a feeling about you. I think you need this.'

I couldn't quite believe I was hearing these words. Didn't the dear old lady have a daughter or a niece or something? I wondered.

'Don't you have family you could give this to?' I looked at her searchingly as I started to push the garment back towards her. What if she was mentally ill? Maybe I should call the police.

'No. And don't ask questions. It's your size, I can just tell. I want you to take it home, hang it up safely and wait for the right moment to wear it. And I promise you, it will change your life, Sienna. But until the day you get to wear it, whenever you feel down, or inferior, or downtrodden by the world, I want you to imagine you are wearing it. I know things are hard for you, I can tell by looking in your eyes. Whenever things are difficult I want you to imagine you are wearing *this* dress . . .' Her eyes narrowed with the sheer passion of what she was saying. I was suddenly aware of a Russian tinge to her accent that I hadn't been able to place before.

Whether she was driven by lunacy or not, I couldn't be rude to this woman. I was simply not brought up that way. I also couldn't bring myself to walk out of the shop with her dress.

'Listen,' I said, putting my hands over hers and pulling her down to sit on one of two fold-up chairs, starting to feel genuine concern about this situation. A middle-aged woman walked through the jangling door but instantly fled when she saw we were having some kind of intimate moment.

'Look, this is so kind of you, and I'm really touched by the gesture. I think your story is lovely and inspirational, and you obviously feel strongly about the importance of being confident. But I just can't take this. I will, however, take a look at your great selection of gymwear.' I started to walk slowly to the other side of the shop, running an enterprising hand over the dusty rails and grinning cheesily.

'Hmm. Fine, do what you want, Sienna,' she said with an indignant expression. She leaned back in the chair and crossed her legs moodily, revealing an ankle as skinny as a goat's knee.

Oh, great. I was going to end up pity-buying the whole shop now. Actually, these things weren't half bad, I thought, as I started to paw through the hangers gently. She must cherry-pick her stock quite carefully. The hangers were old but the clothes were new; there was even some of the Stella McCartney gym range in here, which was hard to get hold of. I hadn't been too inspired by the offerings in other shops. Too much nasty material, too tight, too baggy . . . This all looked quite nice and made the thought of the gym more appealing.

Right. I could get out of this situation quite easily. I would do my gym shop here. I would take the bags and leave, alive, my new friend would keep her lovely dress, and all would be well.

'You take your time and have a browse, my dear girl. You know where to find me.' She disappeared into a dark alcove behind the till, her voice getting considerably quieter as she was enveloped by the blackness.

Trying these things on wouldn't be a great idea. I just picked out some of the best size 10 offerings and started to pile them up on the counter as I browsed. I could hear my new friend carefully wrapping the items in tissue paper. The rustling sound echoed across the shop and into my ears.

My eyes caught a framed picture of a stunning ballerina. She looked a little bit familiar. 'Is this you?' I asked, stepping back in shock.

'Yes it is, my darling. That was me in my salad days. I was nineteen when that was taken. Never thought I would end up selling dance outfits and gymwear, but still. They had me performing all over the world, you know . . .' Her voice had grown louder and suddenly she was standing right behind me, both hands resting on my shoulders. A chill ran up and down my spine again, just like it had when my father was passed out on my bed. Again, I was reminded of the inevitable progress of age, and how it transformed a beauty like this one, smudging the edges until it resembled something quite different. Not necessarily bad, just different. It scared me. It made me want to cling on to the moments of my youth and make sure I lived them until there was nothing more to squeeze out of them.

'He isn't too far off, you know, Sienna,' she said, very quietly now.

'Sorry – I don't know who you're talking about,' I said, thrown into a state of bewilderment again.

'Your man. He will come round to you. It will work itself out.' Her eyes met mine and I felt an ice-cold sensation down my back again.

God, this was weird. But she was definitely nuts and, like a horoscope, frustratingly vague. You will breathe today. At some point in the next forty-eight hours, you will fall asleep. You will change the bed sheets within the next fortnight . . . Well, duh. Ridiculous.

He could be the milkman who owes Dad and me a fiver. *He* could be my uncle who promised he would call last year and just stopped trying. But still, *he* could be, well, you know . . . Nick.

Right. I need to get out of here, I thought. I peeled five £20 notes from my purse and walked out of the shop with my bags. What a strange woman. I considered the madness of the situation as I joined the hustle and bustle of the centre of town.

Couples embraced against walls and street signs; giggling children ran between bollards and bins; lone wanderers looked at stunning cakes and carefully crafted clothing through panes of sparkling glass and smiled at the beauty of it all.

There was something really special about today and it only reinforced my love affair with London. I had been so infatuated with Nick recently that my thoughts had been totally taken up by him. We had spent so much time together that I now had some to myself. And with it, I was going to explore my surroundings more, be independent.

This was the only city where you could meet such a choice selection of eccentrics as I was doing this afternoon.

When I got home, I started pulling my new wares out of their gold bags and carefully unwrapping the tissue paper. You didn't get this kind of treatment in JD Sports.

When I pulled the last parcel out of its bag it seemed heavier than the others. Odd . . . I tore away at the tissue paper and saw a flash of green. A load of silk came pouring like water out of the hole I had made.

Oh my God, it was the dress.

I held it in the air and felt the skirt come tumbling down, swishing against the floor.

'Wow, Sienna. That's absolutely incredible,' came my father's voice as he stood in the doorway behind me, holding on to the wooden frame with a white-knuckle grip. 'What's it for? Are you going to a party or something?' he questioned, a look of wonder on his face.

'No, Dad. I didn't even buy it. I don't really know what to do. A woman I don't know gave it to me today, she really wanted me to have it.' I sighed as I sat back on my bed, guilt and joy rushing over me all at once.

'You'll look incredible in it, Si.' He stood for a minute, looking really proud of me. I didn't know why. I hadn't done anything good.

Unsure of what to do with the dress, I slipped a soft hanger through the straps and balanced it on the door handle of my wardrobe. Dad and I stood and surveyed it like it was a painting in the Louvre.

Was I the kind of girl who could do a dress of that calibre any justice? I really didn't feel like I could, but now I felt a huge responsibility to do so. It was wasted on me, really. It was as if the crisp memory of one woman's youth was now hanging in my room, aching to be relived through some impossible love story. What made it worse was that I wasn't sure if I really believed in love any more . . .

The dress had been playing on my mind all day long. I'd managed to shake it off in the last hour or so, but now, as I looked down at my kitbag, I thought again about this beautiful unexpected gift, given to me by an ex-ballerina I didn't even know. A dancer who took people's breath away as she whirled across stages all over the world. I was in two minds about running it back to the shop.

I met a girl today who *could* wear a dress like that, and that made it all even worse. Her name is Chloe. Now *she* is beautiful.

She's on work experience at the office and will only be with us for a week. She has a mop of crazy blonde hair and a really pretty face. She also has a kind of naughty, bad girl look about her, while seeming angelic at the same time.

She's the kind of girl that makes even the most confident woman look in the mirror and notice new flaws, so it was no surprise I was suddenly feeling so inadequate.

Thank goodness she's only here for a week, I thought.

Being that beautiful, people must make assumptions about you before they know you. I didn't know how she'd wangled a placement from Ant, seeing as he's about as flexible as a wooden ruler, but I think her looks probably helped. She might be a really nice girl with incredible talent and drive, but I guess I'll never know. Girls like that get the things they want in life, I thought.

I looked in the mirror at my long brown hair, which tumbled wildly over my shoulders because it hadn't been cut for a while. I looked at my pale skin, which I had never had the energy or time to stain with fake tan. My nails were self-painted and the varnish had started to chip. My eyebrows needed plucking.

I wasn't fierce. I wasn't even that sexy. I wasn't like Chloe.

CHAPTER 6

'IF I COULD JUST TURN BACK TIME, I WOULD GIVE HER EVERYTHING.'

Nick

The word temp is short for temporary. I even looked it up in the dictionary:

1) adj. 1. Lasting for a limited time; existing or valid for a time (only); not permanent; transient; made to supply a passing need.

When I met Chloe Rogers three weeks ago, I thought she would be with us for a week. It would be temporary. Very much so, and even if Ant did decide to create an extra editorial assistant role, it would not necessarily be her filling it.

There's a lot of competition out there. I assumed there would be a whole interview process where a load of miserable-looking, dejected journalists would turn up, for once having shaved/worn a suit/ wiped off the habitual sulky expression, and go for the job.

But here she is, in all her sexy glory. With her

own desk, being sexy, day in day out. It's extremely distracting. The first email this morning went a bit like this:

To: Redland, Nick
From: Rogers, Chloe
Subject: Tour of Balham needed
Text:
Nick,
I have been with this company for three weeks now and I don't know Balham very well.
I have no idea which café does the best prawn sandwiches, which pub serves the nicest beer and doesn't smell of wee, or how to avoid the local tramps.
Do you think you can help?
Fancy giving me a tour? On a strictly colleague to colleague basis, of course . . .
Chloe
x

Now that is flirting. I may be a little bit slow off the mark when it comes to women, but even I can pick up on the hints in that message. She even did the double bluffing thing with the 'strictly colleague to colleague basis' remark.

Still. I love it, and she's pretty funny too. Funny women are even more attractive than the just attractive ones.

I flexed my fingers and clicked reply, the familiar

butterflies of an exciting new romantic liaison filling my tummy.

> To: Rogers, Chloe
> From: Redland, Nick
> Subject: RE: Tour of Balham needed
> Text:
> Chloe,
> Well, I'm sure I can fit a quick tour of Balham in at lunchtime. How are you set for today? The rest of the week is looking a little chaotic . . .
> I can't promise you much knowledge of the local homeless population, although if it's tramps you're hoping to avoid then just stay away from our car park.
> I can definitely help you on the pub and the prawn sandwich fronts. In fact, let's do both. I know a great pub, which doesn't smell of urine, and serves excellent bar snacks.
> Pick you up (from your desk) at one?
> Nick

But I wasn't going to put a kiss. She put a kiss, but I wouldn't be sucked in so easily. I was going to play hard to get. I had tried playing by my own rules and avoiding office romances, but this would just be a bit of fun – so I told myself.

Wow, she had replied already.

To: Redland, Nick
From: Rogers, Chloe
Subject: RE: re: Tour of Balham needed
Text:
Nick,
See you then. Don't be late.
Chloe
X

A capital kiss this time, nice work.

I leaned back in my chair and looked at my latest illustration. I was quite happy with it. It was a far cry from my frustrated scribblings at the start of the year. In fact, I was quite happy with life.

Just lately I had been feeling really inspired, and I wasn't entirely sure why. I thought a lot of it might be down to just accepting the way things were and having fun. I had spent a lot of time panicking about how my pre-thirty vision was not quite going to plan, and how much I loved Sienna. But somehow, I'd managed to cast all that aside and learned to live in the moment.

It was probably all about enjoying the journey. That's what a stranger told me on a bus some weeks ago, and although it seemed ironic at the time, I really understand it now. Do I really want to hit eighty and regret how much time I spent worrying about the future in my twenties and thirties, when actually everything worked out just fine anyway? I can't think of anything worse. What I'm learning, and slowly, is how to get the balance right. To work really hard, to be ambitious, to be a go-getter, but also to give myself a break when things aren't quite going to plan. If you're trying hard and working to improve every day, then what more can you do?

I still can't help but love Sienna, though. I adore her. Looking at her still makes me melt somewhere deep in my soul. Her presence lifts me up more than anyone else I know. Thinking about her fills me with happiness. What we have is unique. But I have accepted that she will never be mine, so I have to just love her from a distance and move on. It's working. It really is. I am finally achieving peace.

It was tough at first, weaning myself off something that I was so addicted to. It started off strangely. I had all these crazy dreams about her; I could be anywhere – a train station, a supermarket, a shopping centre – and I would see her. I could tell it was her so I would try to tap her on the shoulder to talk, but when she turned round her face was blurred out. Once we were in a library and I could see her through the gaps in a bookshelf. I would try to tell her I loved her, but she didn't know who I was.

So many nights I woke in a cold sweat. So often my finger hovered above her name on my mobile contacts list. I even wrote a letter once, but I screwed it up and threw it away. I felt like I was losing my mind.

Now I realise that I was sweating her out. And

she's gone now. Not literally, obviously – I still see her, and we still hang out, but less often. When I do see her, I go and have dinner with her and George at the flat. It's less intense that way, and her father loves it.

The yearning is more of a quiet nagging, rather than the raging fire it once was. I can see other women now. I can look at them and appreciate them. It's like the blindfold has been pulled from my eyes and I've been set free – and I love it. I can actually *want* someone else.

And right now, I want Chloe Rogers. Not in a 'Let's play chess, go for a stroll round a National Trust property, and have a latte and a toasted teacake' kind of way. I want Chloe in a naughty weekend in the country kind of way, one that doesn't involve stepping out of the hotel room unless a fire alarm goes off. Oh no . . .

It was eleven o'clock, my turn to make the coffees and also time for Tom's weekly prank. It had been a long while . . . A promotion was on the horizon so I was behaving myself more than usual, and working crazy hours to boot.

I rose from my desk and stalked out into the office, my bright blue trainers shuffling against the scratchy polyester carpet. The sound of hurried typing and quiet phone calls could be heard across the room; everyone was deep in concentration including Sienna, who was leaning so close to her computer screen I wondered if she wasn't due for an eye appointment.

Chloe was sitting opposite her; she grinned at me then looked down at her keyboard. I gave her my special smile, the one I reserve for girls I fancy. It's often met with a look of disgust and horror, but she tucked her hair behind her ear and her fingers lingered around the bottom of one of the strands. That's supposed to be a good sign, right? Girls play with their hair when they like you. Fact.

'Boo!' I dug my index fingers into Sienna's shoulders and she almost headbutted the screen in shock.

'For fuck's sake, Nick!' she shrieked, slapping me hard across the stomach and frowning.

I drew a chair up next to hers and started indiscriminately closing all the windows on her computer, one of which seemed to be a heated eBay bidding war for a pair of leather boots.

'Nick, stop it!' she whispered, pushing my hands out of the way and knocking over a small glass of water in the process. She started to laugh.

I tried to help her mop it up but accidentally wiped the majority of it onto her lap. She gasped in shock as the cold water soaked into her dress, giving me another evil look that soon melted into a grin.

'What do you want?' she asked, pushing her smiling face towards mine and flicking great blobs of water into my hair with her left hand. Sienna could never really be angry with me.

She looked lovely today, in a close-fitting flowery dress with tights and ankle boots. Her hair was even longer now. It struck me how much it had grown since I'd first met her.

'Nothing really, Si. Just wanted to annoy you a little and I think it worked. When can we do some city exploring? It's been ages . . .' I gave her my best sulky face. I had learned it from my grandmother's dog, Suki, who was quite literally a spoiled bitch. The queen of getting what she wanted, Suki had skills I wanted to learn.

But I wasn't kidding about it being ages. It really had been. I was all for the giving it some space theory, but this was possibly a bit much.

'Hmm, let me have a look.' She pulled out her burgundy diary and started frantically flicking through the pages. A few receipts fell out, then some guy's business card. I wondered who that was . . .

'Looks like I'm busy for . . . well . . . the rest of my life . . . Sorry, buddy!' She shrugged her shoulders, a cheeky smile painting her features. I dropped my head towards my lap and sighed.

'Just kidding, sweetheart. I'll text you a couple of weekends I have free and we'll get something sorted,' she added, her hand on my arm. 'I do miss you a bit,' she whispered in my ear, looking like she instantly regretted it.

I noticed Chloe surreptitiously peeping over the partition; as soon as her eyes met mine she looked back at her screen.

I shifted away from Sienna a little, aware that our closeness was a bit odd. It was hardly giving off the right vibes if I wanted to get involved with Chloe.

As I started to stand up I leaned towards Sienna, moving a great drape of glossy brown hair away from her perfect little ear. 'I miss you too, Si,' I said so quietly it was almost a breath, and walked away.

A deep and tangible emptiness was returning. Come on, Nick. Be strong, please. You've been doing so well, I told myself.

'Nick!' I heard a familiar yell as I walked towards the kitchen. The call of the Tomcat distracted me from my sudden downward spiral.

My gangly friend put his arm around my waist as we walked into the kitchen, wiggling his bottom like a woman. It was so embarrassing when he did that. It was a wind-up for the sake of a middle-aged lady called Delia, who is something of a homophobe and is convinced that Tom and I are embroiled in some kind of love affair. Delia, who was standing by the kettle, threw her spoon into the sink and stormed out in a huff. Obviously discrimination was still alive and well, then . . .

'Fancy going for a burger at lunch?' asked Tom, pulling out a series of mugs from the cupboard.

'I can't mate, really sorry,' I responded, picking out the green one for myself. I loved that mug. Sienna's dad gave it to me.

Tom threw teabags into the line of cups from a distance, missing most of them.

'Meeting?' he asked.

'No.'

'Wank?'

'No.'

'Dump?'

'No.'

'Doctor's appointment?'

'No.'

'Girl?' came his final guess, hitting the nail on the head.

'No.'

'Oh, come on. It must be a girl,' he probed, running a bony hand through his floppy hair, which was about to envelope his face if he wasn't careful.

'No, not at all. I might, actually, just want some peace and quiet away from babysitting you. By the way, speaking of girls, have you scared away that Fiona or whatever her name is yet?' I laughed, prodding him in the side with a fork.

'No, Nick. It's going really well, actually,' he retorted, flouncing out of the kitchen with one of his shoelaces undone. He was such a weird one.

I grabbed the bag of sugar from the bottom shelf and filled his mug three quarters of the way up with pure sugar granules, then disguised it with a teabag, milk and a tiny bit of water. He was going to love this.

I delivered the sickly sweet concoction to Tom's desk a few minutes later. 'There you go, pal,' I said, careful not to thump the mug down on his desk through the sheer weight of it.

'Thanks, Nick,' he replied, staring at the computer. I skulked back into my office.

Seconds later I heard a cry of 'Pah!' and a loud slamming noise, which resembled the sound of a mug full of sugar being bashed onto a wooden surface.

'Right, that's it!' he shouted, storming into my office. He was laughing already. 'This, Nick, is for you.' He thrust his arm forward and a sudden wave of water washed over me, covering my face, hair, T-shirt and worse, my lap. I didn't even have time to move away from it. The cheeky sod . . .

Tom stood there holding an empty plastic cup with a lot less water in it than there had been a few seconds earlier. He had a look of pure joy on his face, a smile of shock, pleasure and fear all at the same time. Like he couldn't quite believe he had done it. It was a little like the first time you stood up to the school bully, although the first time I did that I got socked in the mouth in the changing room before I had the chance to smile. You had to hand it to the boy. He'd put up with a lot of my wind-ups for quite a long time. It was a good job Ant was out at a meeting though, since as unprofessional as he can be, I doubt this would have thrilled him.

A small crowd had assembled outside my office door; there was a lot of nervous giggling. 'Nice comeback there, Tom.' I rose to my feet and shook his hand. He looked decidedly nervous. Then I picked up my bin and slammed it on his head, sheets of paper fluttering onto the floor and a banana skin hanging over his nose. Ah, that was better . . .

Sienna

'Right then, are you sure you're ready?'

Pete stood opposite me, his hands on both my shoulders. The hair on his chin was growing thick and fast. His bottom lip was cut from where he had tried to bite open the plastic casing on a padlock he'd been given for his backpack. He looked like he had been in a fight.

'Yes I am. Ready as ever. I have a two-hour lunch today, so no pressure.' I started to walk, pulling his arm until it was linked with mine.

We'd had a very hot summer this year, which I hoped had made things a bit easier. He told me he spent most of his nights on his favourite common in Balham, under the biggest tree, with his most cherished books by Dan Brown and Bill Bryson. While I would still rather have my double bed, it was a great comfort to know he was relatively happy, under the circumstances.

We walked quickly, side by side. I was wearing a pair of dark skinny jeans, with high-heeled sandals from Topshop and a black, skinny-fit shirt. He was in his usual get-up of faded T-shirt and brown combat trousers. There was a huge hole in the right knee.

'Aren't you embarrassed to walk with me like

this?' Pete asked me. I could feel his arm tense up as I gripped it close to my ribs.

'No. Of course not. Why on earth would I be?' I pretended not to know what he meant. I really wanted his time with me to be good. He hadn't had much of that lately. I didn't want him to feel like an outcast – I wanted him to belong.

'Well, because I'm homeless and I look awful. And it's just a bit unusual, really. People like you, well, they don't tend to hang out with people like me, that's all,' he said quietly.

'But here's the thing. People like me and people like you are the same,' I replied, smiling at him as the sun beamed down on our heads.

Pete chuckled and smiled back. 'I don't know about that, Si. Not any more. But thank you,' he finished, throwing a lump of gum into a bin as we walked past.

'So what are you going to show me, then?' I asked. I had no idea what on earth it could be. Some might call me a lunatic for going somewhere alone with a homeless man I barely knew. But I had a good feeling about him.

'I can't say yet. But I promise, it's just a ten-minute walk from here.' He looked so excited, traces of what looked like youth creeping into the grey skin on his face. For the first time ever, there was a rosy glow to his cheeks.

They had given him quite a few new outfits at the centre he goes to on a Thursday, but his T-shirt was still pretty tired and for some reason he was wearing these ripped trousers when I knew there were much nicer ones in his backpack. On the other hand, he was also wearing the almost new pair of Merrells I'd found at the charity shop, which looked much smarter than the boots he used to wear.

'OK, I'll take your word for it . . . I got something for you earlier,' I said, digging my hand into my bag. Now this was good food.

'What is it?'

I wasn't going to keep him waiting for this; it wouldn't hold up too well in the heat. I handed him the foil-wrapped lunch, which he opened with his usual hungry enthusiasm.

'Oh, Sienna, salmon and cream cheese bagels . . . I love these!' He pulled my arm tightly into his bony side and grinned. One half of a bagel was soon stuffed into his mouth; white flecks of cream cheese stuck to his stubble.

'Thank you,' he said as he always did, but he didn't need to.

'I knew you liked those, you said a few weeks ago.'

We had some quiet moments as he scoffed his lunch en route. People were staring a bit but I ignored them and thankfully Pete seemed oblivious. The sun was casting its midday glow on everything. It made people look more attractive, and it made the trees look tall and proud. Fruit stalls that looked dark and dismal in the winter were now bright and promising. Everything was colourful, my eyes could barely take it all in.

We navigated the streets of south-west London, a most unusual twosome. The total contrast of his lace-up hiking trainers and my high-heeled sandals. On some parts of our walk the pavements were thick with people going about their daily errands; at other times it was just a dog and its elderly owner making their daily trip to the park.

We walked past rows of tall houses. Beautiful ones that would require me to sell my organs on eBay to even dream of owning one. I could probably afford a cat flap on one of these houses and that would be about it. They stood proud against the blue sky, which had been turned into lattice-work by aeroplane vapour trails.

Some of the houses had four floors, with one down at basement level. They were the kind of houses I would start decorating in my head when I walked past. Cushions. Lots of cushions. I would have a big four-poster bed with the most stunning throw, and maybe a little white window seat with even more cushions on it. And if I was really lucky I would have one of those marble kitchens with the spring-loaded drawers that don't slam when you close them. Dad could have his own floor with a wet room, and everything would be perfect. We might even have a big American fridge with an ice dispenser. An ice dispenser is always a sign that you've made it in life . . .

'Nearly there, Si,' said Pete, who was walking even faster now. He snapped me out of my daydream, which was probably for the best. A dream was all it was.

'Easy, soldier,' I said, struggling to keep up in my heels. I tried to work out where this walk was heading.

Then, suddenly, Pete drew to a halt at the end of the road. Ridley Way meets North Avenue. His face crumpled into an odd expression and I could see that he wasn't very happy any more.

'What?' I questioned him, holding on to his hand because I quickly realised he was struggling with something.

'Now this, Sienna . . . This is going to be hard, but I had to bring you here. It's the first time I've been back, you see, the first time in a long time . . .' He looked down at the cracks in the pavement.

'I don't know what you're talking about, but whatever it is, Pete, I'm here. OK?'

He charged forward, pulling me along with him. His breath started to quicken and I could feel his rough hand trembling a little. What on earth was going on? He was walking faster and faster now, his head pointed forward like a charging bull's. The trees and the bins and the cats and the dogs were starting to speed past us like we were on a train. I had to trot alongside him to keep up.

Then we stopped outside a slightly smaller house and he turned to face it. I followed suit. He looked up and took a deep, deep breath. I turned round too and saw a quaint little house with a small, pretty garden full of colourful flowers and Mediterranean pots. The brickwork and the sunshine gave it a warm, inviting glow. There were white Danish-style decorations underneath the windows. It was lovely.

'What's this, Pete?'

He took another breath, his eyes filling with tears. He put both his hands together as though he was praying and held them to his mouth, clearing his throat. 'This was my home, Sienna. This was where Jenny and I lived before . . . You know, before.'

I took his hand again, winding my fingers between his and squeezing tight.

This was a huge revelation. For him to bring me here was deeply touching, and, I knew, very import- ant for him too.

A red Ford Fiesta was parked in the driveway and I wondered if the new people were home. I wondered what they were like.

'I'm sorry to drag you all the way here to see this, Si, but I wanted to show you my life before. How great it was, and how much love I had,' he said, a tear running down his cheek.

I wiped it away. 'Thank you so much for showing me,' I said, letting the sound of the cars and the birds take over for a bit.

He rubbed his face with a clenched-up fist and sniffed hard, not taking his eyes off the house, even for a split second.

'Tell me more about it, Pete. Tell me about each room and what it was like to be here,' I probed, hoping this would be cathartic for him.

'Well, you see that room up there?' He pointed towards the top right room at the front of the house. I could just about make out the back of a television through the thick net curtains. 'That was our room. On Sunday mornings I would pop to the shop and buy a carton of orange juice and two chocolate pastries and take her breakfast in bed. She liked tea with one sugar, and bits in her orange juice.' He sniffed loudly again.

'That's lovely, Pete. You're a catch!' I said, feeling a huge lump in my throat, dense and hard like a chunk of bread. I had an awful feeling I was going to start crying too, but I couldn't. I had to be really strong.

'Jenny looked gorgeous in the morning,' he continued. 'She had this really funny habit of not being able to sleep without socks on, but she said I had to take mine off because she thought that men looked like barn owls in socks and pants.'

I giggled, relating to her logic. 'Tell me more,' I asked in a whisper.

'Well, that room at the bottom – that was our living room. We had a pet rabbit, because she wanted children but I was a silly bastard who didn't feel like I was enough of an adult myself, so one day she came back with a rabbit. It stayed in the garden most of the time, but in the evenings she would sit with it on the sofa and stroke its ears.' More fat tears rolled down his face. 'And now I would give anything to have her back with me, even with that silly rabbit. Derek, she called it.' He smiled and laughed a little through his grief.

I quickly wiped one of my own tears from the corner of my eye. Come on, Sienna.

Be strong.

'I would have kids with her now, Si. God I would, dozens of them. If I could just turn back time, I would give her everything.' His sobs became louder. A postman gave me a look as he walked past; I gestured that we were OK and he carried on with his round.

'What about that room there?' I asked, pointing towards another window, which now had a black cat sitting in it, staring at the strange pair on the pavement outside.

'That was the kitchen. She would do her evening work on the table for hours. She was such a hard worker, was Jenny. And while she was doing that I made her the best dinners I could. I got all the nicest stuff for her, from the posh section at the super-market.' He paused. 'While I was cooking I would come round to her and give her a little taste on a wooden spoon, then kiss the top of her head.'

I could imagine it all now. Standing in front of this house I had never seen before, I could vividly see Pete and Jenny in every room, being so madly in love it brought a whole new meaning to the phrase. I scanned the other houses around it and wondered what the stories were, what the walls had seen. How many tears had fallen into the carpet. How much blood had been spilled. How much love had been made.

'And what about the back garden, do you think we can see?' I started to walk round the side of the driveway, pulling him with me.

'I don't know if we can do that, Sienna.' He pulled back, his weight on one leg.

'Come on, Pete. If someone comes out, I'll deal with it,' I said and he followed me reluctantly.

We stood on tiptoe and pushed our heads over a dark brown fence, which smelled like it had had a recent lick of creosote. A squirrel ran across the top of the wood like a tightrope walker on speed, using its big bushy tail for balance, its eyes bulging out of its head.

The grass ran wild, and weeds were thick and tangled like a mane of unkempt hair. A burst football was fading in the sun. It was then that Pete really started weeping.

I rubbed my hand on his back and held the weight of him up against me like a prop. I waited and waited. This was going to take as long as it needed to take.

'What happened here, Pete?'

He composed himself. 'This was where I asked her to be my wife.' I noticed that he had the laminated picture of Jenny gripped tightly in his palm. 'And she said yes, again and again, and for the first time in my life I felt like a king. And I'm an idiot because when she died I drank and drank, and smoked stupid things, and popped pills, and walked away from everyone who could help me, and now I've lost everything.'

We stood for a few minutes, just looking at the garden. When he was ready we walked away from the house. We walked down the road in complete silence, away from the postmen and the dogs and the bins and the trees.

'Thank you so much, Sienna. I'm sorry I cried like that.' He looked embarrassed.

'Pete, don't be silly. I'm so grateful that you let me see your old house. It's beautiful – and you know what?'

'What?'

'You'll have a house like that again one day. I just know it.'

Back in the centre of Balham town centre, I took him to my favourite café, where the coffee was strong and the flowers were real. It was bright, airy and lovely and it was just what he needed. 'One filter coffee, a latte and two of those cakes, please,' I ordered, leaning back in my chair and pointing towards some of the most luscious-looking cupcakes I'd ever seen in my life.

Pete looked a little self-conscious, zipping up the cleanest jumper he had so as to cover up his crumpled T-shirt. He ran his hands through his hair in an attempt to flatten it down and prodded at the bags under his eyes in a useless attempt to smooth them away.

'Pete, you look fine, relax.'

'What's happening with Nick?'

Oh dear. The dreaded question. 'Nothing. I told you I'd moved on a while ago,' I said, casually flicking through a copy of the *Sun* that had been left on the table in front of me. I would sooner go through the ten-year archives of 'Dear Deirdre' and other people's weird and wonderful problems than talk about Nick.

'Really? You've really moved on?' he asked as the waitress put our coffees in front of us. 'So if he turned around and said he'd met a girl and fallen in love with her, you'd be OK with that?' he asked, looking deep into my eyes.

The image of Chloe flashed before me, shortly followed by several mental stills of Nick looking at her at work. Sneaky, stolen glances. Long legs. Perfect boobs. *That* hair. She smells divine. She looks angelic. I bet she doesn't even have cellulite. It really is the biggest kick in the teeth I could have, if I'm being honest. I wish she would go out on a lunch run and get lost down an open manhole somewhere.

Fuck. It's official. I am bitter. 'Yes, I'd be OK with that.'

'Really?'

'Really.'

'Are you sure?'

'Yes, I'm sure.'

'One hundred per cent?'

'All right, all right – no, no, no. It's not OK!' I almost shouted out to everyone in the coffee shop. A pair of gossiping mothers stopped their conversation and stared at me. I ducked my head down and blushed, hoping I could climb between the pages of that newspaper I'd just been mentally slagging off and hide somewhere between the tits and the sport.

'I knew it!' Pete shouted victoriously. The staring continued. 'Right, so we're going to do something about this,' he declared, sitting up in his chair excitedly.

'We aren't, Pete, because I think he *has* met someone. She sodding works at my office now, she's everywhere with her sexy tights all over the photocopier and her lipstick all over the bloody whiteboard, for fuck's sake.' I finished my angry little rant and realised that my face was hot and my heart was racing and that sentence had made absolutely no sense.

'I'm sorry – what? Who are you talking about?'

'Chloe. There's this new girl at work called Chloe and she looks like she just fell out of the pages of *Vogue* and she smells good and basically rocks his world.' Wow, jealously was an unattractive trait. But I couldn't help it. It was literally spilling out of me. Jealousy was reaching into my soul, pulling out all the ugly bits and showcasing them in the Tate. I hadn't even known I felt like this until now. I chomped into my cupcake, the sweet icing sugaring my bitter mouth a little.

'This isn't great,' Pete admitted, a look of sympathy clouding his face.

'It's fine. I'm sorry. I didn't know it was this bad

until you asked. I'm going to be OK,' I chirped. I hoped that if I said the words enough they would become real. I. Am. Going. To. Be. OK. All right. Just fine. Super duper.

'I still think you two are going to be together,' he said positively, biting down on the free shortbread.

Although I adored Pete, and he was becoming something of a confidant, I thought he was living in a little bit of a dream world. Playing out his lost love through me and Nick.

The laugh-out-loud, stand-up comedy routine that was me and Nick . . .

Nick

'Have you ever been in love?' asked Chloe, nibbling on her straw and raising a cheeky eyebrow. God, she was sexy. This woman was outrageously gorgeous. I reckon she could get a first-class upgrade on a plane ticket with a simple smile.

This was a difficult one, I thought, pulling on a long thin strand of lettuce that was poking humiliatingly from the corner of my mouth. Why do sandwiches with salad in them always do that? And why do they always do that in front of someone you fancy? 'Er, yes, I guess so.' I paused, looking deep into her mesmerising brown eyes.

'You guess so? Wouldn't you just know?' She flicked some strands of hair away from her mouth and continued to look at my panicked face.

Oh bollocks, I was being cross-examined. 'Well, you know. I've been in a couple of serious relationships, so yes, I guess so.' Nice recovery, Nick. Vague and non-committal.

What I actually wanted to shout out to the whole world was that yes, I had experienced love. Yet the deepest love I had ever felt for anyone was for someone I had never even kissed. I loved her but she didn't love me. But I was over that now, wasn't I?

Strangely enough, the love in question was walking past the pub window with some scruffy-looking guy. I recognised him, but I couldn't work out where from. She had a broad smile across her face, and her hair was shining in the brilliant sunlight. I nearly choked on my sandwich.

'What are you looking at?' asked Chloe, turning her head the second Sienna disappeared from view.

'Oh, nothing. So, er, how about you?' I thumped the tennis ball back her way.

'Yes, definitely, once. I met a guy at uni actually,' she responded, looking down at two rejected prawns that had fallen out of her sandwich onto the plate and were, for some reason, no longer fit for consumption. I could almost hear them calling out to me from beneath their thick layer of mayo. I wanted to dig my fork in and steal them, but you aren't supposed to do things like that with people you don't know so well. I always do that with Sienna, though. I once stole a whole chicken wing from her and she didn't mind.

231

'And do you still, you know . . . love him?' I asked. Please say she doesn't. Please. It would be just my sodding luck for her to still love him, and I could do without any more messy situations and complications right now.

'Oh no. That was ages ago. But it was definitely love. I just know it.'

This was very interesting. *She just knew it.*

'What do you mean, you just knew it?' I enquired, pretending that I didn't particularly need the answer when actually I was desperate to know.

'Well . . . I'll be honest with you here . . . I'd describe it as a wild, almost uncontrollable need to be a part of that person's life. A passion, really. Yes – in fact, the best way of describing it is if you lost everything – your job, your home, your car – but that person was still by your side, none of it would really matter.' She finished her description and her eyes continued to bore into mine.

Shit, what if she was scanning me for bullshit like a human lie detector? I started to sweat. She just couldn't know how I used to feel for Sienna. She just couldn't. It was messy and ugly and painful.

'Do you want another drink?' She gestured towards the bar with a slim arm.

'Yeah, sure, that would be great.'

I watched her get up and walk towards the crowd of midday drinkers in the dingy but painfully cool pub I had chosen. I noticed a seam up the back of her tights, which went all the way to her . . .

'Oi, mate.' A dark, gravelly voice interrupted my mental ascent to heaven; it came from a large, hairy animal who was leaning over the wooden table towards me. Here we go.

'Yes, pal, what's up?' I asked, puffing my chest out like a cockerel.

'Is that your bird?' he said, his tanned face setting off a pair of piercing blue eyes. He was pointing towards Chloe, who was just far enough away to be oblivious.

A thick gold chain hung from his tree trunk of a neck. He was your typical London wide boy, in a sharp suit, smelling of Joop. Men like this irritated me deeply. I would put money on the fact that he had a 'Mum' tattoo somewhere underneath the fake Ted Baker.

'My bird? No, no. She's not my girlfriend,' I told him.

'Excellent,' he responded, rubbing his hands together and swaggering towards the bar like it was a hog roast. Well, at least he'd had the decency to ask.

This could be entertaining. Obviously I didn't want her to have to fend off this horrible, lecherous creature, but at the same time, she was nowhere near being my girlfriend. Not even a naughty, drunk-dialling on a Friday night kind of girlfriend. I watched as he raised an eyebrow towards his equally horrible mates, who egged him on with a couple of hip thrusts and some jeers.

Our elegant suitor tapped her on the shoulder.

I raised the last drops of my pint to my mouth and watched the car crash. I saw her point over to me in a desperate bid to pretend she was already taken. It didn't work, unfortunately, and our urban Mr Darcy continued in his attempts to work his magic. The whole display was dire. I felt really sorry for her.

It was then that she took a chance. One she shouldn't really have taken, considering I was a senior member of staff at the company she worked for. The company she had only been working at for three weeks. In fact, it was verging on ridiculous. She turned around with the drinks and strutted towards me across the floor of the bar, her hips moving in a way that hypnotised most of the punters. Even the women. Romeo was starting to follow her again, so she did something crazy. She kissed me.

I don't know who was more shocked – him or me. But she did it and hell, it was good. She cupped her hand around the back of my neck and pulled my face into hers. For a second the world stopped. In fact, I think my heart stopped. Her beautiful, soft lips melted into mine and she moved her hand from the back of my head and traced her fingers across my stubbly chin.

It must have been quite a sight as I'm pretty sure I flung both arms out in panic, all outstretched fingers and tense legs. I must have looked like a moth in a spider's web.

Then I realised this was just an act to get rid of

him, so I slowly let my hands settle on her waist. Surely she would stop this crazy behaviour any second.

Oh, no, wait . . . She was still kissing me. Still. Kissing. Me. And I was kissing her.

Shit. This was totally inappropriate. We were only supposed to be going out for a prawn butty, but it was so sexy . . . My stomach felt like it was plunging into the depths of the pub floor.

And just like that, she pulled away and turned back to him. 'Sod off,' she said flatly.

He looked embarrassed, crestfallen and particularly angry with me. I could just see the headlines now: MAN'S HEAD FOUND PINNED TO PUB DARTBOARD.

'Chloe!' I whispered into her ear. 'You're going to get me beaten up, for God's sake!' I was genuinely quite angry about what she'd just done, but also very horny. It was a confusing mixture. And horny was definitely winning in this arm wrestle . . .

'What? I just needed him to think I had a boyfriend,' she said casually, taking a sip of her fresh Diet Coke like it was no big deal.

Jesus H. Christ. What a nutter. I quite liked it, though. It might be best not to tell anyone what had just happened, I thought, dropping a carefully placed napkin onto my lap.

CHAPTER 7

I CAN BE ANONYMOUS.
I CAN BE ANYONE.

Sienna

Tuesday night. Treadmill. 4.5 km. 295 cals. 22 minutes and 40 seconds. Two buckets of sweat.

I felt like crap.

The gym is always a bit of a mixed bag. I drag my sorry backside over there after work through rain, hail, sleet – you name it, and I'm in a bad mood the whole way. Yet something keeps me going. Fear, I think it is.

I left school about five years ago now, and since then a large proportion of my friends, apart from Elouise, have put on weight. And I'm not talking a little bit, either. I'm talking additional chins, new stomachs and bouncier bottoms. It scares the shit out of me. So like a hamster in a trance, I move around on these machines in a stuffy ex-warehouse and wish the time would hurry up so that I can be watching *The Apprentice* and painting my nails. Surely no one actually *likes* going to the gym, do they? Do they?

I'd been here for an hour and I resembled a beetroot left in a plastic container on a sunny day. On the treadmill to my left was a tall, slim young girl with extremely long blonde hair. Not a strand stuck to her face. Not a wedgie in sight. Not even a teeny, tiny bit of VPL. All the while, next to her, I plodded away on the black band, drops of sweat running into my eyes and rendering me temporarily blind.

I am mildly entertained by the men in here. It's all tattoos, bulging guns and dreadlocks. Some of these guys must come here every day, I reckon. And they do this really strange thing where they sit in front of the mirror and stare at themselves pumping iron. Looking *at themselves*. The last thing I want to see in this place is me.

I started to think about random things as I went into a running trance, my feet striking the belt, hard. I have a whole pile of ironing to do. We've run out of fabric conditioner. Dad needs to go to the hospital on Friday and I haven't booked the taxis yet. I love my dad. Wow, Elouise's birthday is coming up really soon. Sugar, what do I get her? I keep forgetting to burn that album for Nick. Oh, and I must ask Chloe out for a drink one night after work, it would be nice to get to know her. But where could we go? And so it went on . . .

The pleasure of the gym is I am such a mess that no one bothers me. It's joyous. I can be anonymous. I can be anyone. I don't have to bump into people and talk to them about the weather, the price of stamps or the antics of inane celebrities. I have deliberately avoided talking to people so I can just be known as that excessively damp and angry-looking girl that everyone stays away from. It suits me perfectly.

'Er, excuse me?' came a voice barely audible above the thumping music coming through my earphones.

I ignored it. He was probably talking to Britney Spears next to me.

'Sorry, ahem. Excuse me,' came the voice again, but louder this time. A man's chiselled face was right in front of mine. A man I see here regularly because he owns this overpriced and slightly pretentious boutique gym.

Dear God, he's talking to me. I yanked one of the plugs from my ear irritably and looked at him.

'Yeah, sorry to disturb you. I just noticed something about your gait,' he said, a cheeky grin spreading across his face.

I turned around in confusion, almost slipping off the treadmill in the process. There wasn't a gate anywhere. 'My what?' I said, frantically starting to slow down the machine so I could actually breathe.

'Your gait. G. A. I. T. It's the way you run. I think you overpronate. I hope you don't mind . . .' He looked embarrassed this time.

'I really have no idea what you're talking about,' I puffed as the black strip ground to a halt. I felt dizzy and annoyed.

He obviously didn't pick up on my hostility as he jumped up and started swinging off the side of the treadmill confidently. He was built like Popeye.

'I run this gym. My name's Ben. Basically yeah, it's all about the way your feet strike the ground. It's perfectly normal,' he tried to reassure me but I was starting to take offence. He was doing that thing where you bring the tone of your voice up at the end of a sentence to imply it's a question when it isn't.

This was annoying. 'And what's wrong with the way my feet strike the ground?' I asked defensively, dabbing my face with a pink fluffy towel. I was horribly aware of how much I sweated compared to, well, anyone. Hell, I could outsweat the men.

'It's not wrong, exactly. It's to do with the alignment of your hips and all sorts of things, but it can cause injuries unless you get trainers to accommodate it.'

He was quite handsome, actually, but it was starting to sound like he was trying to sell me trainers, so he could go take a hike.

'Look. Just come over here, would you?' he beckoned. I followed, still pissed off. He put his arm on the bottom of my back as we walked and I jumped out of my skin, almost tripping over a girl doing stretches on the floor.

'Hey! Can't you see I'm a bit hot and bothered here?' I cried self-consciously.

'That's a good thing,' he whispered into my ear.

'It means you're actually doing some work, which is more than can be said for some people.'

Wow. That was a surprise. I thought like most people in here, he would find me a freak of nature and avoid me at all costs.

He led me to a desk and reached over to pull out a file. I was starting to feel really off now, but I took a couple of deep breaths and soldiered on. The muscles in his arms flexed as he lifted the thick pile of documents onto the surface. OK, he was quite nice. But still. He was criticising my legs. What kind of man starts talking to a woman by criticising her legs?

He flicked through the pages frantically, a long fringe falling over his face and covering the top of his perfectly straight Roman nose. 'Ah, here it is,' he announced, pulling out a sheet of paper covered in diagrams. 'Now, this is what your legs are doing. Around 30 per cent of runners have this problem, but it can be easily corrected with the right footwear. With the wrong footwear, you can get problems here, here and, er, here,' he added, pointing out the shins, knees and hips on the drawings.

OK. So maybe he wasn't talking utter trash. There were diagrams and everything, and they looked vaguely scientific because they had the names of the muscles on them.

He looked up at me, a pair of sea-green eyes waiting for a reaction. I felt sick from the exercise; my heart started to thump.

'Are you OK?' he asked, rushing to his feet and

standing in front of me. He had very expensive-looking trainers on and I feared they would soon be covered in my lunch.

'Yes, yes, I'm fine,' I protested. The room was starting to spin.

'Look, I have a banana in my bag if you want that? You look like your blood sugar might be a bit low . . .'

But he didn't get the chance to finish because I ran. And as I ran my legs started to shake, things got whiter and whiter until I found myself lunging in front of the toilet and holding on to it for dear life.

I was sick. Very sick. There was nothing I could do to hide it, either. Some people make it sound like an inconvenient cough whereas I sound like I'm roaring in anger. Embarrassing.

The sharp twinges of acid from my stomach were stinging my nose. Gross. I hadn't thrown up for ages and I'd forgotten how horrible it was. After a couple of minutes there was a gentle knock on the door. My legs were shaking like a frightened animal at the vet and my stomach muscles ached.

'Hi. My name's Naomi,' came a concerned female voice. 'I'm one of the personal trainers here and my colleague Ben asked me to check if you were OK. You haven't been sick, have you?' she asked timidly.

Of course I've been bloody sick. The whole of London probably heard me. Most of the women in the changing room had probably run out screaming in their bras and knickers and promptly cancelled their direct debits. I cleared my throat and whispered through tears, still able to deny the obvious, 'No, no. I'm OK, thanks. Sorry. I'll be fine.'

'All right. Well, if you need anything I'll be near the reception desk, OK?'

I grunted in response. Eventually, when I had composed myself, I found the strength to stand up and peeked my head around the door. Two ladies quickly turned around and fiddled with their lockers.

After I'd showered away my humiliation and sat on the bench for a while, I realised the only way out of this building was to go past Ben. There was no secret exit for people who threw up and were too humiliated to face the world again. If I ever end up owning a gym I will make sure there is at least one of those emergency exits in the floor plan. They should become a mandatory government requirement.

I sheepishly darted out of the door and kept my head down all the way past the weights guys, past Britney and the water machine, and out into the humid summer air. It looked like it had been raining, heavily.

Escape. Maybe I would just never go back. That sounded like a great idea. What a fantastic excuse.

'Hello!' Suddenly I heard the distant shouting of a familiar male voice. Oh bugger.

'Hey, are you OK?' It was Ben. Why on earth

was he bothered enough to follow me out here? It could be some kind of fever-induced vision, but he looked gorgeous.

'Look, I feel really bad about what happened back there. I shouldn't have just stopped you like that,' he said, running his hands awkwardly down his navy tracksuit bottoms. 'What's your name?'

'Sienna,' I answered, wishing I could be someone else. Someone who hadn't just made an arse out of themselves. 'Don't worry about it. I'm so embarrassed,' I added, waving one of my hands in the air and blushing.

'Look, will you please take this?' he asked. As if from nowhere he pulled a banana from behind his back and flashed me a very convincing guilty look. He didn't seem at all mortified by this evening's events, just really understanding.

'Oh no, Ben. I can't take that. And honestly, I can't face eating anything right now. It's very kind, though.' I yanked my black chunky-knit cardigan around my stomach as if to protect it from any incoming food advances. I glanced down at my baggy jeans and trainers, realising what a mess I looked.

'Well, if you won't take that, then you must take this.' He pushed a crumpled piece of paper into my hand, smiled, then ran back to his gym.

Nice bum, I thought. When he was out of sight I carefully opened up the note. The short but sweet message was penned in blobby blue ink, like the biro had been chewed on and was on the verge of exploding all over some poor person's mouth. It was a simple sentiment, paired with an eleven-digit phone number: 'CALL ME'.

I've always been a bit funny about texting a man first and this occasion was no different. In fact, it was worse. It was a situation so difficult that it required dinner and a chat with Elouise. Plus I needed her to take away the pain of the evening's unfortunate vomiting incident.

'Text him, Si,' came her playful response from the open-plan kitchen.

I sank back into the leather of her sofa and sighed. A plastic sword jabbed my ribs so I threw it into the toy box. 'I . . . I . . . I can't, really, El,' I muttered, scrunching up the piece of paper in my fist and shoving it into my bag.

'And why on earth can't you? He owns a gym, for goodness' sake – how cool is that?' she scolded, approaching me with a wooden spoon piled high with the most beautiful-looking paella, a fleshy prawn balanced on top of the orange rice. Now El really knows how to make this dish, but I had thrown up just a few hours earlier so I was feeling more than a little delicate.

'No, El, please,' I protested, but it was too late – the spoon was wedged into my mouth, filling it with a delicious explosion of flavours. She must have managed to find an opening during the 'e' and 'a' vowels of 'please'. Elouise's face lit up and she danced back towards the pan. Suddenly my hunger returned. 'Wow! That's even better than the last one you made,' I said, putting both thumbs up.

'So anyway, what's the problem with you texting this bloke?' she persisted.

I looked over to her and as she sashayed around the room in a pair of skinny jeans and a vest top, I wished I had just a little bit of her confidence. Elouise is a heartbreaker, but not in an evil-on-purpose, bitchy kind of way. It's just part and parcel of being Elouise Dalton. If she needs a marquee for a party, ten will arrive the next day complete with musclebound men to put them up. If she needs a lamp fixing, there will be electricians queuing out of the door. If there's a leak, all of a sudden every bloke including the town vicar will fancy himself a fully qualified plumber . . . You get the gist. She is adored, a sweetheart – and great to talk to about men.

'Well, I don't like chasing men, really, El. Plus, if it goes wrong I'll have to go to a different gym.' I slipped my boots off and put my feet up on her sofa.

'You need to think a little more romantically, my lovely. Just go for it. You're gorgeous, he'll be bowled over,' she said, dishing up the dinner.

My mouth started watering. 'So what do I put?' I asked, gratefully accepting my bowl full of heaven and starting to chow down.

'Just say hi, and ask him on a date.'

'A what?' I shrieked, a tiny shrimp falling from

my spoon and into my lap. I quickly picked it up and dropped it back into my bowl before she noticed.

'Yes, Sienna – a date. Are you sure you're over Nick?' She looked at me doubtfully.

'Of course, El. Yes I am. In fact, I'm going to text Ben right now.' I put down my fork and fished in my bag for my BlackBerry and the piece of paper with Ben's number. I drafted the message. 'How does this sound? "Hi there, this is Sienna, from the gym. Do you fancy a drink sometime? S x"' I considered putting a joke in there about my loving embrace with the toilet pan, but felt it was maybe best to let that one go.

'Yeah, that'll be just fine, Si,' replied Elouise, that sparkle in her eye making me even more excited.

'OK – I'm sending it now,' I said, suddenly wussing out at the last minute and saving the message to drafts. God, I was pathetic. 'Done!' I looked at Elouise and did my best 'I just sent that text' smile.

'Fab. See – it wasn't that hard, was it?'

After dinner, I dashed up to the bathroom and brushed my teeth with the toothbrush I have at El's for those drunken, sleepy nights when I can't face the walk home. I looked a lot better now, I thought, as I pushed my face towards the mirror above the sink. The colour was returning to my skin. God knows what had happened at the gym earlier.

El and I talked for a few minutes before I walked out into the sticky summer evening to get back to Dad. As I made my way towards the flat I felt a vibration in my bag and pulled my phone out, half expecting it to be my father. Instead, it was from a number I didn't recognise . . .

'Hi, Sienna. Lovely to hear from you. Of course I want to go for a drink. How does Thursday night sound? Ben xx'

What a sneaky girl. And how could she tell I was lying? Some people would be very angry about this, but I was glad she'd done it, really.

A smile spread across my face. It was so big, I didn't quite know what to do with myself. What on earth was I going to wear?

16 MONTHS LATER . . .

Nick

'Let's take it slow, Nick.'

That's what she'd said less than a year ago as she slurped on a milkshake by the sea. It was a conversation right at the beginning of our relationship. Sometime after the kiss ambush in the pub, and sometime before I felt it appropriate to take her to weddings and let her use my toothbrush. Round about the period when we were doing posh dinners and cocktails on a Friday night, rather than bickering over plughole hair.

But you see, that phrase is a bad sign – it means the opposite. People are generally quite bad at taking things slow, unless of course it involves paying invoices or walking right in the middle of Oxford Street when you're trying to dash from shop to shop. And they are *particularly* bad at taking relationships slowly.

In fact, I would go so far as to say that as soon as you hear the phrase 'Let's take it slow,' then you should know that things are about to get a lot speedier.

And that's exactly what has happened. She is all over my house. There are pots of Chanel nail varnish on the living-room table, a ladies' razor in the bathroom, unexplained cushions on the sofa and carefully placed lingerie in my bedroom. And it's all a strategic Chloe move to make me feel like I can't live without her.

To be honest, she's doing a pretty good job. She does not live with me. She does not have a key cut. She certainly isn't insured on my car. But she is creeping into my world. It's like a slow infiltration of pink things that smell nice and almost every day I find something new. It always makes my heart race a little bit, but I do think I need to grow up a little. I turn thirty this year, for God's sake. I really need to be able to cope with this, and if I can't cope with a creature as beautiful as Chloe sharing my living quarters, then I'm screwed, really.

She likes to come and stay most nights, which I found quite difficult at first, but I love it now. I think having been single for so long, I became a little bit selfish. You want to be able to do what you want, when you want, and just how you want it.

I love having the warmth of her next to me all night long, and waking up to her nuzzling against my chest. She's gorgeous and I only hope we can go the distance. Plus I fancy the pants off her.

But there's been one major problem in all of this. Sienna. Lately, she has been the subject of quite a few rows. She doesn't have a clue this has been going on. The most spectacular firework finale of them all happened this evening, and it went a little like this:

'Sienna and I were thinking of going to this street art exhibition next Saturday, Chloe, I can't wait. Are you still away with the girls that weekend?' I said innocently as we were driving through Balham.

She had some spa break planned with her mates, most of whom I can't stand. I quietly hoped some of them would get stuck in a steam room and come out much smaller and quieter than they had been before. Though not Chloe, of course . . .

The clouds instantly moved over my girlfriend's face, giving her this angry expression that she adopts whenever Sienna's name is mentioned. And there really is no need for it. I am well and truly over Sienna – and besides, nothing ever actually happened between us.

'Yes I am, Nick,' she said abruptly, looking out of the window and craning her neck so far round it was pretty obvious she was trying to hide something. She was fiddling with a ring on her finger, too; that was never a good sign. She tended to do that when she was really pissed off.

There was cold silence as we drove further away from Balham and out into west London.

'Chloe, come on. You know we love that kind of thing. What's the problem?' I responded, noting how her feet were pushed hard against the footwell in what looked like unexpressed frustration.

Silence. More silence.

I pulled over and stopped the car. This had to be sorted out once and for all. I was getting a little tired of her silent protests every time I mentioned my best friend's name.

'Chloe, I think we need to talk about this,' I began, taking a deep breath and fiddling with a pear-shaped air freshener dangling from the rear-view mirror.

'I don't want to talk about it,' she replied. It sounded like she was gritting her teeth.

'Please, Chloe, just look at me. What's the problem?' I leaned over and touched her arm; she pulled it away sharply and tucked it inside the Zara cardigan that I'd bought her for her birthday. I didn't buy it so she could hide bits of her in it when she was in a mood with me, though.

'Well, we aren't going anywhere until we talk about this,' I declared, putting my hands on the steering wheel and pushing my seat back so I was a bit more comfortable. We could be here a while, I thought.

Drizzle started to hit the windows; I watched as the droplets raced each other to the bottom of the glass. It was captivating. Seconds went by, then minutes . . .

Bang. The passenger door had been slammed hard; the pear wobbled in fear. I turned to see that the seat Chloe had been occupying was empty. There was a small dent in the leather and you could still feel the heat from her body on the surface. She had got out of the car and stormed

251

off into the street, and I could only spot a flash of her blonde hair in the distance. Shit.

I scrambled to my feet and started to run, slamming the door behind me, locking it remotely and chasing her down the street. The rain was really falling now, I could feel the dampness of it through my jeans. My trainers slapped hard against the shiny concrete and my shirt stuck to my stomach. Chloe was walking very fast despite the heels she was wearing. She didn't even look back. Not once.

'Chloe!' I yelled, through the passing pedestrians, dodging children and ducking under spiky umbrellas. I even pushed into one woman by accident, shouting my apologies as I ran backwards and then into a newsstand and its disgruntled owner. Jesus, this was annoying.

When I finally caught up with her she was in a bit of a state, black mascara running down her cheeks. I grabbed her hand and hoped that she would just come to a halt so I didn't have to keep running in this horrible weather.

'Stop, Chloe, please. For God's sake, what is wrong with you?' My tone was angrier than I'd intended but I was getting very frustrated by all this.

'Me? Me, Nick? Are you serious?' She turned away again, storming down the steps to the underground.

Here we go again . . . I ran fast down the stairs, my legs moving so quickly the upper part of my body wasn't quite keeping up and I feared I would slip over and land in a heap at the bottom. I managed to catch up with her. In the small space of the ticket hall, everyone could hear our argument. Bloody marvellous.

'What, Chloe? For Pete's sake, I don't understand what's going on here!' I yelled. A skinny woman with her hair in a tight ponytail tutted and gave me daggers. This probably looked much worse than it sounded.

'*You* want to know what's going on?' she raged, moving towards me now like an angry tiger, her finger pointed straight at me. Well, at least she had changed direction. I suddenly realised that she meant business and backed myself up against the wall.

We were attracting quite a lot of attention by now, so I tried to calm her down with frantic arm gestures. Her hair was matted with water and her plaits were sticking to her neck and cheeks, but she was still so beautiful. I wanted to pull her close to me and kiss her until she stopped being so angry, but I didn't think that would work this time.

'I'll tell you what's going on.' She gritted her teeth again and pushed both of her hands against my chest. I could feel the cold of the tiles against my sopping wet back.

People were really staring now. A group of teenage boys found the sight of a soggy me cowering under my girlfriend's grip very amusing. Tears were welling in her eyes and it dawned on me that this was really quite serious.

'You, Nick, are in love with someone else.' There was a loud sigh from the audience. It was like *Jerry Springer: The Underground*. 'I'm sick of hearing about all the things you like to do together. I'm sick of being told where she is at any given time. I'm sick of hearing about her favourite colour, or her favourite flavour of ice cream. I don't care about her dad and how ill he is, and I certainly don't want to know about your fucking art exhibition. Got that?'

OK, this was quite nasty. An elderly woman covered her granddaughter's ears.

Chloe was definitely slightly less attractive than usual right now.

A wave of anger swept over me but I had to stay calm. She was totally wrong. I was not in love with Sienna. Yes, all right, I had been, but not now. I grabbed hold of her hands and pulled her close to me despite the fury I was feeling. I just wanted to end this circus display, tell everyone to disappear and deal with this in private like we should have been doing in the first place.

At first she resisted as fat tears slid from her eyes, which were now so dark brown they scared me. The colour that I'd once adored now seemed so foreboding.

I could feel her body trembling as she gave in and let me hold her against my chest. She was genuinely very angry and I'd had no idea she felt like this.

'Chloe, for God's sake,' I whispered into her

ear, pulling a great handful of soaking curls away from her face and looking at the assembled crowd with a 'sod off' expression on my face. Some of them took the hint and scuttled back to their lives, which must have been immensely boring in comparison.

'I don't love Sienna like that, OK? But you have to understand how important she is as a friend.' When I said the words I felt her shake against my chest as she started to cry even harder. But I had to be honest with her. 'Chloe, please. There's a real difference. If Sienna and I were interested in each other like that do you not think something would have happened by now? We've been friends for a very long time – you have to understand that, sweetheart. And if you can't, then I'm not sure if we can . . . You know . . .' I trailed off, not sure how I could finish a sentence like this.

But there it was. The big ultimatum. Basically, what it boiled down to was that my friendship with Sienna was more important than my relationship with Chloe. I should have phrased it differently. Now the words were out there I couldn't take them back. I could tell I shouldn't have said it.

In fact I definitely shouldn't have, because the next thing she did hurt. It involved her hand and my face. A collision of the two that left a red mark on my cheek with five clearly visible fingers. I swear I heard clapping . . . Ouch.

And just like that, she was gone.

She really wasn't that kind of woman – you know, someone who thumps men in public. She was a gorgeous, flirty, delicate little flower, who was occasionally feisty, but generally the sweetest thing you could ever be lucky enough to know.

That was the awakening, really; it dawned on me that this wasn't really very fair on anyone. On her. On me. On Sienna. But I wasn't really willing to change anything, either. I was fiercely protective of my friendship with Sienna. I had fought for it, against my true feelings, for years. I had battled so hard to suppress my feelings, and succeeded. I could never let her go.

I considered all this as the two remaining members of the audience stared at me in utter disgust, then turned away as I pressed my fingers to my throbbing face. They were teenage girls in hip-hop style streetwear with ponytails piled on the tops of their heads. They gave me the look of people who know everything when clearly they knew nothing really. Not compared to an adult who had dealt with several real-life relationships. That alone was deeply irritating.

I walked back to my car like a naughty dog, my wet tail between my legs and my ears thoroughly clipped. She had gone. I tried calling her several times, but her phone was off. I resented having to chase her around London when I had done nothing wrong. I hated the whole thing. She had no idea about the torment I had been through with Sienna.

Too angry to start driving, I locked my doors and lit an emergency cigarette from a packet rattling around with the service booklet in the glove compartment. The smoke seeped out through the tiny crack of the open passenger window.

My heart was thumping hard in my chest. There was only one person who could make me feel better right now and that was Sienna. I picked up my phone and held down the 2 button – she was on speed dial. The phone rang twice but I panicked and hung up. Calling her now would be totally inappropriate and I certainly couldn't tell her about what had happened. I had kept all this arguing away from her. It would be too late to explain it all now.

I took more deep drags on my cigarette and exhaled hard, the nicotine rushing through my body, giving me that familiar buzz I craved so much in situations like these. That was when I remembered Ross telling me that night in Brixton how girls and guys couldn't just be friends. But we'd managed it, hadn't we? It's not as if Sienna had feelings for me. Surely not? I knew she didn't like me like that. And I had certainly pushed my feelings aside. No, that was nonsense.

Eventually, when my heart rate had slowed down a little, I drove home, taking deep gulps of air all the way. When I pulled up to my drive I saw the figure of a beautiful blonde girl on my doorstep. My beautiful blonde girl. Thank God.

I was so relieved she was there – now I would

have a chance to talk to her properly. I got out of the car and walked towards her slowly, a little bit nervous after she'd hit me so hard. My skin was still stinging.

'Nick . . . Oh my gosh, I'm so sorry,' she said, walking up to me and putting her hand up to my face. I winced as she touched my right cheek.

'Shit, Nick. I can't believe I did that.' She began to tremble again, clearly startled by the strength of her reaction.

The next few hours we spent soul-searching over tea and chocolate biscuits in my kitchen. I gave her a towel and she mopped herself dry; I put the heating on and hoped we could sort this all out.

'Just so I can understand, Nick. Can you tell me, from the beginning, how you met and how you've become so close? I've just never known a guy and a girl to be . . . well, such good friends,' said Chloe, looking down at her feet resting on the wooden boards. Her socks were draped over the radiator. She had peeled off her soggy jeans and sat in a pair of my shorts. She looked much better in them than I did.

'Please?' she pleaded, raising her eyes in my direction again. She crossed her legs to get more comfortable.

My mind started to wind back to the day Sienna and I had first met. I probably shouldn't tell Chloe that I'd fallen in love with Sienna from the first moment I saw her, over a copy of *Metro*, just when I'd thought my life was crumbling around me.

That it had felt a little like she'd been sent to rescue me. That I still believe to this day that she was . . .

No. I definitely shouldn't mention that. 'Well, OK. If you're sure you're interested,' I said, pouring out two glasses of white wine to replace the tea. It was time to move on to the harder stuff now.

'Well, I guess it all started about two and a half years ago. I'd been to Ibiza and had a week off sick afterwards. She'd started work a couple of weeks before, so we met for the first time at work when I got back from my time off.' I paused. I cast my mind back to the moment those lift doors had opened, and how everything had seemed to go in slow motion. How I couldn't believe my luck when I saw her sitting there.

'Yeah, and then how did you become friends?' she asked quickly, an expression of fascination on her delicate features.

'A couple of weeks later Ant sent us both to a gaming fair in Florida – she went as a writer because Tom was off sick. Yes, that was it – I remember now.' I leaned back in my chair as all the memories came flooding back. Flashes of her hair as we ran around the strip of bars; the lights, the drinks, the food . . . The piggyback attempt that saw us both graze our knees and laugh till we cried.

'And what happened?'

'Nothing, Chloe. But we did get on very well. She's a good friend, probably my best friend now.

And I have to be honest with you here, that's just the way it is.'

She looked really disappointed, but I had to be brave about this. If she couldn't cope with this friendship, she wasn't the one for me.

Even though I was lying a little bit . . .

But it was my business. It was my business who I had loved in the past, not really anyone else's.

'So how did you end up going out together so often, and going to her dad's for dinner and stuff?' I think she was beginning to calm down now, but she still looked quite concerned. I offered her a cigarette and she pushed it between her lips and struck a match, the smell of sulphur filling the air.

'Well, we became good friends when I went to drop something off for her and she wasn't in, but her father was. She'd never told me he was ill, and he passed out on me. I thought he had died, Chloe – there were paramedics and everything. Then she got back and we had a tremendous row and it all kind of came out, all the stress, all the years she had cared for him, everything she'd been through . . .'

Chloe nodded her head in understanding. She was a good person, really, just a little wild some-times. And it was that animal-like behaviour that had made her so exciting in the first place.

She looked relieved . . . almost. 'And so you're telling me that you've never come on to her and nothing like that has *ever* happened between you?' She stared at me, her eyes piercing mine.

A silence filled my ears. My blood ran cold. A sudden flashback filled my brain of that strange, dark night when she'd held on to me for hours and I'd felt like the world was mine. Her body, her warmth – it was all so far away now. But the crash back down to earth had been one of the most painful experiences of my entire existence and I could still feel it, just like I could feel the bruise on my face.

'Nothing has ever happened, Chloe.' Telling her about *that* night wouldn't make things better. Not for anyone.

Chloe fell quiet and ran her finger around the rim of her wine glass, trying to make it sing. She looked tired but her cheeks were still rosy.

'I love you, Nick,' she said softly. It was the first time she'd ever said it. My heart stopped and I felt the heat of fear and joy all at the same time.

It had been a while since she'd said that sentence: 'Let's take it slow.' That one.

And I remembered exactly where we'd been on the beach that day in Brighton and how the wind had smelled. She'd had a banana milkshake and I'd had a chocolate one, and I'd been so glad she said it because it had meant I had time, more time to get my head straight.

Yet here I was, months later, sweating just like I always have done since the second she came into my life.

I couldn't say it back. I didn't feel it yet. But this wasn't a bad thing because I knew I felt a lot.

I had faith in that. I adored Chloe; I worshipped the ground she walked on, the way she left people spinning every time she waltzed out of a room, the way she kissed me. I was so close, but I just needed more time . . .

There are several things I could have said next that would have resulted in either another slap or me being single, or both. Such as: a) Really? b) Gosh, well, what can I say? Or worse still . . . c) Thanks. I am smarter than that, so I took option d), which was to walk over to her, kiss her on the lips and carry her upstairs.

For the first time all night, she laughed.

CHAPTER 8

'A LITTLE BOX I CARRY EVERYWHERE WITH ME . . .'

Nick

The big day had arrived. My birthday. Thirty. That looming number I'd spent my twenties dreading and yearning for in equal measure.

Dreading because I'd had that 'oh dear God, I only have a few years to become something really quite special' feeling, and yearning for in case I woke up on the day and found I actually *was* something quite special.

The reality was, at first, nothing special at all.

I woke up at 8 a.m., which was a nice start. I was alive. It was a nice, sunny autumn day. I opened the window to let some air in; it was fresh and crisp and I loved it. A squirrel jumped gracefully onto a branch, almost within touching distance, before scuttling down the thick, rough bark. An elderly man was walking his dog on the street below, a broad grin on his face.

Chloe wasn't in my bed. I remembered I had deliberately put her off in case I had some kind of panic attack and ended up breathing into a paper bag.

The first big observation was that all my limbs were working just fine. I didn't have a sudden urge to convert my shed into a woodwork den and start recording the birds I saw in the garden on spreadsheets. So far, so good.

The initial step was to go to the bathroom. My joints weren't creaking; all movement was as fluid as it always had been. I stepped cautiously towards the mirror and looked at my reflection. Phew. I hadn't morphed into my father, wonderful as he is. I only had the same four grey hairs I'd had yesterday, and no extra lines round my eyes.

This was going well.

My phone rang so I dashed back into my room to answer it, stubbing my toe on a box full of books. Unfortunately I was still clumsy. My eyes started to water.

'Happy birthday, handsome,' came the purr of Chloe's voice. My mind was instantly filled with images of her in lingerie. That was nice. I instantly regretted sending her home last night. I could be having the first sex of my proper adult life. Maybe I would actually be good at it now . . .

'Morning, Chlo. How are you today, beautiful?' I said, as I sank down onto my bed and climbed back under the covers.

I had booked the day off work. I wouldn't normally bother but I'd genuinely been quite scared that I might have a mini breakdown, and

I didn't want to do that on the third floor of an office in Balham. It's pretty high up. I thought I'd come to terms with it all – you know, the whole enjoying the journey thing. But I'd spent my last week as a twenty-nine-year-old in a state of acute anxiety. Had I been wild enough? Had I been too wild? Should I have done any of it differently? Had I been a bit of a selfish bastard?

'Yeah, I'm great, thanks, Nick.' Chloe's voice broke my train of thought. 'I'm coming to see you tonight to give you your birthday surprise – is that OK?' She lowered her tone; it sounded like my surprise was either ominous or sexy. I hoped it was the latter.

I really didn't want a fuss. I just wanted to get the day over with and then start worrying about hitting forty. It would be a concentrated ten-year task and I needed all the nervous energy I could muster.

'OK, that sounds great. I can't wait to see you,' I responded before hanging up the phone and pulling the soft covers underneath my nose. They smelled of her. Delicious.

Now, what was I going to do with myself? I would really like to see Sienna. In fact, I was quite nervous about this. Even though I wanted my thirtieth birthday to sink into the record books as one of the most unnoticed and uneventful days in history, I would be quite hurt if Sienna wasn't a part of it. This distance was all well and good, but I really did need her today. She hadn't made any plans with me. Nothing. We hadn't spent time together properly for weeks.

There was a hard knock at the door. Wondering who on earth it could be, I sprang out of bed, wrapped myself in a thick, blue dressing gown and tiptoed down the stairs. In the glass I could see the blurry outline of a postal worker. It was the bright red jacket and strip of reflective yellow that gave it away.

Oh dear. Perhaps my mother had sent me one of her homemade cakes again, which often arrived bashed and broken with some awful picture printed on the top of me as a toothless kid in a baggy nappy.

I opened the door and peered through the gap.

'All right, mate,' came a pleasant male voice.

'Hi there,' I answered, a certain level of dread in my tone.

'Right then, this is for you. Can you just sign here?' He handed me one of those screens with the skinny pen, which makes you sign your name like you've just been given anaesthetic.

He handed me a heavy box, wrapped in traditional brown paper. Yes, it was definitely the cake. Bless her. I wondered which horrific photo she'd found this time. They seemed to get worse each year; maybe she'd gone the whole hog and selected the one of me holding a freshly picked bogey up to the camera. Sigh . . .

I carried the box into the living room and made a cup of tea. I wasn't in a huge hurry to open it.

I started thinking about Sienna again. I just wanted to be with her, really. She'd been at the receiving end of all my pre-thirty angst; she'd laughed at me when appropriate and hugged me when it had all got a bit too much. She was wonderful – but where the hell was she now?

I carried the mug back into the living room and started opening the modest pile of cards that had dropped through the letterbox over the past few weeks. There was one from my great-aunt Polly, addressed to 'My dear nephew Daniel on his thirty-second birthday'. Well, at least she'd remembered the date. I made a note to go and visit her soon. It was probably partly my fault that she thought my name was Daniel; I'd been a little preoccupied lately. Still, thirty-two . . .

The next one was from work. Everyone had signed it, even Dill. I was touched. I put it pride of place on the mantlepiece. Then there was one from Ross and the gang – they'd stuck a picture of our group on holiday in Ibiza two and a half years ago. We looked pink from all the sunshine and beer. It made me smile. Inside were lots of silly, mildly insulting messages and a promise of a free night out for me. This really wasn't so bad after all . . .

I recognised the handwriting on the next one, but I wasn't totally sure who it could be. I tore at the envelope frantically and found the name Amelia signed at the bottom in black fountain pen. Oh dear. Now this was a blast from the past.

I suddenly remembered that morning when she'd been slumped on my doorstep crying, and I wondered if she'd found happiness now. I hoped she had. Really I did, because I had found mine.

The final card was from my mum, dad, sister and the dog. It was long and quite soppy and it made a lump appear in my throat, which I swiftly coughed away. It even said they were proud of me. Me. Why? I couldn't help but notice the sentence at the bottom, which read: 'P.S. You have to come over this weekend to get your cake. I couldn't bear the thought of my baking efforts arriving in smithereens this time.'

How odd. I looked over at the brown box on my living-room table with a new level of suspicion. Now I thought about it, it was quite big. And heavy. Too big for the cake. I was starting to worry now. It could be from anyone. It could be a parcel of anthrax from someone I had inadvertently infuriated while going about my day-to-day life.

I pulled it onto my lap and started to tear away the wrapping, uncovering a large shoebox underneath. I took another sip of my tea and pulled the lid off the container. This revealed yet another box covered in newspaper, this time a Topshop delivery box. I pulled it apart. Below that layer was some pink wrapping paper and another smaller casing. I could see what was going on here. Pass the parcel wasn't going to get the better of me at this age . . .

I continued to rip through a plethora of layers

until I uncovered a heavy, hardback book. A black book. This was making me a little bit nervous. I carefully turned the front cover to reveal a faded newspaper clipping. I peered closer and made out a photo of a squirrel on waterskis. Beneath it were the handwritten words 'It all started on a train . . .'

Holy shit. It was from Sienna. A lovely, warm feeling washed over me and I remembered the first time I'd ever looked into her eyes. I started to tremble a little as I turned to the next page.

It soon dawned on me that she had created a book. A whole book, just for me. *The Story of Sienna and Nick*, it was called. It was the most touching, thoughtful thing anyone had ever done for me. The lump returned to my throat and it was as if time stood still. I could no longer hear the noise of the street outside, it was as if the world was on mute. Sienna's gesture had hit me hard, then seemed to grip me in a firm embrace.

The book contained everything: cinema tickets, plane boarding passes, every photograph we'd taken, mini posters for our favourite films. It contained song lyrics, jokes, anecdotes . . . Each joyous memory we'd had the good fortune to experience in our short relationship was in there, spread all over the pages, laid out beautifully with love and care.

I noticed the hairs on my arms were raised. I felt that familiar sensation creep back over me and I started from page one all over again.

269

I put my feet on the coffee table and went on a journey, remembering everything that had happened since I'd met her. I ran my index finger over her face in one of the photos we'd taken in a picture booth in Florida. She was sitting on my lap and laughing. God, she was stunning.

When I first met her she was a baby, really, but so much more ready for the world than I was – or ever would be, I expect.

I could smell it. I could taste it. I could feel the warmth of her right next to me. I'm ashamed to admit it, but a huge tear fell from my right eye and rolled down my cheek. A happy tear. For the first time in my life, another person, Sienna Walker, had taken one of the scariest days of my existence and made it one of the happiest, and she wasn't even here . . .

I picked up my phone with a trembling hand and held down the 2 button, my heart thumping.

'Hello, Nick.' It sounded like she had a huge smile on her face.

'Sienna, fuck. Thank you. Thank you so much. You have no idea . . . how much . . . just how much . . . Ughh . . .' I couldn't even get the words out but I hoped she understood. I realised that my head was in my hands right down towards my lap, the phone tucked between my right ear and shoulder.

'Happy birthday, sweetheart,' she replied, that customary warmth in her voice resonating through the tinny line.

'You didn't have to do this. It must have taken you ages. It's, well, it's incredible, Si,' I said, feeling nervous all of a sudden. Intimidated by the grandeur of her. There was a short pause while I listened to her move into what I assumed were the ladies' toilets.

'I know this might sound cheesy,' she started, taking a deep breath, 'but I adore you, Nick Redland. You've got me through everything. I would be lost without you. So really, it's the least I could do. Thank you for being around.' She sounded nervous.

Her words hit me hard. 'I need to see you, Sienna.' It just came out of my mouth. It was involuntary. The sentence just spilled out because it was the most natural thing in the world.

'We'll see each other soon, I promise. Look, I have to go. Have yourself a wonderful thirtieth birthday, Nick, and be proud of everything that you are.'

And that was it. The line went dead. I looked at the photos of Sienna and me in a supermarket photo booth, and for the first time in a long time, I *was* proud of who I am.

Sienna

It's been 882 days since I first met Nick Redland. That's around two years and five months of happiness, and I'm documenting these moments in a big black book.

'Glue, please, Sienna,' came a polite request from my father, who was holding a cinema ticket in his hands. A blue sequin was stuck to his chin.

'Here you go, Pops,' I replied, passing him a tray of special art glue that doesn't make things go crinkly when it dries.

'This is such a good idea,' he beamed, slicking the viscous liquid neatly over the back of the paper and pushing it down on the puckered white card. 'He's going to love it,' he added, even more excited than me.

I was so glad he was helping. It was something really nice we could do together. And doing stuff together was quite hard nowadays, since he couldn't leave the house for any period of time without falling over and knocking himself out.

Our favourite movie, *Breakfast at Tiffany's*, was playing on the widescreen TV in the background. The sound was low so you could barely make out the clipped accent of Hepburn's character, but you could see her gorgeous little face slicked with rain as she ran through the streets in search of Cat. This was the best bit. Holly Golightly would find herself in a passionate tryst with the man she loved and her ginger pet under sheets of engineered rain. Ah . . . My gaze turned to the window. It was raining here too, but it looked a lot less romantic.

'What gave you this idea, then?' my dad questioned me, rolling the sleeves of his baggy blue jumper above his elbows. I had created him a cushion haven on the sofa, and he was sitting so he would fall onto a soft surface when he passed out. Not if, but when. This was tiring stuff for him.

'Well, I was really stuck about what to give him for his birthday – it's a big one, obviously. Silly gifts and gimmicks weren't really going to do the trick.' I reached over to the pile of mementoes and picked up a strip of photos taken in a booth in Florida. I was sitting on Nick's lap and he had just poked me in the ribs, causing me to cackle loudly as the flashbulbs went. God, I loved him. 'So I was lying in bed one night and I was thinking about all the fun times we've had, and it dawned on me that my room was full of bits of paper, photos, tickets and stuff like that from our various adventures. I got up and gathered them all together and that was when the idea hit me.'

'It's perfect. He's going to love it,' Dad said again. 'You two are quite something, aren't you?' he muttered, holding a photo and peering more closely at it.

'What's that?' I asked. He turned the image round. It was Halloween two years ago; we dressed up as Batman and Robin.

'There is one thing that concerns me a little,' he began, taking a huge gulp from his mug of tea.

Here we go . . .

'He has a girlfriend, right?'

'Yes. Chloe.' Luckily I was over my hideous jealousy by now, otherwise I would have launched

273

myself off a cliff on a motorised scooter. She seemed really nice, actually – not that I knew her that well. She seemed to keep a safe distance from me; the most we talked was when she handed me a mug on her tea round.

'How do you think she'll feel about all this? Hmm?' he probed. He had that look on his face that he always has when I'm doing something a little bit naughty. You know, something you can get away with, but it's still a bit dodgy. Like keeping a tenner you find poking out of a cash machine, bunking the train fare or failing to tip in a really good restaurant.

'You are, after all, quite deeply in love with Nick,' said Dad.

'*Was* in love,' I abruptly corrected him, pressing a theatre ticket onto the page in frustration.

'OK, *was*, sorry. I suppose it was a long time ago you told me all that,' he conceded, sorting through a pile of tickets and receipts.

'Yes, I *did* used to love him like that, but I don't now. Plus I've got Ben. I think Chloe is absolutely fine about Nick and me being friends. That's all this book is about.' I looked him straight in the eye.

He took a deep breath, like he was fighting off his fatigue with a fresh dose of oxygen. 'That's fine, Sienna. I know your intentions are good. It's just, you're a really pretty girl, and I think most women would find your closeness, well, deeply unnerving.'

His words shocked me a little. In comparison to Chloe I felt like some wart-covered creature that

274

had crawled out of a badger set. He wasn't being accusatory or aggressive, just truthful, and that's what I love about my dad.

'Thanks. But no, don't worry. I'll handle it very carefully. It's important he gets this.'

I looked at him as he held a peacock feather towards the halogen ceiling light; its petrol blue and green shades lit up and he grinned. 'What about this one, huh?' He whipped the feather towards my face and brushed my left cheek with it. I pulled my neck back into my shoulders because it tickled.

'We went to a farm once, just for fun. He found it on the ground and gave it to me.'

'And what about Ben?' Dad continued to prod.

'What about him?'

'How does he feel about you and Nick being such good friends? You've been seeing each other for about nine months now, right?'

'Er, yes, that's probably about right . . . I don't think he feels a lot, Dad. We haven't been too serious with each other anyway, as in we don't see each other all that often. And if he has an issue with it, he'll just have to lump it, won't he? I can't be doing with jealous men . . .'

'This must have all been quite difficult for you, really, Sienna,' Dad pondered, gently running his fingers over the feather's circular pattern. 'You know . . . loving someone that much and having to, well, pack it away into a little box and pretend it isn't there.'

That was a very good way of describing it. A

little box. Packed full of love. Love that I had never really been able to express, so it was banging away at the sides and screaming to be let out.

'Yes, it has been. And really, it's a little box I carry everywhere with me, because I guess the love never properly goes away.'

There was a soft thud. Dad had slumped back onto the mound of cushions I had gathered. Bless him.

As the afternoon wore on, I continued to cut, glue and stick the remnants of the last two and a half years of my life onto the book's pages. The film had finished a long time ago, and the DVD menu sequence must have repeated itself hundreds of times. Normally this would have irritated me, but I was in a deep trance. The rain fell faster and heavier as the darkness of the night slowly pulled a thick, black cloak over the daylight. It would be Nick's thirtieth birthday in just three days. I quietly prayed for sunshine so he would wake up and see how good things really are. How he doesn't need to worry about all the silly stuff that crowds his mind, like his career and his age.

The next day I walked down to the post office. Nervous butterflies filled my stomach and made it hard to breathe. I really was doing this, wasn't I? I was basically saying, with photographs and sequins and feathers and glue, I love you. Just as a friend, of course . . .

A grey-haired lady was on the other side of the glass counter. One of those weird jangly chains ran from the sides of her glasses around her neck. What is it that these people think is going to happen to their specs? Quite bizarre . . .

'I need special delivery, please. I really need to make sure this gets to its destination safely.' I meant business.

She looked slightly offended. Well, tough. Inside this box were the best memories of my life, and I wasn't having them delivered to some guy called Bob who would open them, shrug his shoulders and then use them as a footrest.

I wrote Nick's name and address in capital letters, taking care that the numbers were clear, then pushed the parcel through to the woman. According to her badge, her name was Sue, but you could never trust that. When I worked at the supermarket on Saturday mornings I wore a 'Geoff' badge for years, just because they hadn't bothered sending off for a 'Sienna' one.

The parcel was weighed. How much does love weigh, I wondered . . .

'That's £5.90, please,' said Sue, her hand already thrust out expectantly.

I pushed the exact money into her chubby palm and looked into her eyes. 'Please, make sure it gets there safely. Please.'

'Yes, yes, I will.' She finally cracked a smile. I think she knew this was about a boy.

Tuesday came and went. It was uneventful.

Then it was Wednesday. Nick's day. I didn't call or text. I thought I had done enough, really.

'Morning, gorgeous,' said Lydia, rushing over to me in a pair of exceptionally high heels the minute I came out of the lift. Just looking at them made me giddy.

'You look lovely, Lyds,' I said, giving her a gentle kiss on the cheek.

And indeed she did. Her auburn curls were tumbling over a dark grey knitted jumper, cinched in at the waist with a thin patent belt. Underneath that was a pair of tailored black trousers, skinny at the ankle to highlight the glorious shoes. She was like a supermodel. I looked down at my own ensemble, which consisted of black skinny jeans, a grey cardigan and a pair of black ballet pumps. It was a bit boring, to say the least.

'You're going to have to take me shopping soon,' I exclaimed, hoping that just a smidgen of her style might rub off on me if I sat close enough.

She leaned in close to my ear, filling the space around me with her perfume. 'I've met a boy, Sienna. Well, a man. A very sexy man.' Then she moved back again, clasping her hands together and giggling.

'That is so exciting! Tell me more.' I reached forward and held her lower arms in my hands. So that's why she was looking so spectacular today, I thought. I mean, she always looks good, but you can tell when a woman is in the throes of something passionate. She makes even more of an effort. Nails are painted. Legs are shaved. Scented moisturiser is deployed . . .

'Well, he works at an office down the road. We kept bumping into each other in Starbucks every day and he bought my latte last week and asked for my number.' She looked down at her feet, blushing slightly.

'That is so cute,' I gushed.

Then my phone rang, pulling me out of my romantic rundown with Lydia. It was Nick. I gestured an apology her way and dived into the corridor. My stomach filled with nerves again. What if he didn't like the book and I had misjudged the whole thing? Surely I shouldn't worry. Nick was an artistic and creative individual, pretty cool about all that stuff. He wasn't the kind who avoided sequins for fear of turning into a raging queen.

'Hello, Nick,' I answered, forcing a smile across my face so that I sounded upbeat rather than bloody terrified.

He tried to get some words out, but it was a strange sentence which included the words 'fuck' and 'ughh' – if that is even a proper word. I took it to be a good sign.

I pictured him as he spoke. He probably had his face on his lap and his hands clasped around his head. It's a funny Nickism. I wished him happy birthday.

'You didn't have to do this. It must have taken you ages. It's, well, it's incredible, Si,' he said.

Something washed over me. I knew I had to say that I adored him, and say it in privacy, so I rushed into the toilets, hoping they were empty.

It just came out. OK, it wasn't a love declaration. You can 'adore' a friend. But he needed to know that much. I got the closest I'd ever been to telling him that I was wildly in love with him. I realised then that I still was. That I'd never stopped being in love with him.

My words were: 'I adore you, Nick Redland. You've got me through everything. I would be lost without you. So really, it's the least I could do. Thank you for being around.' I said it because I meant it. Putting some scrapbook together *was* the least I could do for him. 'We'll see each other soon, I promise. Look, I have to go. Have yourself a wonderful thirtieth birthday, Nick, and be proud of everything that you are,' I added.

I heard the sudden click of a heel from a far cubicle. Shit. It was Chloe. I could stay here or disappear. Stay here or disappear.

Too late. She came out of the cubicle with a suspicious smile on her face. 'What was that all about? You adore someone? Who is that?' she demanded as she tried to casually wash her hands, her irritation unmaskable.

I went red again and pushed my phone into my pocket as if to hide the whole conversation, but she had clearly heard it all. She knew exactly who I had been talking to. 'Erm, I was just wishing Nick a happy birthday,' I said, trying to sound as nonchalant as possible.

'Did you get him a present?' she asked me flatly as she moved over to the hand dryer.

I had to be honest about this. 'No, I didn't buy anything, I made him a book – just with a few photos in it and crappy old tickets and stuff. I'm skint, so . . .' I replied, trying to play it down, but having to shout a little above the roar of the dryer, which didn't help. When it stopped, she turned to face me, a look of fury painted across her features.

'I see,' she said, turning on her heel and storming out of the toilet.

Nick

'Nick, I have a question.'

It was Tom and he was standing in the doorway to my office holding his laptop, a look of concern on his face. He was wearing a blue checked shirt and the buttons weren't done up in the right order, leaving a corner of material hanging over the top of his jeans. I decided not to point it out.

'Yes, mate, come in.' I moved a pile of magazines from the spare chair.

Tom shut the door behind him. This was likely to be serious. Probably woman-related.

He angled his torso towards me and pushed the computer in my direction, looking very worried now. 'Well, it's my laptop, really.'

God, what was this? I wondered. Still, this was what senior responsibility was all about. I was learning this stuff since I'd been made studio manager, Ant's second in charge. It sounds like it was something I should have celebrated and shouted from the treetops, but in reality I hadn't even been given a pay rise. The company was trying to cut costs as much as possible, and this had been a last-ditch attempt to keep me on the payroll as it was pretty clear I was getting itchy feet. Still, it was great experience and blah blah blah . . . But it also meant people kept coming into my office with strange questions and accusations. Important stuff – you know, Terry's hidden my favourite mug and so forth.

'What's the problem?'

He cleared his throat. His voice was quiet now. 'Well, it's got heavier. I really mean it. It's getting tough to carry it to work.'

I was perplexed. Bemused. Discombobulated.

Then he dropped the bombshell. 'Do you think it's all the files I've put on there? You know, all the stuff I've been saving and downloading?'

I spat my drink all over my lap. 'Are you joking, Tom?' I shrieked, raising my eyebrows and collapsing into fits of laughter. I looked deep into his eyes, hoping this was one of his pranks.

He sat up in surprise. Genuine surprise.

'And how much exactly does a word document weigh?' I shouted through my hysteria.

He still didn't get it and I was really taking the mick now. It almost felt cruel. 'Get out of my office, Tom, please, before I piss myself!' I stood up and handed him the computer, mock dropping it to the floor because of the sheer 'weight' of it.

Then realisation dawned and he must have figured the ridiculousness of his query. He went beetroot. 'Oh shit, Nick. I'm such a div.' He collapsed with laughter.

'I told you, get out of my space before I send out a memo to the whole company,' I laughed, physically pushing him out of my door with both hands on his back. I slumped back into my chair and started laughing again. It was all too much. My ribs were hurting now. I felt kind of sorry for Tom. He was so technically challenged despite being so young. We were talking here about a guy who once got up from his desk and physically closed one of the windows near his desk after misreading an instruction from IT support over the phone.

How did he not know this stuff? He was an anomaly. He'd obviously bunked off IT classes at school. But although I felt sorry for his ignorance, I had to make the most of this. It was an opportunity too good to miss, so I leaped up and opened my door again, swinging my body into the open-plan office.

'Tom?' I called with a smile on my face.

'Yes,' he answered quietly, his red face rising above the screen of his computer.

'How much does an MP3 weigh? Because I was going to get a couple of albums at the weekend and I was wondering whether or not I would need the car. Or maybe home delivery might be an option?'

'Sod off!' he shouted, laughing too.

Everyone looked perplexed. 'Don't worry, guys, Tom just lost his mind for a second. He'll tell you,' I yelled, pointing towards him with a smile.

Suddenly the lift opened and everyone looked towards it, their attention shifting from my mocking of Tom as a massive bunch of flowers with legs appeared under the strip lighting. Holy cow. Now that was a romantic declaration. There were red flowers, pink flowers and white flowers, all tied up in a giant ribbon and secured in the middle with a beautiful bow.

I looked around the office. Who could they be for? I certainly hadn't ordered them for Chloe – I gave her a look before she got her hopes up, then instantly felt like a rubbish boyfriend.

Rhoda has been married to the same miserable git for years, so that was extremely unlikely.

Diane was bitter and angry, and not worthy of such a beautiful explosion of colour.

Lydia had only just started seeing someone. Surely that would be a bit terrifying?

There were a few other girls here, but they were pretty quiet so I didn't know much about them.

Eventually it transpired that the legs actually belonged to the skinny chap delivering them. He seemed to be buckling under their weight. He held a little card close to his face as if he was struggling to read it, great folds of wrinkly skin around his eyes.

'I think you might have got the wrong floor, mate,' I said, walking towards him with my hands clasped together. I was genuinely trying to help.

People's heads were poking above their workstations like they were excitable meerkats.

'No. No. It definitely says the third floor.' He was slightly cross-eyed. He peered at the card again. 'Er, it says Sienna here. Yeah. Sienna Walker?' he called out, stepping back in his steel-toecap boots. His delivery was less than romantic.

My heart sank. Shit. They were from that Ben bloke. And all respect to him, he had really pulled it out of the hat. They must have cost a bomb . . . Still, he does run a cripplingly expensive torture chamber of a gym.

I saw her flinch as soon as her name was mentioned and within seconds every female in the room was running over to her and shrieking like it was the rehearsals for the Cats' Chorus annual summer concert. She went almost as red as Tom had earlier and tried to hide behind her screen.

Why had I never thought of doing something like that for a woman? Or even for her, maybe? Back in the days before I lost my nerve . . .

The delivery man fought through the throng of cooing women and laid the flowers in her arms. 'Sign here, please,' he demanded abruptly, plonking a card and a biro in her hand.

She tried her best to scribble her name but the flowers were impeding her ability to do anything. Sienna hates stuff like this. I know that. She despises being the centre of attention and that's certainly what she was now. It was as if the room had gone into slow motion and I was just watching from a distance. Watching some other guy romance the girl I loved. I mean used to love. Shit.

285

Chloe looked over at me and grinned hopefully. I smiled back. This was going to cost me . . .

'What does it say?' screamed Lydia, who can be very loud at times. She tripped over her own shoe, took the phone with her and just about steadied herself on the desk.

'Girls, girls. Please. I'm really embarrassed. Hold on a minute.' Sienna fished the card out of the grip of a particularly strong Delilah. She sneezed sweetly and then read the card. A beautiful look spread across her face which made me feel warm all over. I was happy for her. Really. Genuinely. Kind of . . .

Lydia could take it no more; she snatched the pink piece of paper from Sienna's fingers and started to read out loud:

'"To Sienna. I know it's not your birthday, Valentine's Day, Christmas or anything in particular. I just wanted to send these to you because you are beautiful and I am the luckiest man alive. Love Ben. Kiss kiss kiss." There's three there, Si, he definitely loves you,' she declared, folding her arms and looking at my best friend with a look of sisterhood. Pride, even.

I hadn't met this bloke yet, but I thought it was about time. He was obviously a good guy. Either that or he was hideously creepy. Whichever it was, I had to grill him. I mean, meet him.

I closed my office door on the scene and sat in the quiet. Thinking.

Contemplating. Wishing.

CHAPTER 9

'I WANT YOU TO
MEET MY PARENTS.'

Sienna

I really am sublimely happy at the moment. So happy that I wish I could play the piano and sing at the same time, just like Alicia Keys. Then somehow I would be able to express this giddy joy rather than laughing to myself on the train like a nutter. It would help if I hadn't rowed with my piano teacher about where middle C was.

Yes, it all went wrong when I was seven years old. Dad organised lessons for me but was deeply humiliated when Mr Davis told him he could no longer teach me as we were having 'artistic differences'. That's a polite way of putting it when you've got a cocky little seven-year-old telling you that you're wrong about a fact. Something that *isn't negotiable*.

You see, at the time I didn't realise that middle C was one of those set things, like times tables and the periodic table of elements. It really isn't open to interpretation. And I regret it now that all I want to do is stick on a really sexy dress and play the piano for my gorgeously handsome boyfriend in the basement of some posh hotel. Bugger.

Ben is everything I'd hoped he would be and more. He is mature, spontaneous, romantic and very good in the sack.

And we were in that sack on Sunday morning at his place, enjoying a love-in, which has become an almost weekly highlight of our relationship.

I literally worship his body. I get lost in his eyes. He is gorgeous.

He is also amazing in bed. The neighbours could probably vouch for this, since more than once they've started banging against the wall, shouting for us to shut up. OK, he does make me feel like a bit of a heifer, but that's always a risk when you're dating a gym man. They generally have bodies to die for.

Despite all this joy, he did shock me a little when he said the three-word sentence.

The one with the words 'you', 'I' and 'love' in it, which it doesn't take a genius to scramble round.

'Sienna, there's something I need to say to you,' he whispered into my ear, a handful of my hair in one hand and my bottom in the other. We had literally just had sex. It was too soon, I was still unable to breathe properly. So much of our skin was touching. We were too naked for this kind of intimacy, and it scared me.

I'd had a feeling this was coming so I panicked and tried to distract him by diving under the covers and blowing a raspberry on his stomach. Possibly the worst way to end an hour of early-morning passion. It was also quite difficult because his torso is hard and muscular with the texture of a spice rack, and has no give in terms of good face to skin reverberation.

He pulled me back up to eye level and opened his mouth to speak.

'Ben, I've had an idea,' I said swiftly, cutting in before he could say anything. Shit, I had to actually follow this up with something. 'Let's play Monopoly!'

'No, Si, it's long and arduous and reminds me of how crap I am with money. Anyway, I was going to say—'

'Ben, I need the loo,' I yelled, diving out of bed and covering my bottom with my hands before frantically putting on my knickers and darting into the bathroom, knocking over a cup of tea in the process.

I ran the taps to hide the fact that I'd been lying and splashed my face with the cold jet of water. I had run and run like a startled little animal to avoid this happening. I didn't want him to say it because he couldn't mean it. I am very hard to love. I do really like him, but . . .

'Sienna, come out here, please,' came Ben's deep voice from the other side of the bathroom door after a good fifteen minutes had passed.

I opened it slowly and he stood there in his boxers, looking hot and very much like he needed to get something off his chest. I put my hands over my boobs self-consciously. I had been hoping he'd think the moment had passed and we could concentrate on getting him naked again, but his face told me otherwise.

'Breakfast?' I suggested. 'I could make you breakfast,' I repeated, starting to march down the stairs, one hand still plastered over my chest.

'Si, we've already had breakfast, remember?' he yelled over the banister with a perplexed smile on his face.

Right, yeah, I wasn't going to get away with this. I plodded back up the stairs and stood facing him. I was a squirrel in the headlights.

'Sienna, will you just stay still for one minute,' he demanded playfully.

'Yeah, sure, what's up? I was horribly aware that my underwear was half wedged up my backside. I tried to pull it out ever so discreetly with my free hand.

He put his arms around my waist and pulled me into his chest.

'I love you, Si,' he said quietly, putting his fingers under my chin and kissing me softly on the mouth. I felt a twinge in my stomach, but it wasn't a happy one. Instead of the joy that should have been flooding over me at that moment, I felt sick. Sick with fear. My mother's face flashed into my mind again and those voices started taunting me. The sentences I had conditioned myself into believing because it was the only rational way to explain my mother's departure.

You're so damn difficult to love, Sienna . . .

My legs felt like they were disintegrating underneath me. I was decidedly wobbly, but he was strong.

Well, there we go, it was out in the open at least, but I was nowhere near ready for this. I thought the best thing would be to kiss him very meaningfully and passionately and take him back to bed. Saying 'thanks' would have been a disaster – that was a bit like taking someone's love, burning it onto the hard drive of your computer just for the memories and giving it back covered in scratches.

I couldn't say it back because I wasn't quite there yet. Like I said, I'm very happy. Can't we just leave it there for the moment?

When he texts me I grin like a loon. When he calls I walk around the hallway twisting my hair and running my toes over the floorboards. When he kisses me, my stomach drops. When I think of him I get excited. It's brilliant. But love may be a bit soon yet.

I'm cautious with the love word because I really know what it means. I've been there, done that and I know what the implications are. I also know that people say they love people when they don't, and it often results in tears and avoidance of bars, supermarkets, even whole towns in extreme cases. I will never be one of those people. I refuse.

Ben rolled back onto his pillow and sighed, the winter sunshine creeping through the window and casting a beautiful light on his face. He has a hairy chest and I love that. I cuddled up to him and started gently pulling at the clumps of hair with my fingers like a monkey. I lifted my legs up and wrapped one around his waist. This kind of closeness – well, I'm not sure I've ever really felt it. To be able to just hold on to someone and be quiet. Not say a word.

'Sienna, I need to ask you something,' he announced after clearing his throat in an official manner.

'Yes, sweetheart?'

'I want you to meet my parents.'

Uh oh. Round two of the panic sweats had kicked in. I'd only just got over him telling me he loved me. Couldn't he give a girl a break? 'Right, OK. I'm sure that won't be a problem. Thanks, I'm really flattered,' I managed to say.

'Well, we've been together for a whole year now and Mum keeps asking about you.'

'What about your dad?'

'Dad doesn't care about anything, really, apart from minding the horses and my mum.' That's sweet, I thought.

He rolled towards me and put his arm around my waist, pulling me closer and closer to him until our faces were touching. I felt beautiful.

Maybe this was it. Maybe he was *the one* and like a really big job interview it was deeply scary but the right thing to be doing. You have to be in it to win it.

'So when were you thinking of us meeting up

with them?' I asked, looking into his green eyes, which remind me of the sea when you're on holiday somewhere really nice.

'Today?'

Wow. There was no time to make up an excuse – he already knew I was free, we were due to spend the day together. I was stuck. 'Today? Right, well, that sounds perfect. I need to get ready, though – got to look nice to meet your rents,' I smiled.

I felt nervous all of a sudden. What if they were horrified by me? What if they pulled him into the kitchen and bitched about me? At least it was happening quickly, like an injection, and I wouldn't spend weeks fretting over it and building it up in my mind.

'Well, we'd better start getting ready then,' he announced, leaping out of bed and wrapping a thin dressing gown round himself.

I tried the best I could to linger. I tempted him into the shower with me and that was a great distraction for at least twenty minutes. Drying and straightening my hair took double time. I wanted to look stunning. Or at least the closest I could get to the word.

I found a black day dress I'd bought from Urban Outfitters a while ago and left at Ben's with a few other outfits and accessories for impromptu days out and drinks with friends. It is nipped in at the waist and shows just enough chest to be feminine, but not too much. I wore it with grey tights and a pair of delicate silver pumps. The finishing touch was a long vintage necklace with a miniature bird-cage at the bottom made out of wire. My nails were still painted a deep red.

Ben had given up and started watching TV as he waited for me to emerge from the steamy bathroom in some kind of presentable form.

'Wow, you're beautiful, Sienna Walker,' he said, kissing me on the cheek.

'Thanks.' I looked down at the floor and went red.

'Right then, pretty lady, get your sexy backside into my car,' he cried, ushering me out of the front door. The ice-cold wind nibbled at my cheeks so I pulled my scarf tight around the bottom half of my face.

The flats, shops and high-rise offices zoomed past as I watched from the passenger seat. Slowly, the numbers of nutters and lost souls started to thin out and the colour green crept in and replaced them. There were proper fields, with horses and donkeys and everything. I saw ponds, too, covered in frost and ice. As we waited at a traffic light, I watched a duck step nervously out onto the surface of one before plonking a webbed foot straight through the surface and into the icy water below. It was lovely.

'Where are we going, Ben?'

'Surrey. They live on a farm, Si – I think I mentioned this a while ago. It's just my parents – I don't have any siblings. They are a bit mad, though,' he warned, turning to smile at me, his strong hands gripping the steering wheel.

I couldn't imagine what it would be like growing up on a farm, or with a mum who had stuck around for more than ten years. The whole idea made me quite nervous.

'Sounds nice. Did you ever help on the farm?'

'Yeah, most of my childhood was spent helping out. When I wasn't at school, of course – but I did my bit before and afterwards. It was hard work.'

I imagined him as a teenage boy, waking up at silly o'clock and helping on some muddy field before the school day had even begun, when most of us were being yelled at by our parents to get out of bed at seven thirty. I had a new level of respect for him.

After what seemed like hours, he pulled his sports car into a long, winding drive. He had to go really slowly because it was incredibly bumpy. Down the driveway and on the right was a modest but stunning farmhouse, surrounded by machinery, some of which looked defunct, some sparkling new.

Ben turned off the engine and looked at me. 'Come on, sweet one. They're going to love you.'

I timidly stepped out of the car and put my left foot into the middle of a deep, cold puddle. Whoops.

'Are you OK, Si?' asked Ben, peering over the top of the car.

This was embarrassing. I tried to pretend nothing had happened, but my foot was squelching as I walked.

'Come here, silly,' he said, ushering me into a small covered area swamped with wellies and green jackets. I put my shoes on a drying rack and tiptoed into the kitchen behind Ben, who was holding one of my hands tightly.

'Ben, darling,' came a female voice, which I could only assume belonged to his mother. A very attractive woman who must have been in her fifties emerged and pulled my boyfriend into an embrace. She looked very much like I'd expected – very pretty and nicely dressed. She had a thick, brown woollen jumper on over a pair of jeans. Her grey bob was nicely styled and she wore a light layer of make-up, which complemented her natural beauty perfectly. Her jewellery was delicate, silver and minimal. Just a small bangle on her wrist and a pair of earrings in the shape of teardrops.

I felt a funny emptiness pull at my stomach. I had always avoided women like this because they reminded me of my mum, who I kept wondering about – and wished was still around I guess . . . I managed to avoid the issue most of the time, ignoring the fact that I don't know my own mother any more. My mother who turned her back on Dad and me, leaving nothing behind but a battered toothbrush and a few credit card bills. From the moment she left, I made a vow that if I was ever lucky enough to have children, I would never abandon them.

'Oh, wow – this must be Sienna!' she said, stepping towards me slowly like I was an unusual and exotic animal. She put her hands on my shoulders and smiled broadly before leaning in and kissing me on both cheeks in a continental style. 'Welcome, Sienna, please come in. We've heard so much about you,' she continued, giving Ben an encouraging look.

He took off my coat and hung it from the back of the door. 'Sienna, this is my mum, Lucy,' he said, sounding even more nervous than I was.

The smells in the kitchen were incredible; pots and pans were boiling and simmering on the Aga. It was exactly how a country kitchen should be. A bottle of wine was sitting on the wooden table with several sparkling glasses around it. I realised how comfortable I felt. This wasn't so scary.

'A glass of wine, Sienna?' asked Lucy, who had clearly spotted me ogling the bottle.

'Oh yes, please. Thanks.'

We went through to the living room, which again looked like something out of a photograph from *Country Life* magazine. Heat raged from a crackling fire, in front of which was an elderly-looking black dog with random tufts of white hair poking out all over its body. It immediately got up and started sniffing at me frantically.

'It's OK, Tara, sit down,' said Lucy.

There was still no sign of Ben's father. I bet he was lovely. Probably all cute and round with a tweed flat cap. Or at least that's what I assumed until a large chair slowly creaked round, revealing a sombre, shadowy figure. It scared the shit out of me.

'Ah, there you are, Dad – I should have known.'

Now Ben's dad was a serious man. Scary, even. He was quite reedy and had combed a thin layer of grey hair over the top of his head to hide his bald patch – which I noticed straight away. In his right hand was a huge glass of whisky. It was only 1 p.m., and it didn't look like his first. He wore dark colours and faded into the blackness of the room like a shadow.

'Hello, Ben,' he said with little enthusiasm. He was very well spoken, but his deep voice had something of an inebriated drawl about it.

'Dad, this is Sienna.'

There was a grunt. Gosh. How rude.

The dog shifted awkwardly, looked up at me and did one of those deep, canine sighs before rolling over on the carpet. I feel your pain, Tara, I thought. If I'm honest, I was deeply disappointed by Ben's dad's reaction, but I tried hard not to show it.

'Er, Dad. Sienna, my girlfriend?' pushed Ben once more, offering me a seat on the sofa. I obliged.

'Yes, I know,' he said, ignoring me and turning back to the golden flames.

'David. Don't be so bloody rude,' snapped Lucy, turning his chair around again. Hard. His whisky almost flew from his glass and onto the floor.

'Oh, for God's sake, darling. I know who it is, we don't need to make a song and dance and scare the poor girl, do we? Now, does she have a glass of wine?' he asked.

I held my glass up towards the light nervously

and smiled, toasting thin air. Everything was fine. Stay calm.

Lucy pulled up a chair and sat almost opposite me. 'So, Sienna, tell me more about you.' She leaned back and smiled, looking genuinely pleased that her son hadn't brought back a piercing-riddled Goth. She was obviously trying very hard to be warm and accommodating to make up for the ignorant pig she had married.

'Well, I'm a journalist, I live in west London. I write for a whole load of different magazines and I love it.'

'Bloody journalists,' came David's gruff tone. 'Always blooooody lying,' he finished, his words flowing even thicker now, like there was treacle in his mouth. It struck me suddenly that my boyfriend's father was a drunk.

Lucy turned red and gave me one of those 'ignore him' looks, but she seemed deeply humiliated by it all. Ben visibly cringed.

It dawned on me that this man had quite a serious alcohol problem, and that maybe Ben hadn't fully realised this. At least David's vitriol wasn't personal. Maybe Ben had been brought up with it and thought it was normal for a man to behave in this way. It wasn't. Of course.

His mother was lovely, though, and I couldn't help but feel an ache. As if someone like her had been the missing piece all along. If I'd had a mum around then maybe my dad wouldn't feel so sad about things. Sometimes he gets really depressed.

'So who do you live with?' she continued to probe gently.

'I live with my dad – just me and Dad. No brothers or sisters,' I replied, hoping she wouldn't start asking too many embarrassing questions, but I was sure Ben would have briefed her on my unusual situation.

'Sienna, I hope you don't mind me asking, but Ben tells me that your father suffers from quite a fascinating illness. Sorry, I don't mean fascinating, I, er, I mean . . .' she stuttered, trying to correct herself and blushing slightly. At least she wasn't pussyfooting around the subject.

'Yes, he has narcolepsy—'

'Narco-what?' I was rudely interrupted by Ben's father, who spat flecks of saliva into the air as he spoke.

'Shut up, Dad,' shouted Ben, clearly quite angry with his father's behaviour.

'It's OK,' I said quietly, holding Ben's hand discreetly. He squeezed it back. 'Basically, it's a condition affecting the neurological system. It's a sleep-wake issue. My dad, George, has cataplexy, too, which is another condition that goes hand in hand with narcolepsy. It means the triggers for his sleep are emotional ones, so when he feels any kind of strong emotion it will send him off. So, in non-scientific terms, it means that he falls asleep pretty much all the time,' I finished, taking a deep breath of the woody air.

I was so hungry now it was making me feel

faint. I took a tiny sip of my wine, aware that it would go straight to my head, and I wanted to stay sharp enough to be on my toes around Ben's father.

'So he could be standing up and he would just hit the floor?' she asked, both eyebrows raised in utter surprise.

'Yes, spot on. Anywhere, anytime. He has really hurt himself, too. It's a constant worry, really. Obviously he can't work. In the eyes of the government, he's disabled.'

'Ah, I suppose he's leeching money off the rest of us paying our taxes, like all the others with depression and ADHD and all these made-up illnesses you lot have nowadays. Basically, he's just chronically lazy,' muttered Ben's father.

Now that was close to the bone. I felt it cut into me like a knife.

My boyfriend erupted. In fact, erupted was an understatement. It was as if someone had dropped a match into a tank of petrol. It made me jump and my heart race in my chest.

'Right, that's it. I've had enough.' He walked round to face his father, who was looking away from him. 'What the hell is your problem, Dad? I've brought Sienna here to meet you and Mum. She's incredible, and your ignorance is shocking. She's hard-working and patient and kind, and you have no idea what she's been through,' he yelled, drawing closer to his dad's face with each word until they were nose to nose. His breathing was fast and his nostrils were flared. A major scene appeared to be unfolding.

'Look, don't worry,' I said, pulling his muscle-bound frame away from the dismissive man sitting in the chair. This was all a bit shocking. Lucy, meanwhile, had escaped to the kitchen.

What an utter disaster. This couldn't actually have gone any worse. Why did Ben bring me here if he knew his father would act like this? I had so many questions to ask. I tiptoed into the kitchen and left my boyfriend and his father to their fight.

The shouting was barely audible through the heavy wooden door I had closed behind me. Lucy sat in the corner of the room, shaking with the stress of it all. I sat down softly beside her. 'Lucy, please don't worry. Please,' I pleaded with her, resting my hand on hers. Her skin was soft and crinkly, so delicate you could see the veins beneath.

'I'm so, so sorry, Sienna. I think we're losing him,' she sniffed.

'What do you mean, "losing him"?'

'I think he has some serious mental problems. He's been acting like this just lately – it's all very recent. It's not all the time, either – sometimes he's sweet and loving, and then he's like this. He isn't the man I married.' She threw her arms in the air in despair.

'So it's not . . . the alcohol?' I asked with trepidation.

'Well, that plays a huge part,' she admitted, tracing her finger over a napkin. 'But now he has these

302

big rants, these angry shouting sessions. He would never have been like that a few years ago, Sienna, never. He would have welcomed you in, cooked for you. Been the man he used to be. He would have adored you – you're lovely,' she finished, looking up at me with hope.

'I'm so sorry he isn't well, Lucy. I know what it's like to live with someone who's poorly,' I said, getting up. 'Would you like some tea?' I asked.

'Yes please, love.'

We only stayed for another couple of hours. Lucy and I had lunch together while Ben sat with his father, trying to work out what on earth had gone wrong. What had come unravelled in his mind? He searched for signs and answers in the angry tone of his father's voice and in his facial expressions. It must have been a hard thing to come home to.

'Sienna, I am so deeply sorry,' Ben said as soon as we piled into the car. It was dark by now and my shoe was still damp.

'Ben, please, don't. I know he didn't mean it. I just feel really bad for you. Really bad.' I turned towards him. I could see the outline of that lovely nose of his in the moonlight.

'I just can't believe it. I don't go back too often, but he has never been like this. To be honest, I kind of thought Mum was exaggerating when she mentioned it on the phone the other day, so I just forgot about it.' He looked down at his lap guiltily.

The journey home was a quiet one. I couldn't

see the geese or the fields in the darkness, but I imagined them. I suddenly realised I was in a proper relationship, a scary one with the 'I love you's and the complex family disasters. While I had been scared about what it would be like to meet a normal family, I soon realised that there wasn't one, really. There were so many family units out there, trying to get by without vital pieces of the typical working machinery. Mum, Dad, the kids and the dog. I thought about my beautiful Elouise, bringing up her little boy on her own, a lone soldier. I thought about Dad and me. I felt lucky in a strange way – lucky that it was just Dad and me, and we loved and understood each other entirely.

When I got back to the flat that evening I watched *Paris When It Sizzles* with Dad, his choice. Then I made him his favourite dinner, pesto pasta with goat's cheese, and ordered some books about colonialism for him online – it was the latest thing he was studying. I also bought some more of the black notebooks he likes to write in. While the day had turned sour in a most unexpected way, it had made me aware of a feeling closer to home: a feeling of gratitude and the simplicity of acceptance.

Nick

'I want to see the book.'
  'What book?'
  'You know which book I'm talking about, Nick.'

'Nope. If you're talking about the Bible, there isn't a copy in this house.' I grinned and started to crawl on top of Chloe, who was lying on the sofa in a pair of shorts and a racing-back vest. I nibbled on her neck but she pushed me away playfully.

'Very funny, Nick. I'm not talking about the Bible. I'm talking about the book Sienna made you for your birthday.' She raised an eyebrow, and wrapped a long, smooth leg around me.

'Oh, *that* book. Sure, no problem.' I got up and went to my room, taking each step very slowly like a child on its way to the dentist. I wanted to postpone the start of the next world war. Deep down I wondered how she even knew about it. I hadn't told her. It had been three months since my thirtieth birthday, and the book was placed in one of my drawers beneath unpaired socks and half-opened credit card bills. I wasn't exactly hiding it, but I didn't think Chloe would understand so it wasn't going to sit on my coffee table. I was a little nervous, if I was honest. Not from guilt, just through fear that Chloe would storm out and leave me with a plate of curry all over my face.

Opening the large oak doors of my wardrobe I noticed five hangers with Chloe's dresses on. This was new, I thought. I pulled open the drawer and felt around for the book, my fingers searching through a mountain of socks and pants until they ran across the edges of the thick paper. There it was.

I gently pulled it out and took it down to my girlfriend, who had now drawn a blanket around her and lit some candles. They filled the room with a vanilla scent, the kind of smell you would only have in your house if there was a woman in it. Nights like this were my favourite kind. It was achingly cold outside, and I was warm inside with a beautiful girlfriend and a takeaway. A chicken dansak, to be precise. A dish I hoped I wasn't about to be wearing.

'Don't you think we should wait until we've eaten and cleared away the food, Chloe?' I asked, wincing at the thought of curry oil blotting the pages and seeping into the photographs.

'No. I think we should look at it now,' she responded bluntly.

Her messy hair was pulled up into a high pony-tail and one of the plaits had become detached and was hanging next to her face. I sat next to her on the sofa, balancing the book on my left knee and her right knee. Some talentless plum was whining away like a dying animal on *The X Factor*, so I turned the sound down.

My pulse started to race. This was quite scary. How was she going to react?

'Right, let's have a look at this,' she said, wiping her fingers on the blanket. I wished she wouldn't do things like that.

The first page was the squirrel article clipping, something I'm amazed that Sienna kept. Even then, when we could have gone our separate ways and simply become colleagues who didn't really like each other very much.

Chloe gently leafed through the pages over the next fifteen minutes as I sat beside her, waiting for the fallout. Waiting for the claws and tears. She traced her index finger over some of the photos, read the receipts and tickets, trying to maintain an expression of calm and happiness. But it was fake. I could tell.

She saw everything: the photo booth, the trip to Amsterdam, even the dry-cleaning ticket from the time I dropped a garlic chicken on her lap in a French restaurant (long story). She reached the end, closed the book hard, took a deep breath and turned back towards the television. Silence.

'Oh come on, Chloe . . .' I said.

'What do you mean, come on? Why didn't you tell me about this?' she said, tears starting to drip from her eyes.

The doom feeling filled my stomach again. 'I was worried you would react like this, Chlo. That's exactly why I didn't tell you.' I sighed, realising this looked even worse now.

She continued staring at the telly, pushing a chunk of fluffy naan bread into her mouth as her chin wobbled. Another fat tear slid down her cheek.

'It's too much, Nick. I don't like it,' she said, wiping the water from her face with a shaking hand. The tears were falling rapidly now.

I shuffled closer to her and wrapped my arms around her slim shoulders, understanding why this would upset her, but knowing I wasn't guilty of anything.

'Listen, sweetheart, I'm sorry I didn't show it to you. She doesn't mean any harm by it. Look, maybe you should get to know Sienna a bit more, then maybe you'll understand what she's really like.' I instantly regretted this.

'Do you think we would get on?' she asked, but I was unsure whether or not she was being sarcastic.

Would Chloe and Sienna get on? Chloe: blonde, feline sexpot with a temper like molten lava and a raging libido. A smoking, drinking, wild child. Sienna: a naturally beautiful (stunning, in fact) angel whose biggest tantrum came when someone stole my wallet in Soho and the police wouldn't take a statement. Even then she just raised her voice a bit and slammed her fist on the desk. Carer to her father and a saviour to her friends. Calm, devoted, loyal and trusting. Probably not.

'Yes, of course you would,' I said, hoping we could change the subject. I suddenly imagined them in various coffee shops, eating shortbread and laughing over the size of my penis. Chloe might even tell Sienna that I fart in my sleep.

'Great, well, let's organise something,' she said. She was being serious.

'What?' I asked.

'Anything.'

'OK,' I agreed, taking a bite of chicken decadently steeped in the most delicious sauce.

'Can I have her number?'

'OK. I'm just eating now, but I'll give it to you later, yeah?' I replied, desperately hoping she would forget.

She nodded and turned the sound up, assaulting my ears with a tone-deaf builder from Stoke who had endured great tragedies in his personal life and now felt the need to torture the great British public live on air to make up for it.

'I got a good film for us to watch, you know,' I said as I cleared away the greasy plates, glad that this hadn't blown up into a proper row. I felt a wave of guilt at the thousands of calories but felt sure I would burn some of them off with a couple of hours of duvet sports. Well, if Chloe wasn't too upset still . . .

'That sounds lovely,' she responded, kicking off a pair of cute slippers. The impending storm seemed to have passed over.

From the doorway I looked at Chloe and saw her lying there with a look of contentment on her face. Maybe it was all over now. All the drama would dissolve and become this silly thing we'd once gone through when we were young and stupid. All the hurt and the confusion would fade into the blackness of a memory. I had found my girl. She had found her man. Simple.

'Chloe,' I called quietly from the edge of the living room.

'Yeah?'

'I love you.'

BEEP.

It was half past two in the afternoon, a Sunday afternoon to be precise, when I got the message. The olive-branch text from Chloe. It was a shock, to say the least.

'Hi, Sienna. It's Chloe. I got your number from Nick. Hope you don't mind. Are you free for a coffee this afternoon? Xx'

So that was how I ended up in an overpriced deli with her, warming my cold hands on a latte. The place was mainly decked out in green marble, with big glass counters displaying a feast of expensive meats, smelly cheeses and strange sticks of bread twisted like strands of DNA. There were numerous strings of salami hanging from the ceiling behind the tills, and the staff looked like genuine Italian food buffs, wiping their rough hands down crisp white overalls. Near the window was a gold freezer containing a plethora of brightly coloured ice cream packed with chunks of chocolate, pecan nuts and ripples of caramel, glittering under the dimmed lights. It was a typical trendy London haunt, selling things I could neither pronounce nor afford. It was nice, though.

Chloe was wearing a pair of light blue skinny jeans and a T-shirt with some band on it that I'd never heard of. As I knew already, Chloe was achingly cool.

I had been a little nervous about this, fearful

that she was going to start asking me about the incident in the toilet on Nick's birthday. The time when she overheard me telling her boyfriend that I adored him. We hadn't spoken about it since, but she was clearly furious at the time.

The café was packed with wealthy-looking couples, some with their children wearing miniature versions of designer labels. It really wasn't my cup of tea. We ordered a plate of shortbreads with little jam hearts in the middle.

'The reason I wanted to go out just us two is because obviously I'm going out with your best friend, and I've heard so many great things about you,' she gushed sweetly, brushing some crumbs away from her top lip. 'I don't know you, but I'd really like to. We work together and everything, but we hardly talk. I feel like you're a stranger, really.'

That was sweet, I thought, as I nibbled the edge of one of the biscuits, which crumbled luxuriously. Maybe we wouldn't discuss the toilet incident. I really hoped we wouldn't. I'd often thought about contacting her too, but she'd beaten me to it. I'd been hoping we could break the ice and shift all this awkwardness that had built up between us.

'Thank you. I'm really happy for you and Nick – he seems so chilled out now you're together.'

She smiled, a look of real accomplishment.

I recognised that expression. It was the look a woman wears when she has discovered the man she wants to be with, the man of her dreams. The one who inspires her to be a better person. And I can hardly blame her. For years he has been the man I want to be with too. He's a catch. And she is so lucky.

'Are you OK with Nick and me, you know, being friends?' I asked, my heart thumping hard in my chest. I believe in honesty and I'm not afraid to ask questions like this.

She looked down into the bottom of her cup and bit her lip. She was so damn pretty it hurt.

'I need to be truthful with you here, Sienna. I haven't always been OK with it. At times I've been really mean to Nick over it, kicked off and stuff because I was worried there was something more between you than there is.'

I didn't say a word; I was starting to experience tunnel vision. The bustle of the people around us seemed to slow right down and I was just looking at Chloe's face until I got double vision. There were two of her now.

'But he's told me time and time again that he's never felt anything for you like that, and that you're just friends.' Chloe almost sounded as though she was sneering. I felt like she was mocking me, but I knew I was only imagining it.

Just friends. I felt a sharp stabbing pain in my stomach as I imagined him holding her close at night and telling her that I wasn't a big deal. Maybe they even laughed about it. About me. But what did I expect? Of course that was what he was going to say. That was all he felt. I'd always known that, but hearing it hit me hard.

I suddenly thought about Ben and felt guilty that the disappointment had cut into me like this. 'Of course, Chloe. You should never feel worried about Nick and I. He's a pain, anyway,' I joked, touching her arm and giggling.

'God, I know!' she shrieked through hysterical laughter as all this energy ebbed from her. Love-fuelled energy, no doubt.

'He has all these really annoying habits, Sienna.' She leaned in and began to whisper. 'He always puts his head in his hands on his lap when he feels stressed or happy – or anything, really. And he doesn't wash up enough, and – oh, this is brilliant – he farts in his sleep!' With this she tilted her head back and started to wipe away a little tear of joy. A bunch of bracelets round her wrist jangled against each other like wind chimes.

I wondered if she really knew him well. Did she know what his favourite book was? How he likes to iron his boxers and put them in colour order? That he has a strange penchant for honey and banana on toast? Maybe she knew him better than I did now. Maybe I didn't really know him at all any more . . .

I imagined them getting married, and me some-where in the congregation with a large black hat on, as if I was in mourning. And how the vicar would ask if anyone had any lawful impediment, and I would have to keep my lips sealed for fear of shouting out that he was the love of my life, and somewhere along the line there had been a mistake. A terrible, terrible mistake.

A cold feeling rushed over my body and I felt detached from the room. It was as if I and the chair I was perched on were rushing backwards, away from the shortbread and the coffee and the Prada handbags, into some unknown world. I felt sick, just like I had that day in the gym.

Come on, Sienna. Wear the dress. I imagined pulling the green gown from my wardrobe, stepping into it and carefully zipping it up my back. I tried to feel tall and beautiful and proud of who I was. A strong, confident woman.

'Sienna, are you OK?' Chloe's voice brought me back and I realised I had been staring at her forehead in silence for quite a long time.

'Yes, sorry, I'm fine.'

But I wasn't. The feeling just wasn't going away. A gut-wrenching sensation, cold and tingling all over, like thousands of tiny needles were biting into my skin. 'Actually, Chloe, I'm not feeling too well. I have to go.' I shot up suddenly, the coffee cups clattering loudly as I bashed the table with my knee. Oh shit, I didn't want to make a scene. I just wanted to get out of there.

'Sienna, honey. I hope you're OK?' She reached out her arm, but it was too late. I was pushing past what seemed like rows and rows of prams all pressed together in a wall. It was like they were speaking, laughing, taunting me.

I felt guilty about leaving her there – she was such a nice, sweet girl. It wasn't her fault she'd fallen in love with Nick, anyone would. But I felt like poison and if I spent any real time with her, I would make her dangerous, just like I was. A bad person who loved other people's boyfriends.

I rushed through the streets and turned corners like they were the pages of a book I was desperate to finish. Street signs were a blur. Faces had no features. People spoke but no sound came out. Maybe I was going crazy. Maybe I should get some help. Someone, please help me.

My heart was pumping and my legs felt like jelly. I just needed to get away from there. As I pounded the concrete in my high-heeled boots I imagined what it would be like to just get the train to Heathrow and fly somewhere and not come back.

I needed to talk to someone, anyone. I jumped on the tube and went to Covent Garden. There were even more people there, thicker, deeper swathes of strangers to wade through. I started to run all the way to that strange dancewear shop I'd visited all that time ago. As mad as it sounded, I thought I could talk to that crazy lady. Maybe she would understand.

I turned one more corner and raced up to the shop window, but the door was closed. It looked dark inside. That was odd, I thought, while I caught my breath. After a few seconds I noticed a crumpled piece of white paper taped to the window. I pushed my nose against the glass and started to scan the wobbly handwriting.

Dear Esteemed Customers,
The Tarasov family would like to thank you all for your custom and kindness to our dear aunt over the years.
We regret to announce her death on 16 October after a brief battle with cancer.
Thanks again for all your support.
Mark Tarasov

I read the notice again and again and let out a deep sigh. My fingers were pressed against the glass and a tinge of condensation was gathering around them. I slid all the way down the window, leaving a sweaty trail with my hands until I collapsed on the dirty ground.

CHAPTER 10

'COME ON FELLA,
NOW DON'T BE SHY.'

Nick

Sienna's favourite singer in the whole wide world is a man called John Legend. Generally, I find her taste in music appalling. So much so that going through her iPod is enough to put me off my food. But with Legend, I can make an exception. His voice is so incredible, you question if it's actually possible for a human being to create such a sound.

I once wondered if he was a robot created in the dingy studio of some record label where they held the world's living musical greats hostage with string and duct tape and siphoned vials of their talent into little test tubes. The voice of John Legend consists of dulcet tones so velvet in musical texture that you almost lose the ability to walk. I swear my pants fell down listening to his album in the kitchen once. He must be a hit with the ladies, that's all I can say . . .

Not only does he sing like it's his last chance, he also plays the piano – and my God, does he know how to handle one of those. I bet he can tinkle out a concerto while flossing his teeth and trimming his toenails.

When I found out he was coming to London, I booked tickets.

'Chloe, do you want to go and see John Legend?' I asked, leaning back in my chair and peering into the hallway. I could see her moisturising her legs over the bath with a towel around her middle. She looked like something from an advert, her skin had that glow to it.

'Urgh, God no. Why don't you take Sienna?' echoed her reply from the bathroom.

'OK.'

Had I been hoping that would happen all along? I knew Chloe would think John Legend was totally uncool.

'Si, have you got a sec?' I whispered down the phone, excitement filling my chest.

'Yes, sweets, what's up?' she replied. I could hear her dad talking to someone in the background.

'I've got a surprise for you.'

'What?'

'I'm taking you out on Thursday night, you and me. You are free then, right? Please say you are?' I pleaded, fiddling with a coaster on my study desk. It was a see-through plastic one with a photo of Ross and me man-hugging each other on a booze-fuelled night out.

'Oh, that sounds exciting, Nick!' she responded before putting a hand over the receiver and checking that someone would be around for her dad.

'Yes, count me in! I'm really looking forward to it, whatever it is,' she giggled, putting the phone down.

I was so pleased she could come. Our relationships meant we had spent little time together recently. This would be our chance to have some fun, like we used to before life got so complicated.

The week went really quickly, and while work was hectic all I could think about was Thursday night. I just knew she would love it, and things had been quite full on with her father lately, so she needed someone to do a nice thing for her. I had the kind of relationship with Sienna that just inspired me to be a better person.

It was a sticky summer evening when I waited for Sienna outside the Brixton Academy. The back of my T-shirt was a tiny bit damp from the tube journey and I sought an escape from the heat by running a cold can of Coke over my forehead. Ticket touts were wandering around, cigarettes hanging from their mouths, trying to sell tickets to people who already had them. I couldn't help but feel they were missing a trick there.

Five minutes melted into ten, then fifteen. Sienna was late, and she's hardly ever late. I started to worry. What if something had happened to her dad? I was wondering if I should call when I suddenly heard my name being shouted from a distance. I looked up to see Sienna running towards me, her hair streaming through the wind, a gorgeous smile on her face. She was wearing skinny jeans with a pair of hi-top Converse trainers and a tight black T-shirt. Even this simple outfit made her look like a model. Mind you, she would look like a model with a bin bag on; it had nothing to do with the clothes.

Men turned their heads as she darted through the crowds of people standing around on the street. She was attracting quite a lot of attention, so I felt very proud when she ran up and flung her arms around me like she hadn't seen me for years. She smelled lovely. Her hair smelled delicious – I wanted to bury my face in it. But no, that wasn't how I was supposed to think any more, so I quickly pushed those thoughts out of my head.

'Now, Sienna, look up there,' I said when I had finally prised her off my chest, and pointed to the big cinema-style letters above the concert venue. I was standing behind her with both hands on her shoulders.

There it was, in bold black lettering: J.O.H.N L.E.G.E.N.D L.I.V.E T.O.N.I.G.H.T

She opened her mouth and covered her face with her hands. Wow, she was really touched by this. I'd thought she might figure out what I'd planned and spoil the surprise, but her reaction seemed quite genuine.

'Oh my God, Nick, thank you so much,' she

said, holding my hands and flashing that megawatt smile in my direction again.

'Come on, then,' I said, pulling her towards the entrance and extending a leg Basil Fawlty style.

As we walked, she gave me a kiss on the cheek. A short, sweet, 'thank you, friend' kiss on the cheek. I wanted to peel it off my face and stick it in a frame.

An impatient woman tore our tickets in half and ushered us through the double doors and into the circular darkness of the venue. The stage was illuminated with blue and green lights. It was so exciting.

We made our way to the bar where I flinched as I paid three times over the odds for a flat beer and a watered-down glass of wine. A famous DJ I've never even heard of was the warm-up act, swamping the room with beats and bass as it filled with chattering people; he was playing a host of hip-hop tunes, which I recognised but knew none of the words to. I suddenly felt old. Sienna, however, was mouthing each and every line. Moving her body gently to the beat of the music. It was so good to see her happy and relaxed.

'How's George?' I shouted above the buzz, squinting as a strobe light was tested right in my line of vision.

'Not great, Nick. He's been a lot worse lately. They've changed his medication and it isn't going so well. That's why I had to make sure his friend could keep an eye on him tonight because he can't be properly alone at the moment.' She stood on her tiptoes to see the stage as it was being set up. Five members of staff dressed all in black were plugging wires into various sockets and tapping on microphones.

I held her hand and pulled her through to a spot very close to the front. 'I'm sorry, Si. Is there anything I can do?'

I realised the absurdity of the comment as soon as I made it. Of course there was nothing I could do. I was about as useful as a chocolate fireguard. I wished there was something I could do to make things better.

'No, no. There isn't anything, thanks. Although he would like to see you soon. He's investigating human sense disorders at the moment – you know, people who can taste colour, smell sound and all that . . .' She rolled her eyes affectionately.

'I'm sure that can be arranged.'

After we'd been standing around for an hour listening to the DJ, Mr Legend finally came out. He was wearing a skinny grey suit and looked so good, I think every man in the room cringed in unison while their girlfriends swooned. Why would you take your girlfriend to one of his gigs?

There was a glossy black piano in the middle of the stage, waiting and wishing, like most of the women in the room, for the soulster to run his expert hands all over it. A small gospel choir was revealed at the back of the stage as a curtain rose. They had those wholesome smiles you only ever see on people who sing their cares away at the crack of dawn every Sunday, as opposed to lying in bed with a filthy hangover.

The room went quiet and he pulled up his stool, playing the first note of the night. It reverberated through the sound system perfectly. I knew this was going to be mind-blowing. Sienna was so excited she could barely contain herself. The music gave me the same warm feeling inside that I get when I am with Sienna. The two combined were setting my heart on fire.

Halfway through the third song Sienna's hand brushed against mine and I thought for a second she was going to hold it. I panicked momentarily before realising it was just an accident. This really wasn't getting any easier. After going to the bar for the second time, I thought it might be a good opportunity to ask how things had been going with Ben.

'Oh fine, thanks, yeah,' she whispered into my ear, keeping her eyes firmly on the stage.

'Just fine?' I asked quietly, horribly aware that the music could go quiet at any moment, leaving me shouting out across the room.

'Well. It's a bit difficult. He seems to have some fairly serious family problems I didn't know about, and instead of letting me help him, he's shutting me out. He just seems a bit distant sometimes and I don't understand why he won't talk to me about it, because you know, I might be able to help,' she finished, her eyes squinting in the glittering lights.

Distant? How anyone could keep any kind of distance from Sienna was beyond me.

'I'm sure he'll be back to his old self soon,' I responded positively.

She nodded silently and I couldn't help but notice how stunning her profile was.

I was trying really hard to be positive about this. I wanted Sienna to be happy, and Ben was by far the closest I had seen a man get to making her happy. The others, quite frankly, had been a disaster. Turning up late for birthdays, calling her the wrong name (no joke, she got called Fiona once), being too young and selfish . . .

We went back to watching the gig when something mortifying happened. I mean genuinely, really, deeply embarrassing.

'So, this next song is for all the people in love,' came the smooth voice of Mr Legend as he addressed the crowd, his hands hovering above the ivory keys in front of him. 'Y'all tell me if you're in love right now, Brixton!' he shouted, rising from the piano until he was standing in the centre of the stage.

The heat coming from the lights was creating small beads of sweat on his skin as the crowed roared out. Oh, come on, surely not everyone in this room was in love with someone, were they? Ridiculous.

Sienna and I stayed quiet, which I guess was a bad thing, looking back. He held the mike casually in his right hand. If I'd been up there I'd probably have started trembling like a leaf and just stood there in terror-induced silence under the spotlight while people threw their drinks at me.

'So for my final song, I want to sing this to some people in love. Do you think I can find two people who love each other in this room?' he cried, waving his arms in the air. More people screamed. One woman near the front fainted.

God, he was cool, I thought. Why can't I be a bit more cool? Then my thoughts were interrupted.

'You, over there in the blue shirt, I want you to come up here,' the singer said, crouching down at the front of the stage and smiling at some poor sod who was about to be hauled on to the stage.

Unlucky git, I thought smugly. Then: that's funny, he's pointing in my direction. I'm wearing a blue shirt too. Holy shit . . .

'Yeah, you, c'mon!' he said once more.

All of a sudden the crowd parted and it was just Sienna and I standing in isolation, our mouths wide open like farm animals selected for the slaughter. The rest of the herd turned and stared at us, smiling and whooping.

'No, no, you don't understand, she's not my . . .' I tried to speak but my voice was a mere squeak. Butterflies swamped my chest and my legs turned to mush. Oh no, I was going to faint like a girl, wasn't I? I could see my face fill the large screen to the side of the stage, the camera pointing straight at me. They were filming this too? Shit. Shit. Shit.

'Come on fella, now don't be shy,' said Legend one more time in his heavy American drawl, the enterprising smile still plastered across his face.

Next thing I knew, two security guards were ushering me towards the stage. Oh bollocks. I thrashed my arms around towards Sienna who was standing there, smiling, both hands to her face as if she was praying. Thanks a lot, Si. I'm going to need a prayer now. She was getting further and further away.

'Guys, guys,' I frantically whispered to the guards, trying in a terribly British way not to cause a scene. 'You don't understand, she isn't my g—'

'Oh, chill out, mate,' said one of them, laughing to the other. I couldn't work out which one of them had the shinier skull. It was like being led to my own execution by two men built like oak trees with bowling balls for heads.

As I was led to the left-hand side of the stage where the steps were, we marched past what seemed like dozens of people all clapping and smiling and waiting for something really romantic to happen. Well, they could sod off. I have a girl-friend, Sienna has a boyfriend, this is all just a big mistake.

I realised something deeply humiliating was going to occur and there was absolutely nothing I could do about it. Yup. I, Nick Redland, was about to be pulled up on stage in front of thousands of people and filmed making an utter twat of myself. And

I'd paid for this. I had paid for my own humiliation. Brilliant.

I have always feared the whole going onstage thing since I was picked out at the circus at the age of five and promptly threw up all over a clown's lap. It was awful.

We reached the stairs.

One. Two. Three. Four. Stage.

'Ah, here he is,' said Mr Legend as he walked towards me and took my arm gently. Everyone clapped. Gosh he was handsome.

'What's your name, bro?' he asked before turning the microphone towards my quivering mouth. I wanted to bite it so it would stop working, but that would have been a bit weird. I'd have definitely ended up in the papers for that. I imagined a picture of me on the front page, a mouth full of metal and blood, frayed wire poking out from between my lips.

'Nick,' I replied moodily.

'Well, everyone, this is Nick. Say hello to Nick.'

The whole crowd shouted my name back to him. Oh shit. They knew my name now and everything.

He pulled me in front of the piano and kneeled down towards the people gathered below him, his eyes scanning back to where we had been standing.

'Now that lady there, in the black T-shirt and jeans, is your girl, right?' he asked, pointing towards Sienna who was probably also soiling herself.

A huge spotlight swung across the audience,

making her the centre of attention and plunging my frantic head-shaking into inky, unnoticed darkness. Damn it.

I mopped my brow quickly and whispered in his ear, 'Mate, there's been a mistake, she's just a—' and would you believe it, I was interrupted again.

'What's your name, beautiful?' he asked, holding his right hand to his ear.

Her mouth was still open and she stared at him in fear and wonder. Speak, Sienna! Speak! Tell him we're just friends, for God's sake. I was hoping I could transmit these messages to her telepathically.

'I can't hear you,' said Legend, looking a little panicked that he might have chosen the most socially inept non-couple in the room.

'Sienna!' she shouted out, shrugging her shoulders at me.

'Now, Nick, I'm going to play this next one for you and Sienna.' His face was very close to mine now.

This was being filmed for his live DVD, which would be for sale all over the world. The globe. That would mean people in China, Canada, Africa, France would be able to watch me, onstage, wondering if it might be possible to pack my own body into a suitcase and carry myself off. A fake smile spread across my face.

'Sienna, come up here, girl!' he yelled, raising both arms towards the blistering lights.

Oh no. It actually gets worse. I saw the heavies

buzz towards her and 'help' her onto the stage. Within a minute she was standing next to me in front of the whole world, with her arm around my waist. I was sweating. Heavily. People were cheering.

Chloe and Ben were probably going to see this. Someone would post a copy through my gran's door, and after finally working out how to operate a DVD player, she would immediately assume I was a cheating bastard and never talk to me again.

'So, here we have some love in the house,' said Legend, walking slowly towards the grand piano, leaving us clutching each other and trembling.

The crowd roared. There were whistles and shouts and more fainting women. My head felt very light, as if it were a little balloon about to roll off my shoulders.

'We're here to celebrate love, y'all. This is what my music is all about, so let's give it up for Nick and Sienna,' he grinned, apparently genuinely believing that she and I were a couple as he started to play the first notes.

A proper couple that slept next to each other every night, packed lunches together in the morning and shared showers. A proper couple that did *the love thing*.

Sienna squeezed me tight around my waist and whispered in my ear, 'OK, Nick. This is obviously very bad. Very, very bad. But there's nothing we can do. So let's just roll with it, OK?'

She turned to smile at me, with those eyes, those cheeks and those teeth, and I suddenly felt like everything was all right. I wanted to kiss her, there, in front of everyone. She was much braver than me, definitely.

'This one's not just for Nick and Sienna, it's for all of you who love somebody. So one by one, I want couples to join our friends here and dance to my song. Do you think we can do that?' There was immense screaming by this point.

Dance? Hold on a minute. I'm not good at that. I prayed for a slow song so that I could just randomly shuffle my legs and it might look OK from a distance . . . And then he started to sing. It was beautiful. I realised I was holding on to Sienna pretty tight. Then she turned to face me under the white lights and put her arms around my waist, her glossy hair tumbling down her shoulders and shining under the bulbs. My heart was thumping so hard, but for a moment it seemed to slow down. It was as if it were just she and I, alone. As if her favourite singer in the world was merely playing from a tiny radio in the corner of the room.

I must have looked frightened because she gave me a reassuring look and pulled my body closer to hers. It was the perfect fit. She was so warm and gorgeous. I put my arms around her waist and rested my nose on her forehead. Her hair smelled fresh, her skin was soft. I started to smile, but at the same time I felt this deep sadness as we slowly danced on the spot in front of thousands of people. I wasn't supposed to be doing this. This wasn't my place. My hands didn't belong around her waist. Ben's did.

One day, Sienna would get married and I would have to go along and wear a suit and a flower in my buttonhole and smile all day. I would have to watch another man marry the woman I love.

Eventually, other couples started to join us on the stage. Thank God, I thought. There were all sorts of people starting to dance around us until we melted into the scene like two dots in a Roy Lichtenstein painting.

We could have got away with letting go at this point and wiping our hands down our trousers like they were covered in bin juice. But we didn't, we kept dancing and just stared into each other's eyes as the people moved around us.

Old people. Young people. Tall people. Short people. Lots and lots of people who all had one thing in common. Love.

Sienna

Pete wasn't on the bench this lunchtime like he usually is. This was strange, but not completely out of character. He loves the common nearby, so I assumed he would be there instead.

The common is only a five-minute walk away, so I decided to head down there just in case. It was a blistering hot Friday lunchtime. London had that summer atmosphere where all men think they can whistle at you from their cars and comment on your bum, and people think it's acceptable to wear sunglasses on the tube. Neither is OK. Even in 30-degree heat.

But maybe this sensational heat was the reason Pete was on the common, rather than sitting in the boring car park behind our office. I could hardly blame him. I strolled through the busy streets that led to the common; people were wearing loose, colourful clothes and had broad smiles on their faces. I felt good, and couldn't wait to tell Pete about last night's gig incident and how funny it had been. I knew he would love this story . . .

As I approached the edge of the common I gazed at the huge expanse of grass stretching out before me. The endless field of leafy green was beautiful. I took in a huge gulp of the summer air, letting it fill my lungs entirely.

On the occasions Pete and I have gone to the common, we've always sat on a huge, fallen-down tree. It's a beautiful shape, full of holes that birds and squirrels dart in and out of as if they're playing hide and seek with each other. I bet he would be there. My trainers sank into the springy grass and I quietly cursed myself for not wearing sandals today. I was going to get really hot sitting in the sun.

After a few turns, negotiating giggling children and smooching couples nuzzling amongst the daisies, the tree came into view. But there was no one there.

My heart sank a little. I'd been looking forward to seeing him. Our little meetings had become a very important part of my life. Despite his absence I went and sat on the tree for a couple of minutes, firstly to catch my breath, and secondly to contemplate whether or not I should keep looking for him. Maybe he just wanted some privacy today.

I eventually stood up and started the short walk back to the office, but something caught my eye as I neared the road. The figure of a man, standing under a tree and looking up through the branches towards the clear blue sky.

Normally this wouldn't interest me at all, but he was swaying and his body language had that slightly eccentric air. The other thing was the man's frame. I would recognise it anywhere. I was sure it was Pete . . .

I shielded my eyes to block out some of the sunlight; it was difficult to be sure, having to squint. He kept swaying, his arms out by his sides. No. Maybe it wasn't . . . I started to walk towards the road again, but something made me stop. The man turned to look at me and then quickly whipped his head away and starting pacing in the other direction. It was definitely Pete.

I started to run towards him. As he walked away he kept turning his head back round, but not looking into my eyes as if he was trying to get away with not noticing me.

'Pete!' I yelled, but he continued to charge away. This was so strange. Not like him at all. 'Pete!' I called out again, even louder. People were looking as I sprinted in his direction, but I didn't care.

Eventually he stood still with his back to me. I caught up with him and clamped my hand on his shoulder. 'Pete! What the hell? Why were you running away?' I cried, trying to make it sound like I was mildly amused rather than slightly irritated. I was definitely the latter.

He hung his head as if he'd been caught shoplifting.

'Pete, turn around. What's going on?' I pleaded, starting to feel a little nervous.

Suddenly a smell of beer hit my nostrils. It was coming from him. That was why he was swaying.

He lifted his head and spun round, a look of utter shame on his face. His eyes had that watered-down look people get when they have been drinking. A lot. He kept his mouth tightly shut. My heart started to beat fast. He looked so strange to me. I was a bit scared, if I'm honest. He seemed like he'd never met me before.

'Look, Sienna, I've . . . I've got to go,' he said, slurring his speech and stumbling violently as he took a step forward. My breath caught in my throat as I noticed he was missing some of his lower teeth. It was a huge shock. The nightmare of when someone you really care about is hurt and you can't get any sense out of the situation. What the hell had happened?

I stood and watched as he swayed away from me, catching his shoe in a rabbit hole and nearly falling to his knees. I couldn't just leave him. Something really bad must have happened.

'Pete, come on! Will you just sit down and talk to me for a bit?' I begged, running up to him again and pulling his arm until his knees buckled and he landed next me on the lush green grass.

There were two main things to address here. The first being that he was pissed. Very pissed. The second was the tooth thing. The lack of teeth in his mouth. Teeth that had been present and correct the last time we'd spoken. I could be angry at him for being so drunk. I could jump down his throat and shout at him, but that would achieve nothing. I had to be very careful about the way I handled this.

'Oh God, Sienna. Can't I be just alone? I mean just be alone, please?' he mumbled, squinting in the sun and yanking a handful of grass out of the ground like an angry child.

I chose to ignore this. 'Something really strange happened last night, Pete,' I said, crossing my legs and hoping that if I could draw him into a different conversation he would calm down and trust me enough to tell me what had happened.

'What was that, Si?' he asked irritably, flopping onto his back and looking into the blue sky. He picked up a wooden coffee stirrer, which was starting to splinter at one end, and began chewing it. I flinched inwardly at the thought of where it could have been. He didn't seem to care at all.

'Well, Nick took me to a concert, to see my

favourite singer. John Legend,' I started, wondering how wise this was.

Pete rolled over so he wasn't facing me. He was wearing a pair of jeans, which he had cut off at the knee to make shorts. These were paired with a promotional T-shirt emblazoned with the Andrex puppy. He almost had style, in a strange 'this was given to me free and I had no choice' kind of way.

'Tell me more,' he said with sarcasm, throwing the splintered wooden stick into the distance. I suddenly imagined some poor terrier choking to death on it, so I ran over to pick it up and put it in the bin. Pete sighed angrily as I returned and continued my story.

'Well, it was all going fine, but then the singer thought we were a couple and asked us onto the stage while he sang a song about love.' I grimaced again, as I had so often today when talking to my friends about this latest 'incident'. I suddenly realised that talking about Nick and me, and my problems, was not a good way to distract him. It actually sounded pretty self-absorbed. I just didn't know how to handle this situation. He groaned, loudly.

I pulled my legs up in front of me and looked down at my bright red trainers, thinking about how badly this attempt at a story was going down. I decided to stop.

Wondering what to do next I started fiddling with the tongue of one of my shoes, which was emblazoned with a vintage Adidas logo.

'How are things going with your boyfriend anyway?' Pete asked flippantly, pulling a packet of peanuts from his jeans. He spat out a piece of chewing gum before he shoved the first load of nuts into his mouth. He definitely smelled of pub now. His tone was loaded with contempt but I chose to answer his question.

'Not great. We went to visit his parents during the winter – I think I told you about it back then?' Pete nodded in recognition. 'Well, I've tried really hard to be there for him, but he's been pushing me away recently,' I said, feeling sadness consume me. The odour of beer wafted up my nostrils again.

'Do you think it has anything to with your closeness with Nick?' asked Pete, in a sharp, accusatory tone which made my breath catch in my throat.

I pulled my aviator sunglasses from my bag and slid them over my eyes, dragging my cardigan under my head in a bid for more comfort. I felt defensive all of a sudden. Pete had always been on 'my team' throughout all of this. Now it was like he hated me.

'It's hard to tell. He's always been really cool about it, actually. Like he isn't at all bothered. I've been trying so hard, trying to be there for him, but I don't know if I can keep pushing it any more.'

I realised how fatalistic this sounded. Like it was the beginning of the end. The start of the last chapter. I was pretty sure that if Ben had loved me, he didn't any more, and that maybe he was too much of a coward to just tell me and walk away. No one apart from Dad can ever love me for long, and it's not like he can really go anywhere. He doesn't have much choice.

Pete groaned again before hiccupping twice, his ribs sticking out through his T-shirt. A pang of guilt assailed me as I realised how long he'd been sleeping rough now, and how I'd done nothing to improve his life apart from bringing him treats and boring him with tales of woe from my excessively complex love life.

'Anyway, enough of me. What happened to you?' I asked, rolling onto my tummy to face him and glancing at his teeth. He sighed angrily and said nothing.

'The thing is, Pete . . . This is hard to say, but you do kind of smell like beer today.' I looked him straight in the eye.

The fact that he'd apparently given up all his vices had amazed me. It had been going too smoothly, really, but I was gutted at the idea that he might be hiding his drinking from me, and that he could be so dishonest to my face. We all need vices – Nick smokes sometimes, my dad has an unhealthy interest in chocolate, I am inclined to binge shop when the going gets tough . . . But when all you have to comfort you in life is the buzz from a can of beer, I can imagine it would be very hard to throw it in the bin. The worst thing was that I kind of sympathised with him, but at the same time, I was scared for him. Scared of my own naivety, too.

He bowed his head in shame and said nothing, but his body language said it all.

'Come here,' I said, reaching my hand gently towards his chin. His bottom lip looked really sore. The smell of alcohol was pungent now. I gently pulled his lip down; he flinched slightly before slapping my hand away like it was a wasp. It made me jump. Any calm we had achieved was gone, since he now looked as angry as he had when I'd first run up to him.

'What happened, Pete?' Tears instantly started to sting my eyes as I saw the aggression in his face again. Just like that time with the photo . . .

'You're just a young girl!' he spat, sitting up quickly, balancing his elbows on his knees and burying his face in his hands. 'What the fuck do you know about hard times, huh? You, with your posh clothes and your good job and your cushty home life!' He pushed his lower jaw out in anger.

His words cut into me. I didn't know what to say, so I stayed silent for a minute or two. 'Did . . . did someone hit you, Pete?' I asked eventually.

He turned to face me again, fury painted across his features, and blinked hard, a funny twitch he had developed some time over the past year. I looked closer at his lip; it was a dark purple.

'Of course they fucking did, Sienna. What, did you think I'd walked into a sodding tree or something?' he snapped.

I jumped a little and a huge lump caught in my throat. I started to sweat. His eyes were boring into mine now. I could see his rage flickering inside like a flame. It was terrifying.

'And yes, Sienna. I am pissed. I got the crap beaten out of me last night, so today I found as much beer as I could get my hands on and drank the whole sodding lot, OK? Happy now?' He spat forcefully onto the grass.

'Well no, I'm not happy, Pete. I'm really—'

But he interrupted me again. 'There's nothing a silly little girl like you can do to help, so why don't you just stop trying, yeah?'

This was all too much for me. 'Just tell me what happened and I'll go,' I said, my voice trembling with fear.

'You want to know what happened? You want to know about the real world? OK, here goes, but I hope you can handle it, Sienna. I was sleeping under the big oak tree just over there and some kids came up to me. They were laughing at me, then one of them kicked me in the stomach for no reason. They tried to take my backpack, but it had my picture in it, the one of Jenny, so I pulled it away from them really hard. I didn't realise my own strength, and one of the kids was thrown to the ground. And then I realised they weren't really kids, they were more like nineteen or twenty. My teeth came out in one punch. I spat them out near the tree. All right?' He was breathing hard now.

I imagined the kids. The taunting. The swearing. The laughter. I had seen it on TV before, in violent films.

'Go away, will you, Sienna? I don't want you around me right now,' he finished, staring into the distance.

Tears filled my eyes and I felt exactly that – a silly little girl. I felt angry, too. He had no idea what I'd been through. I didn't have a cushty home life. Far from it. 'See you around,' I uttered through a lump in my throat before standing up quickly and walking away, tears spilling down my cheeks.

I was furious. Furious with Pete for talking to me like that. Furious with myself for meddling in things that were bigger than me. And furious with the bastards who'd hurt him.

I was a young girl once. 'Silly' had amounted to trying to get a stranger to buy me cider from the off-licence, standing on a worm to see if it really would turn into twins, or asking Elouise to pierce my ears – *not* beating people up and knocking their teeth out. I wiped my tears away and tried to compose myself on the way back to the office. I was shaking.

The air con hit me like a wall of ice as I entered reception; it tickled the back of my throat. It was just Sandra this time, sitting in a bright orange shirt, reading a copy of *OK!* magazine. Her pink lipstick and gold bangles reminded me of the kind of women you see in the Costa del Sol, picking away at their fruit salad in a hotel canteen, hairy-chested husbands in tow.

'Hello. Where have you been, then?' she asked, barely poking her head above her trashy mag.

'Er, just at the common with Pete,' I responded, hoping she wouldn't ask me too many questions and looking away so she wouldn't see my puffy face. She works in reception, of course she would ask questions. She makes it her business to know the ins and outs of everything.

'Who's Pete, love? Your new boyfriend?' She raised an eyebrow cheekily.

'No. The homeless guy.'

All of a sudden I had her full attention. The magazine was on the desk. 'Oh, you aren't still hanging around with *him*, are you? I thought you'd be bright enough to stay away from him,' she said, treating me to a disdainful pout that would give Dill a run for his money.

This reaction annoyed me even more so I pushed the lift button and hoped it would hurry up. I knew if I carried on talking to her I would snap.

'Sorry, Sandra, I just . . .' I muttered evasively. She never heard the rest of the sentence because it wasn't worth finishing. It scared me how ignorant some people were.

I wanted to change the world. Take it all on. Make it better. Dad always says it's my age and that after a while you give up on stuff like that and just worry about what you're going to cook for dinner and how many teabags are left in the cupboard. But I hadn't reached that point yet. I was going to do something good for Pete.

The second I got back to my desk I started searching for information online. Reams and reams of data was available – reports, government guidelines, funding information, case studies, figures . . . I was just looking for one phone number, really. Someone who could help us. And I mean really help us. Not give us leaflets that all led to nowhere.

It was then that I picked up the phone and called the biggest homelessness charity in London. 'Hi. Yeah, sorry, my name's Sienna. Sienna Walker. I have a friend who's homeless and we need some help . . .'

CHAPTER 11

'LOOK, THIS DOESN'T CHANGE ANYTHING, OK?'

Nick

I'm asking Chloe to move in. Yes. I've decided. I'm still scared about her stuff being in my house. I'm *still* not totally comfortable about seeing ornate bottles of lip cream or whatever it is they're filled with all over the bathroom. But I know I really care about her, so I've decided to face my fear. And I'm still scared about being left again, just like Amelia left me before. It's always been in the back of my mind, but it's not logical, is it? You can't tar everyone with the same brush.

I see it a little like a bungee jump or white-water rafting. I know it will be good for me. I know it's the best thing. So I'm going to do it.

I'm absolutely sure I love Chloe. Well, pretty sure. I've said it a few times now and I haven't felt that panic which has taken over when I've uttered it before and realised in retrospect it just wasn't true. I love having her by my side all night. I love cooking together. I love seeing her beautiful silhouette in the glass of the shower door when I'm shaving. I just love the whole thing.

So if this is my final fear, it's time for me to shuffle my toes to the edge of the diving board, look down at the glittering water and let go. Immerse myself in it well and truly, until I've washed away all this fear and bullshit. Everything.

Surely it's normal to feel a bit of trepidation about this kind of thing? Most people do, I expect. Especially when you're inviting someone to make your house their home. Your house where you can indulge in as many guilty pleasures as you want without any prying eyes. Strange sandwich combinations, scrubbing dishes with a flannel when you run out of sponges, and stashing a toilet roll, a tin of gherkins and some extra-strong mints in your room just in case there's some kind of national emergency and the supermarkets are full of panic-buying morons. Well, you *never know* . . .

And I know, I know. I had this thing about office relationships, but it's always gone so well, it never seemed like a good enough reason to walk away from her . . . Chloe is at my place pretty much all the time, so the only thing left to do is fill this little pocket of anxiety with a big, bold move. It really is time I grew up. I'm very aware of this.

Plus, I think it's a move that will push away any last tiny bit of agonising over Sienna. I can't spend the rest of my life pining and wanting and never really doing things properly because I'm hanging on to some impossible crush. Anyway, I pretty much have it all sorted now. This will be the final part of the cure. If Chloe lives with me, I won't be able to spend any time mooning over our photo book or hovering my finger over the number 2 button on my phone for twenty-five minutes at a time.

But before I officially asked Chloe, I decided I should get some advice from Sienna. After all, she is my best friend.

I asked her to meet me in Alexandra Palace, one of my favourite parks in London. From the top you can see what seems like the whole of the city sprawled out in front of you like a perfect painting. Sometimes I sit here and imagine the buildings and the hills have been sketched in thick charcoal, so you can just see the outlines and curves. I imagine what it might be like to try and recreate it as a graphic, but I feel I could never do it justice. Photographers try to capture this scene and sell it in tacky frames on street corners, but nothing beats just being here and using your eyes. This would be a great place to put my demons to bed once and for all, and I couldn't think of anyone better to help me. My beautiful little demon.

I made some sandwiches this morning so we could share them on the hill. The fridge was full of horrible processed ham, stale cheddar, and pickle with new forms of life setting up camp inside the jar. Hell, if it had just been me, I'd have cut the funky bits from the cheese and carried out some excavation work on the pickle, but this was for Sienna too. I was horribly aware of just how beautifully classy she was. She was too good for the vile Betty Swollocks student sandwiches of my past and, sadly, my present. I eventually chose to carve up a relatively fresh cucumber and slice up some sad-looking chicken left over from dinner. It wasn't great.

Still thinking about the battle I'd had cutting the loaf with a brutal hangover and a blunt knife, I gazed at Sienna splayed out messily on a vintage Danger Mouse beach towel. The sandwiches had never actually made it to the park. I felt a twinge of guilt when I remembered myself having second thoughts just before I met up with her, throwing the sandwiches into a bin near the tube station, and rushing into the nearest posh shop to buy some new ones. I hate waste, and this was *very* wasteful.

Her long brown hair was shining, revealing deep red tones that only really appeared when the sun shone. A statement pair of oversized, trendy sunglasses were wedged awkwardly against her nose as her head pressed against the ground. I had to stop myself from gently moving her and pulling them from her face so she could just fall asleep properly, because that was what she needed, really. I found myself looking at her body, my eyes settling on her hipbones, just visible below a navy Franklin & Marshall vest top, which had slid up when she'd thrown herself to the ground.

Now come on, Nick. Be strong. This was supposed

to be the big move that would change my life; I wasn't going to let the childish yearnings of my past get in the way of it. I could finally close the book of Sienna's and my one-sided love story, literally and metaphorically. She wouldn't care anyway. Plus she has Ben, and she has never seen me how I see her. If she did, I know we'd be sitting in my living room right now, holding on to each other tight while watching reruns of our favourite comedies.

We lay there quietly for a while. Then Sienna propped her sunglasses on her head and opened her sea-blue eyes and raised an eyebrow quizzically at me. 'Oh gosh, what? Are my pants showing? I'm wearing horrible pants today . . .' she trailed off, pulling at the band of the offending under-crackers with her thumb. I hadn't actually noticed them, but now she'd pointed them out, they did seem pretty dire.

'So, I made some really posh nosh, Si,' I announced, pulling the culinary surprises cloaked in brown paper from my bag. Sienna sat up sharply, crossing her legs and clasping her hands together in anticipation.

I tore away at the crisp wrapping to reveal some Brie and cranberry offerings, which looked very much like they'd come from the deli counter of an overpriced organic café. I wasn't going to get away with this, was I? I winced inside as the guilty flashback returned. Not only was I passing off carefully prepared food as my own, but my mother's voice rang in my ears, the things she said when she used to lecture me as a child about all the starving people in the world . . . There I had been, just half an hour earlier, at the deli counter of an overpriced organic café, handing over a crisp ten-pound note. I hadn't got too much change.

'I made them,' I said proudly, swiftly scrunching a branded serviette from the inside of the bag into unrecognisable oblivion and tossing it behind me while her head was turned. Why did I feel the need to lie to her about stuff like this? To impress her? Even after all this time? It was pathetic, really.

'Wow, they look so yummy,' Sienna replied, her eyes even brighter than usual. I think I got away with it, you know . . .

'Well, I made some things last night, actually,' she said, that stunning grin spreading across her freckled face. From a small Puma tote she whipped out a home-made banoffee pie. This was followed by a small salad full of plump-looking cherry tomatoes, which were almost panting in the 30-degree heat. Next to that was a fresh, fluffy-looking quiche nestled snugly against a blue freezer block. This was typical Sienna, kind and caring. She'd probably had to wrestle it from George that morning. That would explain the small chunk of missing pie.

'Well, that looks fab, Si, thanks very much.' She'd still managed to outshine me, even with my expensive subterfuge.

'So, what brings us here?' she asked, looking excited about whatever news I was about to impart.

'Well, something huge is going to happen. But I just needed to ask you first, because I'm a bit scared, really. And you're my best friend, Si, and I need you to tell me it's right.'

I realised how needy I sounded. But I really was that needy. Even choosing which pants I was going to wear was difficult without her. I asked her everything, from how much onion I should put in a curry to which shoes I should wear on a date (apparently, if you get it wrong, it can be a deal-breaker).

'OK,' she grinned, pulling a tissue from her bag and dabbing her lips. 'Fire away.'

'All right, I'm just going to come out with this,' I warned her.

I noticed she put her food down and shifted her arms behind her, as if to steady herself. Then she quickly put her sunglasses back on.

'I'm going to ask Chloe to move in with me.'

Slowly she stopped chewing until her face was absolutely still. She didn't say a word.

'Si?' I asked, slightly shocked at her reaction.

'Er, sorry. Sorry, Nick – I'm really tired, you know. That's, that's, well, it's fantastic!' she cried, leaping towards me and wrapping her arms around me with the delicacy and finesse of a baby tiger. She almost knocked me over.

I felt a lump build in my throat. A hard lump right in the middle of my neck, as if I'd tried to swallow a pebble and it was stuck there, hopelessly. I just held on to her for a bit. We sat there for what seemed like forever; it didn't feel bad, or wrong. She was so happy for me, and that was lovely.

The silence was freaking me out a bit so I started filling the gap with comments about which removal company we would use to get her stuff over and where we could go to get cushions, because she wanted more of those, apparently.

An elderly couple walked past and smiled at us. Over Sienna's shoulder I saw a helicopter circle over a tall office block; it reminded me of when I was little and had an obsession with ''copters' – that's what my father said I used to call them, anyway. And here I was, a grown man with proper adult problems, worries and responsibilities, looking at a real helicopter from my favourite patch of grass.

It wasn't until Sienna finally shifted and sat back down that I noticed a damp streak down her cheek. A perfect little line, as if it had been painted on with a tiny brush.

Her shades were so dark I couldn't see her eyes at all. She looked down at her sandwiches.

'Si? Are you OK?' I asked, realising that she must have been holding on to me for so long because she didn't want me to see her cry.

'Yeah, yeah, of course. So what are you doing for the rest of the weekend?' she asked, suddenly finding her salad very interesting, staring intently at the lettuce leaves as though she had dropped her debit card in there.

'Come on, Si,' I said quietly, shuffling my bum

towards hers and sitting by her side so our arms and legs were touching.

'Well, I don't know what you're doing, but I'm going to get some more books for Dad, and then I'm going to visit an exhibition, and then . . . and then . . .' And then she started to cry. My stomach lurched. Shit.

'I'm sorry,' she yelped, between delicate little breaths. She still wouldn't take her sunglasses off and proceeded to poke a tissue underneath the lenses in a desperate bid to soak up her feelings.

'I'm just so happy for you. I'm just so thrilled you've finally found *that* girl, you know?' She sniffed and looked at me.

I looked at her back. 'So you think I'm doing the right thing?' Thank God her tears were happy ones.

'Yes, you silly bastard!' she yelled, pushing me playfully and causing me to tilt to my left and overbalance slightly.

'But don't forget about me, Sienna, please. We can still see each other loads. Chloe loves you. Nothing has to change. Do you promise that nothing will change?' I turned to look at her now, hoping she would make that vow and then everything would be all right. I realised there was a hint of desperation in my voice. I even made a movement with my hands and face to simulate our nights with Donkey Kong and a cigar. She looked away like a hurt animal and stayed quiet.

'Si, please? Nothing changes, OK, that's the deal.' I poked the top of her hand with my index finger. What was that all about? I might as well have started hanging on to her legs and tugging at her trousers like a kid.

'Things will change, Nick. But it's for the best,' she said finally, after taking a deep lungful of the sweet summer air. I could almost feel her rushing away from me; I wanted to hold on to her just so she wouldn't turn into sand and slip through my fingers.

'What do you mean? No it doesn't,' I said, starting to feel like I was pleading with her now.

'It's not fair, Nick. It's not fair on Chloe. I'm not saying we can't be great friends, but if you two are going to be really serious, that's a different level. Do you know what I mean?' She opened her right hand onto her knee, revealing the pale skin that hadn't been touched by the sun.

I knew how those hands felt. They were soft and warm, because I'd held them once when she was sad. I'd peeled them open in the car all that time ago when she'd fallen over on the concrete and wiped away the drops of blood. There was no evidence of that now. No scarring. We heal amazingly well, I thought.

'No, I don't know what you mean,' I answered, starting to feel the lump in my throat again. Fuck off will you, stupid emotions.

'Well, I know you and I are just friends, and that's all it ever has been. But I wouldn't like it if I lived with you. Do you understand?'

I couldn't believe what she was saying. The words

were spilling from her mouth as easily as 'Keep the change' or 'No mayo with that, thanks.'

A football came out of nowhere and smacked me in the side of the head. My ear started to ring. I threw it back irritably, a little bit harder than I'd planned. This was a vital moment, too important to be interrupted by flying objects pelted by boisterous children with despondent parents.

Sienna whipped her head round and watched it sail through the air before it plopped into some water, scaring the shit out of a duck in the process, which quacked in panic and flapped its wings.

'Nick! You threw it into the pond! They aren't going to be able to get that now!' she yelled angrily at me.

'I don't give a shit, Sienna. This is important.' I pulled her arm gently as she started to get up to retrieve it.

She landed back down beside me like a balloon on a string. I could hear the snotty-nosed children whinging like they were right next to my ear. I tuned them out. 'Look, this doesn't change anything, OK?' I said, with a new level of determination. 'She pretty much lives with me now and we can still do everything we did before. It's going to be OK.'

A horrible ache filled my stomach. I was all too familiar with this sensation, and it felt like doom. As though Chris Moyles had casually announced on Radio 1 that the world was going to end, before dropping the needle on an N-Dubz song and playing it on repeat while we all huddled in groups, drinking ourselves to death. It was *that* bad.

'No, Nick. It's not fair on her,' she insisted, lying back down on the grass and curling into a tight ball. She only ever did that when she was really unhappy. She used to do that when Daniel House was being an idiot, which was quite often.

'But there's nothing like that between us, Si – nothing to feel guilty about,' I lied, trying to make it all OK. I guess I secretly hoped that she would just tell me that there *was* something. That there was something more between us than half a metre of lush green grass and the sticky summer air, which was so heavy you could almost dig a spoon into it.

I lay back beside her, lifting my T-shirt up slightly as the sun beat down on us, unforgiving and inescapable as the spotlights the time we were on stage. She pulled a thick layer of hair over her eyes.

'Hey, Si. Are you really happy for me?' I rolled over and faced her, hoping she would stop pushing me away.

'Yes, Nick. I'm thrilled. She's incredible. You're both very lucky,' she responded.

Genuinely. Truthfully. I knew she meant it. 'And you're going to stop all this silly talk about us, aren't you?' I asked.

She said nothing.

Sienna

It's Monday and things aren't good.

Mondays are bad enough as it is. There are more people on the train than on any other day of the week, the corner shop always runs out of croissants by the time I get there, and it's the day of the editorial meeting, where Ant successfully quashes all of our journalistic ambitions in the course of an hour. Even on a sunny day like today, things are distinctly rubbish.

And this Monday I got up and approximately five minutes later, I remembered what had happened on Saturday, and then I felt even more shitty. Yes. There was a blissful 300-second period where I'd forgotten what had happened just two days before. When I remembered, I was in the middle of brushing my teeth, and I bit the head of my toothbrush in frustration.

It had all started at around 9 a.m. when I'd had a text message from Nick asking me to meet him at Alexandra Palace because he had 'something huge to ask me'. I thought this might be it, you know. That moment I'd been waiting for all this time, where he might have chosen a view over London on a sunny day to tell me I was all he could think about.

I quickly prepared a lovely salad, and strangely enough Dad and I had made a quiche and a pudding the night before, just for fun. He insisted that I took them with me, which made me feel bad. 'You never know what he's going to say to you, Sienna,' my father said oddly as he wrapped up the food. He was a cryptic one at times.

'What do you mean?' I asked, suddenly wondering if he might know something I didn't.

'I don't know . . . I just have a feeling about this. And I'll only spend the whole day working my way through it all and getting fat, so please take it with you to share with him,' he added, before sneakily cutting a slice of banoffee pie for himself.

'Anyway, I've really got into this writing thing. There's a lot I want to get down today and I could do without you moping around the house,' he went on, poking me in the side playfully and pointing towards the small pile of black notebooks on the kitchen surface.

I didn't know much about what was written in those books – they were his and his alone – but what I did know is that he wrote about all the things he wanted to see and do, and how he thought they might be. I wondered if his imagination had become super-developed to make up for his inability to experience things for real – rather like the way a bat has incredible hearing to compensate for its blindness.

'I'm going to write about what it must be like to run a marathon,' he announced, grinning from ear to ear and holding up a running magazine.

'Are you going to be OK?' I asked.

'Yes, of course, darling. I promise I'll wear my helmet,' he added, shoving the headgear on, which made him look like an extra from a Saturday night game show.

'Thank you,' I said, before kissing him on the cheek and walking out of the door.

When I arrived at the park gate I saw Nick and he looked nervous. There was something about his demeanour that told me I wasn't going to like his news. Oh God, what if Chloe was pregnant? I suddenly imagined having to hold said child and look really happy. Or maybe they were getting married? Oh Jesus, yes. I bet that was it. He was at that age now . . .

'Hello, skinny,' he said, pulling me into his arms. His body was tense. He was tense. On the other hand, maybe my quiet expectation was correct this time. Maybe he was going to say something about us. Me and him . . . Something good. Wonderful, in fact. But then I could be wrong. Maybe he'd just got a new job or something. That would be pretty bloody bad. I quietly told myself off for speculating so wildly about whatever he was planning to tell me.

But then my sunny day seemed to melt into a moody painting where the colours had all been dimmed, because he told me he was going to ask Chloe to live with him. Cohabit. The temp was permanent. It was official.

I faked the kind of happiness you reserve for the colleague who got the promotion you both went for, or the bloke who reveals a million-pound-winning combination on the scratch card he bought just before you.

Nick leaned back on his elbows, the outline of his washboard stomach showing subtly through a deep green T-shirt emblazoned with a white abstract graphic. His rebellious dark hair poked out from underneath a disgustingly sexy fedora, which cast a shadow against his strong, stubbly jawline.

I didn't know what to do, so I leaped on him and cuddled him. Emotion washed over me like a huge wave. It was utterly overwhelming. I was losing him. I wanted to hold on to him before the gods swooped down from the sky, picked him up and took him away. Forever.

He held me back and as the tears started to come I felt my chest shake. I held my breath hard so he wouldn't feel it. If he didn't feel it, then maybe he wouldn't see the water streaming from my eyes and I would get away with it.

Nick continued to talk about the big decision – how it had come about, cheap removal companies for Chloe's stuff, bubble wrap – but to me it was just a load of mixed-up drivel.

But then he noticed my tears and I unravelled. All I could think about was how our nights of vintage gaming would have to end. No more Donkey Kong or Street Fighter sessions with a few Jack Daniel's and Cokes, followed by a shared cigar with the cherry filter in the garden. Bollocks.

'But don't forget about me, Sienna, please. We can still see each other loads. Chloe loves you. Nothing has to change. Do you promise that nothing will change?' He mimicked moving his thumbs on an imaginary control pad, wincing slightly as if he'd read my thoughts.

I knew deep down that this would be the beginning of the end. Nick had to grow up one day soon, after all, but I just wished it could be with me. Then I pictured Chloe's and Ben's faces and felt guilty about my thoughts. Ben had just gone out for the day, I was due to see him later, yet I'd been daydreaming that Nick would suddenly turn around and tell me he loved me, just like I'd always loved him. If he'd said those words, would I have even given Ben a second thought?

Soon he would be so engrossed in lazy Sundays in bed with his girlfriend, coffee machine and matching dressing gowns that I would pale into insignificance. I suddenly imagined a wedding invitation plopping onto the doormat like a burning turd. We may only have been a worm's bottom's width apart at that moment, but it felt like the distance was already growing. An aching, yawning chasm we could both end up falling into if neither of us spoke soon.

Nick casually lit a cigarette. I had pissed around too long, and now he was about to start cohabiting with the gorgeous office temp I'd dismissed as just another one of those good shags he wouldn't quite be able to commit to. All the others girls had just come and gone, something I'd taken for granted. I'd never imagined that he would actually settle down. He was so carefree – there was something truly magical about him, like he could do anything and get away with it. He was a free spirit, annoyingly unable to stick with just one person for long. But now he was talking about Chloe moving in with him.

Nick was, and always had been, superhuman to me. He even made the lazy curls of smoke leaking from his Marlboro Lights look cool – on anyone else, this would have looked like a small, obnoxious factory chimney hanging out of their gob, the kind that leaves a lingering smell like rotten eggs hanging limply over the surrounding town. Poor Chloe, she had done nothing wrong at all, just fallen in love with one of the most beautiful men to ever grace west London. He was a guy, she was a girl, and all that, and this was a love story. A love story that didn't include me. I did play some part, but a crappy one. Like the time they made me the back end of a donkey in the school nativity.

It was Chloe who interrupted my train of thought as I sat at my desk, chewing my lip hard and remembering *that* Saturday. 'Do you want a cup of tea, sweetheart?' she asked, appearing as if from nowhere. I jumped out of my skin.

'Oh, hi, Chloe. I'm OK, actually, thanks, hon. I have to go to a meeting in a minute and then I've got the afternoon off.' I had no idea why I was telling her this. It had nothing to do with tea.

'Afternoon off on a Monday? That sounds exciting,' she responded, then she leaned in close and whispered in my ear, 'Are you going to a job interview?'

'Oh, no no no. I'm just doing something for a friend,' I replied, hoping she didn't think I was talking about Nick – because for once I wasn't. She waltzed off into the kitchen with a spring in her step. I wondered if he'd told her yet.

When the meeting was finished I left the office and marched to Balham train station where I was to meet Laura. I was nervous. My heart was pounding in my chest. I knew this was a huge move that could potentially change Pete's life forever – for the better. But I also knew that with that move came a risk. An enormous risk. I had seen on more than one occasion the horrible rages he was capable of flying into, and I knew this might well end the same way. This was such a bold thing to do, and I had a terrible fear that he would hate me for it.

As I weaved my way through the people I saw Laura standing by the ticket machines. You could spot her a mile off. Her hair was in thick blonde dreads, intermittently streaked with faded blue and red. She was strange-looking, but in a fascinating and beautiful way. She had a tiny nose piercing and small white teeth, set against a delicate face. A face almost too delicate to be surrounded by such a wild tangle of matted hair.

'Hello, Sienna,' she said, pulling me into a hug.

She wore baggy jeans and a black vest top with a pair of chunky trainers. She was the kind of girl I would have felt intimidated by as a teenager because she was a bit cool. Now I just looked at her and wondered about her past, where she'd come from and how she'd ended up doing this unusual job. An outreach worker, scooping up ruined lives from the city's pavements.

'Hello, Laura, thanks so much for this. I'm really nervous,' I said, realising I was fiddling frantically with my hair.

'Don't worry. We'll sort this out. Do you know where he's likely to be?' she asked, tilting her head to one side enquiringly like a dog. She pulled a large piece of pink bubblegum from her mouth and threw it into a nearby bin. Underneath one arm was a thin black folder with a pen attached to it.

'Yes, I'm pretty sure we'll be able to find him.' I was starting to feel sick now.

This was terrifying. Was I doing the right thing?

'Now, you remember what I said when we spoke on the phone?' she asked, raising an eyebrow at me.

The phone call. The phone call . . . It had been long and I'd been nervous. It was all a bit of a blur now.

'You know, about how he might react? It's very common for people to be pretty aggressive when we approach them. Rough sleepers are incredibly settled in many ways; they can't see a way out so often they've carved a whole new lifestyle, a whole new set of attitudes.' She waved her arm through the air as she said this, as if to emphasise the drama of it all. 'All I'm saying is that it might take more than one try, OK?'

More than one try? I wasn't sure if that was an option. What if he rejected us the first time and then never spoke to me again? What if he ran off and disappeared and I didn't get a chance to explain.

'Come on,' she said, pulling me gently away from the station.

'I think he'll be on the common near here. There's this particular tree he likes, a fallen-down tree, actually, and I often find him there,' I said, starting to shake now. The situation was making me hot with nerves, I could feel that my ears were bright red and my cheeks were flushed. This meant so much to me. It meant the world.

'So, if we find him, I want you to go over just ahead of me and tell him who I am and that you contacted us at the charity, OK? I'll be right behind you the whole time, and then let me take over, yeah?' She looked into my eyes like this bit was really important and I really needed to pull myself together and just listen.

'OK,' I said. I had to trust her. These people knew what they were doing. I had learned all about how we could sort this out when I called them. How if Pete wanted to, he could go to a temporary hostel, which wasn't great, while they got him a better hostel. Then, if he wanted to help himself, he might be able to get a job and a proper house. They would feed him at the hostel. He would have his own room. A chance.

We walked timidly on to the common, which was stretched out in front of us like a huge green blanket. Turning just a few corners revealed the fallen tree and to my relief there was Pete, sitting on top of it and fiddling with a stump of wood at his feet. I walked towards him slowly, the fear caught in my throat. He didn't notice me until I was really close.

'Pete,' I said quietly.

He flinched. 'Oh hello, love,' he responded, looking at the woman behind me in confusion before something shifted in his face as he seemed to realise what was going on. I kneeled down to his level and put my hand over his.

'Pete, I really don't want you to be angry with—' I tried to explain, but he interrupted me, leaning up and whispering into my ear, his stubble brushing my face.

'Who's that woman with the clipboard, Si? Who is she? What have you done?' He sounded angry. His eyes were narrowed and the skin around them wrinkled. I recognised this hostility from the time I'd taken the photo from him for too long, and the time I'd asked him about the fight. I knew where it led. My words caught in my throat and got stuck there.

Laura seemed to pick up on this, and tiptoed into our space. 'Pete, my name's Laura and I'm here from a homelessness charity,' she said warmly, holding out her hand in his direction.

He spat at the ground and grunted, pulling his grey T-shirt over his knees so it stretched to cover him.

The spitting. The fury. They were the traits of

365

an angry, frightened teenager, far from the intelligent man I had grown to love. This wasn't the Pete I'd come to know, the Pete I wanted her to meet. This was the angry Pete who threw beer cans at office windows. I'd been hoping it was just the alcohol back then, but he looked sober now and still as angry. I just wanted him to show her who he really was. How he was a bright, loving individual who had just got a bit lost. Come on, Pete. This is our chance . . .

'What do you want, Laura?' He raised his voice and threw his arms into the air. 'You want to help me? I can tell you now, I'm not worth helping. I got myself into all this mess so I can get myself out. Alone.' He pulled his knees even closer to his chest, the plastic logo on his top stretching and peeling where the paint was being torn apart. He scrunched his eyelids together in frustration.

'OK, I think we should leave it.' I turned to Laura. I'd got this all wrong. I never should have interfered. Laura ignored me and sat herself next to Pete.

'Now, Pete. I just want to have a chat with you, OK? You don't have to do anything you don't want to do. We aren't going to take you anywhere, we aren't going to force anything upon you. Will you just talk to me for a bit?' She looked at him but he kept his eyes to the floor, as if he was trying to bore down and communicate with the worms. I kept my distance, but listened to every word.

'So how did this all start? You don't mind if I write, do you?' she asked, direct and to the point, pulling the biro from its clip on the board, poised for note-taking.

'How can you help me? No one can. There's nothing free in this world,' he muttered, finally looking towards her. I was scared. Terrified, in fact, that I had made a huge error. An error that would undo three years of gentle friendship.

There was silence. Long, deep, cavernous silence. A squirrel ran down the tree trunk, gripping the bark hard with its claws and shuffling around nervously. Pete was distracted, watching its every move and starting to laugh to himself. But it was a strange laugh . . . A wicked one, loaded with frustration.

Suddenly, he seemed to soften, and after a few minutes he spoke. 'My wife died. That's when it began.' He leaned back against the scratchy bark and put his head against it, looking up into the leafy canopy, shards of sunlight cutting through it like rows of glitter powder.

'I was at work when I got the call. I used to be an events organiser – you know, music venues and stuff. I'll never forget it. You would know it as the Oakwood Park rail crash.' He paused again like he had with me so often. It was incredible how his mood could change so quickly. 'The train derailed and she was in it – you probably know all the details anyway. I thought it was a joke so I just said "No" a lot. Then I turned on the news and there it all was – chunks of twisted metal, torn bodywork, like it was a bit of scrunched-up paper. And I knew my beautiful wife was inside, and I hadn't been there to save her, to protect her.' His tone started to grow angry again as he recounted the story.

'What was her name?' asked Laura.

'Jenny,' he said, in a gruff whisper, as if just saying the word felt like bleeding.

'So I take it you used to live with her?' she probed further, scrawling notes onto the paper, the pen scratching the surface hard. I could hear every stroke.

'Yes. We rented a one-bed house in Balham. I couldn't work after that, I couldn't do anything. I tried, but I kept screwing up the bookings. Everything fell apart. Got kicked out of the house eventually, you know the rest . . .' He sounded so angry when he said this. Almost angry with himself.

'I don't really, Pete. Everyone's different. Do you think you might be able to tell me?'

He ran his hands through his hair, the frustration boiling over again, as though talking about this was the last thing he wanted to do.

'Well, I started staying with friends and stuff, family, you know. But as much as people tell you you're always welcome, you aren't for long. You start getting in the way, leaving cornflakes in the bowl too long so they're impossible to clean and stupid shit like that. You do stuff that annoys them, you do stuff differently to the way they've set their lives out, and then they don't want you any more.

'I started to resent this, because I was a bit bashed-up and broken. I got angry and

368

systematically pissed off everyone in my path, until they all shut their doors. That was when I spent my first night on a bench.' He stretched his legs out, as if remembering the feel of the wooden slats beneath his limbs for the very first time.

I listened and thought about all this rubbish with Nick, the stupidity of my pointless feelings. I thought about how we spend all our time thinking we're in trouble because the toaster broke or the Digibox didn't record *The X Factor* when there are people who have been shunned by everyone they know. I started to calm down for a moment as I realised we might be getting somewhere. But I was mistaken.

'Look. I've tried, but you know, I don't want to talk about this,' Pete said bluntly, turning to look at Laura, his lips quivering slightly.

'Are you sure you can't just stay for a few more minutes, Pete?' Laura asked, her body tensing up slightly.

'No. No. I'm not staying. Just leave me alone, will you?' he said as he got to his feet.

He walked towards me and looked me in the eyes. 'Why, Sienna? Why do you keep trying to help me? Just stay away, OK?' he whispered, before charging off into the distance again.

I couldn't cope with this. Emotion was grasping at my throat again. I'd probably ruined it all now. Forever. I didn't want Laura to see me cry, so I squeezed her arm as if to thank her and walked away. Quickly.

CHAPTER 12

I WISHED SOMEONE COULD
TAKE A PICTURE.

Nick

It was green. The most beautiful shade of green I have ever seen in my life. A shade that reminded me of deep, painful, all-consuming envy. It was more than a colour, it was a feeling. An urge. And this colour was draped all over Sienna, touching her curves like the hand of an insatiable lover and dripping down her body like a waterfall. Jesus Christ.

Now *that* was a dress. I wondered where the hell she'd got it from. I'd been dragged around Oxford Street with Chloe enough times to know they don't sell stuff like this in the chain stores. My eyes did that slowing-down thing they do sometimes when she walks into a room. I'd always thought it was a crappy film effect, *but it does actually happen.*

It was our Christmas party. It was a tacky affair, which usually resulted in at least one drunken kiss between people who ended up deeply regretting it, and at least one precarious display of terrible dad-style dancing on a rickety table. In fact, last year Nigel from sales ended up with a cast on his leg from doing just that. The table wasn't so lucky. It's a hideous annual event that sees everyone at The Cube get pissed together and pretend they like each other, whisper all sorts of things over the table and get in major trouble for it the following Monday.

This time everyone's attention was stolen because Sienna had arrived wearing the dress that made us all want to get her into bed. Men and women. And the dress seemed very much out of place in this restaurant attached to a budget hotel. But it didn't matter. I think everyone was pleased she'd decided to wear it. I'd never seen it before, and I've seen most of her 'going out' dresses. I wonder where it came from.

Sienna is twenty-four now, and she's stunning. She just seems to get better and better. It's as if everything that happens in her life, good and bad, just adds to her beauty. I nearly choked on my beer when she walked in with Ben; he was holding her hand tightly and looked exceptionally nervous. He was running his free hand awkwardly down the side of his blazer and glancing down at his shoes a lot. They were nice shoes, too . . . I expect Si picked them out. There's no way a man would select a pair of kicks like that without the help of a woman.

He's a good-looking boy, is Ben, and we've got on pretty well on the few occasions we've met. He's a big improvement on the loser she last went out with, Daniel House. I'd rather pull each and every one of my body hairs out with blunt tweezers than spend another minute in his company . . . Ben was wearing a white shirt with a black skinny tie and a black suit. Together they looked like they were on their way to a film premiere. They looked far too good for this tinsel-clad function room off the M25, and the hotel where we were all about to spend the night.

This place was about as glamorous as my grandma's dentures. Faded red tissue paper was spread over all twelve tables. They were covered in half-hearted decorations, which looked like they'd come from the local pound shop, including party poppers, cheap-looking crackers and confetti in the shape of various festive symbols. In the middle of each table were two cheap bottles of wine – one white, one red – and a tired-looking flower arrangement. A small DJ booth was set up on the far side of the room, which I expected would soon be pumping out the greatest hits of Wham! accompanied by some out-of-sequence disco lights.

Looking at Sienna and Ben standing in the doorway as people clucked around them, I felt like I'd turned up in my pyjamas, despite the setting. I looked down at my trousers and spotted a tiny stain where I'd managed to slop some beer on my lap. Bollocks.

'What are you looking at, sweetheart?' asked Chloe, thrusting her face in my line of vision as she returned from the toilet.

I jumped. 'Oh, nothing. Sienna's just arrived with Ben, look,' I said casually, as if I'd only just spotted her when actually I'd been staring at her for ages. Ben must literally wake up every day and pinch himself.

Chloe looked good too, I thought, as she sat down and started gulping down a glass of wine far too fast.

'Easy, Chlo,' I said, hoping we wouldn't be in for any drama tonight. She was particularly dangerous when she was drinking. As I looked across the table she sat there with a look of mock guilt on her face, in a nude dress that made her seem a lot more angelic than she is. It was a corset number, which she was wearing with a pair of heels that showed off the muscles in her calves when she walked in front of me. It drove me wild. She's trouble, just like all the other girls.

I've had a string of unstable girlfriends and she's the latest in what's becoming a worryingly long list. What with Amelia's crying on my doorstep – a sound which still haunts me sometimes – and Kate, who needed me to be her confidence when she'd lost her own, I thought about whether I had been paying attention to the wrong people. Yes, since she moved in I'm truly beginning to understand just how unstable Chloe is. I seem to be a magnet for women like this. That slap around the face all those months ago was nothing. It was just an appetiser.

We have these arguments, these rows that

involve yelling at each other like crazed animals into the early hours of the morning. And then there's the sex, the crazy 'I love you', 'I'm so sorry', 'Let's never fall out again' sex. The biting, the scratching, the kissing . . . It's complete madness. It's exhausting. I don't know if I can take any more of it. She's jealous, possessive, insecure and angry, but she's beautiful, caring, loving and funny too. She's a double-edged sword. Sweet and sour. Completely bloody bonkers.

'Nick, why are you looking at me like that?' she asked. She slowly and seductively licked the tip of her knife, which had a tiny bit of pâté on it from the pre-dinner nibbles laid out on our table.

'Oh, just 'cause you're beautiful,' I responded, gently pulling her blade-wielding hand towards the cheap crackers and word-processed menus before she split her tongue like a serpent. She visibly melted a little, and ran her hand up my trouser leg under the tablecloth.

'Fuck's sake, Chloe – stop it!' I whispered play-fully, squeezing her hand tight and lurching forwards because it tickled. A candle tipped in the middle of the table and I grabbed hold of it just in time, splashing wax all over my plate.

After Sienna had done the royal parade, shaking everyone's hands and introducing Ben to them, she eventually came to our table. 'Hello, Wolfie,' she said, leaning down and kissing me softly on the cheek with a silly smile on her face.

The scent of her wafted down and rendered me

speechless for a few seconds before I pulled myself together and stood up to shake Ben's hand. She and Chloe kissed each other on the cheek and soon we were sitting side by side with delicate bowls of leek and potato soup in front of us.

Chloe kept licking her spoon suggestively whenever people were looking down at their food. I kicked her shin gently in the hope she would stop. She was embarrassing me.

'So, how are things with work?' Ben asked Chloe and me, smiling knowingly like everyone does when they find out how we met. They must think it's awkward. They're right. I'm just so glad we work in different departments – cohabiting and working directly together would drive me insane.

'They're fine, thanks. And we're really enjoying living together, too,' I responded, pulling a slice of bread from a basket in the middle of the table.

That was a little bit of a lie. It had started really well, true, but now I couldn't escape her mood swings. There was nowhere to hide. On occasion I would come home to find her in a delightful mood, full of joy and love. At other times I wondered if we would make it through the night . . .

'Do you think you guys will live together soon?' Chloe asked, directing her question at Sienna.

I winced a little. It was a bit like asking how much they earned or if they were planning to try for children. You just didn't do that kind of thing, but it was totally Chloe.

'Er, well. Er, I don't know,' Sienna responded, as if it was the first time the idea had been mentioned.

Ben intercepted: 'Well, it's probably a bit soon, really, isn't it?' he said, turning to look at Sienna, who seemed to visibly thank God. I couldn't help but notice how sharp and blunt his response was. Maybe they were just a smart couple taking their time. I wish we had, I thought as I looked at Chloe, who was blowing gently on a spoonful of soup and somehow smiling at me at the same time. Still, she was so sexy. Maybe it would work out . . .

Another bottle of wine arrived at the table, which was promptly shared out. It seemed as though the alcohol was getting to Sienna even before the second course had arrived. She had that relaxed look about her eyes and a pink flush to her cheeks.

'Nick, do you remember that time we went to Amsterdam?' she asked, leaning towards me and smiling, her gorgeous straight teeth almost dazzling me as I started to cut into my roast turkey.

'Yes, I certainly do,' I responded with a grin, memories flooding back. Chloe flashed her insecure look at me. I ignored it.

'Well, you know that weird guy we met? You know, the one who said he was travelling the world, meeting couples and writing love stories about the people he spoke to who particularly inspired him?'

'Let me guess – he's writing about you and Nick?' interrupted Ben, with a smirk on his face. I jerked my head back in shock.

Chloe's mouth dropped open and Sienna scowled

at him. He looked hideously embarrassed almost as soon as the words had escaped his mouth. A crimson shade took over his cheeks.

'No, Ben. What I was actually going to say was that his book's been published. I've seen it online.' She seemed to brush off the comment like it was nothing, but I knew we were all very humiliated by it. I wondered if we could recover. How could I talk to Ben normally? It was clear that he had an issue, and now darkness had clouded Chloe's face, too. There was radio silence, so I decided to break it.

'I'm sorry,' I said, turning to Ben, who was sitting next to me. 'Why did you say that? What were you getting at?'

He tilted his head down towards his dinner and took a breath. My heart seemed to stop in my chest as I realised that this could escalate and I wasn't quite prepared for it.

'I'm sorry, mate, I don't know what's wrong with me at the moment. Chloe, I apologise. I honestly don't know why I said it. Sienna, I'm sorry,' he finished, shrugging his shoulders like he'd accidentally taken my napkin or used his dessert fork too soon. A minor slip.

'No problem. Just as long as everything's OK,' I said, looking at Chloe to reassure her. I genuinely wanted all this shit to end now; it felt like I'd only just managed to convince Chloe that Sienna and I weren't having some kind of affair.

The chatter from the tables around us seemed

to grow louder at this point; I could hear crackers being pulled and loud shrieks of laughter. I hoped the energy of the room would dissolve the hideousness of that moment. A Brussels sprout came sailing through the air and hit me on the back of the head. I didn't even need to look because it was obviously thrown by Tom, but I was quite glad of the distraction. I picked it up from the floor and threatened him with it across the room, laughing to myself as I turned round.

'Well, Sienna, between you and me, I think there might be quite a big job coming up soon,' said Chloe, leaning towards Si and smiling at her. A perfect subject change. That's my girl.

'Really? Tell me more,' replied Sienna, mopping up the gravy on her plate with some bread.

'I think Sarah – you know, the editor of *SparkNotes*? I think she might be leaving in a few months, but you have to keep that to yourself . . .' She had significantly lowered her tone by now.

As the two of them chatted, I took the opportunity to talk to Ben. 'Are you sure everything's OK, pal?' I asked, taking a bold step. I still couldn't get over what he'd just said. Sienna had always made out like he didn't care about our friendship at all, so his comment had come as a bit of a shock.

'I don't know,' he said quietly, leaning forward like the weight of the world was balanced on his shoulders. Oh shit. Here it comes.

'My dad's not well, Nick. Really not well,

mentally. It's all getting a bit much, if I'm honest. I keep ending up saying crazy stuff like that, you know – having a go at people when they haven't done anything wrong. I feel alone. I can't imagine that anyone could understand,' he said.

I admired that about him. His honesty. I could see why Sienna liked him.

'I'm really sorry to hear that. I know what it's like when you're that stressed, you just get wound up by little things,' I said, trying to comfort him in some way.

He leaned close to me now and lowered his voice, keeping his eye on the girls the whole time. 'I'm not treating her right. I just can't be everywhere at the same time. I don't feel like I'm good enough for her at the moment.'

I flinched a little, glancing over to Chloe and Sienna, hoping they couldn't hear. Wow. Now *this* was honesty. And a huge responsibility on my part. Anything I said at this point could have a marked impact on my best friend's future.

I looked over at her in The Dress, which plunged at the neck, revealing her delicate collarbone. She was laughing with Chloe, playing with a strand of hair. They were both engaged in their conversation.

'Right, OK . . . Well, I don't want to say the wrong thing. What are you going to do?' I asked, whispering so quietly it was barely audible. For a moment we were eye to eye. I could almost see the fear in his pupils.

'Leave her,' he said, unblinking.

My blood ran cold. I quickly looked at Sienna in horror, praying to God she hadn't heard what he'd said, but she and Chloe were still engrossed. I shuffled awkwardly in my seat and tried to look inconspicuous. I wanted to grab hold of his shoulders and shake some sense into him. *What are you thinking of, boy?* I felt guilty even though it wasn't me saying the words. Like I was doing her wrong somehow just by hearing this.

'What? Ben, no, come on. I'm sure you can work through this,' I pleaded, hating the thought of her being hurt. Abandoned. Alone. 'She really likes you, mate, come on.' I was starting to beg now.

This was so inappropriate. Why was he telling me all this just a metre away from Sienna? Surely if you could proudly say that Sienna Walker was your girl, you would never let her go. You would kiss her lots. You would hold her every night. You would do *anything* . . .

'Look, I don't want to offend you here, but do you have a problem with Sienna and me being friends like we are? Because if I'm honest, Chloe did. But she knows now, she knows that it isn't . . . you know.' I was struggling to finish the sentence, but I think he got the message.

'I know there's nothing going on, Nick,' he said, turning to face me again. 'But it's hard to know that you're number two, you understand?'

It was as if the sound had been put on mute and his face seemed to blur in front of my eyes.

'What do you mean?' I rested my fork on the edge of my plate, nervous butterflies filling my stomach. I wasn't hungry any more.

'Well, I know there isn't anything going on between you, so don't worry. It's just that she adores you, Nick. She bloody adores you, you're her best mate, and I find it all very hard to live up to.' He looked embarrassed again, but I was deeply impressed by the nakedness of his admission.

His honesty was so rare, yet refreshing. But what would happen if everyone acted like this? 'I'm sorry, but I stopped seeing you because when you took your clothes off, your bum freaked me out,' or 'I moved away from you on the train because your breath smells like the back end of a donkey.' People would get pissed off . . .

I cleared my throat to say something, but I didn't know what to say. My cheeks were burning up. Sienna *adores* me? *Bloody adores* me? *Hard to live up to?* Was I really hearing this? Half of me wanted to shake him out of it, and the other half wanted to punch the air with joy. Ben picked up the wine bottle and tipped the rest of it into my glass as if to wipe my memory of his confession.

I sat there for a few seconds. Seconds which felt like long-drawn-out, hideously awkward minutes. I hadn't realised I meant so much to her. What would I say? I thought, as the predictably awful disco music kicked in, saving me from the intensity of my feelings.

I was finally ready to speak. 'Well, er, right. OK. Er, wow.' I suddenly became aware that I was waffling even more than Hugh Grant did in *Four Weddings*. I was getting frustrated just listening to my own dithering. I tried again. 'That's lovely in a way, Ben – and yes, Sienna and I are close friends. But don't feel like it's something to live up to . . . I really admire you, I get on with you really well. I don't want this to become an issue . . . Pal, she really likes you.' Phew.

He looked relieved, but still troubled. There was marked concern across his features. He was a frightened man and I had a horrible feeling he was still about to run away from her.

'Nick, Nick! Come over here, you have to come and see what Lydia has made out of carrots!' came a sudden shriek from Tom, who was horribly drunk already for the relatively early hour. I put my hand up in his direction as he put his weight on my shoulders and leaned over, laughing hard.

'Tom, please – that sounds great, but I'm kind of in the middle of something here . . . I'll be over soon, OK?'

'All right, you boring bastards,' he said, ruffling my hair as he stumbled away. Idiot.

'Anyway. Come on, Ben . . .'

'God, I'm so sorry, Nick. I'm an idiot. It's fine. I'll deal with this.' He pushed the silverware together on his plate to indicate he had finished.

'Please don't leave her. Please?'

I couldn't believe I was begging him like this. I

just couldn't bear the thought of seeing her hurting. Especially when I looked across the table and saw her smiling, looking like a glittering little star. I turned back and he was gone.

The rest of the night was a drunken haze. Lydia had constructed a naked man out of vegetables, which had been passed around the room on a large square plate. When it reached our table, I managed to drop it, turning me into the most hated individual of the night for ruining her masterpiece. Thankfully it only took a Cosmopolitan cocktail to apologise to Lydia.

Tom managed to get so drunk that he sang *Barbie Girl* through the karaoke machine three times in a row and still wowed the 'crowd' like he was Jon Bon Jovi. Chloe and I danced to the slow songs, my hands around her waist, remembering the last time I'd danced like this.

'Was everything OK earlier, darling?' she asked, placing one of her hands around my neck and playing with my hair. It made all the little hairs on my back stand up.

'Hmm, I don't know . . . I'm not totally sure what's going on with Ben and Sienna. We tried to talk about that silly comment he made earlier.'

'I guess it was only the sort of thing I would have said a while ago, when I was being silly.' She rolled her eyes at the absurdity of it all. 'I love you, Nick Redland,' she said, kissing me on the nose.

'I love you too,' I told her, so glad she was happy tonight. Maybe I would get some sleep.

It turned out quite differently. Chloe dragged me up to our hotel room and that was pretty much the end of the Christmas party and the start of a private one. I tried to stop her – I felt rude leaving so early – but the things she was whispering in my ear were making it very difficult for me to concentrate on anything else, so we scuttled up the stairs, giggling away. She was struggling in her heels, so after a while I slung her over my shoulder and carried her the rest of the way in a fireman's lift.

It was about 1 a.m. and we were just drifting off to sleep when I heard what sounded like a sob in the corridor. Then suddenly – silence. That was strange. I lay there for a few minutes, wondering if I'd imagined it. Well, whoever it was would be gone by now . . .

Then I heard it again. Shit, it sounded like Sienna.

I carefully moved Chloe's slender arm from around my torso and placed it gently on the mattress. Tiptoeing to the door, I put on a T-shirt I'd brought for the morning and pressed my ear against the wooden surface. I was still fairly drunk, but a lot more collected than before. The sound was more distant this time, so I opened the door quietly and shuffled out. Yes, it was definitely Sienna. But where was she?

I followed the corridor round, the red carpet scratchy against the soles of my feet. The walls were illuminated with old-fashioned uplighters in the shape of seashells. Hideous. Despite the light, the corridor was still quite dark and my sleepy eyes were struggling to adjust. I kept one hand on the wall, following it round by touch. There was no one else about, and the only thing breaking the silence was the sound of distress nearby.

There was less sobbing now and more laboured breathing. Cigarette smoke was filling the air. That was naughty, I thought, as my eyes started to sting a little. That was not like Sienna . . . God, maybe it was someone else and I was about to be forced into comforting some complete random. I might even accidentally flash them from the inside leg of my boxers and make them even more traumatised.

I turned one more corner and beneath the haze of thick smoke was a green puff of fabric, and somewhere underneath that was Sienna. She was slightly illuminated by a green fire-exit light to her left.

'Who goes there?' she asked, a drunken lilt to her voice. She squinted through the blur, one eye closed and mascara streaked down her cheeks. A curly strand of hair had come loose from her updo. It hung by her face, lingering around her jawline. Jesus.

I crawled on to the floor and started to shuffle along on my elbows. 'Emergency. Emergency. I need to rescue you from this burning inferno,' I said with my joke robot voice on.

A white cigarette was hanging from between her

fingers, the tip glowing fiercely in the dim light. Somehow, in the midst of her turmoil, she laughed.

I dragged myself up from the floor and sat next to her. 'Miss Walker. What on earth are you doing alone in this corridor? Where's your man? What's happened?' I pulled her legs out from beneath her dress and laid them across my lap.

'I don't have a man any more,' she said, with what sounded like a lump in her throat. She took a deep drag on the cigarette and then passed it my way.

Bugger. 'What? What happened?' Clearly my pep talk hadn't helped at all.

She leaned back against the wall again, the dress pulling tight around her neck because of the angle at which she was sitting. 'He said that things are too hard with his life right now, and that he isn't giving me what I need,' she finished, taking the cigarette back and puffing away at it. It was dangerously close to the nasty letters at the bottom. I pulled it back and threw it out of an open window next to us. She hiccuped.

'Holy shit, Sienna. I'm so, so sorry,' I said, pulling her arms around my neck.

'That's OK. It's not your fault,' she responded in her lovely voice, like a modern Audrey Hepburn.

'Well, I still love you, Panda Pop,' I told her, running a hand through the hair near her forehead to comfort her.

She didn't say anything, but she squeezed me a little tighter. 'Am I ever going to find a nice man,

Nick? I mean, I'm twenty-four now, for God's sake,' she cried, stupidly unaware of how painfully young she was, and just how much there was to come.

'Of course you are. You're a wonderful girl, so I think we can do a bit better than a "nice man". Nice is a crap word . . .' I started.

'It's boring, a bit like a biscuit,' she giggled, finishing my sentence and mocking my voice all at the same time. It was a phrase I'd used a few times before.

'No, seriously . . . What am I going to do?' She looked at me blankly. It was as if she had cried so much there was nothing left but empty questions.

'I wish I knew the answer, Sienna. The man you will marry is walking this earth. He's alive right now, somewhere. He could be in Australia, backpacking with friends; he could be working in a bar in China; he could be a hotshot American lawyer; he could be a musician; he could be going about his life in London at this very moment . . . Any day now, your paths will cross.' She smiled when I said this, like it brought her comfort.

'Where's your room?' I went on. 'I don't want you lying here like this, gassing yourself in a tiny hallway. Plus this dress, it's bloody gorgeous, Si, and you're going to make it smell like a sewer. Where did you get it from, anyway?' I asked, wiping my thumb over one of the black stains on her face. It smeared like charcoal.

She giggled again. 'Er . . . It's a long story. Well, actually, I was told this dress would change my life, but this wasn't quite what I had in mind. My room is 204, I think,' she continued, quickly changing the subject and squinting cross-eyed at her key as she held it in front of her face. What did she mean about the dress? I couldn't seem to get any sense out of her right now.

'Nick, I don't want to go back. Can I just stay here alone? Please?' She was being very strange. But people are strange when they're hurting and pissed.

'No, absolutely not,' I said, standing up and holding her in my arms at the same time. She was light as a feather.

With one hand she pulled the band from her hair, causing it all to tumble out as she tilted her head back in exhaustion. The long swathes of material trailed behind us like the tail of a green dragon. It was beautiful. I wished someone could take a picture.

CHAPTER 13

'DON'T CALL ME. EVER.'

Nick

It all started with a plate. Chloe was standing there in the kitchen holding it tight when I got back from the shop. I'd only nipped out for some cumin seeds and bread, and the next thing I knew the damn thing was hurled across the room, narrowly missing my ear before smashing to smithereens against the wall behind me.

'What the fuck, Chloe?' I shouted, standing in the hallway and trembling in fury. It was terrifying. I mean a bit of rough play and fiery passion were great fun, but this was bloody ridiculous. There were oranges on the side; she could have grabbed one of those instead . . .

'I've had enough, Nick, I really have,' she yelled, holding my phone in the air and storming past me and up the stairs. The screen was glowing in the darkness, lighting up her face and transforming her from sweet, ethereal Chloe to Frankenstein's monster.

I had no bloody idea what she was on about. I stood in the hallway for a bit, droplets of rain seeping into my hair and slipping down my forehead. Only minutes earlier I'd been passing money over the counter of our local shop, talking about the weather and the latest football scores. I'd hardly been ducking out of a brothel or peeling myself away from some illicit lover. This was driving me mad. And that plate was expensive. I dropped the bags and stomped up the stairs behind her.

She was sitting on the edge of the bed in tears. Angry tears.

'Chloe, come on,' I said quietly, trying to sit down next to her but she pushed me away. Hard. My chest jolted as she shoved me backwards.

'No, get away from me, you shit!' she shouted, so loud now I knew the neighbours would hear every word. Make-up was streaming down her face. She was in a right state.

'What have I done? You were fine just ten minutes ago, Chloe, and now it's as if I killed your cat. Come on! I can't take this any more!' I yelled back, aware that I had well and truly lost my cool. If I'd had any in the first place.

'You want to know what you've done? Don't play dumb! Read this.' She thrust the glowing screen of my touch-screen phone against my nose, which immediately cancelled the message. Then she flounced past me again, leaving a trail of anger behind her.

I grabbed the handset and went into my recent messages. Oh shit, it was from Amelia:

'Hey, Nick. I miss you so much. We need to do something about this situation. Call me, please. Amelia xxx' After all this time . . .

'So, what do you have to say for yourself?' she shrieked, stomping back into the room with her heels on, which bashed hard against the wood. I jumped out of my skin.

'Well, I'm simply not defending myself. Yes, it's my ex-girlfriend, from years ago, but so what if she still feels something for me? It's not my fault,' I tried to explain calmly, realising that this didn't look great but unwilling to take responsibility for it.

'Bollocks, Nick. I don't trust you. Why does she still have your number? And what's *this situation*, huh?' She stared straight into my eyes now, breathing so hard her shoulders rose up and down.

This was horrible. 'So she's texted me. I haven't texted her once since we broke up, and yet all of a sudden this is my fault?' I said, following her back down the stairs waving my phone in the air. This was ludicrous. Utter madness. 'And Chloe, can you take your bloody shoes off, please, because you're going to carve up the floor.'

'I'm not taking my shoes off, Nick, because I'm leaving now,' she seethed, pacing the hallway with a huge bag in her hands.

'Oh, Chloe, this is ridiculous. What do you want me to say?' I walked behind her with my arms out. I was starting to feel very irritated now. I had never been mistrusted like this. And I'd never given her any real reason to mistrust me, either. I kind of understood why she'd worried about Sienna, but we'd moved on from that so long ago now.

She started to ram her possessions into the bag. The candles, the cushions, the strange pebbly things she keeps in bowls. She could definitely take those . . . I looked at her and I didn't see the Chloe I fell for, I saw an angry, insecure young woman. I felt sorry for her. There had always been signs of this in her personality, but she'd managed to balance it with the wild love she gave me. I loved her. I said it to her all the time, I whispered it in her ear at night, I wrote it on Post-it notes and left them in her lunch. I *loved* her. Or at least I thought I did.

'So you're leaving, just like that?'

'Yeah, just like that,' she snapped back, almost hissing in my face.

I sank down into the sofa and watched her as she systematically stripped the space around me. If she took my Radiohead CD, I swear . . .

My home. My girl. The two were parting and I felt helpless.

'Chloe, you know I love you. I don't know what else I can say. Is it something else?' I asked, trying to diffuse her fury. I realised that being angry was not going to help in any way; I had to swallow my pride and try to talk her down. Coax her away from this stupid cliff she was about to jump from.

'Well, you've always had eyes elsewhere, Nick, so it's best I go.'

'What do you mean?' I asked, genuinely confused.

392

'When we go to restaurants you stare at the waitresses, when we go to the park you stare at other girls, then there are all those hidden gifts and secret phone calls with Sienna, and now these intimate texts . . . You're a horrible, cheating bastard.'

The words cut into me. *Horrible, cheating bastard* . . . No woman had ever even come close to saying that to me. I looked back at all the meals we'd had and the days in the sun. Had I been looking at other girls? Surely not . . . And I couldn't believe she was bringing Sienna up again – we'd been over that more times than I could remember. I was totally confused, baffled and now pretty angry.

When she had bagged up her possessions in the living room she went upstairs. She'd even taken the DVDs we bought together, but I felt petty saying anything. I sat for an hour listening to her stomping about. I had no idea what to do. What the fuck was I going to do? Did I want her to stay? Did I? Did I really want to be accused of things I hadn't done? Did I want any more of these silly fights and crazy sex like two wild, confused animals?

I needed Sienna. She would know what to do. She always knows just what to do. I sat some more and pulled my head into my lap, hoping if I fell asleep this would all just be a dream. Thanks a lot, Amelia . . .

After a while Chloe had created a pile of bags by the front door, about four in all. Heels were poking out of them, hangers, bottles, a toothbrush.

All of those items that had scared me for so long when they began appearing everywhere . . .

She made her final descent of the stairs. I walked towards them so I could talk to her. She still looked furious. I tried to pull her towards me but she pushed me away again, flicking her arms so my hands flew off them. I lost my grip.

'Chloe, I'm really quite angry about this. I've never cheated on you. So I think this is for the best,' I said, the words just spilling from my mouth.

She pushed her nose into mine once more and scrunched up her features as she said her last words to me: 'Don't call me. Ever.'

Well, that was going to be interesting considering we worked in the same office.

And that was it. The bags were gathered, the door was slammed and I heard her churn up the gravel beneath her tyres as she sped away from my house and out into the open road.

I looked at the cumin seeds and the bread sitting sadly in a blue bag where I'd left them on the kitchen table and wondered what on earth I should do. I sat at the bottom of the stairs and picked up my phone, holding my thumb on the number two. There were two rings and then her voice.

'Sienna, can I come round?'

Sienna

Nick arrived at my door at 8 p.m., looking like a wet dog. A sad, wet dog. A whippet, to be precise.

I've always thought he looked a bit like one of those . . .

'Oh, come in, Nick,' said my dad as he answered the door, holding on to the dado rail for safety.

The second I'd told him that Nick was coming round, he had gathered together a pile of books about the Congo, his latest fascination. I'd tried to warn him that it might not be that kind of visit. I could tell by the tone of Nick's voice.

I was sitting on the sofa when I heard the door go. I stood up as he walked in, slightly shocked by just how wet he was. Droplets were running down his face and his fringe was spiked into dagger-like rows, giving him a greasy boy-band look.

'Nick, what on earth has happened to you? Let me get you a towel,' I exclaimed, making my way to the bathroom.

'Er, well, don't worry. We can talk later,' he said as he sat down next to my father, who immediately started showing him the books. I threw a bright pink hand-towel at him and made my way back to my seat. Whatever Nick had gone through, it was almost impossible to tell as he started listening to the things my dad had learned today. His way with him was incredible.

I made a pot of tea and spread out a selection of biscuits on one of our best plates. I had a warm feeling in my stomach because he was here. It was a feeling I never had at any other time. I sat on the chair and watched as he and Dad turned the pages, pointing at photos and examining the notes Dad had written. It was like nothing else mattered in the world. He had drawn maps, charts, thought processes in pencil. It was incredible.

After a while, when Dad went to the fridge to get Nick a beer, I gently intercepted. 'Nick, are you OK?'

He looked up at me and I could see it in his eyes. Something really bad had happened. 'Well, not really,' he said, sighing deeply and rubbing his hair with the towel.

His T-shirt was stuck to his body and I could see every ripple of muscle. Stop, Sienna. Must. Concentrate.

'Chloe left me tonight. She thinks I'm cheating on her.' He looked towards the table almost in shame. The look was so guilty that for a second I wondered if he had.

I leaned forward so I could be closer to him. 'And you haven't, you know . . . cheated on her, have you?'

Dad sat back down and watched us both. His lids were starting to pull down heavily over his eyes like theatre curtains.

'No, no, of course not. It's ridiculous, really. I went to the shop to get some stuff we needed for dinner. I left my phone in the kitchen and Amelia set me a message completely out of the blue and Chloe obviously just read it.' He looked mortified.

'Oh dear. What did it say?' my dad asked, showing genuine concern.

Nick picked up a chewy chocolate-chip cookie and bit into it, leaving a perfect impression of his teeth. 'Just that she missed me and stuff. I honestly haven't contacted her since the split, and that was so long ago.'

'So what did Chloe say?' I asked him. Perhaps it had been one of their silly rows. The ones that they seemed to have so often . . .

'She basically accused me of cheating on her – she said I have wandering eyes, all sorts of stuff. She packed her bags and left.' He winced as he said it.

'I'm so sorry to hear that,' said my dad as Nick slurped his beer anxiously.

'What are you going to do?' I asked, butterflies filling my stomach suddenly. I wondered why I felt like this. Well, in truth, I knew. Although I really wanted him to be happy and settled, I also knew that maybe we could get back to the way things had been. Me and Nick, having fun . . . I knew I was being selfish. Before he had the chance to answer, my dad cut in.

'Guys, I'm really struggling to stay awake here – no offence, Nick. I'm going to have to go to bed,' he said, his head lolling forward for a moment before he managed to snap himself out of it.

'No worries, George. Thanks for listening,' Nick joked, taking another huge swig from his can.

I held on to Dad and walked him into his room, just in case he fell. He climbed into bed heavily and took some tablets. As I kissed him on the cheek, he said something strange: 'Look after him, Si. He loves you – you know that, don't you?'

'What?'

'Oh, don't . . . don't worry,' he said through thick fatigue as his head dropped softly onto the pillow.

How odd, I thought, as I pulled the duvet over him. He looked so sweet as I stood there for a moment or two, watching him breathe.

When I went back into the living room, Nick had moved onto the double sofa.

'Come here, Si,' he said, hanging his head sadly.

'Aw, sweetheart, don't worry. You never know, you might be able to sort this out. Right?' I asked as I curled up beside him.

My heart was racing. I suddenly felt that nervousness I'd felt before with Nick. When it was just us, spending time together. He pulled my shoulders down and I rested my head on his chest, wrapping my right arm around him and holding him tight. I felt that warmth flood my body. His heart was pounding too – I could hear each and every beat. My hands ran across his ribs, I could feel them under his damp T-shirt. That familiar Nick smell filled my nostrils. I hadn't been this close in a long time. He said nothing, just ran his fingers through my hair. It felt like he was touching my heart.

That ache was returning. The pain that had plagued me for years. I had managed to distract myself from it with new boyfriends, missions to house the homeless and serious but unsuccessful bids for promotion in the office. Now it was back – and I wanted to push it away. I couldn't cope with all this again.

'Have you heard from Ben?' Nick asked suddenly, sweeping a whole handful of my hair away from my neck. It sent chills down my spine.

'No. It's been quite a long time now. I was waiting for him to come running back, but he never did, so I think I can safely give up on that one.'

'Do you miss him?' he asked.

Did I miss him? I wondered about this . . . The weeks after he left me on the night of the Christmas party had been spent with a dark cloud hovering over my head. Every time the phone rang I'd hoped it would be him. I was always disappointed, and then my disappointment had melted into anger, bitter as coffee. Anger because he'd told me he loved me and then deserted me. He couldn't really have loved me, could he? You don't leave people you love. That's why I'd figured my mum hadn't loved me. She could never have packed her bags if she had.

'Not any more. I still think about him, but it's all over, isn't it? No point in dwelling on it.'

He sighed again. The way he ran his fingers through my hair was making me sleepy. I was so relaxed I could feel every part of my body almost sinking into him and the sofa as though they were grains of sand.

The clock struck midnight. 'I should go,' he said, really quietly now.

The thought of him leaving hurt even more. I didn't know why. Then three little words just came out of my mouth. I didn't plan them. 'Please don't go.'

I couldn't believe I'd said it. I swiftly started backpedalling. 'I'm sorry, I didn't mean that. Of course you should go . . .' I trailed off, blushing into his soft T-shirt before peeling myself away from him.

He lay there for a few moments, just looking at me. He was so handsome it hurt. He still made my heart race like the very first day I'd met him on the train, when I instantly labelled him the most gorgeous man in the carriage, if not the world. It was quite an assumption to make for a twenty-year-old girl who had only ever been as far as Paris on a school trip. Ridiculous, really, wasn't it?

I could see the thoughts racing through his mind before he started to get up. 'I'm sorry, Si. Thanks for the offer, but I'm really tired now. I think I need to go home and take stock of this mess.'

I felt embarrassed. I had done it again. For God's sake. Just like that time I thought it would be a great idea to climb into bed with him and cuddle him.

'Don't worry. I don't know why I said it, really!'

He pulled me in for one more cuddle before walking out quietly, his head still bowed like a sad man.

I didn't sleep well that night. Not well at all.

Nick

Nick. Thirty-two. Single.

Nick. Thirty-two. Single.

Oh, here we go again, I thought, as I sat at my desk, photoshopping a pair of breasts for a cosmetic surgery feature. What a sad bastard I am. A sad, sad bastard. Anxiety was nibbling away at me. Where's your wife, Nick? Oh no, you don't have one. Kids? Course not. Running that art studio you always wished for? Dream on.

The door to my office was shut and the blinds were drawn. I was working away like an angry, disfigured creature that had spent so much time in the dark it would turn into ash if it so much as set foot outside.

I didn't want to see Chloe sashaying around the office and looking at me like I'd just been ejected from a pigeon's bottom. *This* was why I had made that promise to myself about relationships with colleagues. I expected that my next tea would be riddled with arsenic . . . She had skipped work for a few days after we'd broken up and I'd kind of hoped she wouldn't come back, but she did.

An instant message popped up and jolted me from my spiral of self-loathing. It was from Tom.

'COME ON, MOPEY HEAD. DON'T BE SAD ☹'

I sighed and smiled. He was such an idiot, but I liked him. 'I'll be fine, Tom, chill. Let's go for a beer later. What do you reckon?'

'YES. YES AND YES. IN FACT, LET'S GO FOR SEVEN BEERS AND SLEEP IN A BIN SOMEWHERE. SOUND GOOD?'

'My perfect night out.'

'SPEAK LATER, BALL HEAD.'

I couldn't help but smile when I thought about the people around me and how brilliant they were. Not brilliant in terms of changing the world, or even changing their underwear, but I was glad to have them in my life. I was lucky to know them. Even if they did throw things at me and call me testicle-related names.

I picked up my phone and texted Ross:

'Ross. Tom and I are going drinking in Balham tonight. From 6 p.m. in the Sheep's Head. Can you come? Text the boys. Nick.'

The boys. I wondered for a moment why I called them that. I think we're still boys at heart, passing thirty hadn't changed that. Even when we're all wearing puffy shoes with special soles and Velcro fastenings and trying not to fall over on the bus, we'll always be 'the boys'. Some day, though, this boy was going to have to grow up . . .

It was 4 p.m., just another hour before I could leave the office and have some fun. My phone rang; it was an internal call. I suddenly feared it could be Chloe. Oh shit. I picked up the receiver with trepidation but it was Ant, thank God. I never thought I would be happy to hear his voice.

'Nick, can you come to my office for a sec?' he asked.

Oh dear. I was probably in trouble, I thought, as I put the phone down. I was going to have to walk across the office floor now. Past my ex who would probably try and staple my lips together or punch some extra holes in my nose. Head high, Nick. Head high. I felt a sharp pang of regret and foolishness for ignoring the no dating your colleagues rule.

I opened my door and walked across the office, my heart thumping in my chest. I could see her in the corner of my eye but I didn't look. I wasn't going to entertain any of her bullshit. After what seemed like an age I finally reached the foot of his stairs. I took a deep breath of relief, but couldn't help but wonder what was coming.

'Come on, Nick – hurry up, will you!' he shouted jokingly from the management tree house, ruining my attempt at being low-key. Anyone who hadn't noticed me skulk past would certainly know I was there now.

I dashed up the stairs, realising how unfit I was when I reached the top and struggled to catch my breath. He was wearing a dark navy shirt with horizontal stripes, which did his growing stomach no favours at all.

'Sit down, Nick,' he said with a wide grin, which seemed to consume his whole face. He certainly meant it when he smiled, that was for sure, even if it didn't happen too often.

'What's up, boss?' I asked, stretching my legs out and placing my hands over my torso.

'Two things, really. The first is why are you such

a miserable bastard?' He pushed a tray of chocolates and biscuits towards me and I had an awful feeling I was in for some kind of management counselling session. But his man-to-man chats always involved ridicule.

'Me, miserable? Really?' I asked, feigning ignorance.

'Yes, you. Look at the state of your face – there's too much hedge going on. And you aren't ironing your clothes any more.'

He had a point. Chloe always used to iron.

'Come on. I heard about you and Chloe,' he said, pushing some chocolate buttons into his mouth with a knowing look.

I wasn't going to be able to escape this, was I? 'I'll be fine. It's been a few days now, anyway . . .'

'Weeks, Nick. A few weeks. And you look like you haven't washed since then,' he said bluntly, crossing his arms.

I *had* washed . . . and it hadn't been *that* long, had it?

'Well, I have great news for you. She's leaving.'

Oh, thank God, I thought. I wanted to shriek with joy. This was brilliant.

I kept my feelings hidden. 'Oh, gosh. That's a shame. Where's she going?'

He peered over my shoulder in some strange attempt to check she wasn't looking, then he leaned in close and whispered, 'Don't tell anyone this, Nick – and it's going to come as a shock. She's moving away, to live with her old boyfriend

– some guy she met at uni or something. I think it's safe to say "negotiations" were taking place when you two were still together . . .'

Holy shit. Cheated on. Again. So that's why she was acting like that. I didn't quite know how to take it. My mind flashed back to the first time we'd had lunch in the pub and she'd talked about love, about how she'd had it once.

I was furious. A raging, blood-boiling fury was washing over me and all I could do was sit in front of my boss and be 'professional'. How dare she accuse me of cheating when she was having it off with another bloke behind my back all along?

'I'm sorry, mate. It shouldn't be me telling you this, but I'm fed up of looking at you in this state and I think you need a kick up the bum to get over it, yeah?'

I nodded my head, but really I wanted to run down the stairs and confront her. She'd tried to make out it was all my fault that she was leaving – she'd almost had me believing it. I didn't know any more. I felt like I didn't know anyone . . .

'And the second thing . . .' Ant interrupted my thoughts just at the right time. Before I imploded with anger and spontaneously combusted all over his office. A foot hanging from the desk lamp and unidentified bits of me all over his face.

'Yes, Ant, what's that?'

'Sarah, the editor of *SparkNotes*, is leaving. She's going travelling.'

A flashback to the Christmas party, and how

Chloe had known about this a long time ago. Urgh, Chloe. But what did this have to do with me?

'I'm looking for a new editor. It's a big job. And I have someone in mind for it, but I need you to convince me.' He smiled again.

I was starting to think he wasn't that bad at all. A rush of warmth came over me – he must be talking about Sienna. I wanted to jump on my chair and preach to him about how wonderful she was. How hard she worked. About how she deserved it more than anyone in this office. OK, it wasn't the editorship of a big national, but it was bloody amazing for a twenty-five-year-old girl who thought there was nothing ahead of her but prescription tablets and making walls out of cushions.

The possibilities started to whizz through my mind. How she would look in her own office, how she could breathe new life into the magazine, how she would have more money so that she and her father could live a better life. Suddenly I wanted this for her more than anything.

He looked at me expectantly. 'Well, come on then, Nick, you've seen her work more than I have. What do you think? Is she ready?'

'Oh God, Ant, she's ready. She's more than ready. She's a superstar, she's talented, she's, she's incredible . . .' I paused, almost out of breath.

He raised a suspicious eyebrow. 'All right, mate, steady on.'

I turned crimson. I could actually feel my face burning.

'Go on, get out of here,' he chuckled.

'You are going to give it to her, aren't you? You are, please tell me you are,' I begged over the desk, knocking a pile of papers onto the floor.

'I'm not totally sure yet, Nick, but when I know I'll tell you, OK? I'll probably deal with it tomorrow.'

'All right. You'd better,' I said.

All of a sudden I felt light and airy as I walked out of the door and down the stairs. I immediately saw Sienna in front of her desk, typing away like a maniac. I was so excited. Chloe wasn't there, thank goodness – she'd obviously gone to make a drink – so I walked over to Sienna and whispered in her ear. It felt strange because I hadn't done that in such a long time.

'Hello, superstar!'

She jumped a little, then looked around her nervously as if I shouldn't be near her at work. 'Nick. What are you talking about?' she giggled shyly.

I winked at her and walked away, ducking into my office. She looked confused for a moment and then continued typing. I was so happy for her. I had to avoid her because I just knew I would tell her if I spent any time with her.

Five o'clock came and went. I slowly opened my blinds to see 90 per cent of the desks were empty, including hers. The office was quiet. The strip lighting was flickering in that headache-inducing way it does. I looked over to the lift and daydreamed about the moment I'd stepped out of it and she became a part of my life.

At 5.30 p.m. I got up and left the office. I had a little while before I would meet the boys so I figured I would sit in my car for a while and call Mum. It had been a long time since I had caught up with her properly. The sun was still out, but it was dimming now, rich streaks of pink slashed across the sky. I had been miserable this afternoon and now I was feeling happier.

'Er, excuse me.' A deep, gruff voice pierced my moment. It was definitely a London accent, but one that had a tinge of well-spoken grace to it, too. Like the person behind it had evolved some-what. I looked around me as I stood by my car. Who on earth . . .?

Suddenly a scruffy bloke rose slowly from the other side of the vehicle. He was scary-looking, but I recognised him . . . I just couldn't put my finger on it . . . It was bugging me. In one hand he was clutching a can of Coke, in the other was a sack full of heavy-looking stuff. Books, maybe? He looked angry. Oh no. What was he going to do to me?

'Are you Nick?' he asked, gesturing in my direc-tion with the Coke can. A great slop of brown liquid landed on the roof of my car and fizzed away at the paintwork. Oh shit. Was he drunk?

'Er, yes. Why?'

'I need to get in your car,' he said ominously.

I don't think so, mate. He looked homeless. There was no way I was letting some homeless nutter into my car. No bloody way. Did I look like a crime number waiting to happen?

I am quite stupid, though, and I pressed the wrong button on my key fob, automatically unlocking all the doors. I panicked, staring at the fob, slowing down my reaction time considerably. Before I even had the chance to press lock, the stranger had opened the passenger door and climbed in. Oh fuck.

He sat in the seat, staring straight ahead, and I bobbed around for a moment, shifting my weight from one foot to the other before running around to the other side of the vehicle. I tried to pull him out, grabbing hold of his thin arm and using all my might to prise his body out of my car. My top lip was starting to sweat. Welcome to London. Full of danger at any given moment. I quietly cursed myself for not being more vigilant.

I kept pulling, but he seemed rooted to the seat, one foot rammed into the footwell, firmly anchoring him in. My hands were getting sweaty and kept slipping off the skin of his arms. I was useless. There was lots of grunting, but I wasn't sure if it was his or mine.

'For God's sake, get out!' I shouted, hoping someone would hear me and help.

'No. Listen,' he said, but I just started pulling at him again. He was gripping on to the roof of the car now and it was impossible to drag him out. The car was rocking slightly under the weight of the scuffle. I even put my leg up on the side of the door to get more leverage, but he was clinging on for dear life and doing a very good job of it. I

409

gave up and breathlessly slapped my hands on my knees, wondering what on earth I was going to do next. Maybe I could punch him? I'm not a violent man, but this was self-defence, surely? I gripped my fist tight and prepared myself.

'Who the fuck are you?' I yelled, my voice echoing around the car park back to me. I sounded like a girl.

'Mate, will you chill out! I'm Pete. You know who I am.'

I still didn't have a clue who he was. Pete. Pete. Now who was he? I studied him. His face had that wrinkled look you get when you spend a lot of time outside; there were lines around his eyes that aged him beyond his years. He was wearing a faded black T-shirt and jeans with holes all over them. Then realisation washed over me.

It was Sienna's Pete. The homeless man she spoke to all the time. The guy I thought she wasted her time on. But he looked so much better than he had before – plumper, clean-shaven. Though still not *sorted* . . . I was totally confused.

'Oh bloody hell, I'm sorry.' I reached towards him, but he pulled away angrily.

'So you should be, you silly sod,' he huffed, shuffling his shoulders so his T-shirt fell back into place. 'Now will you let me sit and talk?'

'Why?' I asked, my feathers still a little ruffled by the run-in. I still didn't know what he wanted from me.

'Because I have something to tell you.'

Coldness washed over my body. Why did he want to talk to me? What was going on?

'Oh, all right then, go on,' I conceded, slinging myself into the driver's seat.

He immediately fiddled with the controls and pushed his seat back until he was almost lying down. Oh, go on then, make yourself at home. Then he put his feet up, a pair of dirty trainers all over my clean dashboard. For fuck's sake . . . I cringed. I'd only cleaned the car the other day.

'What do you want?' I knew he was Sienna's 'friend' or whatever, but if you ask me, he had terrible manners.

'It's about Sienna,' he started, turning towards me and looking me straight in the eye. His eyes reminded me of winter, they were cold and piercing. I suddenly wondered how he had coped all this time.

'Go on then, spit it out. I have to go out tonight, pal.' I was itching for a beer, and I didn't really have time for all this. I'd never shown much interest when Sienna had talked about him. I felt bad about that now.

He sighed and looked down at the footwell, which was now covered in brown scuff marks. I noticed his right hand was trembling slightly. He looked overwhelmingly nervous. This in turn made me overwhelmingly nervous.

'She loves you.'

'What?'

'I said she loves you.'

'Who?'

'Sienna, for God's sake. You're supposed to be clever, aren't you?'

'How do you know?'

'She told me. I mean she tells me. All the time. She has always, always, always loved you.' And with this he threw his right hand in the air, splashing me with more Coke.

I didn't care. I wanted to hug him. I wanted to pull this skinny man into my arms and hold him tight for bringing me the best news of my life. I'd never felt so elated.

'Are you joking?'

'No.'

'Are you sure?'

'Yes.'

I slammed my body back into my seat and ran my hands over my face. 'Please, tell me more,' I begged, turning back to him and hoping I hadn't just imagined the whole episode.

'I don't know where to start, really. She'd be furious if she knew I was doing this. I hope I'm doing the right thing.'

I was speechless, so I just nodded at him instead. He could put his dirty feet anywhere now. I didn't care if he stomped all over my favourite shirt and my expensive curtains, so long as he *just told me . . .*

'She's been in love with you ever since she met you and she's never got over it. Well, she said she moved on, when she was with that bloke – what was his name?'

'Ben,' I squeaked, before clearing my throat.

'Yeah, him. Anyway, I just couldn't take it any more. I lost my wife, Nick – she died in a train crash. The kind of love I know she feels for you is just like the love I had with my wife, Jenny. I can't stand back and not say anything any more. It's been five years, for God's sake.' He tilted his head back and poured the last droplets of Coke into the canyon. 'What do you say? I get the impression you might feel something for her, too? I mean, who wouldn't?' He looked at me searchingly. Hopefully.

'Of course I bloody love her,' I said, slamming both hands on the steering wheel and accidentally pushing the horn. We both jumped.

I was truly shaking now. I needed to calm down. 'What, what, what am I going to do?' I asked him, stuttering.

'Tell her, and for God's sake hurry up, will you? She's a bloody angel,' he said, smiling at the thought of her. 'You're a lucky man,' he added.

I agreed. So, so lucky. I would talk to the boys tonight, and then tomorrow, I was going to tell her. And I was going to make it perfect.

'Do you have any idea what she's done for me?' he asked, looking a little emotional now.

'No. No. I don't really know.' To be honest, I'd grown a bit tired of hearing her worrying about this guy. I'd told her she had enough on her plate. I'd been so wrapped up in myself these last few weeks that I hadn't even realised she still saw him.

413

'She's saved me from the streets, Nick. She got me an outreach worker, and now I have somewhere to sleep. I'm in a permanent hostel. I might even have a job coming up and my own place one day. And it's all because of her . . . I feel terrible that I never thanked her for what she did for me. We fell out in a big way the last time I saw her. I don't know what to say to her to make it better, but I had to do something for her the way she did something for me . . . Look after her for me, Nick,' he said, starting to open the door.

'No, don't go.' I wanted to know more. I'd thought I knew everything, yet behind the scenes she had rescued this man from cold oblivion. From a life of want and hunger.

'You know what to do now. I have to go,' he said, swiftly leaving the car and slamming the door behind him. I watched as he slung his bag over his shoulder and disappeared into the evening.

She loves me. I collapsed on to the steering wheel, wondering what on earth I was going to do next. This was special. I had to wait for the right moment. I sat in the car for a while. A small part of me wanted to cancel the drinks and just drive somewhere so I could think.

I realised I was too shaken to drive, but I felt like I could fly.

CHAPTER 14

IT WAS THE RACK.
IT MADE ME TALK.

Sienna

It was just Nick and I sitting opposite each other on a bench. I didn't recognise where we were, but I knew it was somewhere in London. It was the start of a hot evening. He had brought me here with a black ribbon over my eyes, and I was baffled when he whipped it away to reveal a typical urban street scene that had nothing special about it apart from the fact that he was there.

But I didn't ask questions. I trusted him and his master plan, whatever the hell it was. He had this look in his eyes, one I'd never seen on him before. It was excitement etched with fear, like something really big was about to happen. And even though this bench was on a dirty street somewhere in the city, he was wearing a shirt that made him look like something from a Burberry campaign. He had never looked so good. In his right hand was a flower. A huge red rose that was such a shocking shade of crimson it made everything around it seem black and white apart from the dewy skin on Nick's face reflecting the neon lights from a row of shops.

My heart started racing. What was happening here? I tried to speak but he reached his hand out towards my face and pushed his thumb against my mouth, dragging the skin of my bottom lip down towards my chin. My breath caught in my throat. The traffic around us was a blur and the people seemed to just disappear as he leaned in slowly and pulled his hand away, replacing the gentle pressure with his own mouth. Not quite kissing me, but nearly. So close. I. Could. Just. Melt. He started to speak while his lips were pressed against mine. I felt light-headed. 'Sienna, I just want to tell you that I—'

BEEP BEEP BEEP. Nick and the rose and the bench and the cars were suddenly whipped away from me like a tablecloth from under a four-course banquet. The sound was so sharp it made me jump and I rolled over to silence it. I was sleepy enough that I could hardly see but somehow I managed to locate my phone, which was twisted up in my bed sheets. Bam. Back to reality.

It was a Friday. It would probably be just like all the others, I thought grumpily as I realised that I'd missed 'the kiss' in my only good dream for months. After a coffee I was more accepting of the situation. It was, of course, just a dream – Nick didn't love me, I knew that, and life goes on. Time to get real.

Dad was particularly chirpy this morning, which

pulled me out of my mire of self-pity. 'It's Friday, Sienna,' he said as he lolled around on the sofa on his back, holding a huge map of the world in front of his face. It sagged in the middle and made a loud crunching sound as he punched his fist into the centre to try and straighten it out. The thing looked like it was going to swallow him up inside its folds.

'Yes indeed, Dad,' I replied. 'What are you doing?'

'Well, I'm mapping out the places I'd like to visit if I could just up, leave and go travelling. I'm imagining that you and me are going, little one. And then I'm going to write about our adventure, country by country.' He looked at me with beady eyes. The four great corners of the world sagged beyond his hands and curled around his arms.

This hurt a little. I felt that twinge I get so often with my father when I realise that not only is he accepting of the rubbish cards he's been dealt, but he refuses to be defined by them. It's a blend of piercing sadness and overwhelming pride. A confusing mixture. I can imagine it would be fairly easy to get angry and frustrated, and stop caring about everything beyond the walls of our little flat in west London. But instead of becoming bitter, my father explores all the possibilities like he's out there living them. He does it with HB pencils, leaving shavings behind him everywhere he goes, which I have to clear up with a dustpan and brush. Words. Drawings. Charts. I don't mind at all.

'Wow, that sounds like a massive project, Dad. Can we go to India, please?' I sat down next to him on the sofa, pointing at my destination of choice with a dark-painted fingernail. He put his arm around my waist and squeezed me tight. I squeezed him back.

'Of course, Sienna. Wherever you want to go. I'm going to research each and every place on our route – the food, the way it smells, the customs, all of it. And in a few months' time you'll be able to read all about our travels. We can pick five places each, you and I, and I want your choices as soon as possible, please,' he concluded, turning to look at me like it was real. Like it was actually going to happen. I wanted to squeeze him really tight and not let go for a long time. But I was running late, so instead I gave him a kiss on the cheek and shoved the last bite of toast into my mouth before dashing out to work.

'I love you, Dad,' I said, stopping in the doorway to look at him for a moment as I prepared to be swallowed up by the real world.

'I love you too, Sienna,' he answered, not even looking up from his map.

There was never enough time. Life seemed to be running away from me.

Slipping through my fingers. It was all hospital runs, coffee queues, office meetings and interviews. Absolute chaos.

As soon as I got outside I realised that it was an exceptionally beautiful summer morning and the triviality of my Nick-induced misery started to slip away. It seemed like the whole city was smiling and I was just a tiny part of it all, totally overwhelmed by the majesty of this day. The birds were singing from the rows of tall trees along the road, trees so characteristic of this part of London. Fresh fruit and vegetables were lined up temptingly outside the shopfronts near the station, their colours so bright I could almost taste them.

I felt lucky. It was impossible to experience a morning like this and not be happy. I thought about how much was ahead of me, how maybe one day I would meet The One, and if I was *really* blessed I might have beautiful, happy children. Of course, that was a very long way off, but all of a sudden, everything seemed so full of promise.

I grabbed my morning coffee and a copy of *Metro* before boarding the train. It was full, bodies seemingly squashed into every corner, newspapers folded under armpits and coffees balanced precariously on ledges and seats. As the sweaty carriage pulled away from the station, a modest breeze seeped through an open window near my face. It gently ran its fingers through my fringe, causing it to flap up and down as if someone was yanking it with string. It gave me some relief from the morning crush.

I took a few deep breaths and looked around me. It was one of those mornings where instead of burying my face in a book or a paper, I just took in London and how incredible it is. It made me sit up and soak in the mad city energy. The different faces, the strange things you see on the streets, the sounds and the smells.

Then I remembered. As though it were happening all over again. It was something of a flashback. I recalled looking over the top of the newspaper five years ago to see the most handsome man I had ever laid eyes on, wearing a bright green T-shirt. We'd looked at each other over the pages, and I hadn't known it back then, but something really quite remarkable had begun. It was a love story. But not as you might perceive it.

In most love stories, the guy and the girl like each other the same amount and manage to eventually get over their crippling fear/bashfulness and sort it out. In this love story, I, Sienna Walker, have loved Nick Redland for five years. And what do I have to show for it? Love, yes – but of a rather different sort. Love that comes from friendship, which is almost worth more, really, because friends don't have sex, get fed up, and then avoid each other like the plague.

I could just picture him now, with that gorgeous grin of his revealing a row of straight, white teeth. There was something about his smile that made me want to keep looking. And I haven't stopped looking, all this time . . . I realised I was pulling an idiotic expression while staring at an elderly woman sitting opposite me who looked nothing like Nick. She shuffled uncomfortably. My coffee was going cold, too, so I calmed myself down and took some gentle sips as the train clicked along the tracks.

I wondered how he was. We'd hardly seen each other lately. He'd been distant since Chloe left and then seemed a bit strange yesterday, suddenly coming over and calling me a superstar before going back into his office and not emerging at the usual time. Superstar? I think he was having another of his crisis moments because of what had happened with Chloe. He was probably sitting in silence with his head in his lap. I thought it best not to interrupt him. She's crazy, just leaving him like that. Why would you leave Nick? Just why?

My mind replayed the moment when I'd lost sight of him and thought I would never see him again. How I threw my cup in the bin and walked to the office, almost forgetting I'd ever seen his face. Yet strangely, it had been his face that greeted me when the lift doors opened and . . . Oh, come on, Sienna. Think of something else for a change, will you? I told myself off again. But it never seemed to work.

When I arrived at the office it seemed that Nick was still in a peculiar mood. But rather than looking depressed, like he had yesterday, he was bouncing around the office as if his legs had been replaced with springs.

'Morning, Si!' he shouted as I stepped out of the lift, almost running across the room towards me.

'Morning, Nick,' I said, slightly bemused by the

wild change in his demeanour within the course of twenty-four hours. Maybe she had gone back to him. They might have sorted things out. He had that hysteria about him that could only be the result of hours of make-up bonking. His smile was electric – it was as if someone was tickling his neck with a feather duster.

He looked good. I mean, he always looks good, but since he and Chloe split up he had sunk into this strange quagmire, which seemed to involve a ban on razors and the inability to use an iron. I guess that's what people used to say he was like after Amelia, too. This morning he was wearing a skinny-fit black shirt and a pair of grey trousers. He looked really smart. Yup. This was definitely woman-related. He was wearing aftershave again. The one that makes me want to bury my face in his neck and stay there until the world stops fighting and the price of petrol drops.

'What's with the grin, eh?' I asked as I sank into my chair and started leafing through my diary.

'Oh, nothing, Si. I want to talk to you later, by the way.' He started fiddling with my phone cord awkwardly.

I slapped his hand away. 'Stop doing that, you're going to twist it up. Why, what's up?'

I couldn't face another counselling session, telling him to make things right with Chloe if he truly loved her and all that jazz. It was hard to tell him to do something I so desperately didn't want to happen.

'Nothing much. Can we go for dinner tonight? You know, a nice restaurant or something? Get a few cocktails in.'

I stared at him, directly into his eyes. He looked so wild and strange it felt appropriate to hold his hand and pull him towards me, whispering into his ear this time. 'Nick, what's happened? Do you need to take a day off sick? Are you smoking weed again?'

'No, Sienna, for God's sake. Can't we just go for a drink?'

'Yes, of course, but you just look bizarre today . . .'

As he pulled his face away from my ear, he was smiling like a demented clown. He smelled so good it hurt. I couldn't cope with all this again. Not again.

'Just chill out, I'm fine. Just want to go for a bite to eat, yeah?' he reiterated, poking his right foot at the bottom of my chair and pushing one of the wheels round.

I slapped his leg gently, accidentally feeling his muscles. Wowzers.

'All right, if Dad's OK we can go out,' I said, finally giving in.

'Wicked,' he replied, before twitching a little and prancing off into his office like an imp. Weirdo.

I thought it was just Nick acting oddly. But then Lydia walked over. She was also behaving utterly bizarrely. It must be a Friday thing.

'Hello gorgeous,' she purred, leaning over my desk and twiddling her hair with a strange smile on her face. She looked like she had big news. On the scale of 'I'm pregnant' or 'I'm taking part in next year's *Big Brother*' – you know, life-changing stuff.

'Hello, you, how's it going?' I said, half concentrating on my diary and half concentrating on the ample bosom that was spilling from her top. God knows how men coped – I was well and truly distracted.

'I'm great, thanks,' she said. Then she glanced behind her before wheeling up an exceptionally squeaky chair too quickly, accidentally slamming it into the table leg, and knocking over my precarious filing system in one swoop.

'I heard about you and—' she started before Nick suddenly reappeared and interrupted us, grabbing Lydia by sharply yanking her away midsentence. The chair was left turning on its own in the middle of the room.

Me and who? I watched them scurry into his office and the door was closed hard, causing the blinds to rattle loudly against the glass. Whatever. I'd find out later.

As I fired up my computer I tried to remember what I had on today. My diary was pretty bare . . . it could end up being quite boring. Still, there did seem to be this odd frenzy going on with the people around me. Dad was planning trips round the world, Nick was verging on hysteria and Lydia knows about me and someone, or something . . .

I got up slowly and strolled over to Dill's fish

424

tank, right in the middle of the office on top of a filing cabinet. He would be normal. He couldn't help it. He didn't have the memory for violent mood swings. I leaned forward and peered into the glass, my nose gently bumping against the smooth, cool surface. Dill looked so lonely, I thought, watching him swim around the murky water, past the small pink castle covered in green gunk. He also looked hungry, so I picked up a pinch of fish flakes between my thumb and my index finger and sprinkled them onto the surface. He immediately darted up and started grabbing at them with his little mouth. How cute. The office strip lighting was reflecting against his body, showing flashes of luxurious gold every time he moved. I almost fell into a trance staring at our office pet when I saw a face on the other side of the glass. A face so familiar to me, yet through the layers of glass and water it was stretched out to almost unrecognisable proportions. Dill rushed towards the face squashed up against the glass of his tank and tried to touch it with his mouth.

'Nick, you're so silly,' I said, refusing to move away from the tank because something about this was so cool. It was my romantic fish tank scenario, except with mildew, algae and, well, my friend Nick.

'I know,' he said, peeling his features from the glass and rubbing his cheek. 'Sorry I pulled Lydia away like that,' he continued, his voice quite muffled now.

'Yeah, why did you do that? I thought she was about to give me some gossip,' I replied, in a slightly louder voice this time.

Suddenly his face disappeared and materialised next to me. It made me jump. 'So what's the news?' I asked, turning to face him.

'Er, nothing,' he said, scratching his head with a pencil before casually slipping it behind his ear. It fell straight out the other side and dropped onto the floor. He never does that. What on earth is going on?

'Anyway, Sienna, I was thinking that maybe we could go to Amis tonight, yeah?'

Amis. Amis is a very posh restaurant and bar. Posh as in lots of cutlery, finger bowls and serviettes crafted into the shape of woodland animals. Holy shit.

'Amis? Really? Don't you just want to go to the Sheep's Head or something like that? I hear the Naughty Step has a two-for-one happy hour . . .' I said, tilting my head to one side and looking into his eyes. They had an extra sparkle about them today; the definite tinge of a lunatic.

'No, no. Let's go to Amis. I'll book a table for eight, OK?'

'Er, OK. Sounds great,' I said and watched him walk away from me and disappear into his office.

Oh God, what the hell was I going to wear? And would I have enough time to go home, get ready, and get back into Balham for dinner? Lydia looked over to me and put her thumbs up before pulling her fingers over her mouth to imitate a zip. Hmm.

At around lunchtime Chloe sauntered over to my desk. She also seemed edgy. Her hair was very curly today; she had taken out her trademark plaits. She was wearing a navy blue shirt and leggings.

'Hello, Si,' she said as she sat down beside me. She started to pick the remnants of pink varnish from her fingernails. I felt like an agony aunt for the hysterical. Go on. Roll up a chair. Be weird. Maybe I should get a box of tissues, some potpourri and a home furnishings magazine.

'Hello, Chlo. You OK?' I asked, really hoping she wouldn't give me an honest answer and just say 'Fine.' I'd decided to have no real involvement in her break-up with Nick. It was a dangerous place to be treading, and I wanted nothing to do with it apart from being there for Nick, whenever he needed me. My loyalties lay with him.

'I'm great, thanks. Ant asked me to tell you he wants to see you this afternoon at three for a meeting.'

'Oh no. It isn't bad, is it?' I asked, suddenly seeing myself in a dole queue.

'No. I can't tell you, though, because I don't know what it's about. He just asked me to notify you of the meeting,' she said, biting her bottom lip and looking at her lap.

'Chloe, are you OK?' I asked, suddenly aware that she seemed tearful.

'Yes, yes. I'm just . . . I'm just . . . Don't worry,' she said, whipping her head to look over at Nick's office and then disappearing almost as soon as she'd arrived. I decided not to follow her.

A meeting with Ant at 3 p.m. I really hoped I wasn't going to get fired. I've been trying so hard lately. All I wanted to do was stand out, but what with everything at home I felt like I was sinking slowly under piles of washing, ironing and pencil shavings. I was often late because I had to take Dad to the doctor's or the hospital. Sometimes I had to call in sick just to stay with him at home. Maybe that just wasn't OK any more . . .

I picked up my phone and dialled Nick's line. 'Nick, what's going on? Why am I meeting Ant at 3 p.m. today?' I asked, whispering and ducking my head below the partition so no one could see me. I fiddled with a silver photo frame Elouise had bought me a few months ago; it had our names engraved on it.

'I have no idea what it's about, Si.'

'Come on.'

'I don't.'

'Nick . . .'

'Sienna, I don't bloody know, OK?'

'Nick. You're his right-hand man. Please tell me, am I going to get fired?'

'I have to go, there's someone at the door,' he said in his joke robot voice that I usually found so funny, but not right now.

'Nick, I know full well there's no one at your door,

I can see your office right in front of me and if you hang up I'm going to—'

And that was it. I was cut off. Unfinished. Unresolved. Bugger.

I was in a state of anxiety for the rest of the day. My stomach churned. My hands trembled. What would I do if I lost my job? How would Dad and I cope? These thoughts kept flying around my head until I was finally sitting in front of Ant. He had his feet up on the desk and was leaning so far back in his chair that I felt an accident was imminent. This was not the body language of an axeman, I considered, but that was a short-lived comfort.

'Right then, Sienna. Do you want some tea?' he asked, putting both arms behind his chubby neck.

Tea. That's never good. Tea is a drink used to calm people down. Like for example, 'Here, have a cup of tea – oh, and by the way, your rabbit died at the hands of a demonic, rabid fox last night.'

A box of tissues was sitting in front of me, a flash of white poking from the top and flaring out invitingly as if to say 'Go on, it's been a while, have a cry, *use me.*'

'What's going on, Ant?' I questioned, taking a deep breath to steady my nerves, which must have been as obvious as daylight.

'Right, well. This won't come as a surprise to you, Sienna, because quite frankly your performance here has been' – oh God, I thought, he's seen how preoccupied I've been – 'exceptional,' he started.

Did I just hear that right?

'I have a job for you, a new one. We need a new editor for *SparkNotes*. The current editor has announced her intention to leave the company to travel. I want you to replace her.'

Me? Sienna? I almost turned around to see if anyone else was in the room. Maybe there had been a horrible case of mistaken identity. My stomach plunged with excitement and I stared at his forehead for a while.

'Sienna?' he nudged, pulling his feet away from the desk now and shuffling forwards in his chair, his elbows on a pile of paperwork.

'What, really? Definitely me?' I muttered before realising I should show a little more confidence in myself.

'Of course, Si. You're a star. You probably want to check the details of the job and everything, but I'm sure you know what it entails.'

Of course I know what it entails. It's a job I've been coveting like Brad Pitt's bottom ever since I arrived. It means being the editor of a music magazine read by 500,000 people. Editor at the age of twenty-five, and my own team of journalists. Surely this must be a mistake. I couldn't help but wonder if Nick had had something to do with this . . .

'And of course it involves a pay rise for you, and a car, too,' he said, pushing a sheet of paper towards me with a figure on it much higher than I had imagined. 'I think this will be a great opportunity for you. I really do. I can't think of anyone more suitable to run this publication for us,' he concluded, folding his arms over his belly.

Oh wow. My mind started whizzing through the possibilities. I could do the things I'd always wanted to do – get more social media going, create branded features, inject some more enthusiasm into the journalists by actually listening to them and inspiring them . . .

This was incredible, and completely out of the blue. Chloe had said this job would be up for grabs back at the Christmas party, but I'd never thought it would come to anything. I'd never really imagined it to be a possibility . . .

'Ant. Thanks so much. I don't really know what to say!'

'Say yes, maybe?' he said, with a nervous grin.

'Yes, yes! Of course!' I shrieked.

'Brilliant. Well done,' he replied, handing me a wedge of documents.

'Now get out of here,' he said, chuckling to himself and picking up the phone.

I scuttled out of the office, unsure about what to do next. All I wanted to do was jump for joy. Start making plans. Start my new life. Tell my dad. I just couldn't wait to tell him. I saw my father and me as a team, and I had just scored a home run for us. *For us.*

Nick *must* have known. I guess that was what he

was hinting at when he mentioned dinner tonight. I scuttled back to my desk, grabbed a Post-it note and with a thick black biro I wrote five words:

India. Fiji. Uganda. Argentina. Thailand.

Nick

Tonight my life is going to change. I'm going to tell the girl of my dreams that I love her.

I'm not going to rush into it and tell her everything I've buried deep for so long over the photocopier in the stationery room. Timing is key.

I took a razor to my chin and removed the small forest of facial fluff that had grown all over it. Then I got the iron out and ran it over the garments that had built up in a pile in the corner of my bedroom. This included my red and white striped shirt. The one I'd worn to Florida that time Sienna and I covered the gaming fair. The night we lost all our cares in a strip of uptown bars. I was going to wear it tonight.

I'd felt nervous when I woke up this morning. What if Pete was wrong? What if he was playing a prank? What if I told her and she laughed at me? Oh God, this was terrifying. Aftershave might help, I thought, as I stood in front of the mirror, looking at a terrified me.

Ross had well and truly calmed me down at the pub last night, but this morning I was back to square one.

'She loves me, Ross,' I'd said hurriedly, as soon

432

as Tom realised that he'd got pissed too quickly and had to leave at 9 p.m., walking into a bar stool on his way out.

I'd been itching to say something all evening, but I couldn't in front of Tom. His premature drunkenness was perfectly timed.

'Who? Your mum?' asked Ross, starting to chuckle before patting me on the back. Oh, the 'your mum' jokes – popular at school, rife at university, still unavoidable in later life . . .

'No, well yes, she does, but I'm talking about Sienna,' I said, rolling my eyes in frustration.

'What?' cried my friend, who had only just stopped laughing and was now staring at me in shock. His time at the gym now saw him looking quite a lot like one of those jumbo Toblerone bars you can buy in airports. I could almost hear the buttons on his top shrieking in fear before they tore away from the fabric and pinged into shirtless oblivion.

'Yes. Is it that hard to believe?' I joked.

'Well, a little. After five years? Are you sure about this?'

Thanks a lot, Ross. You could be a bit happier for me. Was it really that hard to believe? Maybe all the muscles he'd developed lately were stopping the blood flowing to his brain properly and rendering him emotionless.

'Yes. Well, it's utterly bizarre. She's friends with this homeless guy called Pete and after work today he was hanging around my car.'

'Right . . .' said Ross dubiously as he played with a ring of water on the table, left by the condensation from his glass.

As I spoke I realised how ridiculous this story sounded. 'At first I didn't recognise him. I thought he was going to mug me or something, so we had a bit of an embarrassing scuffle, but anyway—'

'You tried to beat up a homeless man?' He arched one eyebrow questioningly, starting to grin from ear to ear.

'No, no, no. Well, I guess, almost. For God's sake, let me finish. I realised it was him and I let him in my car, and he told me,' I concluded, throwing both hands in front of me and sitting back in my chair with a look of elation.

'Sienna has loved you for five years and she told a tramp and not you.' The eyebrow twitched again as he assessed me. 'You need to tell me more.'

So I told him. Everything. The whole conversation. The slops of Coke, the dirty boots on the newly cleaned dashboard, the horn-beeping joy of it all.

And then he softened. 'Fucking hell, Nick. This is huge. I'm so, well, happy for you, mate,' he said with a smile. I could tell he was confused and I didn't blame him.

Usually when I met up with Ross it was to discuss something awful or humiliating I'd done, which I think, in a way, gave him great pleasure. But for once things were going my way and I hadn't done something that would have my mate pissing himself at my expense. Now all the stars had aligned for me (for once) and he was unsure of what to say next.

'So you've told her how you feel, right?' he asked, shoving a handful of peanuts into his mouth.

'No.'

'What?'

'I said no.'

'You idiot!'

'Thanks. Why am I an idiot? What have I done now?'

'So basically, the girl of your dreams loves you, even though it was as obvious as the nose on my face—'

'You do have a big nose, pal,' I interrupted him.

'You've loved her for five whole agonising years and yet as soon as you find out she feels the same, you're sitting in this dingy pub with me, your fat friend, drinking overpriced, flat beer.'

'You're not fat, Ross, you just took the body-building a bit too far.'

He ignored me. 'So you're sitting in the pub with your fat friend rather than knocking down her door and sorting this out?'

'I was waiting for the right . . . moment?' I said, a cold wave of realisation washing over me.

He looked at me. I looked at him. He had a point. There was almost a minute of silence while we mourned the loss of something. My common sense.

'Should I go now?' I said, suddenly standing up

and grabbing hold of my jacket, ready to sweep her off her feet.

'No, no, no,' he said, pulling me right back down again.

'What? You're confusing me.'

'It's nearly ten, Nick, and to be honest you look like a homeless guy yourself. Plus, judging by the look in your eyes I reckon you're about 60 per cent drunk, which means you'll probably ruin the whole thing.' He took a huge gulp of his pint, keeping an absolutely straight face.

I'd imagined this moment to be a little different to how it had turned out. I'd thought it would involve lots of smiling, backslapping and deep man-talk about love that would make us so emotional we'd both have to clear our throats and 'go for a quick walk outside'. I didn't know if it was the alcohol, or the knowledge that Sienna felt the same, but it seemed as though I was walking on clouds all the way back home that night.

But my nerves seemed to treble when I saw her walk into the office this morning, and rather than locking them away somewhere quiet like I should have done, I bounded over to her before she'd even had the chance to sit down. I think I might have freaked her out.

Lydia almost blew my cover too. I'd bumped into her in the lift earlier. 'Hey, Lyds,' I said, folding my newspaper in half and starting to read the front-page story. Again. I'd attempted to read it a few times this morning but my eyes kept hovering over the first line. I was too excited to finish the rest, never mind actually open up the paper. Do. Not. Tell. Her. Be strong, Nick. Mouth shut. Keep quiet.

'Hey, Nick. You OK?' she asked, standing next to me, looking lovely and smelling like fruits of the forest. As usual she looked nice, but there was a lot of boob going on today . . .

'Oh my God, Sienna loves me,' I blurted out as the lift started to pull away from reception. Well done. Idiot. It was the rack – it made me talk.

She turned towards me with her mouth wide open and a look of sheer joy on her face, as if she'd been told she'd won the lottery. 'I know she does!' she shrieked, jumping up and down in a pair of treacherously high shoes.

The lift shook a little so I threw out my hand to stop her. Lifts were scary enough as it was. She knew too? I wondered how many other people knew. And why hadn't they bloody well told me?

We stood and stared at each other in wonder for a few seconds. 'She's liked you for a long time, Nick. I'm so happy for you both.' She giggled, elbowing me in the side before the doors opened, then flounced off way too fast.

But wait . . . It had been such a brief conversation that I'd forgotten to say the most important thing, which was 'Don't say anything, I haven't told her that I know . . .' So later, after Sienna had arrived and I saw Lydia pull up a chair next to her, I had no option but to yank her away. I admit I did tug pretty hard on her arm, but it seemed to work. So far so good. Disaster averted.

It was about 11 a.m. when the phone on my desk rang, waking me from a daydream.

'Right, Nick, I've asked Sienna to come and see me at 3 p.m. about this job.' It was Ant and this was a decision that would change her life forever.

'Brilliant! That's great, Ant. You won't regret it, you really won't,' I said, realising how clichéd this all sounded. But I knew he wouldn't regret it. No one had ever given Sienna responsibility and regretted it. She was more capable than the whole office put together. She was amazing.

'OK, but keep your mouth shut. I'm not talking to her until 3 p.m., and she might even turn it down,' he instructed, before rudely hanging up on me. I didn't care this time.

I thought about her father and how proud he would be. I knew George quite well now, and I knew that this would bring him great joy. But someone like George couldn't go out and do the things other fathers would to show their pride. Chocolates. Balloons. Flowers. Whatever. I knew this would be a bit of a risk, but I was willing to take it. I picked up the phone and dialled. It rang a few times and then eventually there was a click on the other end of the line.

'Hello, George Walker speaking,' he said in an unusually gruff voice. He had obviously been asleep, I thought.

'Hi George, it's Nick,' I replied, feeling a rush of anticipation all over my body.

'Oh, Nick – it's so nice to hear from you.' He sounded really sleepy. I was worried about putting strain on him if he was having an off day.

'You too. I think you need to sit down for this,' I said, knowing that imparting this news while he was standing up would be a bad idea.

'Yes, definitely – hang on a sec.' I heard him sink into his leather chair, which always squeaks when you sit on it. I could just picture him in the flat. Notebooks and plates everywhere, mugs collecting on the table.

'Sienna has achieved something quite amazing today. I don't want to tell you exactly what it is, because that's her job, but she's been given a great promotion,' I started, feeling a bit sick now. I took a deep breath and looked at my noticeboard, which was covered in photos, including one of Sienna and me on a company team-building day. I looked into her eyes and just knew I was doing the right thing.

'Oh, really?' he said, his voice starting to twinge with emotion already.

'It's something so big, it will make you feel very proud.' The hairs rose on my arms as I was saying this.

I heard him breathing heavily down the line. In. Out. He didn't say a word; I knew he was fighting off the dark cloak of sleep.

'You there, George?'

'Yes,' he said quietly.

'OK. If it's all right, I'm going to order some flowers and balloons from you for Sienna. I hope I'm not crossing the line by doing this. It's just, I know you can't go to the shop . . .' Oh dear. I hoped I was doing the right thing.

There was a long pause before he spoke. 'Really? That's ever so kind, Nick.'

Phew. 'Well, it's nothing. They're from you – I don't really have anything to do with it. It's just . . . this is big news, George, and I want you to be able to celebrate with her . . .' I trailed off. I felt I'd handled it OK and I was glad.

'Thank you, Nick. You mean a lot to us both, I hope you know that,' he said, very slowly now.

'You too, George. I'll order them now so they arrive by the time she gets home. I'll tell the company to leave them in the cupboard by your door if you're unable to answer it.'

There was some more heavy breathing and then the phone clicked off. He was probably asleep.

I ordered the most beautiful bunch of flowers, a bottle of Moët champagne, a card and two big helium balloons. I couldn't wait to see her for dinner later. I was going to tell her.

Tell her I love her and always have, since the day we met.

CHAPTER 15

'DAD. TEA'S READY.'

Sienna

It had been an agonising countdown for the clock to strike five so I could rush home to tell Dad. He'd be so happy I reckoned he would fall asleep immediately, but that would say it all, wouldn't it? That was more than enough for me. Then I was to go out for dinner with Nick to celebrate. I just couldn't wait. This was so exciting.

As soon as the second hand reached the right spot I quietly packed up my things, trying hard not to seem so desperate to leave the office. I wanted to run outside and tell the world that everything was OK. Everything had worked out just fine . . .

The usual suspects had already scarpered, shaving an extra five minutes off the working day. Yet I knew that Julie and Alan in admin would pretend to be working for at least an extra hour for those horrible office Brownie points they seem to be dying to collect. They stumble into the office early with their shirts inside out and a piece of toast hanging from their mouths, and leave sometimes several hours late, almost frothing at the mouth with hunger and exhaustion. And what does it really achieve?

No, tonight I was going to be strict on myself. I was leaving at five, and wouldn't be pulled into all this bullshit, so I could see my father and then have some fun with Nick. I was going to present my list to Dad so he could start writing about our adventures. I waved goodbye to the last clingers-on and peered into the small office that would soon be mine. Luckily it was quite a distance away from Nick's. At least now his window would be out of sight, so I'd be able to focus on the task at hand. And what a task it was.

The office was small but bright and all the walls were painted ivory. I imagined myself sitting in there, living out my dreams. This was really going to change my life.

The car alone would make a huge difference. This would mean we could go out. Dad and I – out. I imagined walking him slowly to the front seat with an arm around his shoulder and driving him around at weekends so he could see more of the world. He could breathe the fresh air of the seaside and eat fish and chips with the door open. I could take him to Yorkshire where he could see all the pretty stone walls cutting across the fields like scars. He could actually get out and experience the world rather than tottering around our balcony garden, with its thick, high fence just in case he falls. Maybe he would snooze for a lot of the journey, but still . . .

This was the start of a new chapter for my dad and me. I could take him to visit family, even though they never came to him. It would be all too easy to hold a grudge, but that wasn't the point of life, was it, to hold grudges? Babies had been born in our family. New lives, new beginnings. And my dad hadn't been any part of it. I didn't think my dad had held a baby since I'd been one. And I wanted the youngsters in my family to grow up knowing my dad. Not to know my father is to miss out . . . The thought of the places we could go to brought a lump to my throat. I could wholeheartedly say it meant more than the promotion itself.

As I walked towards the station listening to Ellie Goulding through my earphones, my head was swamped with the wonderful memories I had yet to experience. I was walking on air. And tonight I was going out with my best friend to celebrate the occasion. I almost broke into a run to get home once I'd left the train, but everyone seemed to be getting in my way as if the world was conspiring against me. Charity touts were approaching me, plying me with their guilt-inducing spiels, newspaper stands seemed to be all over the pavements, and there were lots of people with those suitcases on wheels, all making it difficult for me to navigate my path. Still, I wouldn't let it deflate my mood.

The crowds were like treacle until I neared my road and then they dispersed to clear the way. My chest was full of excitement as I prepared to tell

Dad all about my news. How would I start? So, Dad . . . I mouthed the words under my breath as I hurried along the streets. I have something to tell you . . . Dad, I got promoted – things are going to be very different for us now . . . Dad, I made it! Whatever way I imagined it coming out, it all seemed so corny, and just not really my style. I decided to ad lib and let it roll.

I turned the key in the door and as soon as it opened I was greeted by a huge bunch of pink and white flowers, which sat on the doormat looking lusciously at me, a small card wedged inside. Unable to speak, I reached down and opened the card. I immediately recognised the shaky writing. It must have taken him ages to do this – but how had he known? I hadn't even told him yet. A thin line of biro trailed off from one letter where he must have fallen asleep mid-word. The third kiss was particularly wobbly.

To you, Sienna, my gorgeous girl,
I am more proud of you than I have ever been.
We are family, you and me, however small the
unit.
  Thanks for being my world.
  Love, Dad
  x x x

'Dad!' I exclaimed, choked up with thick tears. 'Thanks so much! I'm so happy, you literally have no idea . . .'

Nick must have told him. What a sweetheart, I thought as I hurriedly kicked off my shoes, losing my balance and nearly knocking over our coat stand in the process. I managed to steady myself by gripping on to the radiator. Phew. I scooped up the flowers and buried my head inside; the most crisp, stunning smell wafted up my nostrils. I stood there for a minute, taking it all in before speaking again. Amazing things like this didn't happen very often. I wanted to seize the moment to take a picture in my mind, so I could remember this in the hard times.

'Dad?' I tried again. Silence. 'Dad!' I shouted, even louder. Nothing. Probably asleep, I thought with a smile. I turned into the living room; it was pretty dark and so quiet I could hear the clock ticking as if it was right next to my ear. I would find him snoozing in his room, I bet. Hmm, I thought, that's a shame – I was busting to tell him. I decided to make some tea.

I turned into the kitchen and saw something that struck me as odd, but not totally out of the ordinary. The bottom half of Dad's legs on the floor, poking out from behind the kitchen counter. A pair of fluffy brown slippers at the bottom of some black tracksuit pants. My dad. Two pink helium balloons floated in the air, bobbing sadly against the ceiling. Bump. Bump.

My stomach plunged. I couldn't look. Please, no. *Please.* I stood still, my heart thumping in my chest. Nausea started to rise in my throat. Now

445

come on, Sienna, I told myself sternly. It's probably just one of his usual falls, he's likely to still be passed out. I looked over at the sofa. His crash helmet was sitting uselessly on a cushion, staring back at me. Shit. He wasn't wearing his crash helmet.

There was silence, broken intermittently by the gentle thud of the balloons, which were shifting in the cool breeze from an open window. Calm. Quiet. Peace.

I took a deep breath and one step forward. I saw my father lying face down on the floor. My eyes seemed to zoom in and out, trying to make sense of a small pool of blood surrounding his head. The balloons were streaming from his right hand, which was gripped into a fist. The ribbons ran through his fingers. My heart sank, and my head started to spin immediately. Adrenalin trickled into my legs like alcohol. I felt weak. No. This was some kind of sick joke.

I rushed down to his body and pressed my trembling hand against his cheek. It was cold. I instantly started to cry, my whole body shaking as if I had been left outside on a wintry night. I felt the distinct moment when my heart broke into tiny little pieces. It was like a tearing in my soul, each twist and rip made me feel like the world had really ended. I was losing my grip, losing him.

I pushed my fingers against his lips, into his neck, on to his chest, frantically searching for a sign of life. A heartbeat. A breath. *Anything.*

'No. No. No. No. No,' I started to say again and again. I shouted it out in my empty flat so loudly it echoed around the walls and came back to taunt me before the ticking of the clock took over again.

'Please, no, not my dad!' I shouted it so piercingly this time I felt like the world might hear it. My throat felt as if it would split I yelled so loudly, and my voice cracked under the strain.

I lay across his back, crying so hard it hurt. My lungs rattled. My breath was choked with tears. This physically hurt.

Not my dad. No, please. Please. Please. I ran my hands over his face, then wrapped my arms around his chest, gripping on to him. I squeezed hard. Nothing happened. My mind started to twist and turn as I lay there.

Eventually shock set in and I calmly got up and put the kettle on. No, this wasn't right. I was definitely imagining the whole thing. I'd been under a lot of stress lately. This was just a figment of my imagination. You hear about this kind of thing all the time, don't you? Don't you?

The water boiled so hard that the kettle rattled against the work surface. Teaspoons clattered in a pot. I got two mugs. One green. One blue. I poured the water into them, on top of teabags and sugar. I needed to be good to myself. Give myself a moment to take in my promotion, everything that had happened. Dad will wake up soon, I thought. I poured a splash of milk into each cup, watching it infiltrate the muddy brown water.

After a time I slowly picked up the mugs and walked into the living room. I sat there for what seemed like hours, just absorbing the silence. I needed to give myself a break. I was clearly going mad. A doctor's appointment. That might help. I would tell my doctor that I was seeing things. Imagining things. Terrible things that weren't actually there. My phone rang. It was Nick. I ignored it. I looked at the clock, it was 7.30 p.m. already. Darkness was creeping into the summer evening, slowly, through the blinds.

A while later, I broke the chasm of quiet. 'Dad, your tea's ready,' I said quietly. He would come in any minute, I just knew it. Shuffle shuffle. That was my father's trademark noise. Maybe I should get his tablets ready, I thought. But then the stabbing realisation started to creep into my mind, and the image of him on the floor kept flashing before my eyes. The haunting silence remained unbroken. I rubbed my eyes hard with my fists, trying to wipe the visions away. It never happened, OK? My bottom lip wobbled uncontrollably.

I tried again, just to be sure. 'Dad. Tea's ready.' My voice was getting hoarse now.

No sound. Tick. Tock. Tick. Tock. 'Your tea, Dad. Come on, hurry up – it's getting cold.'

Tears started to leak from my eyes again, but I felt nothing. Numbness had spread like anaesthetic. They dripped on my lap and my fingers. They collected in the base of my neck like a swimming pool. I bent over and touched his mug. It was cold. Stone cold.

Nick

It was half past ten on Friday night when we broke into Sienna's flat. Her neighbour Jack and I. He told me he'd heard her screaming, had knocked a few times but no one had answered.

'I was supposed to be meeting her for dinner hours ago,' I said to him as we stood in the dingy hallway. I was wearing the red and white striped Florida shirt, my nicest pair of trousers and some posh shoes.

He looked extremely worried. I'd never met him before, although I'd heard of him. I knew he'd helped Sienna and her dad in the past. He had thick, wiry white hair which poked out in tufts and whirls; the skin on his face was grey and wrinkled but there was a warmth about his features. A kindness.

I'd found him hovering around in the hall when I came up to the flat. Pacing up and down. Sienna hadn't answered my calls. I was already concerned, but when I saw him, I knew I had good reason to be troubled.

'I think we need to smash the door down,' he said calmly.

'But she might have just gone out,' I protested, eager not to make a scene. I knew George was probably in there, sleeping quietly with no idea we were outside. Maybe she'd been screaming with happiness about her job, got carried away with it all and forgotten to meet me. Was it really necessary to smash the door down?

'But Nick – it is Nick, isn't it?' I nodded. 'I heard her, mate. She was shouting, she sounded really distressed.' He reached out and put his arm on my shoulder, trying to get some sense out of me.

My heart sank. He was right. This probably was bad.

'She's not the type to just not answer her phone, is she? Not turn up?' he asked, his fists clenched in what I could only assume was unexpressed tension.

'No. No, she isn't,' I conceded, shaking my head.

'Well come on, then, we're going to have to bash this door down.'

I looked at it. It was big and strong and tall. Bigger and stronger and taller than me. I had no idea how two men like us were going to open it.

'Come on,' he urged, taking a few steps back and pressing his body against the wall. He beckoned me to stand next to him. 'And go!' he shouted, and we both ran towards the door, slamming our combined weight into it hard.

I was more of a literature and chess kind of chap than a strong man capable of knocking down mighty structures. It showed. My arm started to throb immediately and my skin tingled as I pulled away. We had made no impression whatsoever.

Then, suddenly, this fire ignited in my soul. I

had to get to her. A strength rose from inside. A force I hadn't even known I had. We ran towards it, again and again, until it was thrown open, launching us both into Sienna's living room.

The door swung violently backwards; the sound of metal parts pinging away and hitting the walls greeted my ears. I could hear wood tearing and cracking, and then it hung sadly from the bottom hinge. I was breathless. Nervous. It was dark. it took a while for my eyes to adjust and then I saw her with her back to us, sitting on the sofa in the pitch black. She didn't even turn around. Oh God. I rushed over to her and threw myself next to her small frame, which was bent right over.

'Sienna, sweetheart. What's going on?' I asked frantically, shaking so much now I could barely hold it together.

She just looked ahead, staring into nothingness. I touched her face gently. It was wet, and more tears were running from her eyes like a tap had been left on in the back of her mind. I held her, so tight. I wrapped my arms around her body and squeezed. I could feel her heart thumping in her chest. She started to shudder.

'Sienna, listen to me.' I grabbed hold of her face now, starting to feel desperate. Then her body became limp and I found myself supporting her weight. 'What's happened?' I begged. She didn't say anything, didn't even acknowledge my presence.

I felt a tap on my shoulder. It was Jack. 'You need to come here,' he said softly in my ear.

I peeled myself away from Sienna, who sank into the cushions, and followed him into the kitchen. A small amount of light was coming from a lamp he'd switched on. There he was. George. Lying face down on the floor, his hands wrapped around the balloons I'd ordered earlier. Oh no, no . . .

I ran back to Sienna and held her again. Grief overwhelmed me and I started to cry. I gently moved her face towards my chest and stroked her hair. I had to protect her from this. Save her. But it was too late. She'd gone through this alone.

'Nick, what are you doing?' she asked, pulling herself up and pressing her nose against mine. Her face was expressionless and her tone was flat.

I put both hands on her cheeks and kissed her nose. 'Si, we need to call an ambulance and the police, OK? We need people to come and help us,' I whispered through my tears, again feeling just as clueless as I had all that time ago when George collapsed on me. *An ambulance*, I thought, unsure of what you're actually meant to do in situations like this.

'No one needs to do anything with my dad. No, they don't,' she said, starting to sob.

I kissed her nose again, this time keeping my lips pressed against her face for longer. 'Look, you just stay here, OK? Lie down. I'm going to sort this out.' I scratched my head and wondered what on earth to do next. She just shook her head and stayed still. 'Please, Sienna – listen to me, OK? I'm going to look after you. I'm going to call the right people who can help us, and then you're coming back to my house with me, all right? I need you to be with me for your own good.'

Eventually she stopped shaking her head and lay down on the sofa, defeated and exhausted. Jack had already started to call the emergency services; he paced around George's body with the phone pressed to his ear, a troubled look across his face.

I rushed into Sienna's room, searching for a bag. I eventually found one and threw as much of her clothing into it as possible. I couldn't even think straight. I managed to pick up her winter coat but swiftly stopped myself as I tried to stuff it in. It was summer, for God's sake. Toothbrush. Shampoo. Shower gel . . .

Soon the flat was filled with green overalls and the sound of ripping Velcro. Sienna eventually stood up from the sofa and watched as they carried out various tests, pushing their fingers into his neck in search of the life that had fled his body. She watched it all but said nothing. I wasn't sure whether I should shield her from it. Cover her eyes. Protect her. Instead, I let her observe them, but held her tight the whole time. I felt it was important that she knew he was in good hands. She said nothing.

When George had been transported from the flat, I took her home. Away from it all. Jack dealt with everything incredibly well. I saved his number to my phone and told him I would call as soon as I could to let him know how Sienna was doing.

The journey was difficult. Driving was difficult.

When she finally agreed to get into the car she started to shake again, but it wasn't because she was cold. It was shock. She stared out of the window for ages, not saying a word until we were about to pull into my driveway.

'He's dead, isn't he, Nick?'

I took a breath and turned off the engine. 'Yes, Si. He is. I'm so sorry.'

She just nodded and opened the door. Something odd had swept over me. My tears had dried and the hysteria had vanished. I had to be there for her and I couldn't do that while I was falling to pieces. I had to be strong. So somehow I was.

That night she slept in my bed with me. She refused to eat and crawled into my bed fully clothed. She was too tired to put on her pyjamas, so we just turned out the light and lay there. Her breathing was totally normal now as she soaked it all in. I didn't want to confuse her with words so I stayed quiet, pulling myself under her body and wrapping my arms around her again, holding on to her tightly. Sorrow. Stillness. Frustration.

Eventually she fell asleep. I didn't. I stayed wide awake, like an owl. There for her. I made a vow. I was going to be there for her for the rest of our lives, if only she would let me.

Sienna

Grief. I don't know how to describe it other than as a rollercoaster that drops you into the pit of hell with the rats and the demons, and then lifts you up above the clouds to the place where heaven begins.

When I was down, I wondered if I would ever dig myself out; and when I was up, I waited by the gates, calling out my father's name in the vain hope he would answer me. I like to think of myself as a positive person, and I think it was this that got me through it.

And Nick, of course. I spent a fortnight at his house, filling every room with the stench of my loss. I felt dirty no matter how much I washed. I felt tired no matter how much I slept. And I slept a lot. The first night I slept beside him fully clothed, but after that I stayed in his spare room, apart from during the day when Nick was out and I would creep into his room just so I could be close to him in some way. While Nick worked I tangled myself in his sheets. The only comfort in this world was the smell of him all around me. I pushed his pillow into my face and took in its warmth, and it was just like he was with me, holding me close. Because really, that was the only time I ever felt calm, when I could imagine he had his body wrapped around mine.

My skin was pale and there were red streaks under my eyes as if someone had painted them on in some strange African ritual. My hair hung limply from my head, greasy and straggly. Sometimes Nick got back from work and we didn't even speak because I'd gone back to the spare room and slept the whole way through the evening. He would come and check on me as I snoozed, and all I could utter was a grunt before pulling the duvet over my head.

Sometimes I wanted to do weird things like play board games and watch *Friends* repeats until four in the morning because it was the only way to lessen the pain. And it *was* pain. A pain I'd forgotten about, which brought all the memories of my mother's departure straight back to me. Now I had no parents at all. Pain like this physically ached. It was a different feeling, more poignant and tangible than anything I'd ever experienced. In the course of fourteen days I felt angry, sad, confused, even hysterical at times.

But despite all the hurt, creeping in amongst it was a kind of happiness, like soft velvet. Strange happiness. Joy because I'd been lucky enough to know my dad for all the time I had, twenty-five beautiful years. Sure, it had been hard – I'd cared for him for nearly fifteen years of that time, but they'd all still been moments I would treasure for the rest of my life. Twenty-five years. Some people don't even get that long . . . Things had been hard – sometimes more than that – and at times I'd wondered how we would make it, but somehow we did.

Even though he'd been so cruelly taken away from me, it was difficult to remember him without a smile. Without this warm feeling that infiltrated the pain and pushed it away, even if it was just for a few minutes at a time.

Nick stayed off work for the first two days because he was frightened to leave me. I told him that he had to go back before my misery infected him too. He called me all the time, though, and the phone calls, if answered, went a little like this:

'Si, how are you doing?'

'Fine, Nick.'

'Look, you don't sound fine – I'm going to come home, all right? Give me twenty minutes.'

'No, please. Just stay at work. I promise I'll be fine.'

'Are you sure?'

'Yes.'

There were at least four of these exchanges a day.

Friends came to the door; sometimes I answered, sometimes I didn't. On the first day, Elouise arrived alone. Nick let her in. I hadn't realised she was coming. I was barely paying attention as I sat in the kitchen trying to eat some toast. When I say *trying* to eat, I really mean that. It was like attempting to swallow sandpaper with jam on it.

'Si?' she said, with tears in her eyes as she stood at the door. I didn't have any tears left. She was wearing a white T-shirt with some boy-fit jeans and a pair of ballet pumps. She looked lovely. I looked up from my toast and felt so glad she was there, but I was too scared to speak. I didn't know what would come out. She walked towards me slowly and I stood up almost on ceremony, unsure about what to do with my arms. I didn't know what to do, or what to say. She just cuddled me. Held on to me tight for what seemed like an age. When she eventually pulled herself away and looked at me, black lines of mascara were smeared down her face like an oil spill. Her eyes were red.

'I'm sorry, Si, I shouldn't be the one crying,' she apologised, sniffing hard while pulling out a wooden chair for herself. Nick stood in the doorway and watched for a while before making us tea and then slinking off upstairs. The steam rose from the mugs and I wrapped my hands around mine, needing more warmth.

'What am I going to do, El?' I said, starting to feel my chin go again.

She grabbed hold of my hand across the table and held it tight. 'You're going to be OK, you know. I bloody love you, Sienna – I'm like family, you know. I'll always be here for you, and so will Nick.'

I felt the tears well again just when I thought they'd finally dried out. Surely it wasn't humanly possible to cry this much? I looked down at the knots in the wooden table and started to trace my finger around them. They felt smooth. My head was heavy and I wanted to put my face against the cool surface, but that would have been a bit strange.

'Thanks,' I said.

'Is there anything I can do to help?' she asked.

To help. All I wanted was my father back. Even if he was asleep. I just wanted to watch him snoozing like I used to. To make him dinner, listening to his ramblings about whatever world topic it was he was studying, read to him. I wish I'd been there to catch him when he fell. If I'd just come home earlier . . .

I'd been dreaming about it, dreams that made me sweat and tremble. Night terrors. In my dreams, Ant told me I could leave early. I got home and Dad and I were both standing in the kitchen together, laughing and joking as usual. Then, when he fell, I spotted it and tried to catch him, cupping my arms under his back. But he was too heavy for me, I wasn't strong enough, and he hit the floor and disappeared. I started looking for him, on my hands and knees, grabbing at the floor to try and find him. But he was gone. I'd woken up twice now, scrabbling at the mattress, looking for my father.

What could Elouise do apart from stay in my life? She couldn't bring him back.

But I hoped she would never disappear like he had. Never be taken away from me. But there were no guarantees any more. Life was fragile, temporary. It scared me.

'Can we have a Disney night?' I asked.

She laughed a little before realising I was serious. 'Well, yes, of course we can. I'll come over with wine and takeaway and we can watch Disney all night if you like.' She brushed her fringe from her blotchy face and smiled.

'Yes please,' I said.

'How about tomorrow?' she asked.

So that's what we did. Nick, Elouise and I. We sat together on the sofa, Elouise to my left, Nick to my right. We watched *Lady and the Tramp*, *The Little Mermaid* and *The Lion King* all in one sitting. And we drank wine like it flowed from the kitchen taps. I'm not sure why I asked for Disney, but something about it was so comforting at the time. It made the world seem better. Sometimes I didn't even have the energy to open the door to my friends.

We ran out of milk one day and I tried to go to the shop, but I felt so overwhelmed by the fresh air and the loudness of it all I couldn't cope, so I came back inside. It was a fortnight that felt like a month, maybe a year. A jumble of almost callous and torturous timelessness where three in the morning might as well have been lunchtime.

On the fourth night it really caught up with me. I'd finally drifted off when the nightmare struck and woke me up within a few minutes. I was so disturbed it made me tremble. Nick was sleeping soundly in his room; I could hear his breathing from across the hallway. I tried to focus on that, but it wasn't helping the pressure in my chest that was getting tighter and tighter. Rather than lying there and trying to calm myself down, I woke him. I just couldn't get through the night without him.

'Nick, Nick,' I whispered as I prodded his arm gently. I felt like a lunatic.

'Eh?' he said sleepily as he woke up, rubbing his

fists in his eyes. 'Si, what's wrong?' There was panic in his voice.

'I'm sorry, I'm sorry,' I mumbled as I began to cry again, sitting on the side of his bed and feeling like a fool. 'I just can't cope. I don't know how I'm ever going to get through this,' I choked, pulling my vest down over my knees to protect myself from the humiliation of this moment.

He sat up and pulled me towards him by wrapping his arms around my waist. I felt light as a feather. He started stroking my hair. That was all I needed. Almost straight away I felt the anxiety rushing away from me.

'I'm sorry, I know I shouldn't wake you,' I said, trying to see the alarm clock through the murk of his room. It was 3 a.m. I could feel him, his body perfect under a soft, crinkled T-shirt. I was so embarrassed, but totally unable to get through the night without him.

'Shh, Sienna, never apologise. You know that I'd do anything for you,' he said in his deep voice.

I held on to him even tighter now. I thought about how much I loved him. How deep it ran. How it was more than the heady lust I'd often experienced – something much more powerful. Deeper than the pain I was feeling, and the lake of tears I'd cried. I immersed myself in his love. It was healing me . . . I realised I was now lying down next to him and he had both his arms around me. I was stroking the hair on his right forearm.

461

'Sienna,' he said, just as I was finally drifting off in my state of emotional exhaustion.

'Yes.'

'You know I'm never going to leave you, don't you?'

There was quiet. 'What do you mean, Nick?'

'I just . . . er, I'll always be a part of your life, in whatever way. I'm never going to just go,' he said in a whisper.

But how did he know? How could anyone promise that? I said nothing and drifted into sleep.

Somehow, by the end of a fortnight I was feeling a lot better. These things take a long time to heal – years, in fact – and I know that even when I'm an old lady, I'll look back on these days and feel something tremendous wash over me, although I don't know what it is yet. But slowly I came round. I started cleaning the house when Nick was at work. I had to pull myself out of this misery. It made me feel better. I scrubbed taps, vacuumed the floor to within an inch of its life, I even dusted the ceilings.

And I started making elaborate meals for him, involving exotic spices and giant prawns, things I'd never tried before. I was finally able to venture outside and I started going to Borough Market where I could buy all manner of exciting ingredients. I smelled them, I touched them, taking in all the textures and colours. I had to be strong, and somehow I found some kind of solace in this crazy marketplace with all its bustle and vibrancy.

There was something new and exciting there. The stallholders measured things and sliced them and poured them into little boxes and wrapped them in paper. I loved it.

On Friday afternoon, the door went again. Nick wasn't in. I saw a tall male figure through the frosted glass but I didn't know who on earth it could be. I slid the chain over and opened it partially, just to be sure.

It was Pete. I'd had no idea he knew where to find me or why I was there. In fact, I'd assumed he would never want to see me again. He looked so much better – it was a shock, actually, but in a good way. I couldn't understand this. It was so confusing. I thought he hated me since I'd brought Laura to the park and it had all gone so wrong. I hadn't seen him or heard from him since . . .

As I peered through the gap I could immediately see he'd put on some weight, and he was even wearing a shirt. His skin looked good. Wow. He had a big bunch of yellow flowers in his hands, the colour so bright it made me squint. I slid the chain back and opened the door.

'Come here,' he said, cuddling me before I even had the chance to speak. There was something about his hug that told me he was sorry and scared all at the same time. Scared about how *I* would react, this time. To be honest, I didn't have the energy for wild reactions. And I'd missed him too . . . I was so glad to see him. Despite this, though, something about his past made it even harder to be around him. His grief had been so destructive and so profound that it had taken him to hell and back. That worried me.

We sat in the living room.

'Sienna, I'm so sorry,' he began, putting his face between his hands.

'Oh, don't worry, that was ages ago now, Pete . . .' I replied, feeling a little overwhelmed by all this.

'No, no. Not just about all that. About your dad,' he said, with a look of deep regret in his eyes. 'I had no idea he was ill. I didn't know anything, Sienna, and I spoke to you so badly. I was so rude to you.' He was leaning towards me now, his body language full of remorse.

'How did you find out?' I asked.

'Nick got hold of me – he contacted the charity and found me.'

'Nick? But you two have never met . . .'

Pete stumbled over his words as he mumbled something almost unintelligible about plucking up the courage to go back to Balham and ask people at work where I was.

'How does Nick know about the charity? I never told him – and I thought you hated the idea of them interfering and didn't want anything to do with it?' I asked, suddenly very puzzled.

'Oh, er . . . I don't know. Listen, Si. That day you and Laura came to the park, and I stormed off like a selfish kid . . . Well, you see, I came back. I turned round after a couple of minutes and saw

464

it was just Laura there. You'd gone, and we got talking, and . . . well, they helped me.'

I felt a sudden wave of happiness wash over me. I'd had no idea he'd gone back.

'Gosh. That's incredible, Pete. I'm so pleased.' I felt like everything suddenly made sense now. But then I remembered what had happened with my dad and felt that sadness immediately take over again.

'I wanted to contact you and tell you, but I was worried you'd never have time for me again after the way I behaved. Then I heard about this and I just had to find you . . .'

I didn't know what to say. I was just so glad he was here now. 'Pete, this feeling, does it ever go away?' I asked, looking at the TV, which was on mute. My stomach was empty, but not for lack of food. There was some awful game show on; I'd been watching it with the sound off before he arrived.

'Yes and no. You know, I had a very hard time, but I'm not like you. I'm not as strong . . .' He trailed off, looking ashamed of himself.

I didn't know what he meant. He was a man, several years my senior, who'd spent the past few years sleeping on the cold, hard ground. He was stronger than I would ever be.

'But you. There's something very special about you, Sienna, and I just know you'll take this and turn it into something good.' He locked his gaze into mine. I'd forgotten how cold those eyes of his were. How blue.

'Thanks,' I said, unsure of what he meant.

'It never really goes. You'll think about this for the rest of your life. But I promise, it will get easier. Your feelings will twist and change, but he'll never stop bringing you joy because it's all up here, all those memories.' He tapped his finger against his temple.

His words were of great comfort to me. But I couldn't stop the fear from gripping my throat and chest.

'What's going on with you, Pete? Are you in a hostel now or something?' I asked, hoping to concentrate on something more positive.

He smiled. There was a look on his face I hadn't seen before. Positivity, I think.

I leaned forward and held his hands.

'Yes I am, and it's brilliant, Sienna. I've met some really nice people, and I went for a job interview today.'

'You what?' I almost jumped off the sofa in sheer delight.

'Well, yes – they sorted me out an interview with a small private firm in Camden. It's just an admin role, I don't think I'll get it, but it's a good start, isn't it?'

I really hoped he would get it. It would be the start for him; one day he'd be able to live in some kind of comfort again. 'I'm so proud of you, Pete. Well done. How do you think it went?'

'I was stupidly nervous, Si,' he said, leaning even closer to me and exposing the gaps where his bottom teeth had been.

I giggled for what seemed like the first time in ages. 'What, as in wee yourself nervous?' I asked, laughing a bit more.

'Ha! Not quite, but I was in a right state. I got on the wrong bus and everything because I couldn't see straight from the fear.' He held his hands together now, his fingers intertwined. 'I just wanted to thank you, Sienna,' he continued, looking much more serious now.

'Oh, don't thank me. It's no biggie, Pete. Really. It was all you – it was you who made those choices, it was you who walked back and talked to Laura. You're not weak, Pete. You're something else . . .'

I was so proud of him at that moment. I really meant what I said. Achievement is relative. Whether he got the job or not, he'd earned more respect from me for climbing out of the gutter than some of the executive high-fliers I'd come across. His accomplishments so far were his and his alone. No one could ever take that away from him.

'No, really. I'm not sure I'd be alive if it wasn't for you.' He looked really serious now and his eyes had started to water ever so slightly. 'To me, Sienna, you're an angel.'

I felt emotion pulling at my chest again but I tried so hard to hold it in. I looked at the TV once more; it was an ad break, and some woman was holding a bottle of bleach up to the screen and pointing at it as if it was the answer to all the world's ills.

I was no angel. If I was an angel I would have saved my father. That's what angels do.

I changed the subject. 'Please let me know when you hear about the job. Please?' I begged him, desperate to know how it went.

'Of course I will. I also wanted to ask you though . . . When's the funeral?'

Oh yes. The funeral. It had been a nightmare to organise, and to be honest I was absolutely dreading it because I knew that would be my final goodbye.

'It's on Monday, Pete,' I said, unable to hold the tears back any more.

CHAPTER 16

TOTALLY IN AWE OF HER.

Nick

The church was big and we were small. A modest group of people were scattered across the wooden pews, united by loss, but divided by fear. There was an ample gap between each and every bottom, family members embarrassed because they had never been around enough, friends ashamed of their neglect. Crimson cheeks hiding behind their crumpled white tissues. And amongst those people was a small handful of human beings who had never let Sienna down. They could hold their heads high, safe in the knowledge that they had been there. Properly.

It's always difficult when someone dies. Things are left unfinished, regrets gape wide open like a wound with no one there to stitch it all together and make everything all right again.

Sienna had lost a worrying amount of weight over the past two weeks, but she still looked beautiful. She was wearing a jet-black dress with small frill details around the sleeves and a square neckline which revealed her collarbone. It was tight around her waist, flaring out to a skirt that stopped just above the knee. She was wearing the dress with a dark pair of tights and some heels, and on top of her long, glossy hair was a small, grey, angled hat with a large feather curling away from it. She looked like something from a magazine, her blue eyes contrasting against her skin. Her cheeks were so rosy it was as if she was the epitome of life and all that was beautiful about it.

If her father could see her now, and I was sure he could, I knew he'd have looked at her and not wanted to have changed a thing about his life as long as she'd still been a part of it. He adored her. He loved her more than the air that filled his lungs. And so did I.

I'd been holding her warm hand tight all morning, her fingers interlaced with mine, trying in some small way to make the day easier for her.

It was hard to let her go as I watched her walk up to the front of the small crowd. The air filled with the smells of incense and mahogany. She turned to face us and smiled, running her hands down the front of her dress as she looked ahead nervously. My stomach was in knots and I felt nauseous. I swallowed. Hard.

She cleared her throat. 'My dad,' she started, before taking such a deep breath in through her nostrils that everyone automatically copied her without even realising it. She composed herself and continued. 'My dad, George, liked to sleep,' she said, starting to giggle quietly and looking down at her hands, which she gripped together in front of her waist. Her dimples were showing and it made me smile in spite of the sadness of it all. Her voice echoed across the room and as she laughed, the feather on her hat bobbed gently. Friends and family members started to laugh with her. Quietly. Timidly. Thankfully.

I smiled as I remembered all the times George had collapsed. Backwards. Forwards. On cushions, books and plates full of pasta, he wasn't choosy. And it had been such a shit situation that you had to see the funny side. He certainly did.

'Yes. As you all probably know, he was a pretty tired man, and our lives were far from being normal . . .' She paused again, clearing the hurt that was caught in her throat.

I glanced back to see Elouise leaning forward from the bench behind me; she looked at me, tears filling her eyes. I took hold of her hand and smiled at her reassuringly before turning back to Sienna.

'But despite all his tiredness, his exhaustion, he was full of life to me,' she declared, a look of total joy spreading across her features.

Tissues were blotted against faces. Sobs were drawn close to the chest, muscles taut. No one wanted to make a sound, so we were all silently choking on the memories. I gritted my teeth to stop myself unravelling right there and then. All I wanted to do was run up to her and hold her hand while she spoke. Look after her. It was hard to sit back and watch her like this, but I had to.

'I was so blessed to know my dad for the time I had with him, and I wouldn't change a thing. He loved me whatever I did, good or bad. It was unconditional,' she said, biting her lip vulnerably as she stood so strong. 'Not so many people can say they have truly been loved unconditionally.' She made eye contact with me for a moment before carrying on.

'Things were really hard for us, but I would do it all again for him. Every single thing. Even though I'm hurting because he's gone, I can't help but feel like a very lucky young woman.'

As she said this, I noticed the glittering sunshine through the stained-glass window. It plunged her into a glorious spotlight. Just her. No one else.

She looked up at the ceiling as if he was there, talking to her. 'Thanks, Dad,' she said.

Elouise ducked behind the back of a pew to hide her grief, her fingers slipping away from mine.

'My dad had not been outside into the real world for years, not properly, yet he learned about more of it than any of us.' She gestured towards his coffin, which was adorned with flowers. 'This man, right here, wrote about outer space, running marathons, African tribes, crop circles, you name it . . . He learned by studying other people's experiences and beliefs, then describing those experiences as he'd have liked to live them. And I can't help but wonder how many of us struggle to look further than our office windows every day.'

She started to walk slowly towards his coffin.

'My dad was a hero to me. Not because he ran marathons and not because he travelled the world, but because he was able to imagine it all. He never grew bitter, or jealous, or selfish. He wasn't afraid to learn about a life he would never truly be able to explore.' She put her hand on his coffin now, running it over the smooth, varnished wood.

'He always listened to me. Even when he was sleeping. Somehow we got through it, Dad and I. I will miss him for the rest of my days, but I'll forever be thankful that I knew him, and loved him. I will always love him . . . Always.'

A tear dropped from her face and landed on the wooden surface. She ran her fist across her cheek and wiped it gently as more followed.

'So if you ask me if I'm sad, I'll say yes, I'm sadder than I've ever been in my life. And if you ask me if I'm angry, I'll say definitely, because I feel like he's been stolen from me. But most importantly, I'm happy. Happy that I was lucky enough to call him my dad and my friend. So happy that it was worth all the struggle, and the fear and the pain, because without all of that, you can never truly say you experienced the best bits.'

I felt emotion rise in my throat. I was so overcome I didn't know what to do with myself apart from start to fiddle with a tissue, quietly tearing strips from the middle and rolling them into balls between my fingers. My stomach muscles started to pull in sharply as I desperately tried to keep it together.

Sienna turned to face George's coffin now, both her hands on top of it. 'I love you, Dad . . .' She had held it together for so long, but now the tears came. They flowed from her eyes and into a tissue, which she pressed against her soft skin. I ached inside because I needed to be with her, but I had to stay here and let her do this alone.

There was complete silence again, broken only by sobs and sniffles as she turned her back to us. She said goodbye with two hands on his coffin, her frame shaking hard as she silently wept. I could see the sides of her stomach trembling. She started to whisper to him now – final goodbyes that were not for our ears. They belonged to her and George.

The light brightened even more, creeping in through the clear panes of glass. I like to think that light was George, telling her in some way that he loved her, and would be with her forever in whatever ways he could.

Eventually she leaned down and planted a gentle kiss on top of her father's coffin, before turning away from it and slowly walking towards me. I studied her face and saw not desperate sorrow, but some kind of joy because she had experienced such powerful love. I could read all this just by looking at her face, because I knew her so well now.

Sienna was magical. A hero to me. She could see the best in all situations, and somehow get through anything. Her strength scared me, but conjured such inspiration in my soul at the same time. It was as if she was walking in slow motion, her eyes locked into mine. I had never felt so proud of anyone – I was totally in awe of her. I wanted to run away with her somewhere where there were no people, no cars and no buildings, and just tell her how much I loved her, and how amazing she was to me.

Eventually she was sitting next to me, her warm body against mine. I held her hand tight, tucking all of her fingers between my own. The coffin slowly started to fall out of view, and as that happened she squeezed my hand so hard I feared her heart was breaking right then and there.

I put my mouth to her ear as she watched George disappear. 'You're incredible, Sienna Walker. Stay strong, for me. Your father was very proud of you, more than you'll ever know,' I whispered softly.

Another giant tear rolled from her crystal-blue eyes and I reached my index finger out and wiped it away. As soon as the coffin had gone, I pulled her face close to mine and looked into her glassy eyes until her breath was calm and the church was empty.

Sienna

'Are you sure you'll be all right on your own tonight?' asked Elouise, who was standing in my kitchen, nibbling on a biscuit. The flat seemed so empty now, but I needed to be alone for the first time. It was something I had to do. I finally felt ready. Well, I thought so, anyway.

'Yes, I'll be fine, sweetheart,' I said, faking positivity. I pulled my sleeves over my arms and wished I could climb inside my cardigan and hide for a while until things felt normal again. It had been a blisteringly hot day, the kind of oppressive heat that gives you a headache. Now it was melting into a stunning, salmon-pink evening with rich streaks of purple tearing through it as the sun went to sleep. I could see the splendour of it all from the windows, which were wide open to let in the fresh air. I traced my bare foot over the floor and felt the cool tiles on my skin. I caught a flash of myself in the mirror. I looked like I hadn't slept for days, my skin tinged with grey.

Elouise tilted her head to one side and smiled, popping the last chunk of shortbread into her mouth. 'Really? Because I can't help but feel it might be too soon . . .' she said dubiously, her thick, blonde hair sweeping over her right shoulder. A look of concern spread across her pretty face.

'Yes, really. I promise,' I responded.

'Well if you start feeling horrible, just call me. I'll be round like a shot. Do you promise you'll ring if you're struggling?' she asked, almost begging.

'Of course I will. But you know what, I think I'll be fine,' I said, really hoping I would be. I'd had this exact same conversation with Nick a couple of hours before. It had been almost impossible to get him out of the flat. I'd eventually had to push him out of the door, tickling his sides because he can't defend himself when I do that.

'Look, El. I promise everything will be OK. I'm feeling so much better now.' I really meant that, I thought, as I looked around me at the place we used to share. My dad and I. I had to learn to be alone. I was going to have to spend evenings in solitude without talking to myself, or racking up huge phone bills by calling horoscope hotlines. Cats weren't an option either. I was far too young to have a flat full of them, weeing all over the place. I felt just about ready to take on my new life now. Acceptance had come rushing in, and it was doing me the world of good.

'I'll have my phone on loud. All night,' Elouise told me, leaning up on her tiptoes and kissing my forehead. It made me grin. She and Nick had seen me through this whole thing. It would be hard to truly feel alone ever again.

As she walked past me, she left a trail of her perfume in the air and I breathed it in deeply, holding the memory of it close for the dead of night when I might need her. I wasn't going to call her, or Nick, or anyone. Not even Mystic Margaret from south Ealing with her premium-rate phone line.

'Love you, Si,' she said, turning towards me as she stood by the door, her small frame almost swallowed whole by a trendy T-shirt.

'You too, pretty one,' I said, standing by the counter.

The door closed slowly and quietly. I looked around me and took a few deep breaths.

That night I was hungry for the first time in ages, so I made my favourite dinner, medium rare sirloin steak with mashed potato and Mediterranean vegetables. Nick had brought all the ingredients round for me. I think he was worried I was going to end up looking like a bag of bones if I didn't put some weight on soon. He had a point, I thought, looking down at my trousers, which were gaping at the waist.

I spent at least an hour preparing it all as the last dregs of the day slipped behind dark clouds. I put the radio on and sang along to every song. Great songs. Shit songs. It didn't matter what it was because it was a way of expelling all the tension, even if it did involve screaming Aerosmith at the top of my voice and using a courgette as a microphone. I could sing as loud as I wanted and I knew no one would disturb me. This night was all mine.

I chopped up onions, sliced mushrooms in half and divided juicy tomatoes into quadrants. I put a steak in the pan and listened as it sizzled satisfyingly, the smell wafting up my nose and making me even more hungry. I had a bottle of wine and a small chocolate pudding in the fridge. I was going to treat myself. Relax, and bathe in the happy memories. Because they were happy, and they would never be stolen from me like my father had been.

After dinner I curled up on the sofa, put on *Breakfast at Tiffany's* and sipped a huge glass of cold wine. I was content for once. I didn't feel scared, I felt safe and happy. Wasn't I supposed to be crying like a lunatic still? Was I in denial? I looked over at the chair opposite me and wished my father was sitting in it. I wished so hard that I imagined it before my very eyes, his lovely, kind face and his thin frame, draped in a jumper and a pair of chequered trousers. The thought of it made me smile so wide I forgot for a moment that the film was on. I just stared at the emptiness where he used to be. When I turned back to the screen, I was reminded of all my favourite scenes. Audrey Hepburn's passion for parties, diamonds and sleeping until midday. It was a magical world I could lose myself in. I just wished I could live like that, wandering around with a cigarette and a sexy smile, needing nothing else in life but the date and whereabouts of my next social gathering.

And then I remembered my dad's notebooks. Reams and reams of writing I had never looked at because I hadn't wanted to intrude. They were scattered all over our flat and I hadn't touched them. It had felt wrong to move them, and when Elouise, Nick and I sorted through his possessions, I'd begged them to leave them where they were.

I could see them now, all around me. Big books with thick, black covers, white labels with dates on. They were stacked in neat piles, some on the shelves, a few on top of the TV and a whole load more in boxes under his bed. I sat for a moment and wondered what it would be like to read them.

Would it be too soon? Would it rekindle all the fear and agony, or would it be like he was with me all over again?

I paused the film and sat for a while, taking a few more sips of my wine and wondering what to do. I picked up the book that was closest to me and ran my hands over the smooth, cool surface. A flash of lightning shot across the skyline and I pulled a light blanket over my body. A storm must be coming, I realised, thinking back to how hot and stuffy it had been today. I wasn't scared of it. Not at all.

I held the book, slipping my fingers between the pages, feeling the thickness of them, which seemed even denser now they were covered in scribblings, the words pushed into the paper where he wrote so hard. Would he mind? I wondered. I opened it at the middle, greeted with his familiar handwriting, which had so often been scrawled on a Post-it note on the fridge, little reminders to me of the things we needed. Peanut butter. Cooking oil. Soap.

My eyes glazed over the letters, too frightened to read but too curious to look away. More flashes of lightning bolted across the summer sky like strobe lights. They illuminated the room in brilliant white for a split second before plunging me back into the warm light of the candles in the middle of the table. Rain started to patter on the windows. What would I find? Would I discover that he'd been deeply unhappy, but kept it from me? Did he ever think I'd neglected him? Let him down? My heart started to thump as I began to read.

It is mile twenty-three and hurting is an underestimation. The streets of London are lined with crowds, screaming and shouting. There are lots of names, none of them mine, but I can hear my daughter cheering me on in my head. It's the only thing that will get me through the last three miles to the finish line. I can see her face, too, ahead of me all the time. My beautiful daughter. I know she is waiting for me at the end. She would never let me down, I just know it.

My legs feel like raw meat and some of my muscles are starting to spasm now, twitching and jerking under my sweaty skin. It's just a pounding sensation reverberating up my calves and thighs. Thousands of steps melting into one huge effort. To be honest, it just feels like a funny dream. I panic for a few moments as I'm unsure whether I will make it to the end or not. I can't let her down.

A water gun is squirted from the sidelines over the runners, and some of the droplets land on my face. It's so cooling I want to hobble to the water station and tip a glass of it all over me, feeling it run into my mouth and down my throat. But no amount of water would quench my thirst now – it's as if I've been wrung out like a flannel. I'm sweating so much it's getting into my eyes. Stinging. Hurting. Everything hurts. I need the loo, but stopping would be the end of me. It feels like my muscles would seize up and dry, fast and thick like concrete. Got to keep going.

People around me are really struggling now, breathing is laboured, groans and sighs like a crowd of zombies in expensive sportswear. Got to keep going.

People are dropping like flies, collapsing on the pavements and falling onto grass verges. I don't want to look at them because it scares me. Somehow I'm still going. I don't know how, and the more I think about this, the more terrifying it is.

The soles of my trainers feel like squashed steaks when they started off like clouds. Each movement is painful, each breath is sharp. I know it isn't far to go. I've run miles and miles in training, but my mind is playing tricks on me. Suddenly it feels like three miles is an awfully long way. But Sienna is on my mind, because I know she will be there, waiting for me.

My vision is blurred, my brow furrowed with concentration. People in brightly coloured fancy dress are confusing to me. The shapes and the colours seem to morph in front of my eyes. I'm angry, scared, yet euphoric, because I know the end is coming. I know that I'll have run a marathon, and I'll have achieved it after all this time. All the hoping and wishing and dreaming. I could start to walk now, but I won't.

Thud. Thud. Thud.

There is pain in my shoulders, acid in my stomach and my guts are ruined. I have to make it. This is my mantra. There is a balloon up ahead, a big pink one suspended by a string. I keep my eyes on that and follow it as we navigate the streets of London. Familiar tourist attractions are now mere inconveniences on the way. Roads are just something I have to defeat before I can truly taste achievement.

As I turn one corner a woman is holding out a tray of energy cubes. I grab one like a monster, groaning my thanks and shoving it into my mouth, which is so dry it makes my taste buds twitch. I feel the jelly melt into my tongue as the flavour of blackberries explodes on my taste buds. It's so intense and I need all the energy I can get.

I turn more corners, winding roads, small ups, small downs. Nearly there now. After what seems like an age the finish line is ahead, covered in yet more balloons. Sound is going now. It's all muffled and the only thing I can hear is my breathing, rattling through my brain. My long, positive strides have turned into drags, one leg after the other, like wading through treacle. Closer. Closer still.

It is then that I see her, near the end of the race. My beautiful daughter, standing against the railings and cheering me on. Her lovely smile is all I need. There are so many people around, but I can spot her immediately. She is distinctive, one of a kind. Strikingly beautiful and every day I wake up and wonder how I created something so special. How I didn't screw it up like so many other things in my life.

That was all I could read. The emotion was tearing at my chest again. It was too hard. I slammed the book shut. His imagination astounded me, and I'd had no idea he felt so proud of me until then. I knew he would 'finish' the marathon. It was my dad, of course he would. I believed in him, but I had to close it, just for a short while, otherwise I would trip up and fall down that hole of grief I knew was so difficult to climb out of.

I wiped a single tear from the corner of my eye, wondering what secrets the rest of the books would hold. The film was flickering in the background now. Curiosity got the better of me. I poured another glass of wine and went into his room, pulling from under his bed a large box, which was full of notebooks. It shocked me how many there were. I wanted answers. I wanted a sign. Something.

I wanted to know my father better. So I closed my eyes and picked a book. Any book. One of at least fifty, I think.

I clutched it between my fingers and carried it back into the living room, sitting on the sofa and drawing the blanket around my body once more. The rain was beating so hard against the glass now that the noise took my breath away. It was one of my favourite sounds: nature battering the world around me, leaving me safe in my little man-made box, sipping wine and reading.

I looked at the label on the front of the book. 1 JULY 2006. Wow, this was ages ago, I thought. I'd only been in my job for a couple of months then. Things had been very different. Again, I braced myself before opening the pages. I could handle this . . . and if it was too much, I would put it away and come back in a few months' time. No one is forcing me to read this, I thought, peeling it open with trembling hands. I flicked through the pages, my eyes scanning over words. In a flash I saw Nick's name pop up. How strange . . . I'd only have known him a short time by then. I leafed back to the place where I found it, and started reading.

It's hard having kids. How much do you show them the way and give them the answers? I've always been the kind of dad who let Sienna make her own mistakes, find things out for herself and solve her own problems. I won't just give her all the clues.

485

I want her to be able to stand on her own two feet one day because to be truthful, I'm not sure how much longer I'll be here. Anything could happen. Well, anything could happen to anyone, that's certain, but with me there's so much more risk when I could collapse at any given moment.

I promised myself, before I got ill, that I wouldn't just buy her the things she wanted. No, I wanted her to work for them so she truly knew their worth. I don't tell her all the wonderful things people say about her, because I want her to realise her talents and value on her own. I want her to truly see them for herself as she grows up.

I hope this makes sense and doesn't make me sound like an exceptionally selfish human being. I mean, if she was in trouble then of course I would jump in and save her. But if it's not urgent, and if it makes her stronger, I would rather she went about it all her own way. I watch from the side-lines, like a hawk, and swoop in to get her if she needs me. And don't get me wrong. I am watching (when I'm not asleep – then I'm just listening), but now I'm in a bit of a situation. One that I'm in two minds about.

She has this friend called Nick, a man she met at work. He's an artist at the publishing house she writes for. She adores him. In fact, she loves him. She's only young, but I think I can safely say this is pretty big for her. Although she won't admit it . . . I had never met the bloke before until yesterday, when he just turned up at my house to 'drop a CD round' on his way into town.

Now I'm a man, and there's no way he was just casually on his way to the shops. I could tell that he loves her by his dopey eyes and his bashful demeanour the minute I opened the door. It was the look of a man in love – and he seemed like a great bloke.

Sienna wasn't in and I think it's safe to say we had something of an incident. I collapsed. Now it seems that Sienna never told Nick about my condition, because the poor man thought I'd had a heart attack or something. He was wailing like a banshee. Panic wasn't the word. He was making me worse because the more I wanted to scream out to him that I was all right, the deeper I was pushed into sleep. There I was, lying in my body, which I couldn't move, but able to hear everything. Everything.

And he said something. He told me that he loves her. I'm sure I didn't mishear him. He was pleading with me, and I think he said, 'I love Sienna, she loves you, and she needs you. Don't go anywhere . . .'

So how do I handle that? He might have

just said it in the heat of the moment, or he might have meant he loves her as a friend. And however he meant it, is it my place to tell her the things he said when he thought I was knocked out for good?

But if it is love, real love, then I want them to find each other. Because I believe that love is an overwhelming, all-consuming force, and when it's genuine you can't really ignore it. No matter how long it takes. It knocks down your door by force. It keeps you awake at night. It plagues your thoughts and burns your soul. If it is love, they won't need me at all. By telling my daughter that the man of her dreams loves her too, would I not be getting in the way? Meddling with fate?

Anyway, I tried to tell her, but I couldn't. Something inside was pushing me to keep it quiet. And if he loves her, I hope to God he sorts it out soon, because she's one of a kind, my daughter. Really quite special.

Nick

Sienna has gone home and now I'm left like a lonely, sad zoo monkey. A miserable creature whose considerably more attractive monkey wife has been exported to a zoo for better-looking animals on the other side of the world. *That's* how bad it feels to be without Sienna. How will I sleep without knowing she's just across the hall? What is there to come home for if I know she won't be here?

No. I had to be cool about this. It's important she spends her first night alone. I must give her some space. I have my phone on loud, though. And vibrate. And in a glass dish so it rattles really hard if she calls me while I'm sleeping.

I lay down in my bed and decided I would try to read a book. Yes. Maybe I could find something to distract me in Charles Dickens's *Great Expectations*. As far as I'm aware it has nothing to do with stunning, blue-eyed girls from west London. You know the type – the ones who steal your heart and leave you floundering helplessly without it for half a decade, shoving other things into the gap where it used to be, but finding that they don't bloody fit.

A book is probably the best option because everything else reminds me of her. TV shows. Music. Films. Radio. Even cereal boxes (she cut a couple of holes in one a few months ago, put it on her head and crept up on me while I was washing up. I actually screamed). So as raindrops hurled themselves against my window, I climbed into bed and started to read. Chapter one. Here goes.

But my thoughts were intruding. Maybe I should call Sienna . . . You know, just check that she's OK. No. Give the girl some space, for fuck's sake. Now let's try again.

Chapter one . . .

But she might be upset, she *might need me*. Come on now. Concentrate. Chapter one . . .

I could take her some of those little lemon cakes she likes so much. I wouldn't even have to see her. I could just leave them on the doorstep, ring the bell and run away. Oh yeah, now that wouldn't be in the least bit creepy, would it, Nick? You freak. Chapter one . . .

No. This just wasn't working. I hadn't got past the title. I sat bolt upright in bed, pushing the book face down into the covers in sheer frustration. A few of the pages crinkled in the middle. What was I going to do to distract myself? Maybe I could make a model castle entirely out of matchsticks? Find a new formula for banana muffin mix? Or I could rewind all my old VHS tapes and put them in title order, just in case there's some kind of sonic boom which renders modern-day equipment useless and the ancient video player is the only surviving technology. People might have to queue outside my door because I'd be the only house on the street that could show films . . .

Oh God, I think I'm losing my mind. Is there a place you can go for this kind of shit? You know, a little white room with a chair that's really hard to get out of and an endless supply of tissues and pizza. 'Er, excuse me, I've loved this girl for five years and every time I try to tell her I screw everything up and it's driving me nuts.'

Maybe I could tell her tonight. It's been a while

now, I thought. Obviously, when George died so suddenly like that, thoughts of telling Sienna how I felt were completely wiped from my mind. It had been a terrible shock and it was certainly no time to start declaring your love like a hapless, bungling fool. It would have been about as well received as a fart in a two-man zorb. But now, maybe? Possibly?

I peeled myself out of bed and opened the window slightly. A warm breeze tickled my nose and droplets of rain lashed against my face. It was lovely, despite the fact that a ferocious storm was kicking in. I looked into the distance; there were lots of lights everywhere. The glow from lamps in cosy windows, twinkling headlights. A glittering city lit up in brilliant white as bolts of lightning slashed through the sky. I looked over in the vague direction of Sienna's flat and wondered what she was doing. Was she frightened? Hurting? Could she feel my love from all the way over here? I concentrated on my feelings for her and let them run riot, but it seemed like my heart was going to burst into flames.

I closed the window and pulled a packet of cigarettes from my drawer. Smoking in my bedroom, now this was new . . . Sitting on the edge of my bed I lit one, smoke drifting into intricate curls all around me. I looked at my reflection in the large mirror stuck to the wardrobe doors. Silly me, smoking a cigarette in my boxer shorts. Tufts of hair here, there and everywhere. Hairy, knobbly knees. God I'm ugly, I thought. I kept taking deep drags and blowing the smoke out into my bedroom.

This was disgusting. I needed a woman to come and save me before I started living off pork pies and Lucozade. As soon as I started spending the afternoons in betting shops I'd know I was screwed, but we hadn't reached that point yet.

The rain was getting harder now. I wanted to be outside immersing myself in it, cooling myself down, washing away all my insecurities. I have two options, I thought, as I bent down and flicked the ash into an empty mug on the floor.

1) I could sit here like the vile creature I am, smoking cigarettes and wondering where I left my boyish good looks.
2) I could go to Sienna's house, right now, and tell her I love her.

Option one was easier. It involved less humiliation. Option two would change my life forever. But was it the right time?

Time. It's a funny thing, that. I've known her for five years and every time I've tried to tell her how I feel I've been interrupted by a variety of different things. Paramedics, boyfriends, excruciating insecurity. You name it. And now, while she recovers from the greatest tragedy she's ever experienced, I feel a little selfish throwing this at her. OK, fair enough, according to Pete she *does* feel the same, but it doesn't seem right. And as more weeks pass since Pete and I had 'the chat', the whole idea seems more and more surreal. Like I might have imagined it or something.

No, I thought, pushing the cigarette butt into the bottom of the mug. I'm going to get back into bed and try my best to sleep myself out of this funny mood I'm in. This terribly strange mood of mine.

Sienna

'*I love Sienna*'. I read the line again and again before putting the book down on my lap, my mouth hanging open. But that was about four years ago, I thought. Why didn't he say anything? Why did he go out with other girls? Why didn't he cuddle me back that night in bed? Questions were racing through my mind like a train. Had he not been able to tell that I'd fallen madly in love with him the moment I met him?

Something started to creep into my tummy. Happiness, I think it was – real joy that made me want to dance around the flat. He loved me all those years ago. Maybe, if I'm really lucky, he just might love me now . . . You know, in *that* kind of way. A way that involves being nothing like his sister or any other female relative. I know he loves me as a friend, but maybe, just maybe, it could be more than that. Just like I always dreamed it would be.

My brain scanned through a host of memories

493

as if I was flicking through a picture book. I was searching for clues. The things he'd done and said. Maybe I could call him. No. No. There's no way I can call him. What the hell would I say? 'Oh hi, Nick, just found out that you might have quite fancied me four years ago. How's that going, by the way?' Ridiculous.

And bless my father. I understood his reasoning. *But why, oh why didn't he just tell me?* Then I suddenly remembered the times he'd obviously got so close to uttering those words, the odd things he'd started to say that had confused the hell out of me, but I'd just shrugged them off. It was all coming back to me now, huge flashbacks which took over my brain. The TV in the background was white noise, the images blurred into one. I was like a woman possessed. I picked up my phone again, holding it in my palm and looking at the numbers. Yes. I should just call him. Come on, it's Nick. I can tell him anything. Can't I?

Maybe I could tell him that I love him more than anything in the whole world and that if he would just give me the chance, I could love him better than anyone. All those crazy girls he's dated with their weird mood swings and cheating ways. I know I would give him the love he deserves. Without question. I would make him toast in the morning, do a Christmas stocking every year, and look after him if he was ill. Loving him would be my life.

I started to scroll through my contacts, my

494

thumb hovering over the call button when I found his name. No. I can't, I thought, cancelling it suddenly and throwing my phone onto the chair opposite. It was a really long time ago. Things might have changed.

I forced myself to watch the film, turning the sound up a bit more to drown out the rain lashing the windows all around me. My favourite bit was starting, where Holly Golightly is running around the streets of New York in the rain . . .

Funny, that, I thought, looking out of the window again.

Nick

Right. This is bloody ridiculous. I'm going. Now.

I shoved a pair of jeans over my legs and grabbed a T-shirt from my wardrobe. I pulled it down so fast and hard that my head got stuck in one of the armholes and I was temporarily blinded by the black fabric. I thrashed my limbs around in frustration before working out where the head hole was. One more big tug and I could see again.

Shit, I really should have a shower, I thought, angling my nose down to my armpit. No. There's no bloody time for showers. I've been showering and pissing about for five years and it's got me nowhere. I'm going to get my girl. My heart started to pump in my chest, hard.

I rushed down the stairs and stomped into the kitchen, picking up my car keys. No, actually, sod the car. Knowing my luck it would probably break down, or I'd hit roadworks in the half-mile between her house and mine. In fact, I could almost guarantee that if I got into that car I would probably find a herd of obstinate cattle in the middle of the road. Totally unwilling to move. In the city. Miles away from any fields.

Now *where was my sodding jacket*? I wondered as I rifled through a pile of clothes on the kitchen chair. I gave up on that and peeped through the patio windows, wincing at the rain. Fuck it. I didn't care. Office furniture could fall out of the sky. Volcanic ash. Ten-ton weights. Hundreds of tiny ball bearings. Whatever. I would take on the lot. I was going to get there, whatever happened.

The blood was pulsing through my veins. Nothing would stop me now. I was going to stop being a pussycat and I was going to tell her.

'Sienna Walker, I love you. OK?' I said to myself under my breath, realising that it sounded like more of a threat than the cripplingly romantic declaration of a 21st-century Romeo.

I reached into the cupboard under the stairs and finally found my waterproof jacket, which wasn't all that waterproof. I'd discovered this on a recent lunch-break outing, which had left me shopping for a pair of emergency underpants and trousers, I had got that wet. No one wants a damp bum at work. No one.

I slipped my phone into my trouser pocket, turned out the lights and opened the door. Great droplets of rain hit my face and hair straight away. Lightning was flashing in the sky. I slammed the door behind me hard as I marched out into the summer night, wondering what the odds were of me being struck by a bolt of lightning. I'd be very angry if that happened.

It was the kind of rain that was so strong it made you feel as if you could drown just walking in it. It battered against my face as if I was on the deck of a ship in the middle of a catastrophic storm. It trickled from my hair and down the back of my neck. Within just a minute or two it had soaked into all of my clothes. I tore off my jacket and stuffed it into a nearby bin. It was completely pointless and it was warm anyway. I walked purposefully along the glistening pavements, the water rushing down gutters and flowing out of drains. The trees swayed frantically, branches creaking and leaves tumbling to the ground. An orchestra was playing dramatic music in my mind, violins and cellos creating the kind of sounds that send shivers of electricity down your spine. Love coursed through my veins. I was so close, and yet so far.

Sienna

Pacing. Backwards and forwards. Up and down. Side to side. Like a desperate little molecule. The possibilities had taken hold of me and I didn't know what on earth to do with myself.

497

Call him, Sienna. Just pick up the phone, for God's sake. I know, I'll ring El. She always knows what to do. I held my phone up to my ear, my hand shaking. I was so full of emotion I wondered how I would get the words out.

She answered instantly. 'Oh God, Sienna, what's happened? Right, that's it. I'm coming over, now,' she declared, with what sounded like indelible determination in her voice.

'No, no. I'm OK. It's not that,' I said in a wobbly voice. I ran one hand through my hair, hoping I could calm myself down somehow.

'I'm leaving now. Damn, where are my keys? I can bring Luke in the car, he's sleeping anyway.'

'No. No, El, please listen to me.'

There was a brief pause where all that could be heard was my heavy breathing.

'What? What is it?' she shrieked, clearly frantic with worry now.

'I've just found something in my dad's diary, El. It's about Nick, and how he told my dad he loved me, years ago. He loved me, El. What do I do?'

There was a pause while El obviously considered how to word what she said next. '*Loves* you. Not loved you.' I could hear a smile in her tone.

'What do you mean?'

'I've seen the way he's been with you over the past few weeks. He adores you. Love isn't even the word . . .' she trailed off.

'You think?' I asked, more excitement bubbling inside me. Tears of happiness filled my eyes as I forced myself to sit down. I couldn't believe my eyes or ears any more. I needed her to give me the green light.

'Yes! For God's sake, Sienna. He's completely taken you under his wing for the past two weeks, had you stay at his house every night, and that look he gives you, *that look* . . .' She was whispering now.

'I'm going to tell him I love him, El. Tonight.'

'Please do. Please just tell him, before I do,' she pleaded with me. 'Oh, and good luck,' she added, giggling a little now.

'Thank you,' I replied, so choked with emotion I could barely say it.

I hung up.

Nick

Road signs seemed to blur into one. Hedges and glittering streetlights were bleeding into each other. I was walking faster and faster now, but it wasn't getting me there soon enough. I started to run. My feet pounded against the pavement, making great slapping noises as I struck the water under my shoes. The streets were deserted and cars were few and far between. Nothing could get in my way. One more corner . . .

I stood at the entrance to her block of flats and stopped suddenly, my heart beating so fast I feared it could explode. I bent over, my hands on my knees, desperate to catch my breath. This is the right thing to do, Nick, I told myself as I slowly pulled my body up again. Lights were glowing from some of the windows, but hers was dark. What if she'd decided to go out? No, surely not . . . Fear suddenly kicked in. Trepidation. The unknown.

I pushed the door to get inside; the locking system hadn't worked for years. The stairs seemed to go on forever, but eventually, after climbing what felt like the emergency steps in Canary Wharf, I was finally at the top, my gasping lungs echoing in the hallway.

I stared at her front door and paused. I must be mad. I should turn back. Yes, I should go home. It was too soon. What was I thinking? I stood there for a moment, listening to the sound of my own heart beating.

Sienna

I'm going to go round there. But I need to look good. All this crying has given my skin a ghostly hue and I haven't given my hair any real attention in weeks. This was no way to woo the man of your dreams. No way at all.

I rushed into my room and tipped out the contents of my make-up box, frantically rifling through dozens of pencils and pots for some much-needed foundation. That would help. Then maybe he wouldn't think Halloween had arrived early and throw sweets through the letterbox in a desperate bid to get rid of me. Colour. That was what I required. I squeezed a big blob of foundation onto my fingers and started to rub it into my skin. I was shaking so much this proved very difficult. Eventually it seemed even enough.

Then I dipped a big brush into a tin of bronzing powder; I was so clumsy I managed to knock a load of it onto my sheets. Oh well. Who cares. I'll buy new sheets. I pushed the soft bristles against my face, swirling it over my cheeks and forehead. I was starting to look a little less like I'd been locked in a slimy dungeon for the summer and more like I'd spent a season in Ibiza. That was more like it. Mascara – now this was the toughest bit. I was trembling so much I managed to miss my eyelashes completely and jab the wand into my eye socket, covering my skin in sooty blackness, which seemed to multiply every time I blinked. Bollocks. I quickly wiped it away and started again. Come on, Sienna, pull yourself together.

Eventually a pair of thick, black lashes sprung out from my eyelids. I was starting to look human again. I pulled the band from my head, my hair flowing over my shoulders as it was released from its ponytail. I ran a brush through it, backcombing it a little so it had a bit more body.

Another wave of nerves swept over me. I felt sick. Doubts were creeping into my head. What if he didn't feel that way any more? What if I wasn't enough for him? And then I remembered the dress, hanging in the wardrobe. OK, it hadn't helped me much at the Christmas party, but maybe that was missing the point. Maybe, if I could just put it on, it would make me feel better. That was what the strange ex-ballerina had said, wasn't it? That whenever I felt scared or downtrodden I should imagine I was wearing the dress . . .

I walked over to my wardrobe, pulled the doors open and there it was. My eyes were greeted with an electric flash of the most beautiful green ripples of fabric. Just like water. Yes, I was going to put the dress on. I wouldn't wear it to his house, because that would be weird. But I could wear it for a few minutes and then get changed again. Hmm, I'd probably had a bit too much to drink, but I was going to do it anyway.

I rushed out of my clothes, abandoning them in a messy pile at my feet and stepped into the dress. The soft material slid over my legs as I pulled it up around my neck. It was perfect apart from a tinge of cigarette smoke still clinging to the fabric.

I *love* this dress, I thought. All of a sudden all the memories of the Christmas party, and Ben leaving me the way he did, vanished to make way for new ones.

Soon I was standing in front of the full-length mirror, looking at a version of myself I hadn't realised existed. She was right. And all I wished was that my father could see me now . . . This really was the dress that would change my life. OK, I wouldn't be wearing it when I told Nick I loved him, but I would in my mind. I rose to my tiptoes and did a twirl, the green silk splaying all around me like the petals of a flower. I took a deep breath and felt all the tension rushing from my lungs. That will do, I thought, staring at myself in the mirror. I'd better get changed now. No time for fancy dress . . . My vanity was interrupted by a knock at the door.

Nick

I did it. My body was telling me no, but somehow my heart took the reins and I knocked at the door. The brand-new door I'd fitted to replace the one I'd had to bash down, nearly breaking my arm in the process.

I felt sick. Terrified. Water was dripping from my clothes, my hair, and creating a small pool at my feet. I looked a state. Eventually the door slowly opened, and there was Sienna. She was wearing the dress. You know, *that dress*. The way she looked in it literally took my breath away. I felt like someone had punched me in the stomach. Hard.

Looking at her now, she was what all the romantic writers of the past hundred years had been trying to immortalise.

She seemed shocked. Embarrassed, even. She blushed suddenly as she stood there with her mouth open. It wasn't, initially, a look of happiness. My legs felt like jelly and my breathing was so laboured now my chest was visibly rising up and down. Sod it. I was going to tell her anyway. It was too late to pretend I needed to borrow some sugar.

'I love you, Sienna. I'm sorry but I bloody love you,' I said, between gulps of much-needed air.

Our eyes were locked. She said nothing for a moment. Silence. I hoped the girl I knew so well would not be a stranger to me now.

Slowly a smile spread across her face. The biggest one I had ever seen. She reached her hands out towards me, great waves of fabric swishing forward as she did so.

'I love you too, Nick. So, so much you wouldn't believe it,' she replied, tears filling her eyes.

Oh my God. Pete was right. I didn't know what to say so I rushed forwards through the door. I held her face, dripping water all over her and the dress. She pulled me close to her, digging her fingers into my wet back. I wanted to kiss her, right then and there, but I couldn't just yet. I had to savour the moment. I was breathing hard onto her nose and her cheeks as I pressed my mouth to her face, holding her hair in my hands.

'Nick, is this a dream?' she asked, pulling away and looking into my eyes, tears spilling over her skin.

I didn't say a word, I just picked her up slowly and held her against the wall, looking deep into her eyes. I could feel her softness beneath the green silk that trailed down and tickled the floor.

The door was wide open. We didn't care. A thief

could come in and take everything, slide past us with the TV in his arms and gold jewellery hanging out of his backpack and we wouldn't have stopped him. Because the truth is, this is love, and it doesn't matter if you lose everything. Your job. Your home. Your car. Not as long as you have that person by your side.

I buried my face in her neck as she wrapped her legs around me, her back pressed against the blue wallpaper. We stared at each other for a few moments, before I softly kissed her lips.

'Please don't go anywhere. I need you, Nick. I love you, I love you, I love you,' she said breathlessly.

And I just knew this would be the happiest moment of my life.